P9-EGD-883

TOR BOOKS BY MARY ROBINETTE KOWAL

The Glamourist Histories

Shades of Milk and Honey

Glamour in Glass

Without a Summer

Valour and Vanity

Of Noble Family

Of No
Famil

Of Noble Family

Mary Robinette Kowal

A Tom Doherty Associates Book
New York

This is a work of fiction. All of the characters, organizations, and events portrayed in this novel are either products of the author's imagination or are used fictitiously.

OF NOBLE FAMILY

Edited by Liz Gorinsky

A Tor Book
Published by Tom Doherty Associates, LLC
175 Fifth Avenue
New York, NY 10010

www.tor-forge.com

The Library of Congress Cataloging-in-Publication Data
is available upon request.

ISBN 978-0-7653-7836-1 (hardcover)
ISBN 978-1-4668-6123-7 (e-book)

Tor books may be purchased for educational, business, or promotional use. For information on bulk purchases, please contact the Macmillan Corporate and Premium Sales Department at 1-800-221-7945, extension 5442, or write to specialmarkets@macmillan.com.

First Edition: April 2015

Printed in the United States of America

0 9 8 7 6 5 4 3 2 1

For my brother

Dr. Stephen K. Harrison

aka Apeface

Let other pens dwell on guilt and misery. I quit such odious subjects as soon as I can, impatient to restore everybody not greatly in fault themselves to tolerable comfort, and to have done with all the rest.

—JANE AUSTEN, *Mansfield Park*

Of Noble Family

One

Cherubs and Monsters

The presence of an infant in any gathering offers all the substance for conversation one might require. In some instances, the child's behaviour might occasion a desire to leave the room, but it will still provide something to discuss, even if it is only the infant's volume of squalling. In other circumstances, the conversation might turn to which parent the child most resembles.

In the case of Jane's new nephew, their current visitor, Herr Scholes, appeared content to make faces at the infant upon his knee. The celebrated glamourist widened his eyes, rounded his mouth into a circle, and made the most ridiculous noise. The whole of his expression was at odds with his reputation as one of the great glamourists of the ages.

Young Tom giggled in response and waved his plump fists. Even under a lace cap, the richness of the infant's red curls was apparent.

"Oh, what a *Rotschopf* you are. Like one of Rubens's *Cherubinen*, eh?"

At that, Tom's gaze drifted from the elderly glamourist's face, as if he were watching something that attracted him. Every infant Jane had known stared as Tom did, seeming to fix upon random patterns in the air. Yet, if one switched one's vision to the ether, the object of the infant's fascination would be clear. Loose strands of natural glamour floated in front of Tom.

Jane glanced across the room to where her husband, Sir David Vincent, sat by the window, with a faint smile warming his features as he watched Herr Scholes play with their nephew. During the four months they had been in residence in Vienna, Vincent had taken the opportunity to refresh his acquaintance with his old mentor, Herr Scholes. Their time in the city had led to a softening in Vincent, who seemed to have shed layers of disquiet. His blue coat of superfine hung to advantage on his broad shoulders. Once the strong line of Vincent's jaw had seemed incapable of anything more than disdain. Now, he was captivated with Tom to the point of offering to watch the boy while Jane's sister and her husband made calls. Truly, Jane thought that Vincent might even be pleased that Tom's nanny had been taken with an ague.

"There." Vincent sat forward as Tom snatched at the empty air in front of Herr Scholes. "He is reaching for the glamour."

"Love, he simply has not yet learned to distinguish between the corporeal world and the ether."

"But he is forward for his age, is he not? To reach at only two months?"

Jane laughed at her husband. "Melody was reaching for glamour threads at least this young. Likely sooner, though it is hard to tell before they begin to acquire some coordination."

Herr Scholes wrinkled his nose at the little boy. "Lady Vincent, would you be so kind as to indulge us both with a little glamour? My hands are rather full."

"Of course."

When Jane had first met Herr Scholes, she had been too intimidated by his reputation to perform glamour in front of him without a great deal of persuasion. But he had been so generous with his attention that Jane soon lost her fear. Seeing him make faces at Melody's baby only endeared him to her further.

She let her gaze shift to view the ether and pulled forth a fold of glamour, twisting the ray of light into a simple red ball, which she bounced between her hands. It took so little effort that her heart barely sped at all. Tom's gaze followed the arc of the ball with lively curiosity. Jane bent the strands that created the illusory ball so that it came closer to the infant. He snatched at it as it swung by, frowning as his hand passed through it.

"Very good, my little man." Herr Scholes nodded with mock seriousness. "Now. Will you keep the ball moving, but alter the threads so that it is not in the visible spectrum? Let us see if he reaches for it then."

"Give me but a moment . . ." Jane let her own vision shift from the corporeal world into the second sight of the ether and loosened the strings of light that made up the red ball. She let them slacken into nether-red, the area of the spectrum below visible sight. In her own second sight, the strands of glamour glowed. They stretched out of the ether, wrapped around her hand and twisted into the shape of a ball. Her view of the corporeal world was little more than a dim, grey perception of the room.

Still, she could see Tom clearly enough to know that he, too, watched a ball that was no longer visible to normal sight.

"Ha!" Vincent clapped his hand upon his knee. "Surely this is exceptional."

"Yes. Yes. He is exceptional." She could not help but laugh at her husband.

"When he starts folding glamour, then we may call him exceptional. Until then, he is merely interested." Herr Scholes crossed his eyes for the boy. "And adorable! To give you better understanding, my daughter's second child was working glamour the week before he was delivered."

"Surely not." Jane was so astonished that her vision snapped back to the corporeal plane. "That cannot have been safe for the mother or child."

"And how do you tell a baby to stop working glamour?

Hm? It never lasted long enough to be a concern, but was quite astonishing." He winked at Jane. "I should not be surprised if you experienced a similar spectacle some day."

Vincent cleared his throat. "Are you sure it was not a prank? Recall M. Chastain's flood?"

"Oh, that was clever. But no. This is a genuine, though rare, event. Your pranks, on the other hand, were far from rare."

It was unnecessary, but Jane was nevertheless grateful for Vincent's consideration. Her miscarriage was far enough in the past that remembrances of their childless state did not provoke the sharp pain it once had. Her nephew did much to soothe her, as did the reminder that with infants came a long list of messes that were kept in check by only the presence of a nanny. Still, it was awkward that everyone expected her and Vincent to have children by now. Three years they had been married, while Melody and Alastar had been wed little more than a year and had Tom to show for their time.

Jane let the glamour she was holding unravel back into the ether. "Did you say pranks? You must imagine my curiosity at my husband's exploits. Pray, do not keep me in suspense."

Herr Scholes gave a little chuckle. "Oh ho! Well should you pray. Your husband is one of the most devilish—"

Again, Vincent cleared his throat. "I suspect I shall regret this topic."

"I was only going to tell Lady Vincent about the fishpond."

"Ah—Um." Vincent's blush was most becoming.

Jane asked, all innocence, "Fishpond?"

Her husband shifted in his seat and rubbed his brown curls into an even more riotous mess. "I may have been caught while attempting a bit of subterfuge."

"Three times! I thought he would never learn. I had only three rules, and one of them was that my pupils must be in the house by midnight."

"You said it was so that your housekeeper did not need to wait up to let us in. I did not make her wait, did I?"

"Only because you were opening a window and stealing out of it. He left a ladder by the window, Lady Vincent, masked by a glamural, so he could come and go at his leisure. And I do need to give him credit: it was a very pretty illusion. This was before he had developed the *Sphère Obscurcie*, so he had needed to weave a glamural with all the details of the view that would have been visible if the ladder had not been present."

"It was not terribly complicated, being against a stucco wall."

"If it had not been so nicely done, I would have noticed it sooner. Now, the window was not so high, but there was a small ornamental fishpond next to the house, and he used the ladder to span it. The first time, I simply removed the ladder."

"I was practised at slipping out, so I slid my legs out the window, trusting the ladder was there, lost my balance, and landed in the pond."

"Woke the house with his swearing!"

"It was cold."

"You were embarrassed, and the anger came from that."

Vincent rubbed the back of his neck and gave a dry grimace. "Shall I hold Tom for you? Perhaps he needs changing." Her usually gruff husband appeared to be an embarrassed schoolboy. Given his height and the breadth of his shoulders, it was an incongruous expression, rather like one might expect from a chagrined bear. He adjusted the cuffs of his coat, a blush still high on his cheeks.

"Tom is perfectly content where he is." The glamourist tapped the infant's nose with his forefinger. "Are you not, my boy?"

Tom gurgled with delight, offering no escape for Vincent.

"The second time, he lifted part of the glamour that was masking the ladder and looked before stepping out. But . . ."

With a pained chuckle, Vincent took up the next section. "But he had placed a second glamour beneath the first to show a ladder there. It was not. Mind you, the illusion was brilliant. The support structure was woven so that it looked like drifting bits of natural glamour. We had not yet begun to study Wohlreich's treatise on opticks and the possible uses of poorfire threads as anchor points in glamurals. I had not known the etymology of poorfire until then, and find it quite fascinating. Did you know it was a corruption of 'porphyry,' after rocks the color of the shellfish blood that the ancient Greeks used to dye their gowns purple?"

"Oddly, I did. It was mentioned in *A Girl's Primer on Glamour.*"

"Ah. The benefits of being encouraged to study the womanly arts. My own education was somewhat more autodidactic, until Herr Scholes."

"My dear . . . I believe that you are using a discussion of craft to change the subject."

"And you will not let me?"

"Did you land in the pond again?"

"I did."

"With as much swearing as before!" Herr Scholes laughed.

"Although not for the same reasons this time. Cold and wet, yes, but I was more angry that I had been tricked by glamour. It was an affront that my dignity disliked more than the dousing."

"And yet, that did not stop you from attempting to slip out again." Herr Scholes lifted a finger into the air. "The third time, he had hidden the ladder in his room, to safeguard against its removal."

"So I made it out the window and across the pond, thinking myself in the clear. Until my teacher threw a basin of water on me." Vincent shook his head, laughing now at the memory. "How did you know that I would be stepping out that particular night? I have never been able to satisfy myself as to that. It was weeks after the other attempts."

Herr Scholes winked. "I did not know. I was not there, in fact."

"But—but, I saw you. And let us not forget the basin of water." Vincent tilted his head, staring at the older man in disbelief. "Glamour? No—no, I was unequivocally wet, because I remember dripping on the floor and hanging my clothes to dry afterwards."

"A string stretched across the path emptied the basin. I heard the swearing—again. It awakened the household, and gave me time to step into an inverted Cruikshank's weave that I had woven earlier on my balcony. I then had a clear line of sight to your path. Had you crept out during the day, I would never have been able to get away with it, because the image does not have the detail to be plausible in daylight. But in the dark, to an angry young man, it no doubt looked very much like I was standing on the path."

Vincent's gaze went a little distant, as though he were looking into the ether or into memory. "Oh. That was beautifully done. And you did not speak, then. Simply pointed back to the house. When I had changed out of my wet things and you were waiting at my door, I thought you had followed me. Truly artful. I am embarrassed anew that I did not sort that out."

"I am pleased to see that being embarrassed no longer makes you angry."

"Not usually."

Jane asked, "But why were you stealing out?"

Vincent's smile slipped a fraction. In the hesitation, she saw him consider avoiding the question. Then he gave a little shrug. "This was not long after I arrived. I had been free of my father's influence for just over a year and had trouble sleeping." For a moment the memory of his father's abuse haunted his face, then he cleared his expression, as if from habit. "Walks helped clear my head. That night, Herr

Scholes advised me to use glamour as a release. It has proved to be more efficacious."

"I will tell you now, my intention that night had been to expel you. I thought you were off visiting a maid, and if you had dissembled in the slightest, I would have carried through with that intention, though it would have broken my heart." He shifted Tom to his other arm. "I had given you three chances only because I was not prepared to let go of my best pupil."

"You had better pupils. I was merely—"

"Mr. Vincent!" Herr Scholes glared at Jane's husband. She shrank back in her chair herself, even though his look was not turned upon her. "What have I told you, repeatedly, about undervaluing your work?"

The abashed look returned, and Jane could imagine her husband as a pupil of one and twenty. He knit his hands together, ducking his head. "I must not undervalue my work simply because I enjoy it. A working artist understands his worth and lives by it."

"Good. Though I suppose I should apologise for speaking to you as a pupil. I am still unused to calling you Sir David."

"To be honest, I would prefer to be Mr. Vincent still, but one does not say no when the Prince Regent wishes to confer a knighthood."

The door swept open, and Jane's sister entered with a smile. From the hall behind her, an unmistakable bustle announced that the rest of Jane's family had arrived back from their excursion. Melody spied their guest and gave a squeal of delight. "Herr Scholes! What a pleasure. Will you stay for dinner? Do say you will. And have they made you hold Tom!" Melody had retained a pleasing plumpness to her figure after the birth of Tom, though that was hardly surprising given the rich food in Vienna. Jane's own clothes were growing tight from the abundance of *knödel* and *strudel*. Not that a little bit of plumpness would do anything to balance her overlong nose, but it might soften her sharp chin. On Melody, the fullness gave her a merry cheer that supported her already sunny disposition.

Herr Scholes relinquished Tom with a sigh. "Mrs. O'Brien. It is a pleasure to spend time with your son. My grandchildren are all too old to have much time for me."

Entering behind Melody, Alastar O'Brien crossed to shake the glamourist's hand. "It is very good of you, nevertheless. And allow me to repeat the invitation to dine. Cook has promised *Erdäpfelknödel* for dinner."

"Thank you. I accept."

The next few moments were occupied with a procession of parental figures as Jane's parents and Mr. O'Brien's joined the merry gathering. Mrs. Ellsworth repeated the invitation to dinner and continued to press Herr Scholes to stay, as though he had not given his assent several times already. The conversation turned back to the health of Tom and the pleasures of having an infant in the house, though this latter became more dubious as the young man began to add his own contribution to the volume of noise.

While they were attempting to quiet the boy, Alastar escaped the small circle and went to Vincent. "There are some letters for you."

"Ah. Thank you." He took the small packet, clearly grateful for an excuse to avoid the bustle, and sat with them by the window for better light.

Herr Scholes smacked his forehead with the flat of his palm. "Letters! I was so taken with young Master O'Brien that I forgot I had a reason for calling. Have you given thought to what you will do when you return to England?"

Jane shook her head. "I am afraid not. We had originally thought to seek some new commissions, but with the state of the nation presently . . ."

"Princess Charlotte." Melody sighed in commiseration, making those necessary arrangements to attend to her son. "Such a tragedy."

The Prince Regent's daughter had died birthing her stillborn son the previous November, though news travelled so slowly that Jane and her family had not received word until recently. With all the resources the royal family had, and with excellent medical care, it did not seem possible that Princess Charlotte should come to such an end. Yet women died of childbirth so often, it should not have surprised Jane that even a member of the royal family could be felled.

The entire nation was in mourning. For the year after the death, the streets of London would be lined with crape-covered windows. Ladies would dye their wardrobes black, and gentlemen would wear a band of black upon their sleeve. Glamourists would be briefly employed to strip homes of glamour for the duration of the mourning period.

It was such a desolate tradition. When Christ had risen after the third day, he had let the disciples stick their fingers in his wounds, saying, "Let there be no illusions here." So, while in mourning, a house stood bare to the eye to remind the inhabitants of the one who was lost. Even here in Vienna, Jane and Vincent had pulled the glamour from the house as a gesture of respect for the death of the Prince Regent's heir and her son. As bare as a house in mourning . . . which meant that there would be little work for glamourists in Britain in general and none at all for the Prince Regent's glamourist.

Herr Scholes cleared his throat. "Well, I had a letter from one of my pupils, who is starting a school for girls in London and has asked me to help her find glamourist teachers. She is one of Sir David's former pupils, so I naturally thought to ask if you and he might be interested."

"Possibly." It would be very agreeable to remain in one place for a while. Their tour of the continent had been extended rather longer than they had originally planned. Jane turned to get Vincent's opinion, more than a little surprised that he had not expressed some curiosity about the project.

He sat in the window in a state of shock, though not at Herr Scholes's news. His face was a blank mask, breath held, as he stared at one of the letters that Mr. O'Brien had brought in. From Jane's seat, she could make out a black border on the edge of the paper. That, with his rigid expression, could only mean that he had received word of a death.

"Vincent?"

"Hm?" He shook himself and looked up. "Forgive me. I was not quite listening. What were you saying?"

Melody, who was less acquainted with his moods, said, "Herr Scholes has a possible situation for you."

"That is very kind." He looked down at the letter again, folding it so the border no longer showed.

"It is a school for glamourists. In London! Is that not grand?"

"Indeed."

"Speaking of learning glamour . . . Herr Scholes, would you tell my sister about your grandson's first use of the art?" Jane tried to draw the group's attention away from Vincent. He was clearly discomfited—or, rather, it was clear to Jane that he was distressed. To another, he might appear merely distant or unconcerned. His agitation was marked by a layer of excessive calm spoilt only by a faint tremor in his hand as he turned the folded letter over and over.

He made a show of listening to Melody and Herr Scholes compare notes about infant glamour, but his gaze stared through them as if he were watching the ether. Jane tried to think of some errand that could offer her an excuse to take Vincent out of the room and find out what news he had received. She now rather wished they had not invited Herr Scholes to stay for dinner.

Before she could think of a ruse, Vincent stood and crossed the room to Jane. He leaned down, handing her the letter, and whispered, "My father is dead."

Two

A Letter of Note

At his words, Jane looked up sharply from the letter he had handed her. "Are you all right?"

"I hardly know. Will you forgive me if I . . . ?" He flexed his hands in an unconscious gesture, as if he was already reaching for glamour to calm himself. Or, if not to calm himself, at least to work himself to exhaustion in an effort to clear his head.

"Of course." Louder, she said, "Would you mind fetching that book we were discussing?"

Vincent nodded in thanks. "It is upstairs." With apologies to the small gathering, all of whom were so occupied with Tom they paid him little mind, Vincent slipped out of the room.

It had taken Jane a long time to understand his need for privacy while he contended with his feelings. He had spent too long trying to be the model of manliness that his father expected, to be at all comfortable freely expressing any troubles. Still, she planned to look in on him later.

The ceiling creaked overhead as Vincent paced in their apartments upstairs. She could picture him with his chin tucked deep into his collar in thought, hands clenched behind his back, as though he were a lecturer. When his strides overhead stopped, the picture changed to him standing in the middle of their bedchamber working one of his vast abstract glamours.

Even in death, Vincent's father had the power to disturb his sensibilities. If she had not already abhorred the man, his ability to distress her husband would have provided her with ample reason. She slid her chair back a little from the group and unfolded the letter, to acquaint herself with the details of Lord Verbury's death.

Verbury Court
5 January 1818
Sir David Vincent
My dear Vincent,
I do not know if I still have the right to call you brother, but I am writing to you as a brother, so shall take that familiarity. Our father is dead. I do not expect that you will mourn him, but it is necessary that I tell you of his death. He died at our West Indian estate in Antigua last August after suffering a stroke. He had been weakened by yellow fever and I understand did not linger long.

The second death that I must tell you of weighs more heavily. Our brother Garland celebrated his ascendance as the newly made Earl of Verbury with the purchase of a barouche-landau for himself and invited me out for a drive to Lyme Regis. The roads are not always the best in September, and our carriage was upset. I do not recall the details, but the results I know too well. Garland was killed. I was left with a broken arm and a foot so injured that it had to be removed.

Garland's death leaves me the earl. It is not a position in which I ever thought I would find myself.

It is on this point that I write to you to beg for your help. I know that you have long been estranged from the family and that I did nothing to ease the suffering that our father inflicted upon you. I was a coward. The fact that I told you this in our youth does not excuse it. I simply want to acknowledge that I have no right to expect aid, when I did not extend the same charity to you.

There is apparently a newer will in Antigua, which will be released only to one of his sons. It does not say which one. I cannot go. Would you be willing to be a Hamilton again, long enough to set the estate in order? You are, let us be honest, better suited to the task than I, in ways which have nothing to do with my health. You studied at university. I studied only horses, the cut of coats, and the inside of gin houses. I was a second son. I expected to die without ever having any more responsibility than to avoid embarrassing the family. You left and fashioned a new path.

I do not wish to drag you back into the tangled mess that our father left, but I am at a loss. Please. For the sake of our mother, if for no one else, will you go to Antigua? Will you help us?

Regardless, I have arranged for funds to be made ready for you in Vienna. Call at the office of Lord Flower-Horne, who will make any arrangements you desire, including telling me to go to Hell.

With deep regret,

Believe me at all times with sincerity and respect, your faithful and obliged brother,

Richard Hamilton

The Right Honourable, The Earl of Verbury

Jane had to read the letter again to fully comprehend it. She looked up, expecting night to have fallen outside, but the late afternoon sun still shone on the buildings across the street and caught on the mullioned windows. A gentle breeze shook the strands of bobbing ivy that twined around the frame.

Lord Verbury, dead.

She did not expect Vincent to regret that fact, but she had no idea how he might feel about the death of his eldest brother or the accident that had disabled his middle brother. She had only met the men once, and it had been an evening fraught with tension. She rubbed her brow, trying to order her thoughts. When she lowered her hand, Herr Scholes was watching her.

He pushed his chair away from the conversation, which seemed to be about the trials of teething, and drew it next to Jane. "Is Sir David well?"

Jane smoothed the folds of her dress. If her mother had asked the question, Jane would have given a polite fiction, but Herr Scholes had filled the void that Vincent's father had created long before his death. "He has received word that his father and eldest brother are dead."

"Ah." A wealth of unhappy knowledge rested in that simple exhalation. He rubbed his bare scalp. It was a gesture she had seen from Vincent many times, and Jane suddenly realised where he had learned it. Herr Scholes looked at the ceiling as if he could see through it to Vincent. "Forgive me for an impertinent question, but does he still have nightmares?"

"Not since we arrived here. They were particularly bad after the Trial." Jane was aware that she spoke of it as if there could be no other trials, but when one stood accused of treason by one's father, as Lord Verbury had done to Vincent, there could be no other. The Trial was over a year behind them, yet Jane knew that Vincent's sleep would be disturbed tonight. "Have you any suggestions?"

"I am certain that you know him better than I by now, and you have heard the sum of my wisdom about using glamour to channel your emotions."

"He does work himself to exhaustion when upset."

"Hm. I am familiar with that . . ."

"Was he so often upset?"

"Angry, more than anything. Understand that, given our

profession, I was accustomed to pupils who had been told that glamour was too feminine an art for them to pursue. Most of the young men who came to study with me bore the scars of their choice in some form or another. Your husband was marked by fury, made worse because he was so used to containing it that he often did not recognise his own anger." He sighed and scrubbed again at his scalp.

"I think he was still struggling with that when we met. I thought he was angry at me, at the time."

"You? You have done wonders for him. I saw him laugh more today than in the two years he studied with me. I think he—"

An abrupt sound from above, as of a body striking the floor, caused Herr Scholes to break off. Jane was at the door to the parlour without any memory of having stood. She glanced back at Herr Scholes, who met her eye with a knowing look. It was the sound of Vincent falling unconscious.

Fortunately, only family was present, and they were familiar enough with Vincent's history that Jane needed to make only a hasty apology for her exit. She hurried out of the parlour and up the stairs to their room.

Vincent had not been gone long enough to risk a seizure by working beyond his capacity. Even so, it was rare that he pushed himself to the point of fainting. His stamina was impressive and one of his great strengths as a glamourist. Still, Jane would not be easy until she saw him.

When she pushed open the door to their chamber, the remnants of glamour floated in the room. Unlike the detailed, precise illusions that they created for the houses of nobility, this consisted of raw strands of glamour pulled straight from the ether. Reds and blacks swirled around the room in a thundercloud of distress.

His voice came from behind the small sofa set in the middle of the room. "On the floor."

Jane shut the door and hurried around the sofa. Vincent lay on his back in his shirtsleeves. Sweat had soaked the fabric, sticking it to his chest. It plastered his hair to his head and stood in great drops upon his forehead, but he was clearly not in any danger.

Jane knelt beside him. "You worry me."

"I did not faint."

"And yet, you are on the floor."

"I was dizzy and caught my heel. It seemed simpler to lie here and wait for it to pass." He wiped the sweat from his brow. "You read the letter?"

"I did." Jane still had it in her hand, in fact.

Vincent covered his face with his hands, letting out a long breath that approached a groan. With his fingers resting on his brow, he rubbed his temples.

"Does your head ache?"

"A little."

She suspected it was more than a little. Since the concussion he had received when they were in Venice, he seemed to be more prone to headaches and dizziness, but he did not like to discuss it. Jane counted it a victory that he had admitted any discomfort at all. She set the letter on a side table and shifted to sit by him. "Would you like me to rub your forehead?"

"Thank you." He moved so that his head was resting in her lap and sighed again as she began to rub his temples. His brow was fevered and still damp with sweat, but no worse than she had seen him at the end of a normal day of work. Where his collar lay open, the strong beat of his pulse counted the time passing. For some minutes, they remained together in this manner, as Jane waited for Vincent to order his thoughts.

The beat of his heart slowed under her touch and his brow cooled. Vincent lay with his eyes closed. She could almost hope that he had fallen asleep, were it not for the fluttering of his eyes beneath his lids and a crease between his brows.

Inhaling, Vincent opened his eyes. "Muse, I do not know what to do."

"Must we do anything? Your brother is quite right that you have neither reason nor obligation to assist."

"I am less confident in that." Vincent lay still for a moment, the muscle in the corner of his jaw clenching. "My brother. . . . Both of them, really, but Richard, my middle brother—even were his injury not a consideration. . . . He was ill-used by my father."

"I think that is a common condition for your family."

"Ah yes, but—" He stopped and for a moment appeared to hold his breath. A small, thin stream of air escaped in an almost inaudible keen. Though she had pointed out that he made this noise when conflicted, he had yet to break the habit, and she did not encourage him to do so, as the sound proved a useful indication of his state of mind. He grimaced, looking up at her. "Not a word of this, Muse. If you meet Richard again, you must pretend not to know. I know I can trust to your discretion, but promise me nevertheless."

"Of course. I shall say nothing."

Vincent nodded, jaw still clenched. "Richard is six years my senior. When he was fifteen, my father found him and one of the stable-boys engaged in carnal acts. I ask you to make no judgements against him—I cannot blame him for seeking what comfort he might find in a comfortless household, and nothing merits what my father did as punishment. For reasons known only to him, my father seated the three of us on a bench in the stable." Vincent sat up abruptly so his back was to her. He blew out air in a huff. "He tied the stable-boy to the wall and whipped him. If we looked away, he beat us, too."

"My God."

His laugh was ragged. "No God was involved in that. He saw my interest in glamour as a sign that Richard's propensities had transferred to me, so he included me as a warning. All of which is to say that when Richard says that he did not extend any aid to me, it is because he knew the consequences of doing so."

"But you risked being beaten and still—"

"No. No, you do not quite see. It was not the bodily pain, though I am certain that my father beat Richard as well. But my brother saw someone he loved whipped bloody and turned out with no recommendations and no place. I was too young to think of such things at the time, but I doubt the stable-boy lived much past that night." He turned to speak over his shoulder, the planes of his face dark against the evening sun. "It is that memory, in part, which causes me to be conflicted about what I ought to do. I now have the opportunity to mend a relationship that has been broken for years, and yet . . . and yet, is it something that I wish to entangle myself with again?"

"Did you have good relations aside from the pressure of your father?"

He shrugged. "By the standards of your family, no. I learned to guard my tongue at an early age and had few honest conversations until I came to study with Herr Scholes. But he was never cruel. Richard, I mean. Richard was never cruel to me."

All of Jane's training was inadequate for this. She had been raised with an understanding of the proper forms and etiquette for mourning. With another family, the death of a father and an elder brother would be a signal to begin deep mourning. She knew to drape the mirrors and to undo the glamour. She knew to procure black cravats and gloves for Vincent. She knew to order the stationery bordered with black, and the black sealing wax. For a year and a day, they would carry out the mourning period . . . or, rather, that is what they would have done for a different father.

With Vincent's, she was at as much of a loss as he.

He looked forward again, shoulders slightly hunched. "The mourning period for Princess Charlotte means no glamour in England until November. . . . If we cannot work there, there is nothing that would prevent me from going to the West Indies."

In the hall, the stairs creaked with a slow and steady tread. Jane turned to stare at the door, willing the person away. A gentle knock sounded, in spite of her efforts.

"Jane?" her father called softly.

"Yes, Papa?" She made an effort to keep her voice even.

"Your mother sent me to inquire if everything is all right."

Jane ran her fingers down Vincent's back, feeling the old scars through his shirt. "Please tell Mama that my husband is not dead or even ill."

"I already did, but she wants to know what the noise was."

Vincent raised his voice. "I tripped. No broken bones or sprains. Only a bruised ego." He turned his head to Jane. "You should probably tell him."

Sighing, Jane clambered to her feet. She loved her family, but there were times when their concerns—or, more especially, her mother's concerns—overwhelmed the actual difficulties. Jane crossed to the door and opened it, slipping into the hall where her father waited.

Mr. Ellsworth's white hair stood out in a silver halo. He wore a rare furrow on his brow and compressed his lips as she shut the door. "I am sorry, Jane. I told your mother that if Vincent needed medical attention then you would call for us, but you know how she gets."

"I do." She bit the inside of her lip, imagining what would happen when her mother heard the news. "Papa . . . Vincent's father is dead. And his eldest brother."

"What? Both?"

Nodding, Jane related the contents of the letter with as few words as possible, but she could still see her father's shock. His brows drew closer together with each word she spoke. "How is Vincent taking it?"

"Distressed. Uncertain."

"And you?"

"Also uncertain. I think we will likely go to the West Indies, and I dread what the trip will do to him."

"There, now . . ." Her father pulled her into an embrace, and Jane let some of the tension she was carrying transfer to him. "There, now. From what you have implied of his father, he has survived worse, and he has you with him to face this trial."

"I wish I knew what to do for him."

Her father set her back and tilted his head down to look at her. "Shall I tell you what I do for your mother?"

"You cannot seriously compare Vincent with Mama."

"Well, he has more sense than she, I will grant that readily enough, but—" He held up a finger. "But. You must always remember that her fears are real to her. She wants to know that she is not alone."

"She wants attention."

"Yes. That is how I let her know that she is not alone." He made a little wave of his fingers. "Granted, distracting her is easier. But, as a start, make certain that Vincent knows he is not facing this alone. Meanwhile, I shall give you both a great and noble gift."

Jane could not help but smile at her father. "And what is that?"

"I shall be the one to tell your mother." He pressed his hands to his bosom in a martyr's pose.

"Oh! That is a great and noble gift. You are too good to me."

He winked at her, turning to go back down the stairs. Listening to her father's footsteps recede towards the distant murmur of conversation below, Jane quieted her breathing in the same way she might after working an especially challenging piece of glamour. She inhaled to her fullest extent, until her ribs pressed against her short stays, then let the breath out through her mouth. It did not help. She still felt as though she would be ill. There was no correct choice in this matter, only a lesser evil.

Jane put her hand on the latch and tried to assume an air of calm that she did not feel. When she opened the door, Vincent had moved to the window and was standing with his back to the room. He tossed what appeared to be a jet of fire from hand to hand, directing the glamour with little twists of his fingers. As the door shut, he turned his head and snipped the cords of the illusion. The flames winked out. "Is your mother palpitating?"

"So it seems, but Papa has promised to reassure her as to your health." She came to stand next to the window, just behind Vincent. She could see the angle of his cheek and the edge of his brow. "He also offered to share the news of the letter for us. So we have only to wait until Mama has time to calm down."

His cheek rounded a little. "I do not know if I can remain

in the room so long as that. Might we have our meals sent in?"

"Hush. She is not as bad as that. Sometimes. Occasionally." Jane worried the inside of her lip for a moment. "What do you want to do?"

"Ah, Muse . . . I do not trust my own judgement at all."

"Well . . . let us think through the various particulars." They would go, it was clear to her that they would; but in his current state, Vincent needed help trusting his own instincts. "You left your family to pursue your art and are not bound by any code to assist with the resolution of the will. In fact, given that your father tried to have you executed, can you truly be considered a son?"

Vincent waved his hand, shaking his head. "I am certain that my father would have made arrangements so that we were, at worst, shipped to Australia. No doubt he would have brought us back after a few years, once he thought we had learned not to cross him."

"How can you possibly think so?"

"He would never dispose of an instrument. You have no idea the amount of effort he put into shaping me."

"First of all, your father might have arranged to have *your* sentence commuted, but not for any of the others on trial, and perhaps not for me."

Vincent tilted his head to the side. She could imagine the wince upon his face. "Likely you are correct."

"Second . . . trying to remake you according to his own principles is utterly selfish. If he had rescued you from execution and exile, it would have been for his sake, not yours."

Jane inhaled and held her breath, trying to cool her sudden anger. Every time she considered what that man had done to his son, she became enraged anew. But that would not help her husband sort through the question before him. She let her breath out in a slow stream. "On the other hand, if we set aside your father from our deliberations, your eldest brother's death should surely be mourned, and Richard's infirmity should be pitied. It does seem as though there is a motive for us to go."

Vincent turned. "You would go with me?"

"Vincent." Jane took his hand in hers. "Given all that we are discussing, I would not feel safe or right letting you go alone."

"So you think we should go?"

"I do not relish the prospect, no." The way his thoughts kept offering reasons to go and none to refuse the request told Jane all that she needed to know. It would be difficult but would perhaps at least provide him a means of closing certain chapters in his life. She suspected that if he did not see his father's grave, he would spend his life wondering when the man might appear again. "But it will do us no harm. Going to the West Indies will not put you in contact with any of your living family, as they are all in England. If nothing else, I have not been to the West Indies, and it will be instructive."

Vincent rubbed his face, pressing the palms of his hands against his eyes. Jane let him think and waited until he finally nodded. He lowered his hands and reached for hers. Lifting one of them to his lips, he kissed it gently. "Thank

God for you, Muse. I should be lost without you. I do not wish to go, either, but think we must."

Jane squeezed his hand in return. If Vincent was to go to the West Indies as Lord Verbury's son, then he would need to be a Hamilton again, at least for a short time. That meant observing mourning. She knew how to do that, and she thanked the stars that they need only observe the forms. Nothing could induce her to truly mourn the death of Vincent's father.

Three

Travels and Travails

Vincent's brother, newly made The Right Honourable Earl of Verbury, had been as good as his word. When they called at the office of Lord Flower-Horne, they discovered not only that arrangements had been made for an ample travel allowance, but also that Lord Flower-Horne had already secured passage for them with the Falmouth Packet Service, which regularly sent the mail via packet ships to Jamaica. The vessel would make a stop at Antigua on the way and could drop them off en route.

Though Jane regretted leaving her family, in particular her sister and new nephew, she could not think of allowing Vincent to go by himself. No amount of hysterics on the part of her mother could sway Jane from her intentions.

Even the thought of the trip had been enough to renew Vincent's nightmares. In the three weeks it took to travel across the continent to the English Channel, dreams woke him no fewer than four nights, and he showed signs of disturbed slumber on other nights.

More than once, Jane woke to find Vincent weaving glamour in the bedchamber of whatever inn they had stopped in for the night. She did not alert him to the fact that she was awake for fear that he would take to late-night walks to avoid disturbing her. She had reservations about the trip herself, given how their last voyage had gone, but took comfort from the knowledge that those particular circumstances would not repeat.

A letter had gone ahead of them by fast courier to England to let the newly made Earl of Verbury know that they were en route to Antigua. Vincent had called at the post before they left the port in Falmouth, and a letter from Richard had awaited them, full of such unreserved gratitude that it made Jane a little easier about their decision to go. Still, Jane could not help but think that affairs in Antigua would be much altered eight months after the late earl's death.

One of Jane's true concerns as they finally set sail for the West Indies was that Vincent would be unable to work glamour as a means of distraction at sea. She had packed a few books and their painting supplies, but her best hope lay in the *Verres Obscurcis* they had made in Venice. Vincent was ever a theorist, and puzzling out a conundrum would be just the thing to occupy his mind.

Their berth upon the *Marchioness of Salisbury* was a small room, no more than five feet long and six wide, though it was large by ship standards. Jane could touch the ceiling with a flat hand without standing on her toes. Vincent had to duck to enter the room at all, and he stood with his head cocked to one side, as though he were afraid he would knock it upon the ceiling. Its two narrow bunks, one atop the other at one end of the room, made it clear that Vincent, who was rather over six feet in height, would be sleeping bent the entire voyage. A desk stood built into the forward wall with a variety of cunning shelves above it. Each had a rail to keep the items on it from tumbling off as the ship rolled.

When they first boarded, the movement of the ship troubled Jane not at all. In the morning, however, she was barely out of her bunk when she was afflicted with unexpected nausea. With an urgent necessity, she availed herself of the chamber pot and emptied her dinner from the night before.

Vincent sat up in the top bunk and knocked his head upon the ceiling. With a hand to his head, he clambered out of the bunk. "Muse, are you all right?"

Jane's answer was apparent as she was sick for a second time. When the heaving had passed and Jane had wiped her mouth upon the cloth that Vincent provided, she straightened. "That is most vexing. I hope that I did not acquire an ague at the last inn."

"Might you simply be seasick?"

"I never have been before." Her stomach churned again

and, as if her body needed to voice its disagreement, Jane was sick for the third and fourth times in rapid succession.

"Would you like to lie down?"

"Yes." Jane caught her breath, grateful that she had not yet put on her stays. "I think I might."

By the afternoon, Jane's stomach was improved enough that she felt she might venture forth. She stepped into the dining hall that divided the main cabin. A long narrow table ran down the middle of it, under a skylight that showed an abundance of sail overhead, and beyond that a brilliant blue sky. Jane walked to the front of the cabin and climbed the short ladder, which led up and out.

Stepping over the raised threshold and onto the deck brought her almost immediate relief. The fresh salt air brushed away the lingering nausea. A stiff breeze whipped past her, clutching at her gown and playing with the ribbons of her bonnet. If Jane had not tied it snugly down, she would have lost it to the sea in moments.

That great body of water surrounded them, grey-green and rolling. The passage to the West Indies would be close to a month, and Jane could only hope that she would not be ill that entire time. The ship was filled with men in smart blue uniforms working on the various tasks. Though most were of European descent in appearance, a few Black Africans and a slender Asiatic man worked amongst the others. She could not pretend to understand what any of them were doing with the ropes, beyond adjusting something in the rigging, but the boys scrubbing the deck were obvious enough.

The ship pitched, and Jane grasped the rail as the deck tilted beneath her. A moment later it levelled, and then tilted the opposite way as the ship climbed the next swell.

"Look at the horizon, madam." A Black African sailor stood on a platform a few feet away, steering the boat. He spoke with a curious accent, almost as though his words had been flavoured with sweet jam. He had a broad forehead beneath close-cropped curls and had a long, narrow, nose. He wrinkled that nose and smiled at her. "If the motion of the ship troubles you, the horizon is steady."

"Oh. Thank you." Too ill to be much disturbed at being addressed without an introduction, Jane swallowed and looked out at the far horizon. "Were you much troubled your first time at sea?"

"Oh no, madam. I was sailing with my father before I have memory. But I have seen other Europeans turn your particular shade of green."

"Ah." Staring at the horizon did seem to help. "I thought that Africa was a desert sort of place. I had not thought of sailors there."

He laughed. "It is a large continent with a significant coastline. Somalia, where I am from, has a navy to make the British take notice."

"I confess surprise." She inhaled and let her breath out slowly. "Thank you for the advice about the horizon. I am not usually troubled by seasickness, so have no methods for assuaging it."

"Tell the cook that you have a delicate stomach. He will make a broth for you that will help you steady. If you need anything else, ask for Ibrahim."

"Thank you." Jane kept her gaze out at the horizon, grateful for Ibrahim's advice. Perhaps the trouble had simply been that she could not see anything at all from their cabin. She resolved to spend more time on deck until she became used to the motion, though there was little to see but waves. England had vanished with more speed than she had expected.

"Is there anything else I can help you with, Mrs. Hamilton?" asked Ibrahim.

For a moment, Jane did not answer, before recalling that "Mrs. Hamilton" referred to her. "I was looking for my husband. Mr. Hamilton."

He would, of course, know to whom she was married. It was more to accustom herself to using the name than anything else. For their entire marriage, they had lived with the surname Vincent. It had originally been her husband's given name, as The Honourable Vincent Hamilton, third son of the Earl of Verbury, but he had taken the name David Vincent long before he had met her, so that he could pursue a career as a glamourist. Now, though, given the terms of the late earl's will, it seemed best to be Hamiltons, at least briefly.

The sailor laughed. "Just look to the midship. I think you will spot him readily enough."

Cautiously, Jane turned her gaze towards the front—no, towards the bow of the ship. Beyond the box of the skylight, a great, billowing opalescence of unformed glamour rose above the ship. A cheer went up from a crowd of sailors bunched around the rail. "What in heaven's name?"

"Lightworks. It's a game we play with glamour sometimes, since the use of fireworks is prohibited on ships."

"I thought it was not possible to work glamour at sea." Indeed, she and Vincent had made an effort last summer and had barely been able to catch hold of it. Why had no glamourists written about this habit of sailors?

"Oh, there is no managing it. All it does when you try to catch it is make fragments of rainbows, and you lose those pretty fast. It does serve some utility, if you need to communicate with another ship from a distance and have lost your signal flags." He shook his head. "The game is to see how long a rainbow they can conjure before losing their grip."

A ribbon of undulating light flowed back in the wake of the ship. The sailors counted, beating the deck with their heels. "One, two, three, four, five, six, sev—oh!"

The rainbow evaporated into a sparkling mist. Laughter rose from the group as the sailors shifted around to let someone else have a go. Vincent stood in the middle of the sailors, with his head cocked to one side in an attitude of concentration. He had lost his hat, although Jane hoped he had simply neglected to put it on, so he stood with his brown curls ruffled by the breeze. He nodded in response to something that a grizzled man said and reached into the ether.

A jumble of colours streamed from Vincent's hand as he let the glamour fracture into a long banner made up of the spectrum. As one, the sailors started to count again. When they reached ten, the nature of the chanting changed a little. It took on a tone of disbelief and swelled as the men's enthusiasm grew with each number.

At fifteen, Ibrahim grunted in surprise. "I have never seen anyone go past twelve."

"My husband is—" She bit off "the Prince Regent's glamourist" before she could say it aloud because, of course, Mr. Hamilton was not. That title belonged to Sir David Vincent, and even then it was questionable given the state of mourning in the royal court. "He is given to rivalrous competition."

The glamour fractured amid shouts of, "Nineteen!"

Panting, Vincent leaned forward to brace himself with his hands upon his knees. Jane lost sight of him as the sailors clustered about him with congratulations. Well . . . at least she need not worry that he would go mad without being able to work glamour.

"If you will excuse me?"

"Of course. Don't forget to talk to Cook."

Jane thanked him and made her way forward to the cluster of sailors. Vincent straightened slowly, nodding his thanks at the cries of approbation. The moment he spotted her, his brow turned up in concern. Jane raised a hand to wave and reassure him that she was well. He relaxed, but he still made his way through the sailors to her.

"Feeling better?" Vincent put a hand to her cheek as if to check her temperature.

"Much, thank you. I think it just took me some time to

acclimate to the ship's motion." She nodded to the group of sailors, who had resumed their game. "I feel that I should ask if you are well. That was quite the display."

"Eh? Oh—Lieutenant Price had an interesting trick to how he let the glamour spool out. Instead of holding it directly, he is, in essence, holding an opening in the ether and letting the motion of the ship draw the glamour out." Vincent gestured with his right hand. "Shall I show you?"

"Yes, but may I suggest that you not succeed quite so well this time?" Jane tugged her gloves off, intent on having a go herself, once he had shown her the technique.

"Hm? Why not?"

"Because the helmsman seemed astonished by your display. He said that he had not seen anyone go past twelve."

"Oh. Lieutenant Price said that he knew a fellow who could go to thirty. Mind you, I do not know how. It feels as if it is drawing your breath out with the glamour. I have never been winded so quickly. And the heat! Were it not for the breeze, the heat would have undone me. Here, I will show you." Vincent extended his hand into the ether.

Jane let her vision shift to the second sight to watch what he did there. He spun his hand so the palm was up. With his thumb and forefinger, he reached forward, as though to pinch a speck of salt, then spread them wide almost like a set of scissors opening. It was not an uncommon motion, but rather than catching a strand of glamour and drawing it forth, he held the gap in the ether open and used his remaining three fingers to guide the glamour that streamed out of the opening. Without that little bit of direction, it would not have retained enough distinctness to be visible. Even so, bits and pieces shattered around his hand in a phosphorescent mist. The stream of rainbow that emerged from his hand spread and diffused almost immediately as it streamed back down the length of the boat.

"I think I have it." Jane tilted her head and considered whether there were any changes she might make to alter the position of the hands. Attempting a contrariwise Bellinger's grip might improve it, but only if she could catch hold of the glamour in the first place.

Letting the glamour dissolve, Vincent wiped his brow. "Thank heavens. I had to watch three or four times before I could spot what they were doing."

"You always say the kindest things." Though she teased, Jane was secretly pleased that her ability to trace and understand patterns was superior to his. Dipping her hand into the ether, she parted the curtain and let glamour flow out. The effect was as if she were managing a massive fold and spinning it out at enormous speed. Her breath quickened till she was quite panting, but she held on, perversely intent on reaching at least a count of twelve. At a count of six, Jane felt her stomach churn. Perhaps this was not so clever a plan after all. She released the glamour.

"What did you think?"

Jane swallowed back her uneasiness, though it was significantly milder than it had been that morning. "It seemed to require as much exertion as working a large fold at speed. Do you suppose . . . do you suppose that the glamour itself contains an energy? Might that be what causes the corporeal effects rather than exertion?"

"I had the same thought. Certainly light does, though glamour is composed of only waves, while light consists of both waves and particles." Vincent leaned against the rail, looking back at the white wake the ship left behind them. "Perhaps it is the friction of the waves? That might account for the unhealthy effects of some of the glamours outside the visible spectrum. Too rough for safety, or some such."

Jane considered the art involved in managing glamour. It seemed likely that if one were able to do more than produce an oily rainbow, then Napoleon would have found a way to control that power for use during the blockade. The fact that he had *not* certainly added weight to the old belief that glamour was not possible while at sea. It was simply too difficult to control the relationship of the glamour both to the ether and to one's own self given the constant motion of a ship. However . . . if one did not have to maintain the relationship with one's own body . . . "I should like to see what happens when we use one of the *Verres Obscurcis*."

At the mention of their experiment in glass, Vincent pushed himself away from the rail. "By Jove—yes."

"Should we make the attempt, so exposed like this?"

Vincent returned to the rail, looking around them. "If it works, then we shall be invisible, and if it does not, then we simply have a ball of glass."

"And if it works imperfectly?" Jane gestured to the men working around them. There was not a place on board the vessel where they could go and be unobserved, save their own cabin. That was not an option, since the *Verre Obscurci* required full sunlight to work. "The dining room is unoccupied and, with the skylight, should have enough direct sun to make the experiment."

"I acknowledge the superiority of your plan."

"As you should."

Laughing, he offered her his arm and led her across the deck to their cabin.

As they reached the back—aft—of the ship, Ibrahim smiled and nodded towards the horizon. Jane nodded back, to let him know that the remedy seemed to be helping. She hoped that going below deck would not cause her nausea to return, but Vincent was moving with more life to his step than she had seen since they received the news of his father's death. A little seasickness was worth that.

The dining room was still thankfully unoccupied. The sun was overhead and a little behind the ship, casting brilliant rays across the table and into the front of the chamber. Vincent ducked into their cabin as Jane sat on one of the long benches affixed to the table. The lamps that hung over it swayed with the motion of the ship and did her nausea no good. She looked up at the sails visible through the skylight as she waited for Vincent.

He took only a few moments to reappear from their cabin. Under one arm, he carried the small chest that held two of the glass spheres they had made in Murano the previous summer. They had decided to pack the rest and ship them back to Long Parkmead, Jane's family home in England, rather than bring them all to the West Indies.

Vincent set the chest on the table by Jane. "I am glad you thought to bring these, Muse. It would not have occurred to me until we were on the ship, and then I would have cursed their absence."

"You were distracted, with good cause."

He grimaced. "Yes, well." Fishing the key out of his pocket, Vincent undid the lock on the little chest and opened it. Inside, wrapped in a length of black velvet, lay two of the smaller spheres they had made. So long as they were in shadow, the effect would not take hold.

Jane said, "If you stand back some feet from me, you will be out of the influence of the *Verre*. If it works, you will be able to ascertain that quickly."

"Hm. And why do you get to be the one using the *Verre*?"

"Because I am already sitting." Besides which, her stomach was still uneasy. "And I like to watch your face when the sphere works."

"Oh?"

"You have the most charming smile."

Chuckling, he ducked his head and gave a little bow. "As you wish."

When he stood some feet back, Jane loosened the wrapping around the glass sphere. She threw the cloth back. Sunlight caught in the faint inclusions that twisted around the otherwise unblemished crystal. From within, she could tell no difference at all. A properly woven *Sphère Obscurcie* would bend the light around the glamourist at its centre, while leaving their view of the world clear. A *Verre* was their own invention for capturing glamour in glass, and it worked the same way. The thing in question was if removing the human element would allow glamour to work upon a moving ship. A quick look into the ether showed that the sunlight at least seemed to be acting upon the glass in the same manner as it had upon the land.

Jane lifted her gaze from the *Verre* to where Vincent stood with his hands upon his hips. He really did have the most charming smile. Throwing his head back, he laughed.

"May I take it that we have success?"

Vincent fairly skipped forward in response, slipping into the *Verre*'s influence. "Oh, Muse, it is as steady as if we were on land."

"Therefore, the only thing that prevents glamour from working at sea is human error." She studied the sphere, paying particular attention to where the glamour departed the glass. It did billow a little, although clearly not enough to spoil the image. She shifted her vision back from the ether to address Vincent. "Do you think—what?"

He took a step closer, careful, so that his shadow did not cross the Sphere. His smile was still present, but had become smaller and more intimate. "I think . . . I think that I am a very fortunate man."

"And why is that?" Jane's heart sped in a way that had nothing to do with glamour.

"Because no one can see us now."

Her breath was taken quite away.

Jane and Vincent discovered that two determined individuals could fit in one of the narrow bunks. After their experiments with sleeping arrangements the night prior, Vincent had retired to the upper bunk for slumber.

On their third morning at sea, his long legs hung over the side before he hopped down. For a moment, his nightshirt caught on the raised edge of the bunk and offered an appealing view of the backs of his knees. Not even that was enough to quiet Jane's heaving stomach.

Remembering the sailor's suggestion that a view of the horizon would help, Jane rolled upright. She would dress quickly and go out on the deck for fresh air. Surely that would—

She did not manage to do more than stand before her plans were overturned. Jane barely made it to the washbasin in time.

"Muse!" Vincent had his hand upon her back to steady her.

"Oh . . . oh, I am so sorry. I have made a mess." She clung miserably to the side of the small table.

"Do not concern yourself about that." He felt her brow. "I should have insisted that you stay in bed yesterday."

"I think it is the bed that is making me ill. Something about the motion when I am lying down. Truly. When I am outside in the fresh air, I am better." She paused to establish that she was not yet better. Groaning, Jane hung her head over the foulness. She had not been this ill since she was with child . . .

Her thoughts slowed and tripped upon themselves.

Was it possible? Her cycle had always been irregular, but she had not had her flower for . . . four months—no, nearly five now. Usually it was not more than three months that she skipped, and then only when working heavily with glamour. They had worked so little in Vienna because their attention was elsewhere, what with Melody's confinement. Her clothing had also been getting snug, but Jane had thought it was simply due to the rich food in Vienna. The illness now put everything into a different light.

Good lord in heaven. She might be with child.

Four

Lines of Heritage

Jane did not tell Vincent of her supposition immediately. At first her reason was that Vincent was already taxed with enough cares and she only *might* be with child. Given that they were in the middle of the Atlantic, there was little that could be done, and since she had once miscarried, he would fret if he knew. If there were no reason, if she were merely seasick and plump, then why concern him?

With a groan, she rolled over and pushed herself out of the narrow bunk. Her stomach was uneasy. After the past days, this was no longer a surprise. She stood with one hand against the top bunk, hoping that if she took deep breaths and stared out the window, that she might get past the worst of the nausea.

Alas, that remedy proved unequal to the task. Jane had enough practise now that she had no trouble making it to the small pail that Ibrahim had provided for her troubles. She rather thought he found her retching amusing. As she hunched over the bucket, the door to their cabin opened.

"Jane?" It took Vincent only a single stride to reach her. "Poor thing . . . I thought it had passed."

"Usually, I—" She lost the ability to speak for a moment.

Vincent slid an arm around Jane to offer support as her stomach heaved in time with the ship. He paused, with his hand upon her stomach. For a moment, she heard a small, high whine, as if his breath were imperfectly held around a thought that was slowly leaking out. He must notice the change. Surely, he could remember what her health had been like the last time and note the likeness. He had, perhaps, suspected for some time, but the standards of polite society indicated that one did not discuss such delicate matters in mixed company, even with one's wife, unless pressed. And Jane had said nothing, because doing so would make the child real. If she miscarried without ever acknowledging that she was increasing, then she would not need to mourn again.

But Vincent had trusted her with his fears about this voyage and more. Jane could trust him with hers.

She straightened and took the glass of water he offered her. She rinsed her mouth and cleaned her face with the damp cloth he handed her. Folding the cloth, Jane said, "I think I might be increasing."

He exhaled forcibly, almost a laugh, almost a cry, as if

the thought he had been holding escaped all at once. For a moment, the mask of deep reserve that was his habitual expression snapped into place, his face appearing calm, but with a suspicious lustre to his eyes. Then he shoved aside the years of training with a shake of his head, and all his wonder became visible. "Truly?"

She nodded, averting her gaze from the joy in his. "I did not want to tell you in case . . ." In case she miscarried again. "In case I was wrong."

"But we might have turned the ship."

Jane drew back a little to stare at him. "To what purpose?"

"Well—well, you should not be travelling in this condition." Vincent raked his hand through his hair. "I wonder if the ship's surgeon has any experience with childbirth."

"We shall not be on board long enough for that to be a concern. And, truly, aside from the illness, I am little troubled. I would be just as unhappy on land."

"But you should have had access to a proper doctor. The best medical—"

"The best medical opinions did nothing to save Princess Charlotte."

Vincent drew up short, eyes widening. Jane instantly regretted her words. As a man, he had never been privy to a circle of women discussing the horrors of childbirth. It seemed every married woman had at least one friend who had not survived her lying in, and they all felt compelled to relate those stories. Her mother seemed to collect the tales.

It had been all Jane could do to keep Mrs. Ellsworth from telling a new one every day to Melody.

She slid her arms around him and leaned into an embrace. "I am sorry. I ought not have said that."

"No. No, you are right to remind me of the burden you face."

"Burden?" Jane snorted and squeezed his ribs where he was most sensitive. Vincent gave an involuntary laugh and twisted away. Jane pursued, tickling her impossible husband until she chased him into a corner. "You are the only burden I carry. Do not even contemplate coddling me, or treating me like delicate china, or shutting me up in this cabin."

Breathless, he held up his hands in surrender. "No! No. I cry mercy."

"Do you promise to continue on as if my health were unchanged?"

For a fraction of a second he hesitated. Jane made a move towards his ribs. With a nervous laugh, Vincent caught her hand. "I promise not to treat you like a delicate china cup, but you must allow me room for some solicitude. Please, Muse?"

"Hm."

"Fetching your tea. Warming your slippers by the fire. That sort of thing."

"As we shall be in the West Indies, I very much doubt I shall want my slippers warmed."

"We will not be there when your confinement comes. I shall see you safely back in England long before then." He raised a hand and traced the line of her cheek. "Are you . . . ? I recall that you were unhappy during the first . . . before. Will you let me do what I can to make you content this time?"

Jane pulled his head down and kissed his cheek. The rough brush of whiskers told her he had not yet shaved that morning. They tickled her as he pulled her deeper into an embrace. She sighed, settling against him. "Vincent, the last time we had been married but three months, and I had not known you for long. It was my first time away from home and family. I was terrified and uncertain in ways that are well in our past. While I do not relish that my condition requires me to give up glamour for months, it is the best possible timing for such a prohibition. We would have little opportunity to practise our art due to the mourning period for Princess Charlotte. I have better reserves now, and plans for how to occupy my time."

"You are a wonder, Muse." His voice rumbled in his chest as he pulled her tighter. "What are these bold plans of yours?"

"First, I thought I might write a book."

"A book, eh? A novel such as Melody reads, perhaps? Full of young women pining for arrogant men?"

"Oh, no. While I would argue that I have some experience regarding arrogant men, I thought to indulge in my own interests and write a book about glamour."

He ran a hand down her spine and settled it at the small of her back. "I approve of this plan."

"Good, since I do not know that you have much say in

the matter." Jane trifled with one of the buttons on his waistcoat.

He chuckled. "You said 'first,' which implies you have other plans."

"I thought to paint, since the landscape of Antigua will be new to me. And also to work on my music. Perhaps I will finally learn the harp." Jane worked the button free and felt a certain subtle shift in Vincent's posture. "And attend to my husband's needs, of course."

He cleared his throat. "Is that safe?"

Jane undid another button. "His papers and correspondence? I shall be certain to take care when sharpening his quill."

He groaned. "Muse, you are at times wicked."

She tilted her head up to kiss the tender part of his neck below the line of his jaw. "I learned that from you, Rogue."

"I would argue against your case."

The remainder of their argument took place without much language, and through their combined efforts Jane and Vincent were able to resolve any marital difficulties that arose.

The weather became progressively warmer as their route carried them farther south and west. Jane began to regret that she had brought only black gowns. She quite longed for a simple white muslin. Her parasol had been of no use at sea, but the moment they docked in the calm harbour of St. John's in Antigua, Jane was happy to avail herself of its shade. Even the shelter of her bonnet was not entirely adequate for the tropical glare.

The small town that had arisen around the dockyard was a tidy affair of modern stucco buildings. Green hills surrounded the brilliant blue of the harbour, and palm trees waved overhead. Everywhere around them, people moved with a purpose. More interesting was an alteration that took Jane a few minutes to notice. Aboard the ship, she had been surrounded by Englishmen, with some few men of foreign extraction thrown in among them. Here, Jane saw Black Africans everywhere she looked. For the first time, Jane understood why the term *Black African* was used, as the skin of the workers unloading their ship was very dark indeed. There were very few faces as pale as her own. She had spent a good deal of time in London associating with the Worshipful Company of Coldmongers, the young men who provided cooling glamour to the great houses of London. As they were largely descended from slaves, she had become used to being around young men of colour. Compared to the dockworkers, those young men had been as fair as she. There were men of colour in the lighter range of brown that she was accustomed to, but they were fewer in number.

Ibrahim stood at her side on the deck. They gazed at the bustle of the port while they waited for Vincent to finish the business of finding lodging, which Jane and Vincent would need until they could arrange transport to his father's estate. She had their small case on deck, so she used it as a seat. Their larger trunk was still in the hold, and would be sent on to the estate when they were ready.

Jane tilted her head back to look up at Ibrahim. "Have you been to Antigua often?"

"We call here every two months or thereabouts, being a regular packet ship."

"That long between ships?"

"Oh no. Packet ships arrive every two weeks, but it takes us a month to get here and another month to return to England." He squinted against the sunlight. "I do not go ashore here. But the food is very good. You must particularly try the black pineapple."

Vincent strode towards them, his complexion marking him out from the crowd of labourers, even if his height did not. He was followed by a brown man in livery. The fawn-coloured knee breeches and coat seemed out of place among the rough linen shirts and rolled trousers surrounding them. The footman's skin was nearly the same shade as the fawn cloth, and Jane wondered for a moment whether he had been chosen to go with the fabric or the fabric with him. The black mourning band on his arm and his close-cropped hair were the only points of contrast. When he boarded, she saw that he was quite young, probably no more than a year and twenty. For all that, he had a peculiar sense of familiarity.

"Mrs. Hamilton." Vincent addressed her formally now that they were in company. "Ibrahim. This is Zeus from my father's estate, come to meet us."

"Zeus?" A curious name, though with a sister named Melody, Jane could not make a mock. Mothers chose odd names for their offspring. She ran a hand along the front of her dress to smooth it. "I am grateful for your assistance. How did you know we would arrive today?"

He gave her a bow and, with eyes so low he might have been addressing the ground, answered, "Mr. Frank, the house steward, he sends the carriage on those days that a packet ship is expected. I am to convey you to the Greycroft estate and make arrangements for your trunks to be brought after." Zeus's voice had a slight softness to the consonants and a novel syncopation. He stepped smoothly to Jane's side and took her parasol, holding it over her as if this were a dance whose steps they had already rehearsed. With equal ease, he picked up their small case and stood waiting to guide them.

Ibrahim bowed over her hand. "It has been a pleasure to have you sail with us, Mrs. Hamilton."

"Thank you, Ibrahim. I do not think I should have survived the crossing were it not for you."

He winked at her. "I wish you joy." And he was away.

Jane followed Zeus across the crowded dockyard. "How far is it to Greycroft?"

"The great house is just above three hours, madam." He turned from the dockyard and onto the street fronting it. "Here we are."

An enclosed chaise with a matched pair awaited them. It was in the older style, but still in good repair. Another liveried man stood with the horses, his skin a match for Zeus's in tone, though his face was broader in the cheeks. Still, it was clear that they had been chosen to be a matched pair quite as much as the horses. The noble houses in

England often chose their footmen along similar lines, selecting two of the same height, but here. . . . This man was not simply a servant, but a slave.

She looked back towards the harbour. All of the men must be slaves. Now that she took notice, she saw there were scattered men with whips among them. Until she arrived, Jane had not truly comprehended what going to the West Indies would mean. Like most people in London, she had signed abolitionist petitions and rejoiced when the slave trade was ended in 1807. She even had an abolitionist engraving with the motto *Am I not a man and a brother?* in one of her commonplace books. In England, it had been easy to think that they had triumphed over the evil of slavery itself, rather than merely the sale of slaves.

Vincent handed her into the carriage while Zeus folded her parasol and passed it in to her. A moment later, her husband climbed in, shutting the small door. The glass windows reduced some of the noise from the dockyard, but also the breeze. Jane produced her fan from her reticule and attempted to stir the air a bit. What she would have given in that moment to be able to weave a breeze from glamour, but that was restricted for some time yet.

"Shall I open the window?" Vincent reached for the catch to let down the glass.

"Thank you, yes." She had half expected him to offer to weave a breeze, but of course that made no sense, as they would depart once their trunk was secured. "You seem concerned. Is something troubling you?"

He compressed his lips and shook his head. The glass

lowered easily, letting in a hint of a breeze. "Only anticipating the work ahead."

Jane settled back in her red velvet seat to watch the streets of St. John's roll past. It was a tidy, modern town, with tall stucco houses and bright painted shutters. As they moved away from the dockyard, she saw more white people, but most of those they passed were some shade of brown. "Are they all slaves?"

"No . . . I believe there is a healthy population of freedmen here and in Falmouth." Vincent rubbed his forehead and stared out the window. "Muse, would you mind terribly if I closed my eyes for a bit?"

"Not at all." His nightmares had resumed as they had drawn closer to Antigua. She doubted he would sleep, but any sort of respite would be of use.

He nodded in thanks and leaned back in the seat, stretching his legs out in front of him. Vincent rested his head against the corner, shutting his eyes with a sigh. She watched him settle, taking advantage of the time to appreciate her husband's figure. With his buckskin breeches tucked into tall boots and black coat, he looked more a nobleman's son and less an artist. If she could convince him to wear gloves, which he avoided, as most professional glamourists did, he would make quite the convincing young man of fashion. The tension slowly eased out of his frame, and his breathing slowed until she thought that he might actually be asleep.

Beyond him, the nature of their surroundings had changed. As they left the centre of town, the houses became smaller and meaner in appearance. Single-story structures appeared, made of wattle and daub and topped with thatch woven of palm fronds. Through the open doors, the bare earth floors were clearly visible. The people here were chiefly coloured and in rough homespun, much patched and faded. Then even those houses dwindled, and they rode through a stand of tamarind and palmetto trees, which entirely guarded them from the intense heat.

Jane had seen palmettos at Brighton, and had even included them in a glamural at her parents' home. But those were poor scrubby specimens compared with these. These were from forty to sixty feet high before they put out a branch, and as straight as a line. The dense growth of leaves overhead created shade, as though the trees were topped with an umbrella made of ferns. When she returned home, she must make the trunks of the palm trees in their glamural smoother and lighter in hue, almost a silver satin.

These trees quickly gave way, and they entered the first of the sugarcane fields. Save for that brief stand of trees, the fields seemed to reach nearly all the way to town. They were divided into plots by hedges of different kinds, but they bore no resemblance to the rolling green fields of England. The cane towered overhead in great waving stands. The wind kept the heavy reeds in constant motion. The whisper of fronds could be heard even over the steady beat of their horses' hooves and the creak of the carriage's springs.

It was remarkably tranquil. The easy motion persuaded Jane to lean against Vincent and fall asleep.

A shout awakened her. Jane sat up, for a moment thinking she was still on board the ship. She rubbed confusion from her eyes as Vincent stirred awake beside her. Their carriage continued its way up a winding slope. Outside the window, the tall fronds had been cut away in a long stretch of churned dirt. Beside a wall of canes, a group of enslaved Africans worked cutting down the thick stalks. Their machetes rose and fell with a double *whick* as they cut the top and bottom of the cane.

Near the road, a light brown man held a whip. A darker man knelt, shirtless, in front of him. A line of red trickled from his mouth.

Then they were past the scene and the heavy canes masked the view. Jane turned towards Vincent, but he was yawning and scrubbing his eyes. It was clear he had not seen anything.

The view out his side of the carriage was entirely different. The side of the road opposite the canes dropped down towards the valley floor. More wattle and daub houses clung to the side of the road, smaller and even meaner than the ones in St. John's. A gang of very young children played in the dirt in front of one of the houses without a stitch of clothing on. Jane blushed for them and turned her gaze away.

Vincent pulled his watch out of his waistcoat pocket and peered at it. "Getting on near six o'clock. I think we must be on my father's land now."

"Do you see these—I hesitate to call them houses."

He frowned and sat forward. Rubbing his mouth, he

stared out the window at the crude sheds. "I shall speak with the overseer about them. Surely we can do better. I would not keep a horse in such conditions, much less a person."

The carriage rounded a bend in the road and the final stretch of their journey lay clear before them. Atop a rounded hill, surrounded by a level plateau of cane fields, stood the Greycroft great house. It had a high, peaked roof of cedar shingles, with a broad veranda wrapping around the building to provide shade. Tall windows, with shutters thrown back, gave the whole an inviting prospect. Tidy gardens and groves of orange trees surrounded the house, which stood in marked contrast to the conditions they had just ridden through.

As the road wound up the hill to the great house, the cane fields dropped away and the wattle houses almost began to look like thatched-roof cottages in the distance. An invigorating scent of jasmine and orange filled the air as they turned around the last bend to the great house's front sweep. The sound of the carriage seemed to provoke activity in the house, for as they drew near, liveried servants came out to arrange themselves by the double staircase that led up to the veranda.

The carriage stopped precisely in front of the entrance. Zeus jumped down as another servant—no, a slave; Jane must learn to remember that the circumstances were different here—a slave ran forward to hold the horses' heads as another set a step by the carriage door. Vincent climbed out, stretching, then turned back to hand Jane down. In an instant, Zeus had her parasol open above her.

One of the slaves, an older man of Vincent's height, stepped forward to meet them. He gave a stiffly correct bow. "Mr. Hamilton, Mrs. Hamilton. I am Frank, the house steward for Greycroft."

As Frank straightened, Jane could not quite contain a gasp. He looked like Vincent. Though older and cast in a deeper hue, the unmistakable stamp of the Hamilton family was visible through his brow and strong jaw. Jane turned to where Zeus stood at her side and understood why he had looked familiar. He, too, had the Hamilton brow.

"Thank you." Vincent shifted his weight as if seeing the same thing that Jane had. "It was considerate of you to send the carriage to fetch us."

"I trust that Zeus and Jove took adequate care?" Frank stepped back, welcoming them to the house.

"Indeed." Vincent followed him up the stairs and into the welcome cool of the veranda. "Is the overseer present? I saw some things en route I should like to discuss."

A bare hesitation preceded Frank's answer, which Jane might not have noticed were she not looking for additional similarities between him and Vincent. "Mr. Pridmore is indisposed. But you must be tired. Allow me to show you to your rooms."

"That is most kind." Jane murmured, wondering what brand of indisposition the overseer was afflicted with.

The entry of the great house opened onto a long gallery

that spanned the width of the house, lit by tall windows overlooking the veranda. At either end of the gallery, broad doors opened onto parlours, through which yet more windows showed views of the valley below. The house had a fortune in glass alone, to say nothing of the furniture filling the rooms. They were led to the left into a charming blue parlour whose tall ceiling was open to the roof. A door at the back of the parlour opened to a short hall, where they found their rooms.

The apartment was well appointed and had more elegance than Jane would have expected. The tall bed was hung with thin lawn curtains, drawn back presently. The mirrors were still hung with crape, and not a scrap of glamour appeared anywhere.

Jane pulled off her bonnet and set it on a small table beside their bed. From the door, Frank said, "When you are settled, I will take you to your father."

Vincent grimaced. "I suppose it is best to have that over with."

Jane, too, would rather have waited to view the grave, but the forms of propriety must be obeyed. Putting off the task would make it no more pleasant. Then, too, she was hoping that seeing the grave would put Vincent somewhat more at ease and allow him to concentrate on the attendant tasks associated with the disposition of the estate. She picked up her bonnet and followed the men back to the front of the house. Frank led them across the long gallery to the other wing, a route that was much appreciated as it kept Jane out of the sun for a bit longer.

The parlour at this end of the house was white and airy, with ferns on stands scattered around the room. Frank opened a door set in the back of the room. Vincent stepped through and stiffened. Jane could only stare past him.

In the room was Lord Verbury, quite alive.

Five

Discreet Matters

At the sight of Lord Verbury, Jane drew back involuntarily. Vincent's father was much changed, wasted and bent, but unmistakable. His mouth was a little open and he wore an expression of clear shock. She could not understand why he should be shocked when he had sent the carriage for them. That brief unguarded glimpse lasted only a moment before he turned to pick up a cup of tea, as though there were nothing unusual in meeting them like this.

Vincent had frozen upon entering the room. Not out of fear, but as though he had, on instinct, stepped into the role of a young man of fashion, full of cold disdain. His shoulders drew back and his posture stiffened into a frosty perfection. Tucking his hands behind his back, he clasped them together. When he spoke, his voice was so even that Jane could scarcely credit it. "I thought you were dead."

"You were meant to." Lord Verbury sipped his tea.

"The stroke?"

"I was not expected to live, and am as you find me now." He nodded towards his left side. Only then did Jane see that his arm was twisted into a claw next to his body. "It seemed expedient to allow the falsehood to stand, rather than return to face charges of treason."

"I see." Vincent remained in the same precisely etched posture. "The conditions in your will make keeping that secret rather difficult."

"Not at all. Only Garland and a handful of the slaves know." He tilted his head back and contrived to look down his nose at them, in spite of being seated. "Why are *you* here?"

Jane inhaled sharply. He did not know about the carriage accident.

Vincent tilted his head to the side, studying his father. "There was an accident. Garland is dead."

A spasm ran through Lord Verbury, slopping tea over the side of his cup. His mouth worked, but no sound emerged.

"Richard is the earl now, but crippled in the same accident. Not knowing you were alive, he asked me to attend to business." Vincent straightened his head, and pursed his lips slightly. "No doubt you have much to think about. We will speak later."

He backed out of the small room, shutting the door on his father. Frank still stood in the parlour, his expression as fixed and remote as Vincent's. Looking out the window, Vincent wiped his mouth and took a slow breath. "Frank, would you attend my father? He has received a shock."

"Of course, sir."

Turning so that he almost looked at her, Vincent put a hand on Jane's back and drew her away from the door. Without softening his posture, he strode through the parlour and down the long gallery. His free hand went to his mouth again and covered it. He dropped his hand from her back and sped his steps, almost to a run.

He flew through the blue parlour and flung the door to their rooms open. Jane entered the bedchamber in time to see him step onto their veranda. He leaned against the rail and braced himself there, as if he were about to be sick.

"Vincent?"

"Shut the door." His voice was a grating wheeze. "Please."

Jane did, her heart finally remembering to beat again when the door shut. Lord Verbury was alive. She shuddered. Of all the things she had expected to find here, that had not been a consideration.

Behind her, Vincent retched forcibly.

Turning from the door, Jane extracted her handkerchief from her reticule. The square of lawn and lace seemed inadequate, but she carried it to her husband.

His hand shook as he took it from her. "My apologies." The other gripped the rail, and he remained hunched over it. His breath grated in his throat. "It has been some time since I experienced this. I fear it will not be pleasant for you, Muse."

"For me? I assure you, my thoughts are more occupied with you." She put a hand on his back.

He flinched away from her touch. "Again, apologies. I am not myself."

Jane withdrew her hand and stood back, aching for something to do for him. "Should you prefer to be alone?"

He shook his head.

She waited as he leaned against the rail. He wheezed like an asthmatic with each deep breath he drew in. Jane crossed her arms, clenching her hands into fists. Witnessing this unprecedented level of distress, she could not imagine the effort it must have cost him to be so composed when addressing his father. A rush of anger heated her through at the thought of that man. Jane bit her lips, finding it severely taxing to conceal her vexation. She must be steady for Vincent.

He coughed once and cleared his throat. "Is there water?"

"I do not—yes." By the bed, she spied a carafe of water with slices of lime floating in it, and she sent a silent blessing to Frank for having it ready for them. Jane hurried to the bed and poured a glass. A pair of fine linen napkins lay on the table, so Jane picked up one and doused it with the water. Thus armed, she returned to her husband's side.

Standing well back, she held them out to him. Still not looking directly at her, he reached for the water. Tremors shook his hand, but when it closed on the glass, the shaking was nearly concealed. He took a sip, staring at the horizon, then spat the water over the side of the veranda to rinse his mouth of the sick.

God. Her heart ached for him. Jane held out the cloth again, longing to embrace Vincent and keep him safe. Right now, though, he was as a man flayed.

"Thank you." He took the cloth, setting the glass on the broad rail of the veranda. He wiped his mouth, and then slowly let his breath out. Much of the wheeze was gone. Vincent cleared his throat again. Lowering the cloth, he coughed into his fist, still looking at the hills in the distance.

The sun had touched the horizon, turning the clouds into a confection of orange and pink. With the blushing of the sunset, the wattle and daub houses were picturesque shadows in the distance, the neglect and dirt masked by the warm evening light.

Vincent turned a little to sit on the rail. "Forgive me, I should have asked sooner. Are you all right?"

"Well enough." Truly, Jane was by turns angry at Lord Verbury and frightened for Vincent, but he did not need to hear that in the present moment.

"Good." He glanced down to the flowerbed below the veranda and scowled. "Well. Someone will report the mess to my father. It has been years since we have had that conversation. How delightful to revisit old times."

Jane could only stare at him, aghast.

"Muse . . . I know I look a fright, but it is not so bad as it seems. There was a period at Eton when I did . . ."—he gestured at the mess in the flowers below them—"*this*, with some regularity. I enjoyed school, until the holidays, when my father would come to fetch me himself. He terrified me."

There must be something she could do. "What helped you in the past?"

"I replaced my fear with anger."

Accompanied by pinpricks of chill, Herr Scholes's words returned with force: *Your husband was marked by fury . . .*

"Truly, Muse, it will pass, and I ask for your patience." His voice did sound steadier, and when he sighed, the wheeze had gone. He glanced at her, then away quickly, as if meeting her gaze hurt. "But he will take great joy in reminding me of my weakness."

She swallowed. "I do not think anyone saw."

He surveyed the grounds. "Perhaps not, but with shrubbery this extensive, he must have a gardener who tends the flowers with regularity, and I did make a notable mess."

"We could tell people that I was sick. I have reason enough."

"God! No!" Vincent rose, eyes wide with terror. Then he caught himself and screened his expression with an unlikely laugh. "I would rather he not know you are with child."

"We can hardly hide it for long."

He looked at her midriff with the sort of calculation he usually reserved for glamour. "Unless someone were to know you, the fact that you are increasing is not yet obvious. You might only be stout. I think the secret is still safe."

"The birth of a child will give the game away eventually."

Vincent shuddered. He turned to the rail as if he were going to be sick again, but only leaned against it.

"He has no hold on you. We have an independent living through our work as glamourists, and even were that not the case, he is an exile and a traitor to the Crown."

"Yes, well, I also thought he was dead, and you see how well that is working," he snapped. Then he winced, lowering his head. "Sorry. My tongue might be a trifle keener than I would like tonight."

"I am not surprised. You handled yourself well in the moment of discovery."

"The irony is that we may thank my father for what control I had. Years of training in governing one's expression under duress. Like so—" He shifted his posture, standing once again in that painfully correct manner, with his hands clasped behind him and his chin tucked into his tall collar. "My hands shake when I am angry, so this posture hides that. With my chin down, the collar masks that I am clenching my jaw. Also, it makes it easier to sneer, which is greatly prized."

"I had no idea so much thought went into your deportment."

"And the way I walk, my speech, my handwriting. . . . There is little about me that did not receive corrective training." Vincent grimaced. "Muse . . . sometimes my first instinct comes from *him*. I am shaken enough that you may see a side of me that I dislike. Vehemently."

"Is there anything I can do for you? Patience I have in abundance, but if there is anything more than that . . ."

He stared into the growing darkness. After a moment, he shook his head. "Thank you. Having you here is a comfort, though at the same time, if I had known my father was alive I would never have permitted you to come."

"Then we are well matched, as I would not have permitted you to come, either."

He gave something like a laugh. "I wish there were a moon tonight so we could leave now. It is too dark for the road to be safe."

"Oh, thank God." Jane sagged against the rail. "I was afraid you would insist on staying here to see things through out of some misplaced sense of duty."

"If I were not terrified of what he will do when he finds out that you are with child—and he will find out; you are right about that—perhaps I would. As it is, I propose that we return to England, expose my father's fraud, and leave the entire thing in someone else's hands."

"That sounds entirely sensible."

He compressed his lips in his small private smile and held a hand out to her. Biting back a sob of relief, Jane took his hand. She had not been certain how long he would keep her at a distance. She slid into the warmth of his embrace and leaned against her husband as the last rays of the sun sank behind the horizon.

Vincent kissed her on the forehead. "Thank you, Muse."

"For?"

"Only thank you."

When Jane awoke in the morning, she was alone. The sheets beside her were cool, so Vincent must have arisen some time earlier. The sheer lawn curtains had been tucked back under the mattress to protect her from mosquitoes, and they fogged her view of the room. She pushed them aside to slip out of bed. The room was astonishingly cool given how warm the day had been. That might have been due to the door to the veranda standing open.

Jane pulled her shawl from where it hung over a chair and went to the door. The veranda was in shadow, but the air had already begun to acquire a certain muggy warmth. She had fully expected to find Vincent engaged with working a massive glamour and was a little relieved to find him sitting quietly with a newspaper. He had a wicker chair that she did not think had been there the night prior, and he sat with his feet up on the rail. He was still in his nightshirt, with only a banyan robe wrapped around him for modesty.

"Did you sleep at all?"

Vincent shook his head, and then lowered the paper. "Did I wake you?"

"No. Thank you."

"How are you this morning?"

Jane opened her mouth to reply and stopped. She had not a trace of nausea. "I feel quite fit, actually. Perhaps I was merely seasick after all."

Vincent raised a brow and looked pointedly at her stomach. Though the fullness of a day dress still obscured her figure, in nothing but a shift, it was obvious that Jane was increasing. He cleared his throat, lowering his feet. "I am glad you are better. Frank has sent someone ahead to reserve a place on the *Marchioness of Salisbury*. Although . . . if the ship's motion makes you ill, I wonder if it is advisable to travel in your condition."

"Vincent, I am not staying here a moment longer than it will take me to dress."

"Not here. Clearly. But we could stay in town until after your confinement, and—"

"No."

"Jane, I am only thinking of your health, and—"

"No. First of all, my health will be best if I am near my family. Second, and more significantly, you are not staying anywhere near that man. He was here for close to a year before the stroke and yet had not been removed to England to face trial." She almost stopped, seeing his face grow pale, but felt the need to make it clear to him why they could not stay. "Meaning that someone is in his debt here. But in England, he is very much out of favour. Let this be someone else's concern."

Vincent lowered his gaze and folded the newspaper in half. "You are right, of course." He folded the paper in half again, smoothing the crease. "Of course. I should know that better than you."

"Shall we dress?"

"Yes." He stood, tucking his hands behind his back.

Jane looked at the posture and tilted her head in consideration. "Are you angry with me?"

"What? No." He looked down, seeming to recognise his posture and what he had told her about it. "No. It became a habit to stand this way always, so that it did not give me away when I needed it."

"Herr Scholes. . . . He said you were angry all the time when you came to him."

Vincent gave a cheerless smile. "Why do you think I learned to work such shapeless glamours when I was discomfited? No fine control."

And what could she say to that? He had once kept his past as the Honourable Vincent Hamilton entirely separate from his life as Sir David Vincent. She had long understood why he kept such a rigid wall around that former life, and she had respected the boundary. The fact that he now trusted her behind that wall was a sign of how much their marriage had strengthened, and yet, every glimpse of Vincent's history made Jane ache for him.

As they dressed, the black of Jane's mourning clothes seemed to make a mock of their situation. She clenched her jaw against anger, starting to have some understanding of why Vincent had learned to stand with his hands behind his back. While growing up, Jane had had little to vex her beyond the frustrations of being a plain girl with a very pretty sister. Those old cares seemed trivial now, and she was ashamed of herself for having ever been put out by such a trifling thing. She shoved her gown into their small case with more force than strictly required.

Vincent cleared his throat. "Have I ever told you that you frighten me a little when you are angry?"

"Forgive me. It is not directed at you."

"I know. You are still a force of nature when disturbed."

She closed the case, taking care not to slam it. "Well, let us hope that I have no reason to—"

A knock sounded at the door. Both of them stiffened, staring at it, until Vincent relaxed and murmured, "He would not knock." Raising his voice, he called, "Enter."

Frank opened the door, stepping into their room. "My apologies. Zeus has just returned from town. The *Marchioness of Salisbury* left with the tide this morning."

Jane had fully expected Vincent to curse. Instead, he picked up the paper and folded it into a narrow roll. "I see. And when is the next ship bound for England?"

"It may be a month or more, I am afraid."

"A month!" Jane frowned, shaking her head. "But Ibrahim told us that packet ships call every two weeks."

"That is correct, but they do not all return directly to England."

"But there were so many other ships at the port."

"I am afraid that none of them are bound for England." He tilted his head, considering. "You could take the *Lady Arabella*, which departs in three days, but it is going to Portugal. You would have to make your way back to England from there."

Vincent twisted the paper around, likely doing the same math that Jane was. A month sailing and then another month from Portugal to England . . . It would take as long as waiting a month in Antigua and then sailing directly, but with a more arduous trip. Given her history, that seemed imprudent, even to Jane. "What about lodgings in St. John's? Could you arrange for a place for us to stay until the next British bound ship?"

"Yes. . . ." Frank wet his lips and eased the door shut. "However, may I ask you to reconsider your departure? While I understand your wish, the great house is large, and Lord Verbury does not leave his rooms."

"I am afraid remaining here is not possible."

"For my own benefit, may I ask you not to go?" Frank turned his attention from Jane to Vincent. "There are serious issues with the estate, as I am certain you saw on your way in. I have charge only over the great house and grounds, but can see what is happening with the rest of the estate. I have concerns that the overseer—" He cleared his throat. "While his lordship was in good health, matters ran smoothly. However, Lord Verbury's stroke has put the estate heavily into Mr. Pridmore's hands."

"I commend your concern for the rest of the estate, but this does not require my presence." Vincent's voice was coolly aristocratic. "Once my father is removed, then I will recommend to my brother that he replace the overseer. Will you arrange for the carriage?"

Frank stared at him, expression guarded. Then he shook his head. "I cannot allow you to go."

"Pardon?" Vincent tilted his head. "You cannot allow us? Cannot *allow*?"

"That is correct."

"I think your time managing the house has led to a misapprehension of your circumstances—"

"I am a freedman, sir. Not a slave." Frank's hands were behind his back. His chin was tucked into his collar. "When I say that I cannot allow you to go, I am in full possession of my senses."

Jane put a hand on Vincent's arm to stay his reply. "Forgive me, but you must offer a more pressing reason than his lordship's poor health. Neither of us has reason to grant him any charity."

Whatever tricks Vincent had learned to govern his expression, Frank seemed to have learned them as well. No hint of his emotions peeked through his smooth façade. He stared at her coolly for a moment, gaze moving between her and Vincent, and then back again. He gave a small nod, as if coming to a decision. "Lord Verbury freed me in exchange for my assistance in hiding him. At the time, I accepted it as a gift, but as a freedman, I will be charged with aiding a traitor to the Crown."

Vincent cursed, suddenly and liberally. He turned away from Frank and walked to the window. "That is like him. To offer a gift that will then hang you."

Jane asked, "But why not simply leave, or turn him in yourself?"

"Lord Verbury still has friends in the Admiralty. And even if I could find someone impartial, he has an additional assurance for my continuing aid." Frank's control faltered for a moment. He paused to clear his throat before continuing. "Lord Verbury still owns my family. If I cooperate, they stay on the plantation, with a promise of being freed later. If I betray his lordship in any way, including allowing

Mr. Hamilton to depart, then they will be sold to different people. In particular, my daughter has been promised to the overseer. He has already expressed his . . . interest in her."

Vincent pressed his fingers against his temples. "Did my father offer you suggestions on how to stop us if we choose to go? I presume he told you to play upon our sentiments in this manner?"

Jane was frankly shocked that Vincent's mind leapt straight to that conclusion. It was true that her motivation to depart had weakened significantly upon hearing that Frank's family was in danger, but it had not occurred to her that this might be a scheme.

Frank shook his head. "He suggested that a carriage accident would be unfortunate."

"And you agree?"

"No, but neither will I allow Zeus or Jove to take you to St. John's." He studied the floor, and not even his high collar could hide that his jaw was clenched. "I would rather that we worked together to resolve our mutual difficulties."

Jane took a step closer to him. "Could you give us some time to discuss matters?"

"Of course, madam." Frank offered her a bow. "Sir."

He left them standing in the room with no more ceremony than if he were simply a house steward dispatching his duty. Jane bit her lip. His duty. She supposed that *was* what he was doing. She only wished that his duty did not involve holding them captive.

Six

A Frank Discussion

When the door had shut behind Frank, Jane let her breath out in a rush. Her stomach churned, but the nausea had little to do with her morning ailments. Vincent remained at the window with his hands still pressed to his temples. He would need some time, and, truth be told, so did Jane. She pressed her hand to her mouth, trying to think of what choices they might have. The carriage was out of the question.

How far away was the port? Three hours by carriage, but part of the way had been uphill, so perhaps it would only take four or five on foot. They could take the small case, but they would have to leave the trunk. She sighed. Well, they had lost their clothing before, and Jane would gladly be shed of the mourning clothes.

Vincent dropped his hands and turned from the window. "I think I must talk with him."

"Your father? To what purpose?"

"To find out exactly what his conditions are for Frank's family to be freed and for us to be allowed to depart."

Jane opened her mouth but could not form a sentence to fill it. Confounded, she shook her head and tried again. "You intend to stay?"

"Not willingly, but I do not see another way."

"We can walk."

"Muse, I cannot risk your health."

"I am not proposing that we run to St. John's, but that we walk. You recall that Melody's doctor told her to stroll. With the *Verres Obscurcis* we will be in no danger of being spotted and can stop as needed. There is no more risk than if we were walking to church."

Vincent sighed heavily, and she could see that she had won the point. "The next packet ship arrives in two weeks. That will give us time to weaken my father's hold on Frank."

"The fact that Frank is willing to keep us prisoner does not trouble you?"

Vincent shook his head. "I know what it is to be controlled by the Earl of Verbury. My suspicion, knowing my father, is that he suggested the carriage accident to Frank in order to exert additional pressure, but will not issue the order."

"Can we not simply free Frank's family?" She would rather they freed *all* the slaves.

"I do not have the authority."

"But you are here as the executor of the estate."

"Yes, but freeing slaves requires the signature of the owner himself, not merely the executor. I think Richard would grant it, but—the time. It would take two months at best to get word back from him, and there is no end of mischief my father can do in that time."

Jane gnawed at her lower lip, trying to think of things that she could do. She did not want to stay. She did not want to leave Vincent anywhere near that man's influence. For the next two weeks she would have to do everything she could to protect him. "I do not like it."

"Nor do I, but with luck we can sway Frank and take the carriage. Otherwise, we will try your method with the *Verres*. But—if we are to remain for the next two weeks, then I must convince my father that he has won this battle, so I need to talk to him."

"Do you want me to come with you?"

"No." Vincent raked his hair into greater disorder. "I will have to argue with him. He will expect it. I would rather you not be there."

"I have seen you argue with him before."

"Oh no, Muse. . . . You have only seen him on good behaviour." He turned to the mirror and tweaked the dark cloth of his cravat to make the bow uneven.

She considered, very seriously, the possibility of using a *Verre Obscurci*. The angle of the sun was such that the veranda on that end of the house was fully lit. She could walk down to the windows easily and eavesdrop. But no matter how easy it would be, the fact remained that her husband would feel spied upon, so she had to ask.

"May I watch? Not—" She held up her hand to stop his gathering protest. "Not be in the room with you, but may I stand outside on the veranda using the *Verre*? Not knowing frightens me more than anything I might witness."

"It is not. . . . It is less my father's treatment of me that I wish to avoid showing you, and more who I become when I am around him." In the mirror, the man who smiled back at her was cold and bitter and no one she recognised.

"Vincent—"

He sighed and lowered his head. For a long moment she thought he would refuse again, but he nodded, still with his head down. "If it will help you. I only ask . . . I am not likely to wish to revisit the conversation afterwards."

"I shall not mention it."

"Thank you." He rubbed his forehead, his scowl darkening. "I need to go before I lose my resolve."

"Of course. Do not wait for me." Jane bit her lower lip as he nodded his thanks and strode out of the room.

She went quickly to their small case and withdrew a *Verre Obscurci* from its box within. Jane rose, and then hesitated, looking back at the case. If a servant were to come in while they were both out. . . . She knelt again and pulled out the box, relocked it, and shoved it deep into the wardrobe.

Shaking her head at her own excessive caution, Jane carried the *Verre* out onto the veranda. Trying to look as though she were merely taking the air, she walked down the veranda in the shade. On the grounds, gardeners worked at trimming the shrubbery. At the corner, she paused and peered around to make certain that none of them was looking at her, and then she stepped into the sun.

The sun, which made sweat spring from her skin, flowed through the thin inclusions in the glass to render her invisible. She walked past the windows of the white parlour towards the back of the great house. Like the room that Jane and Vincent occupied on the far side of the house, this had louvre-boards upon the windows to allow a breeze. She could just barely see through them.

Lord Verbury's voice was clear before she saw him. "I expect you to do your duty. What is the point of having you here otherwise?"

"I would gladly leave. Believe me, sir, I have no wish to be here." Had Vincent not spoken to her in their bedchamber, she would not have known he was agitated. His voice was cold and sneering.

"Of course not. You have always run when something became too difficult. How many times did I have to fetch you back home when you were a child?"

"If you had beaten me less, perhaps I would not have had reason to run."

"You see that I am racked with guilt for trying to make something of you. Your eldest brother—"

"If he were still alive, then I would be in Vienna with my wife. Instead, out of respect for Richard, I came here to attempt to manage the estate."

"I have an overseer to manage the estate. I need you for an heir."

"You have Richard for that."

"You must acknowledge that he is unlikely to produce one."

"Richard's business is his own."

"You will have to divorce your wife, of course."

Vincent's laugh made the sun cold. "I see. Thank you for making your position clear."

"Fortunately, being barren can be grounds enough among the peerage."

Jane shivered, her entire body breaking out in gooseflesh. She wrapped an arm around her stomach, as if that would protect the child she carried. She now understood why Vincent wished so strongly to keep her condition a secret.

"I should advise you to tread carefully, sir."

"How did she catch you? I have never been able to satisfy myself as to that. A mannish thing with no heritage to speak of. . . . I suppose you are more like Richard than I had hoped, if that is what catches your fancy."

"Stop."

"Do I trouble you because I come too close to the truth? Yes, I saw how it upset you on the witness stand at the trial when the questions bent towards your tastes. Men's clothing? Is she truly a woman, or just a boy to serve as your punk?"

Vincent turned towards the door without a word.

"There he goes. The conversation touches difficult ground and he runs. You always were a coward."

Jane crept back along the wall as Vincent opened the door to the white parlour.

"You know . . . it has only just occurred to me. Garland made a half dozen bastards before he married, and not a one from you. Perhaps you should ask Mr. Pridmore to show you how to handle your wife."

Vincent stood in the door, his face clearly visible through the white parlour's windows. Rage had bared his teeth and made the muscles in his jaw into knots. Like a glamourist at work, his gaze went vacant for a moment. He seemed to seize all the anger and push the tumult within himself. His face cleared with a speed that frightened Jane more than that glimpse of fury. Turning, Vincent leaned against the door-case. With tones that belonged only to the most aristocratic of families, he drawled, "Really, Father . . . if you think that threatening my wife will convince me to aid you, then your judgement has slipped more than I thought. Good day to you, sir."

Vincent pulled the door shut as he stepped back into the parlour and stood for a moment supporting himself against the door. Jane stepped into the parlour, the shade of the room stopping the effects of the *Verre*. At the sound of her foot on the broad wood boards, Vincent spun, his face mottled red with fury.

The moment he saw her, colour drained from his features. Vincent swallowed heavily, glancing back to his father's room. He raised a finger to his lips.

Jane nodded to let him know that she would not betray her presence by speaking.

Still half-turned from her, Vincent pointed to the front veranda with his brows raised in question. Jane gave a little nod and followed him along the veranda to the front of the house. Even once there, he waited until they had progressed across the shaded stretch away from his father's wing of the house.

He coughed into his fist, clearing his throat twice before speaking, and still his voice was hoarse. "Are you all right?"

"Only concerned for you." She put the tips of two fingers, no more, on his arm, and yet he flinched under her touch. "Are you well?"

He glanced behind them. Through the long stretch of windows that spanned the front gallery of the house, a maid was quietly polishing a table. Vincent turned to face the yard again, gaze resting now upon a gardener trimming a shrub, and then upon a groom walking a horse in a circle upon the walk. None of them so much as glanced towards the Vincents, and yet Jane became aware of their presence as she never was of servants back home.

When Vincent spoke again, his tone was painfully calm, as if he were saying that the day was a fine one. "Well . . . you had expressed curiosity about what I was like as youth. Now you know."

In spite of the heat, a chill washed over Jane, as if a coldmonger were weaving glamour directly on her skin. *Your husband was marked by fury. . . .* His apparent calm worried Jane more than agitation might. She could see a preservative shell hardening around Vincent, and they had not even been in Antigua a full day. "There will be more of this. If we stay here."

"Yes." He looked over the horizon of the estate, appearing for all the world like a man at ease, if one could disregard the rigour with which he gripped the rail.

"Shall we go inside? To escape the heat."

The skin around Vincent's eyes tightened slightly before he looked down and lifted one hand just a little above the balustrade. It shook as though he were palsied. He lowered it again and said, with deliberate mildness, "I think it might be best if I were to walk about and look over the estate. If you are truly all right."

"I am. Truly."

"May I further ask that you to wait in our rooms? It would . . ." His voice faltered, and then his jaw locked around whatever emotion was there. "I should like to know where you are."

She tilted her head, studying him. Though it felt alarmingly like being set upon a shelf for safekeeping, if she stayed in the room, then he would not have to worry about unpleasant possibilities. Jane controlled a shudder, aware that something in his past prompted this . . . difficulty. More than anything, she wanted to pull him into her arms and provide shelter, but she instead kept her hands by her side and her voice low. "I understand. I will wait for you in our rooms. Only . . . please do not ask me to make a habit of it?"

"I will not." He hesitated for a moment, balanced on his toes as if he was turning to go, but then turned back towards her. Vincent leaned down. There was a brief pause, as if he had to force the contact, before he brushed her cheek with the scantest of kisses. "Thank you."

Still without meeting her gaze, Vincent went to the stairs.

He took them two at a time, and then walked straight across the lawn.

Zeus, the slave who had driven them there, hurried down the stairs and followed behind him. Jane clenched her jaw in a mirror of her husband. She had no hope that Vincent would enjoy any privacy.

Jane returned to their rooms with the intention of taking up a book and awaiting Vincent's return upon the veranda. While it was not strictly speaking within their room, sitting outside would allow her to see his return that much sooner.

She rounded the corner from the parlour to the hall of their room and slowed. The door to their room stood open. Fabric rustled within. Her heart sped far more than such a simple sound merited. Jane and Vincent did not travel with their own servants, so it was likely just one of the maids setting their room to rights, part of the perfectly normal routine of their arrival.

Remembering Vincent's consciousness of the servants when they were on the veranda, Jane took a moment to secure the *Verre* more discreetly in her shawl and stepped within.

A young mulatto maid stood at the wardrobe, hanging one of Jane's dresses within. Her skin was very brown, but, from its transparency, her complexion was uncommonly brilliant; her features were all good; her smile was sweet and attractive; and in her eyes, which were very dark, there was a life, a spirit, an eagerness, which softened even the

Hamilton brow. She had her thick hair twisted back into a chignon and wrapped under a lawn kerchief that was held in place with a black satin bow. She wore a simple black round gown with a lace fichu covering her bosom.

Jane cleared her throat.

The maid spun with a speed that reminded Jane of Vincent's flinch and told her more of the state of affairs in the house than any lecture. When the young woman saw Jane, she dropped her eyes and bent in a low curtsy. "Mrs. Hamilton. My name is Louisa." Her voice was a pleasing contralto with hints of the Antiguan accent tempered by aristocratic consonants. Born here, clearly, but taught to sound British. "Lord Verbury sends me with his compliments to act as your lady's maid while you are in residence."

Whatever had been pleasing in the young woman's countenance now took on a foreboding cast. Given Lord Verbury's statement that only a small number of trusted slaves knew he was alive, that meant he trusted her, or, at the very least, had some hold over her. Jane could be certain of Louisa reporting anything she said back to Verbury.

"That is generous of his lordship." She stepped farther into the room. While it made her uneasy to have Louisa as her maid, it might present an opportunity. Perhaps she could mislead Verbury by what she chose to say to the maid. "You must be familiar with the household arrangements."

"Of course, madam." Her head still down, Louisa hung one of Jane's multitude of black dresses in the wardrobe.

If only the maid were not quite so close to where Jane had

hidden the box of *Verres*. "Leave that for the moment. Perhaps we should start with an orientation, which will enable me to assist my husband while we are here."

Dutifully, Louisa stepped away from the wardrobe. "I believe that Mr. Frank has arranged for a tour of the grounds this afternoon, with the intention of introducing you to the staff. There are fourteen slaves total in charge of the maintenance of the house and grounds. Another one hundred and eighty in the fields and distillery."

"So many!"

"His lordship's estate is the third largest on Antigua."

"How are you treated?"

"Mr. Pridmore is a professional and attends to his job thoroughly. Shall I begin by telling you which of the other staff are aware of the situation with his lordship?"

Jane sighed. "Thank you, yes."

"Cook is aware. As she has charge of the kitchen, it was necessary to keep her informed. Mr. Frank, of course. Miss Sarah, his mistress. Then Zeus and Jove, for the occasions when his lordship must be moved."

"Really?" It was easier to comment on that last surprise than on the fact that Lord Verbury still kept a mistress, given his current health, or that she was listed among the staff. "Where does he need to be moved?"

"In and out of his wheeled chair. They also fetch Sir Ronald, his lordship's physician, in the carriage."

Jane sighed and settled into one of the chairs, conscious of the glass sphere tucked in her shawl. It was tempting to hide it behind a pillow, but she had seen maids arrange them too often in other houses. "Louisa, would you fetch some paper and a pen for me? I should like to take some notes."

"Of course, madam." The young woman hurried out of the room.

Jane waited until her footsteps had faded down the hall and stood. She went to the wardrobe, reaching into the back corner where she had left the box that they carried the *Verres* in. It was still in the back of the wardrobe and locked tight. Jane tucked the other one inside the box and let herself relax a bit to see both spheres of glass within. After some thought, she left it in the back of the wardrobe, but slid it to a different corner so that the folds of one of her black dresses masked it further.

That accomplished, Jane returned to her seat and took up a book, in an effort to look at ease. Two weeks. They need only be this suspicious for two more weeks.

Seven

Property and Propriety

Jane and Vincent were sitting in the blue parlour taking tea when Frank appeared at the door. Really, she did not see how he could move down the long gallery so silently when she made noise even in her slippers. He paused until Vincent looked up from the account book he was going over.

"Mr. Grenville Pridmore, the overseer, and his wife, Mrs. Pridmore."

Vincent exchanged a look with Jane, which managed to convey his concern for her sensibilities when presented with the man that Lord Verbury had implied had certain . . . appetites. She smiled in return, to reassure him that she was not as fragile as all that. Thus appeased,

Vincent shut his book and rose, as a hearty man of five and thirty strode into the room.

Beneath sandy hair, Mr. Pridmore's face was rough from the sun but came equipped with a ready smile. He wore a linen coat and trousers, although without the waistcoat that was *de rigueur* in Britain. His wife, a good ten years his junior, had managed to retain her pale English rose complexion in spite of the tropical sun. Her brown hair had a natural curl to it and set off her oval face neatly. She wore a green lawn dress with a black ribbon as a generous nod to the mourning that the house was under.

"Oh! Mrs. Hamilton, I am so very sorry for your loss." She dropped her husband's arm before he had a chance to address either of them and crossed the room, hands outstretched to Jane. "It is so good of you to come all this way."

"Of course. I could not let Mr. Hamilton come on his own." Jane was surprised into a smile at having her hands clutched with such sincerity.

Behind the two Pridmores came a third person, a mulatto maid of middle height with general prettiness, a clear brown complexion, and a face that was round rather than long. She took up a station against the wall with her eyes downcast. Neither Pridmore acknowledged that she was in the room.

By this time, Mr. Pridmore had reached Vincent. "Indeed, you have my sincere sympathy. Frank told us the news last night. We expected your brother and had not the slightest idea that something had occurred. Dreadfully sorry to hear it."

"It was a shock to us all."

"Frank said you wished a tour of the estate today? Are you certain? There is nothing so pressing that it will not wait a few days to give you time to recover from your journey."

"Now, you gentlemen must take your business elsewhere. I have charge of making Mrs. Hamilton feel at home in our little rustic estate, and simply cannot do it while you are speaking of business. Have you been out on the veranda, Mrs. Hamilton? I say that there is nothing like a veranda for taking in the air, provided that it is in the shade, of course. Here above all other places, one does not want a brush of the tawny. People might get the wrong idea. But you have not that difficulty at all, I am certain. With my dark curls, I do have to be so very careful."

"I did have the opportunity to enjoy the veranda attached to our rooms last night." Though *enjoy* was perhaps the wrong word, given Vincent's illness.

Mrs. Pridmore squeezed Jane's hand. "Oh, I am so glad you have come. I have been ever so lonely."

Mr. Pridmore laughed at her. "Lonely? Why, you are chattering all day and all night with Betsy. Honestly, Mrs. Hamilton, she does not go anywhere without her maid."

"Indeed?" Jane raised a brow and turned back to Mrs. Pridmore. "Betsy must be a comfort to you."

Wrinkling her nose, Mrs. Pridmore waved a hand to chase the idea away. "Oh! As to that, it is not at all the same as the company of an Englishwoman. You have lived in London, I understand. I do so miss London, but no matter how much I tease, Mr. Pridmore will not agree to our going."

"My dear, you know well that I cannot be away. I have business to attend to for his lordship. "

Vincent cleared his throat. "Speaking of business, I should like that tour of the plantation."

Mr. Pridmore closed his mouth around whatever his first reply was and gave a nod of his head. He smiled. "Of course. I see that you are a man of business, like your father. I admire that. Mrs. Hamilton, should you like to accompany us on the early part of our tour? You might like to see the shrubbery."

Jane stood, brushing off her dress. "I should be delighted to come. It would do me good to see where we are to live."

"What?" Mrs. Pridmore cried. "Oh, you cannot mean it. Mr. Pridmore, you are not thinking of the heat today. You would be much better to stay in the shade of the veranda. Really, the heat quite does one in when you first arrive. I fainted my second day here, truly I did."

Mr. Pridmore waved her objection away. "We will start close to the great house so that you may return easily." He picked up the bell on the side table and rang it. Jane might have been affronted to have him call their servants, were it not for the fact that as overseer he had charge of all the workers on the estate.

Frank appeared in the door on the instant. "Sir?"

He addressed Vincent, but Mr. Pridmore answered him.

"Fetch Mr. Hamilton's hat and send Mrs. Hamilton's maid with her parasol and bonnet. Betsy? Go with him to fetch our own."

Betsy curtsied and left the room, all without raising her eyes.

Jane smiled at Mrs. Pridmore. "You must have become used to having this house empty."

"Oh, indeed we did! How lovely to have neighbours again. I do so miss Lord Verbury. You must miss him terribly. He was such a sweet old man, and always so wonderfully condescending with his attentions. Why, do you know that he gave me an orange tree to plant at our house when we married? Such a kindness. It has grown quite tall, and bears such lovely fruit. Oh! And I have just had a thought. As we walk, I shall be able to show you our house. You must come to take tea with me as soon as you are settled."

Louisa entered then with Jane's black bonnet and her parasol. She offered the bonnet with a curtsy and Jane noticed that she had a second bonnet hanging by the cord. "We are only taking a tour of the property, Louisa. I do not think I shall require you. Perhaps you could attend to Betsy while we are out?"

"Oh!" Mrs. Pridmore put a hand to her bosom. "But I could not do without Betsy on our walk. Who should hold my parasol?"

Louisa donned her own bonnet. "Indeed, madam. You are not used to the climate here. I should be remiss in my duties if I did not carry your parasol."

And of course, it would also be difficult for her to report

to Lord Verbury about Jane if she did not accompany them. "Thank you, Louisa."

Once they were all equipped with bonnets, hats, and parasols, Mr. Pridmore led them out the back of the great house. The two wings of it extended to make an open yard at the back. A broad stretch of lawn had palmetto trees at intervals to provide welcome shade. In the centre of the lawn stood a narrow brick building. It had a low ground floor, and then a set of steep steps leading up to the first floor. Iron shutters hung open from the windows. Vines twined up trellises affixed to the sides, which did something to relieve its harshness.

Mr. Pridmore gestured to the building. "Our counting house. You and I shall be spending quite a bit of time there, eh, Mr. Hamilton?"

"Likely." Vincent followed him with his hands clasped behind his back.

As they rounded the building, strolling towards a shrubbery at the back of the yard, Mr. Pridmore stopped by a heavy iron door. "This is for you, Mrs. Hamilton. I don't expect you'll have much interest in the accounts, but you will be glad to know where the safe house is."

Mr. Pridmore produced a key from the ring he carried and unlocked the door. Inside astonishingly thick walls was a low room without any windows to relieve the dark. Several beds lay within, as well as barrels and shelves of food. The simple brick floor had been covered with a braided rug, but there was no other ornament of any sort.

Vincent removed his hat to avoid knocking it off on the

low ceiling and stepped inside. He put a hand to the wall, frowning. "Are you so worried about uprisings?"

"After the rebellion in Haiti? Yes. Every plantation put them in." He pulled a copy of the key from his ring and handed it to Vincent. "Every couple of years, some planter is happy they built one. Food is there. The large barrels hold water. The small ones have rum, though we have to keep that locked down."

Jane moved farther into the room and looked at the stores. Impressively, the safe house had modern Appert jars to hold fruits and vegetables. She picked up one of the jars and frowned as the lid shifted. The food inside was quite spoilt. Putting it back on the shelf, she took a quick survey of the other jars and could see that nearly half of the visible ones had spoilt.

Vincent stooped over one of the rum barrels. "When was the last uprising here?"

"The last bad one was back in 1736. We've had some minor incidents. Sir Thomas's estate on the north part of the island had trouble with arson for a while. Lost most of the harvest. But he came out himself, and has had no troubles since."

"And this estate?"

Mr. Pridmore frowned and counted on his fingers. "Eleven years ago? Before my time, that. Do not let it worry you, though. My introduction of the Rock Dungeon has reduced the number of incidents considerably."

Jane shivered and wrapped her arms around herself before remembering what it did to her gown. She lowered them quickly, hoping that the dim room hid her movement.

"Oh, you have frightened poor Mrs. Hamilton!" Mrs. Pridmore attached herself to Jane's arm and directed her outside. "It sounds horrid. I should know, having lived here as long as I have. But there are nearly forty naval forts, so you only have to wait a little before soldiers come to put the uprising down."

Jane extricated herself from Mrs. Pridmore's grip. "Have you had occasion to use one?"

"No! Heavens, no. Mr. Pridmore is much too clever to allow anything like an uprising to occur. Our slaves—that is to say, your slaves—are all contented."

They were at least silent. Louisa and Betsy both moved to stand by the ladies as they left the shade of the safe house. After her experience with the coldmongers in England, Jane could not think that either woman was content.

"How is it ventilated?" Vincent reached up to touch the low ceiling before ducking back out into the sunlight.

"Oh. I—I am uncertain. . . ." Mr. Pridmore frowned back into the room. "It must be—er . . . I, um . . ."

Jane walked at her husband's side as they left the safe house behind and headed down the hill towards the slave quarters. Louisa stayed close by her, keeping the parasol in place with a diligence that was impressive. In a low voice, Jane asked, "No ventilation, really?"

Frowning, Vincent settled his hat back upon his head. He offered her his arm and glanced back at Mr. Pridmore, who was still looking for ventilation. "There is a gap at the base of the door, so it would be a simple matter to smoke someone out."

"I should add that many of the preserves are clearly spoilt."

Vincent gave a little snort. "And the wax seal on the rum barrel has already been cracked."

"Mr. Hamilton! Wait—the shrubbery is this way."

Without checking his pace, Vincent said, "I am not interested in the shrubbery."

"But the ladies—"

"Can see well enough where it is." Vincent tucked his chin into his cravat. The dark cloth framed his face with even more severity than his usual. "What I am interested in seeing next are the slave quarters. The ones we passed on the way in had significant decay."

"It's shameful, really, how lazy they are." Mr. Pridmore took Vincent's arm. "Allow me to show you the gardens, lovely places."

Vincent looked at Mr. Pridmore's hand on his arm. "Perhaps later."

"Oh, but the ladies have no wish to see the slave quarters, I am certain. They are vulgar places."

"Jane?"

Jane smiled at her husband. "I am not afraid of a little dirt. At least it is only dry dust here. You know how my gown gets when I go walking in the shrubbery after a rain."

"Then we are agreed." Vincent walked forward, but he dipped his head and murmured to Jane. "You will let me know if you become fatigued?"

"As we have thus far walked no farther than the length of the house, I am in no danger of fatigue."

"But you will let me know."

She sighed. "Yes."

He pressed his hand over hers, where it rested on his arm. "Thank you."

Mr. and Mrs. Pridmore stayed close on their heels, with Betsy and her parasol providing continual shade. As they passed through the hedge that formed the boundary of the lawn, Mr. Pridmore cleared his throat. "I must say again that this is not a place to take a lady, quite apart from the dirt. They are animals, and frequently engage in carnal acts, quite in public, that a lady should not see."

"Mr. Pridmore!" His wife fluttered her handkerchief. "It is not genteel to speak of such things, and most especially not in front of Mrs. Hamilton."

The overseer seemed to come to his senses about the topic he had been discussing. "I beg your pardon, Mrs. Hamilton. We are so unused to being in company that I forget how such things must seem to one who is newly to our island. I do not tend to think of it as any more untoward than discussing the breeding of hounds."

"And yet, it is quite different."

"Of course. Of course . . ." He did not seem as if he quite agreed with her, but he had the grace not to argue the point further. Turning at an angle to the hedge, he gestured along a well-beaten path through the lawn "Well . . . this way, then, to the slave quarters."

Vincent frowned. "I recall them being closer to the road."

"You are thinking of the old buildings you passed by on your way in. These are closer, which would be better for the ladies, do you not agree?"

Vincent inclined his head and gestured for the overseer to lead on. As they walked, Mrs. Pridmore drew even with Jane and engaged her in conversation about fashion and music, to which Jane had very little to offer, as the overseer's wife was more than capable of carrying on nearly the whole of the discussion by herself. Due to the narrowness of the path, Louisa and Betsy were forced to walk in the grass to either side of them in order to keep the parasols overhead.

They rounded the slope of the hill and came upon a set of little white cottages, surely no more than one room apiece. Each had a small garden plot of vegetables in front, and one had pea vines trained on a trellis up the side.

Mr. Pridmore gestured broadly. "There you are. Pretty as a picture, eh?"

Jane counted ten houses and then thought of the number of slaves that Louisa had said were on the estate. There was not enough space to accommodate anywhere near the two hundred slaves she had mentioned. "And where are the others?"

"The others?"

"The other houses. I wonder if they have so pleasant a prospect."

Vincent narrowed his eyes and strode towards the nearest cottage. "The quarters by the road are still in use, are they not?"

"Yes. . . ."

"Why are not all of the slaves supplied with cottages such as these?"

Mr. Pridmore laughed, slapping his hands together. "Oh ho! A romantic. My dear sir, once you have an opportunity to go over the accounts you will see that we have too many slaves to make that economical. Given the mild weather here, those are more than sufficient. Cottages such as these are reserved for the house slaves. In general, the coloured slaves are more adept than the blacks, but they are also more delicate in constitution, so cottages such as these are necessary. It comes from the mixing of the bloodlines, I fear. Their rate of births is alarmingly low."

Vincent humphed as he walked down the row of houses.

Mr. Pridmore appeared to take that as an encouragement to continue. "I have been thinking of starting a breeding catalogue to improve the stock. After all, cattle ranchers do it to great effect. It would be a simple matter, I would think, to breed for a docile temperament. Why, take Betsy here. As calm and steady a maid as you could ask for. Why not breed her with someone like your Frank? It might improve the birth rate as well."

"Mr. Pridmore! Remember Mrs. Hamilton!"

"I am not concerned for myself." Jane studied Betsy, who walked behind Mrs. Pridmore with an elegant deportment but two spots of red upon her cheeks. "But a change of subject would be welcome, I think."

The maid's eyelids fluttered as though she was restraining the impulse to look up. In no other manner did she display that she had even heard the conversation. Jane was accustomed to pretending that servants were not in the room, in part because that social convention made it easier for them to go about their work rather than requiring constant courtesies, but she was not used to, nor comfortable with, the idea of discussing them as if they were not present.

"Ah—yes." Mr. Pridmore cleared his throat. "My apologies. Should you like to go in one of the cottages?"

"I have seen enough." Vincent's hands were behind his back, and he had tilted his head down into his cravat. More telling to Jane than his habitual stance was the tension around his eyes and mouth. "The rum distillery should be next, I believe."

"Of course." Mr. Pridmore gave a little chuckle. "Though, to that, I really must insist that we not take the ladies. It is not safe."

"If it is safe enough for you gentlemen, then surely it is safe enough for me." It might have been Jane's imagination, but she could not help feeling that his reasons for avoiding the distillery had little to do with her safety.

"I am afraid not, Mrs. Hamilton. Should there be an accident with the boiler, or simply a careless movement by a slave, your muslin would be inadequate to protect you."

Vincent turned from the group and met Jane's gaze. He then glanced from Mrs. Pridmore to Mr. Pridmore. Someone who was not intimately acquainted with him would see no more than that. Jane took it to mean that his next sentence would be for them, not for her. "Perhaps you should return to the house with Mrs. Pridmore. I am afraid we have business to discuss that could not be of any possible interest to ladies."

He gave a slight tilt of his head towards Mrs. Pridmore with an even smaller head shake. Jane inhaled with understanding. He thought that Mrs. Pridmore did not know about Lord Verbury. Her continued presence meant he could not be direct in his conversation with the overseer. "Of course, but I hope you will tell me all about it when you return."

He relaxed ever so slightly as he saw that she understood. "You have my word. I am looking forward to seeing what Mr. Pridmore chooses to show me. The tour has been instructive thus far." Again, beneath his words and in the slight shift of his weight when he said "chooses" lay another message for Jane, which confirmed her own thought.

Mr. Pridmore had been steering the tour very carefully. Given what they had seen, she was certain that the rickety sheds by the road would be far from the worst thing. She did not like letting Vincent bear the burden of this alone, but given Mrs. Pridmore's tendency to chatter, Jane might be able to gain a different perspective of how things lay without them present.

Jane gave her husband an encouraging smile. "I shall find ways to occupy myself while you are busy with men's work."

"I am certain you will." His eyes almost twinkled in response. "You have always been accomplished at the womanly arts."

Eight

Customary Restraint

Jane had gathered little of substance from Mrs. Pridmore, other than what she had already suspected. By the lady's occasional lapse, it was clear that she and Mr. Pridmore had become accustomed to thinking of the estate as their own. Vincent, too, had found conditions as he suspected. The distillery's boilers had been poorly repaired and little maintained. He found not only men working in the deplorable heat, but children working among the vats of boiling cane syrup. The whole of it seemed designed for disaster, and, while he had been there, a dropped bucket had scalded a youth across his legs. The boy had been beaten for dropping the bucket and then sent back to work. When Vincent had spoken to Mr. Pridmore about it, the man had brushed his concerns aside and said that he was following Lord Verbury's instructions. He invited Vincent to take it up with his lordship.

That conversation had not gone well.

Monday, their third full day in Antigua, found Jane and Vincent in the counting house. Jane, in a wicker chair by one of the tall windows, was attempting to help him sort out the affairs of the estate and now sat looking through pages of cramped text in the slave registry. It pretended to show the birth and death dates of each slave owned by Lord Verbury, as required by the London Registry, but it had been carelessly kept, and many names were missing. Often a slave was noted without any parentage, even when the dates made it clear that he or she had been born on the estate.

Jane rubbed her eyes and sat back in her chair. The large metal shutters had been thrown back to let in a breeze, which helped somewhat with the afternoon heat.

Across the room, Vincent and Frank were bent over an account book going over the finances of the estate. Seeing them with their heads so close in conversation made the familial resemblance all the stronger. Frank's skin was darker, and his hair had begun to silver at the temples, but their silhouettes were very much alike. Jane sighed and turned back to the ledger again. She had, at least, begun to gather some sense of what Mr. Pridmore had meant by the low birth rate. An alarmingly high number of women lost their babies shortly after birth or never came to term at all. It was not, in her condition, the most comforting of reading.

Still, it gave her an idea for a distinctly feminine way of determining the state of affairs. "Vincent . . . my family used to do charity work with the people in our village. We would take such supplies as they could not afford and ensure that they had any medicines they might need."

"You are thinking to do that here." Vincent nodded slowly, clearly recognising her deeper meaning. "Though I am not certain it can be accounted as charity if they are people who . . . whom we are so directly responsible for."

She swallowed. Of course it would not be charity to take better care of your property—even that thought made her ill. She could not shake the English way of thinking that those working on the estate were free. "All the more reason, then. Would that be useful, Frank?"

"It is, in fact, one of the things that your husband and I are attempting to address." He placed a finger on the account book to hold his place as he gave her his attention. "The slaves are responsible for growing their own food. While the tending of sustenance plots is common on the island, Mr. Pridmore recently cut their salted fish and pork rations. He felt it unnecessary, since the field slaves are raising chickens."

"That—that is absurd."

The corner of Frank's mouth twitched. "If *you* were to ask Louisa to arrange for a cut of bacon from Cook, no one could say that was wrong."

"Thank you." She sighed, turning back to the ledger. "Meanwhile, would it help if I were to fill in the missing information? If we are supposed to be providing the London Registry with a full accounting of the slaves owned by Lord Verbury, then we are sorely wanting." Jane drew the book a little closer. "For instance, it has a record for Amey, who has two children, but only Solomon is named. There is a date listed for the birth of the second, but no name, and no death."

"Eleanor, I believe. Thank you, it would be appreciated if you could sort this out. I can assign one of the older women to go over it with you. They know who everyone is." He almost smiled. "You know how old women can be."

"I do. You should meet my mother sometime." Jane took up a quill and wrote the name of Amey's child in the ledger. "It is really shockingly kept. There is no record of Zeus and Jove at all, for instance. Or you, for that matter."

"That may be because Zeus and Jove are just what his lordship chooses to call them." He bent his head back to the account book. "See if there are a Zachary and a John born in 1805."

"I thought those were peculiar names." Jane turned to that year and traced her finger down the list of births. "Ha! Here we are. Thank you. Should we call them by their real names?"

Vincent answered, "Not while we are trying to keep my father happy."

"Surely he would not know. He cannot even leave his rooms."

Frank cleared his throat, and let that be the whole of his remark. Jane sagged in her chair. It was so wearying, having to attend to the desires of a man who was supposed to be dead.

She wiped her pen clean with more diligence than was perhaps merited, considering that she was not done writing. She had never abhorred someone as thoroughly as she did Lord Verbury. "And you? Is Frank not your real name?"

"It is a nickname given to me in my youth." Sliding his chair back from the table, Frank reached for another ledger on the table behind him.

"I should be happy to call you by your real name, if you prefer. In spite of his lordship." Jane waited, but Frank only set the new ledger down on the table in front of Vincent and began leafing through it.

Vincent straightened in his chair slowly. "Frank . . . Frederick. You are named after my father, are you not?"

Frank stared at the ledger pages, his expression set. Then he shut the book and pushed it away from him. "Yes, sir. My name, for your wife's ledger, is Frederick Hamilton II."

There was no reason why Jane should be shocked. His parentage had been obvious from the moment she had seen him. What surprised her was that Lord Verbury had been proud enough about the birth of a slave child to name him after himself. "You were his firstborn."

"Yes, madam. You will find my birth on the page for the year 1773."

Incongruously, Vincent laughed. He covered his face with his hands and leaned back in his chair. It was so out of character and out of keeping with the conversation that Jane could only gape. Frank, likewise, stared with his mouth stopped at the beginning of a word. Vincent wiped his eyes and sat forward again. "I am sorry. It is not amusing. It is only that when he was disappointed with me—which was always—he would say, 'My eldest would not speak to me this way.' I thought he meant Garland."

Frank opened the ledger again and pulled it towards him. "I suggest that we—"

"Ah!" Jane made the cry before she understood why. She pressed a hand to her stomach, terrified.

Vincent's chair clattered backwards, as he sprang to his feet. "A doctor. Fetch a doctor!"

The pang repeated, a sharp blow from inside. The baby had kicked. "No! No, I am fine."

It was not a cramp. She knew all too well what that felt like. She had felt this, too, from the outside, when Melody's baby had kicked.

When Jane had been expecting previously, it had not lasted long enough for their child to quicken. Which meant that she must now be further along than she had thought. Jane put her hand to the spot and willed the child to kick again. Vincent knelt in front of her. When had he arrived?

Frank was halfway to the door. If he got a doctor, then her condition would be clear to everyone. Jane put her hand on Vincent's cheek and forced him to look at her instead of her stomach. "It was a bit of indigestion. Something I ate did not agree with me. Nothing more."

"But—"

"Frank!" Jane looked past her husband. "Truly, I was only surprised by how . . . indecorous my digestion was."

He slowed and eyed her. "Should I tell Cook to use fewer spices?"

"The meals have been delicious, but perhaps . . . perhaps I should have something plain for dinner tonight." Jane turned back to the ledger she had been working on and drew a scrap of paper closer. Taking up her quill, she wrote: *The baby kicked. All is well.*

Vincent stared at the little piece of paper as if he could not read. He lifted it off the table and sank back on his heels, gazing at it. After a moment, Vincent covered his mouth and gazed up at her. He raised his hand as though to touch her stomach, but caught himself before he did. If Frank had not already guessed, he surely would have then. Clearing his throat, Vincent folded the paper in half and tucked it into his waistcoat pocket. "If your digestion is troubling you, perhaps you should lie down?"

Frank was staring at them. He knew. He must know. Jane laughed with a gaiety she did not feel, hoping that she could somehow convince him that nothing was amiss. "Do not be silly. It was a touch of ill vapours. Just be happy that the windows were open and we have such a pleasant breeze. Now go on, back to your numbers. I have some ancestry to sort out."

As Vincent stood, with an admirable display of ease, Jane turned her gaze back towards the ledger. Her attention, though, was fixed internally, as she waited for movement within.

Jane's husband was a man of enormous will and restraint. It took all of Jane's power to remain in her chair, but Vincent lasted nearly a full hour before lifting his head to regard her. "Were you considering visiting the slave quarters today?"

She set down her quill. "I had thought to, yes."

"I need to stretch my legs a bit, so will walk part of the way with you when you go." Vincent pushed his chair back, making it clear that he meant for her to go now.

Frank shut the ledger in front of him and rubbed his eyes. "We are at a good stopping point, and I have some matters to attend to in the house as well."

Jane slid her chair back and neatly arranged the small stack of papers and books she had been looking through. Looking "at" would perhaps be more appropriate, as she had spent much of the time waiting for the baby to kick again. Aside from a few brief flutters that truly might have been only the vapours, their child had quieted.

"I presume you want to go to our room to fetch your bonnet and parasol first." Vincent's manner was calm, yet he kept touching his waistcoat pocket where the little slip of paper was.

Jane suppressed a smile, trying to match his demeanour. "I could not think of going without either."

He walked beside her down the steps and across the short stretch of lawn to the great house. The space between them began to fill with unsaid words, and by the time they reached the door to their rooms, the silence seemed nearly as gravid as Jane herself.

They stepped into the room, and Vincent shut the door.

Leaning against it, he closed his eyes and let his fatigue show. Jane sometimes forgot that Vincent was younger than she—only by a year—but the differences in their lives gave him a countenance far older.

She took his hand, so much broader than hers, and placed it against her stomach where she had felt the kicks. "I do not know if it will happen again immediately."

He opened his eyes. "I thought—"

"I know. I did too, for a moment." Jane concentrated, willing some movement to occur. "But it means that I am likely well into my fifth month."

Scarcely breathing, he nodded.

Jane pressed his hand against her more firmly, but their child seemed as stubborn as Vincent and refused to perform on command. "Have you thought of names?"

"I have been a little afraid to do so."

"Well . . . let us begin. If a girl, is there anyone you would like to honour?" That seemed a safer question than asking about boy's names, considering their situation.

He wet his lips. "My grandmother? Lady Vincent. Her given name was Grace. Would that . . . ?"

"Grace Vincent." Jane rolled the syllables around on her tongue. "That is a lovely name, and as the woman who first taught you to work glamour, I think it appropriate. May I also suggest Virginia?"

"After your mother?" He seemed almost surprised, though it was the most commonly done thing.

"Mama has tried to do her best for us and would be so pleased." Jane frowned, thinking she felt a flurry of movement, but Vincent showed no signs of marking it. "Grace Virginia Vincent—oh. No, that is entirely too many Vs, even if she is going to change surnames upon marriage. Perhaps Elizabeth, taking Mama's middle name?"

He raised his eyebrows in disbelief. "Your mother's name is Virginia Elizabeth? Truly?"

"My grandfather wrote a book on Queen Elizabeth that was very well received."

This made Vincent chuckle for some reason.

"He was an amateur historian of some renown. You do not need to laugh quite so hard. Elizabeth is a perfectly lovely name."

"To be sure, but you must see the comedy in Virginia Elizabeth."

"To be sure, I do not." She was fully aware that Virginia Elizabeth referred to the Virgin Queen. It had not been an accidental connection. While she was glad to see him laughing, it had been a very good book on the queen. There was a copy in His Majesty's own library.

"It is only that—"

The baby delivered a swift rap to Jane's side, silencing them both. Vincent inhaled convulsively as a second kick followed the first. His semblance of calm melted, leaving only an expression of open wonder. "That was . . . kicking?"

"Or punching." She ran her fingers through his hair.

His brows drew together with concern. "Does it hurt? You should sit. Why am I keeping you standing? You should sit."

Jane laughed at her husband as he led her to the small sofa in their apartment. "It can be surprising. That is—" The baby kicked again. "—all. Though I've been told by Melody that it can get uncomfortable later. Tom was apparently quite the pugilist."

Vincent settled her on the sofa with an absurd amount of care. He sank to kneel in front of her and looked for permission before putting his hand back on her stomach. "Do you think it is a boy?"

"And if it is, what shall we call him? What is Herr Scholes's name?" That should be safe enough.

His attention had returned to the sensations beneath his hand. "Leopold Sebastian Faustus Scholes."

"Faustus? That will never do. Leopold Vincent?"

"I was thinking Charles."

"After Papa?"

Vincent looked up, a shyness in his brown eyes. "Would that be all right? His conduct is exemplary."

She leaned forward to kiss his cheek. "He would be honoured and delighted." She took both of his hands and pressed them to either side of her, so that whichever way Charles or Grace kicked, her husband could feel it. In quiet, intimate moments, she had seen Alastar sitting like this with Melody, with a similar expression of stunned joy. Jane traced her fingers through Vincent's hair and across his forehead. That line between his brows had finally smoothed.

The door to their room opened.

Jane pushed back in the sofa, aware that their pose made

her state all too clear. Equally startled, Vincent sprang to his feet, eyes widening. And then he replaced the fear with anger. He reached for it like glamour, wrapping rage around him, and spun to the door.

"How dare you enter without leave!" His shoulders seemed somehow broader, with his hands held away from his sides and flexed almost into fists.

Louisa flinched back into the door. She ducked her head, shrinking into a curtsy. "I'm sorry, sir. I—Mr. Frank told me to see to Mrs. Hamilton."

"Knock. You must always knock before entering." He towered over her, moving his hands behind his back and clasping them tightly.

"Vincent." Jane stood.

Her voice seemed to recall him to himself and he rocked back on his heels.

"Thank you, Louisa." Jane's heart knocked against her ribs. While she settled her nerves, she turned from the young woman as though to fetch her bonnet. Vincent rarely raised his voice and had never shouted at a servant before. "Would you be able to acquire cuts of bacon from Cook? I should like to visit the slave quarters."

"Yes, madam. Mr. Frank made the suggestion, so I have already arranged for Zeus to carry it for us."

"You are not seriously going out." Vincent spun on Jane, and she took an involuntary step back. He clenched his jaw. The effort he took to moderate his tone made the next sentence excessively calm. "That is to say, I thought you were tired."

She took up the bonnet and went to the mirror. "Not so much as to stay in."

"But—" He cleared his throat. "In this weather?"

"We are asking people to work in this weather. Surely I can make a walk." Jane settled the bonnet, trying not to flatten her hair still more. If she could pretend that all was normal, then perhaps he could steady himself a little.

"But it could wait until tomorrow."

"And would tomorrow be any cooler? Likely not."

Vincent narrowed his eyes. It was clear that he was trying to think of a protest that did not amount to telling Louisa that Jane was in the family way. He finally nodded and said, "Well. I shall see you this evening."

He turned to the door and stopped. Louisa still stood by it, her head lowered. Vincent let out a slow breath. "Louisa, I apologise for raising my voice. It was needlessly rude."

Louisa looked up, brows rising as her eyes widened, but she quickly masked the surprise with a curtsy. "Thank you, sir."

When he walked from the room, his hands were still clasped firmly behind his back, but he had apologised, and that was not something that his father would have done.

Jane let out a slow breath when the sound of his footsteps had faded. Vincent had warned her that his behaviour would alter, but she had not reckoned with how quickly or how much. This was only their third day in Antigua, and the pendulum of his emotion frightened her more than a little.

Nine

A Charitable Call

Seen from the great house, the wattle and daub houses had a picturesque charm that did not survive closer inspection. To be sure, the vegetable plots surrounding them lent them some softening verdure, but they were little more than sheds, with dirt floors and crumbling mud walls huddled together around a dirt yard. The low roofs, constructed of plaited palm fronds, made the ceiling of the ship's cabin seem high.

A gaggle of children chased each other, giving off infectious squeals of laughter. One little girl wore a ragged shirt as a dress. A boy of no more than five ran past wearing only trousers. Sitting in the dirt, patting at the dust, one toddler wore nothing at all. Watching over them were a pair of old women and an old man. The man leaned back on a bench in the sun with his head resting against the side of one of the sheds. His occasional snore was audible even over the laughter of the children.

As the children ran past the women, a spider the size of a draft horse rose out of the dirt. It gave an incongruous, bubbling laugh. Squealing in mock terror, the children scattered.

It had taken only a moment to recognise that the red and black creature was a rough glamour, but it still made Jane's mouth quite dry. Even Zeus had started back when it emerged.

The children, however, were not fearful. Their squeals quickly changed to laughter as they joined together on the far side of the yard. The older of the two women smiled and waved her hands in front of her, making the spider unravel into the ether. She nudged her neighbour and they worked together, clearly reweaving the glamour that had sprung out at the children. Jane bit down on the inside of her cheek to keep herself from shifting her vision to the ether to see what they were doing. Every movement and twist of their fingers spoke of working glamour, but she could see none of the threads. With matched grunts, they tied off their work.

So quickly! Jane fairly itched to see their process.

The younger of the two sat back while the elder nodded to the children to begin their run. The children started off cautiously, and Jane soon understood. The women had placed a trap for the children. They had to play their game around it, not knowing when the spider would jump out.

One of the little girls spotted Jane and came to a halt in

front of her. She remained stuck to the earth, staring first at Jane, then at Louisa and Zeus with his basket, and finally back to Jane. The girl's braid went into her mouth as she stared.

So riveted was the child that Jane almost expected her to scream. One of the little boys spotted them next. Then a flurry of movement had all of the children standing in a group in front of them, save for the toddler, who still played in the dirt. Jane counted nine of them in various states of undress, none appearing to be more than ten years of age.

The old women moved more slowly. One nudged the other, who answered with a little grunt before heaving herself off the bench.

Louisa, next to Jane, gave a little sigh.

"Good afternoon." Jane greeted the children first, to give the old woman time to make her way to them.

They looked at each other and one of them giggled. What she would not give to be able to perform glamour right now. It had always been how she had made friends with children in the past.

"What were you playing?" Jane smiled and addressed the first little girl. She backed away upon being addressed, her braid still in her mouth. One of the older boys caught the girl about the shoulders and wrapped her in a hug. On Jane's other side, Zeus shifted with his basket. She turned to him and said, "Shall we set up on the bench over there?"

He hesitated. "I would wait until Nkiruka tells you what to do, madam."

Jane made note of that hesitation and his advice. It spoke

worlds about the woman's stature in the community. "May I take it that that is Nkiruka approaching us now?"

"Yes, madam."

The woman was a deep ruddy brown, all lines and wrinkles folded around a mouth that seemed designed to disapprove. Or perhaps just to disapprove of Jane, since she had been smiling broadly while playing with the children. She wore her hair under a kerchief, but the bits that peeked out at the temples were grey. She gave a sharp hiss at the children, and they scattered like water on a hot pan.

Jane nodded to her. "Good afternoon."

The woman rested her hands on her lean hips. When she answered, her words clung together as if they wanted to stay snug. Jane had to think for a moment before she understood her to say, "If you say so, ma'am."

Jane gestured to the basket that Zeus carried. "My husband, Mr. Hamilton, and I have only just arrived in Antigua. I thought you might want some meat for your dinner."

The woman continued to stand there, her gaze occasionally darting to the children as though she wanted to return to playing with them and Jane was keeping her from it. To be fair, Jane *was* detaining her, so she cut straight to the point.

"I took the liberty of bringing a side of bacon as a gift, thinking it might keep." Though truly, how anyone could keep anything in one of these sheds was beyond Jane. If they accomplished nothing else in the next two weeks, they simply must do something to address that.

"Bacon?" Nkiruka studied Jane for a moment, compressing her lips. Then she turned her back on them and headed for one of the sheds to the side of the yard. "That good. Amey go lub dat."

Jane had to struggle for a moment to understand the woman. She had thought that Louisa and Zeus sounded Antiguan born, but even these few words made it clear that she had barely heard the Antiguan accent. She frowned, trying to make the alteration in her understanding.

Louisa misinterpreted the frown and spoke in a low tone to her. "Please forgive her, madam. She is old, and as a field slave, has not learned to be around the master or any other white people. The manners of the others, too, may be coarser than what you are accustomed to."

"I am aware that I am not in a drawing room." Jane picked her way across the yard, glad that she had worn one of her shorter day dresses. The hem would still need attention, but at least it would not drag in the dirt.

At the door to the small shed, Nkiruka stuck her head into the dark interior. "Amey! Lady from de big house ya fu see you."

A moment later, a woman of colour who was heavy with child emerged from the house. Though not so dark as Nkiruka, her skin was still deeper than any of the house slaves, with a dash of freckles across her nose and cheeks. She wore a ragged dress, and the swell of her belly lifted the front hem to the middle of her shins. She had a hand against her back and squinted against the sun as she stepped out.

Jane's gaze was dragged back to the woman's stomach. She must be very near her time. Perhaps it was only the threadbare frock that made her appear so large, but Jane could not help brushing her hand down the front of her own gown. Her stomach had not increased even half so much, and she already felt enormous.

If Amey had not attempted a curtsy, made clumsy by her condition, Jane might have stared for another five minutes before collecting herself. The social forms gave her an anchor. She returned the curtsy before remembering the difference in their stations. She hoped the young woman would not take it as a mockery. She quickly brushed past it by introducing herself and stating her purpose in visiting.

"That is kind of you, ma'am." Amey turned to Zeus. "A table inside."

He nodded and carried the basket into the dark interior.

Louisa called after him. "The little jar in the basket—bring it with you when you come back." She murmured to Jane, "I brought a bit of candied ginger for the children."

"Oh. Thank you, that was thoughtful of you." In spite of the records that she had looked at, it had not occurred to Jane to bring a sweet. She waited, awkward in the silence, for Zeus to return. The children whispered to each other, all seemingly curious about her. Nkiruka, too, watched her steadily. Jane became keenly aware of the paleness of her own skin. She had not given her complexion much thought before, besides wishing that it were not quite so sallow. Clearing her throat, she offered the old woman a smile. "The spider you worked earlier was an interesting glamour."

"Anansi?" Nkiruka shrugged as if that were no great thing.

"I was curious about what folds you were using to lay it. It seemed clever—"

At that moment, Zeus appeared with the little jar. Jane's interest in candied ginger had never been lower, but the children who had followed them to the house all stared at it with something akin to awe. He handed the jar to Louisa, who in turn held it out to Jane.

Jane shook her head. "It was your idea. Please."

"It is more proper coming from you."

"Is proper really a concern?" Jane moved to the nearest bench, which had the dual advantages of being shaded by the shed and removed from the chaos of the children. She pulled her bonnet off, though they were yet out of doors. She was enough in the shade to prefer a breeze to the stifling closeness of the straw brim. "May I sit?"

"If you want."

"Will you join me?"

With a shrug, Nkiruka settled next to her on the bench. Zeus and Louisa moved a few feet away and opened the jar of candied ginger. One girl reached out to touch the cotton of Louisa's gown, but otherwise, their attention seemed fixed on the jar. Zeus smiled and held out a piece of ginger. She had not seen him smile before. It quite changed his face.

Her chief interest, however, lay in Nkiruka's spider. "Am I correct that you were using a *frottis mélange* to slip the spider outside the visible spectrum?" It was the only thing that made sense, for them to have created the spider earlier and then colour-shifted it away.

Nkiruka frowned at her for a moment, then shouted into the house. "Amey!" She followed that with a string of language that Jane did not recognise at all.

The young woman poked her head out of the house. "Mama. Remember Mr. Pridmore want us to speak only English."

"Bah. Let dem tell." She shrugged. "Me too old fu punish."

"You know that not true."

"Maybe. But still, tell me wha she say."

Amey turned to Jane. "Sorry, ma'am. You can repeat the question? I'll try an' help my mother understand."

"Of course. Thank you for your help. The spider your mother made. I wanted to know if she used *frottis mélange*."

Amey bit her lip. "Hm . . . I don't know that word either."

Too late, far too late, Jane understood that she was asking about a formal term of art that neither woman would have had opportunity or reason to learn. "It . . . it is a word that relates to using a thread of poorfire . . ." That term received nearly as blank a look as the French had. "Using a thread of glamour that is above the visible spectrum—that is, light that we cannot see with normal vision. So, *frottis mélange* means using that thread to anchor a fold elsewhere. I—I think my explanation was so disordered that it barely made sense to myself, but did you catch my meaning?"

"I think so, ma'am." Amey turned to her mother, who

waited patiently through the exchange. Amey changed to a rolling percussive language and the two had a rapid conversation, including hand gestures that Jane thought might be glamour.

In fact, as they continued, she became more certain that it was. It alarmed her to see a woman who was increasing work glamour. "Please—there is no need for you to work glamour on my account. Not in your condition."

The two women stopped. Nkiruka looked at her, then at Amey, then back at Jane. "Why?"

"Well . . ." She did not want to discuss such a delicate subject, especially if it would alarm Amey, but without the benefit of an education, they might not know of the danger. "Well, glamour is not safe for a woman in the family way."

"You t'ink glamour mek woman lose dem baby?"

"I have been taught that, yes." It was, in fact, common knowledge in England.

Nkiruka laughed at her, shaking her head. "No, no."

Jane shook her own head. She had miscarried before while working glamour. "I have evidence to the contrary."

"Ha! If working glamour mek woman lose picknee then no new slave woulda born."

"I understand your point, but must, respectfully, disagree. All of the best medical science says that the energy toll on the mother's body from working glamour is a danger to both her and the child."

"English medicine. You t'ink glamour all one thing." Nkiruka shook her head and held up three fingers. "Is three different magics. Two safe. Sound and scent. Even light all right, if not too much. Like walking. Walking good for de mother. Running, no."

The memory of running through a field of rye with a stitch in her side stopped Jane's breath for a moment. She shook her head to brush the past away. "But the overseer says that the birth rate here is extremely low. If your expectant mothers are working glamour, might that account for it?"

There was a shift in Nkiruka's posture, but Jane could not determine what it was. A glance passed between Amey and Nkiruka. The moment passed so quickly that Jane might have imagined it.

Amey struggled up from the bench, steadying herself with a hand against the wall. "Don't worry bout me. The only thing that hurt is that hard bench. I goin' inside. Call if you need me."

"You lie down." Nkiruka watched her daughter go, then leaned back against the wall. "My daughter tell me what you asking 'bout de spider. You wan' know how I do it."

"Yes, thank you."

"Language hard for dis. Come, let me show you." She moved her hand and, in the centre of the yard, the spider rose from the dust.

Jane frankly gaped. When Nkiruka had worked the creature before, she had been sitting on a bench on the other side of the yard. Any threads she had to control the glamour must have been anchored there, and yet she worked it from here. Generally, the further one was from the illusion, the harder it was to maintain the threads and folds involved in creating it. Nkiruka showed no sign of even breathing hard. Jane swallowed in astonishment.

"I am afraid I did not quite catch the weave." To be more accurate, Jane had not seen it at all.

"Dat ah your first trouble. Folds. Weaves. I do not use those."

"Pardon?" It had clearly been a glamour. "May I ask, then, how you created it?"

"Is different where I come from. We don't try an' mek glamour behave like cloth."

"Oh—oh, well, neither do I. It is only that the language of fabric is so useful for discussing what is an otherwise intangible art."

"An' it set what de English can do."

Jane thought of the detailed glamurals that she and Vincent had created for the Prince Regent. Months of care had gone into creating a representation of an undersea kingdom that could be mistaken for real. Even Vincent's pranks when studying with Herr Scholes had apparently looked quite real. Nkiruka's spider was impressive only because of the distance involved. The illusion itself was quite crude. "I think, perhaps, you have not had the opportunity to see what a professional glamourist can do."

Nkiruka snorted and gave Jane a look that made her feel quite small.

"I—yes, my apologies." Jane clasped her hands in her

lap, but undid them when she noticed the fabric of her dress smoothing over her stomach. "How . . . how do you approach glamour, then?"

"Glamour is it own thing. Why mek it subben else?"

Jane considered this, recalling a conversation she had once had when attempting to explain glamour to a little girl. The child had wanted to know why glamour used borrowed words. "Do you not think that a metaphor makes it easier to understand?"

"Babies understand glamour." She gestured with her chin at the children. "You ha fu teach dem fu see dis world. Fold? Weave? Stitch? Wrong words."

"I confess that I have spent my whole life thinking of glamour in these terms, so it is hard to think of it any other way."

"Ha! See? Dat ah de trouble. Look." She drew a fold of yellow glamour out of the ether and fanned it out so that a sunrise seemed to be in her hand. "Now. You do this with a fold?" She slid her other hand across the length of the glamour and . . . Jane bit her lip in frustration. She could see the sunrise change smoothly from yellow to red to blue, but not how.

"No. Can you describe what you just did? I am afraid I did not see it."

"Yes, *m na-eke ya ka a na-eke ịsị aka*, and then *ị dọ ya-adọ ka ịwedata ugwu dị na ya ka hancha dị na-ala.*" The woman stared a challenge at her.

Jane took her point and sighed. "Would you show me again, please?"

Maybe Jane could hazard a guess from watching only the visible parts. She would not chance even peeping into the ether, as much as she was tempted. It likely would not hurt, but before, when she had first been with child, even looking had made her dreadfully ill. Concentrating, she watched Nkiruka's hands, trying to match the movement with techniques that she knew, but was confounded completely. "Did you stretch it?"

"See? T'inking 'bout fabric stop you." She raised her hands. "Again."

Jane shook her head. "Thank you, no. I am afraid I cannot see what you are doing."

Nkiruka looked at her as though she were stupid. Jane ducked her head, irritated that she could not explain that she was prohibited from working glamour, because to do so would be to tell Louisa and then Lord Verbury that she was with child. A little of her old distress returned. She was accustomed to being good at glamour—and not merely *good*. Jane would never admit it aloud, but she knew that her work could be accounted brilliant. So to be suddenly too stupid to even see a fold vexed her. Crying about it would be nonsensical, especially when sitting here surrounded by people who barely even had clothes enough, yet Jane's eyes began to burn. She picked up her bonnet to go.

As she lifted it, she saw Nkiruka look down at her stomach and make a small, "Ah."

Jane's heart staggered, and, as if in response to her agitation, the baby kicked hard against her side. Only the fact that she was holding the bonnet kept Jane from touching the spot. She could not even weave a sphere of silence around them so she could beg Nkiruka to hold her tongue.

Turning her back to Zeus and Louisa, Jane mouthed, "Please," and put her finger to her lips. Tears wet her cheeks, which vexed her. Crying would only make things worse: they would ask why, and what could Jane say then?

"Glamour interesting, nuh?" Watching her for a moment, Nkiruka's eyes narrowed. Her gaze darted behind Jane to where Louisa and Zeus talked with the children. Nkiruka's hand moved, slightly, and the conversation became muddied, as if she had done something to the sound. "Me tell you de truth. You can at least watch glamour."

Jane remembered her prior sickness with such distinctness that she thought she would be ill right there.

"Perhaps . . . perhaps you might come to the great house to discuss glamour? My husband would be very interested to hear about your approach." Jane's voice came out too high and breathless.

"Maybe. They not goin' want me there."

Jane wiped at her cheeks, trying to get her breathing under control again. "Well. I will make it clear that *I* want you."

"Den we talk bout if you can do glamour."

Nkiruka knew. She did not merely suspect that Jane might be with child. She *knew*. Nkiruka's hand slid through the air and the conversation behind Jane became clear again. Nkiruka raised her voice. "It too warm out here fu you. Zeus! Take her home out of this sun. Get her a coldmonger."

In other circumstances, Jane might have protested that she wanted to stay to talk about glamour, but she put her bonnet on and hid in the shadow at its depth. If Nkiruka wished for her to go, then she would go and do nothing to upset the woman. "I trust we will see you at the great house soon."

"Madam!" Louisa's voice sounded indignant. "She cannot come to the great house."

"Why not? I want her to speak with Mr. Hamilton about glamour, and he hardly has time to come down here." A moment of inspiration struck Jane. "Besides, I need help correcting the ledgers, and Frank had suggested that I ask one of the older women for help. If Nkiruka is willing, that is."

"I willing." She shrugged. "But, I tell you, they not goin' want me there."

"But *I* do." The fact that Louisa found the older woman an improper choice made Jane only more determined to have her for an assistant.

Ten

A Theory of Glamour

Jane stared at the page before her. She had already crossed out three different attempts to explain what she had seen the giant spider do that afternoon. Whatever she had thought about writing a book was clearly mistaken. Attempting to describe a visual medium in words proved much harder than she had anticipated.

Hearing Vincent's footsteps in the long gallery recalled her to herself. He paused in the door. "Muse, you have ink on your nose."

"Do I?" Jane set her pen down and wiped at her nose. When had it grown dark outside?

"Indeed. More, now, I think." He produced a pocket handkerchief and knelt in front of her. Catching her chin with one hand, Vincent applied the handkerchief to her nose. "What are you working on?"

"There is a folk glamourist in the slave quarters who used the most interesting technique to create a giant spider. She constructed it outside the visible spectrum and then shifted the colours. At least, I think that is what she did."

Vincent pulled the handkerchief away from her nose, his brows contracting a bit. "You were not working glamour, were you?"

"No." She gave him a sharp look to signify that she was not simple. "It was quite provoking, actually, because I am afraid to look into the ether. Even that much made me sick—before."

He looked down, folding the handkerchief so that the ink spot was inside. "It will not be much longer."

"I know." Jane bit the inside of her lip. They were already skirting too close to the issue. "Shall we retire to our bedchamber? It is nearly time to dress for dinner."

The skin around his eyes tightened with concern, but he held his question until they reached their room. Once inside, Vincent shut the door, without taking his eyes from Jane.

"What happened?"

"Am I that transparent?" Jane loosened her fichu and pulled the lace shawl from around her neck. "Do not answer that, I know that I am."

"Not to others. Except sometimes your cheeks betray you." He grimaced. "And I was far worse today."

She wrapped her hands in the lace, pulling it tight. "My concern . . . and please understand that it is only a concern, not a rebuke . . . my concern is that we have been here only three days, and the effects on your sensibilities already seem severe."

"I know. It troubles me as well." Turning a little away, he walked to the balcony door and stared out. He reached back to clasp his hands behind him, and then stopped himself. His hands hung at his side for a moment, as if he did not know what to do with them beyond that posture. With a little sigh, Vincent crossed his arms over his chest. "When I shouted at Louisa . . . that is never appropriate, and given her circumstances—" He shrugged further into himself. "I left the room, and all I could hear was how much I sounded like my father."

"You are nothing like him."

"But I was, was I not?" He dared a glance up at her and away. Jane's heart ached at that brief glimpse of pain, and yet she was grateful that he was able to overcome his training to show her even that much. He cleared his throat, again looking out the window. "You were going to tell me what happened to you today."

Jane had to swallow twice before finding her voice. "The glamourist I mentioned, Nkiruka. She guessed. About me. We were talking about glamour, but she does not know the formal terms for what she does, so she was trying to show it to me. I said I could not see it and—and she guessed."

He turned his head, almost looking at her. "Do you think she will tell?"

"I do not think so. I hope. It was so stupid of me."

"Truly, it does not sound as though you were anything but curious."

"Yes, but so many women hint that they are in a delicate condition by first announcing that they cannot work glamour." Jane walked away from him to sit on the bed. "Though according to Nkiruka, that is only European women."

Now he looked at her, head cocked to the side with the curiosity and interest that discussions of glamour always provoked. "What do you mean?"

"According to her, working glamour holds no innate danger for a woman while with child."

"Jane . . . I would not put much stock in what a field slave tells you about glamour."

She rubbed her forehead, feeling a little like her husband as she did so. "I did not at first. But she pointed out that if it regularly caused miscarriages, then no slave would willingly carry a child to term."

He frowned at that. "Mr. Pridmore did say that birthrates were low here."

"Yes, but I have spent the past day looking at the records. Births are low, but not completely absent. On top of that, many of the infant deaths are due to failure to thrive after delivery." Her voice had become strange, too high and too rapid. She tried to slow down and sound calm so that Vincent would not be alarmed. "So what I keep coming around to is that if she is correct, then perhaps my miscarriage was not because I worked glamour, but because of other factors. The carriage, the running . . . or simply me.

That last is the one I cannot shake, because it is the one I cannot guard against. I can avoid glamour. I can avoid running. But what if I have inherited my mother's troubles? What if I cannot carry a child to term?"

Vincent crossed to her. He sat, pulling her into his arms. That undid all of her resolve to present a placid countenance. She buried her face in his coat and inhaled the salt and horse scent from his day's activities.

"There, now." He kissed the top of her head. "There, now. Hush."

She gave a fragile chuckle. "You sound like Papa."

"I was doing my best impression. Did you like it?"

"Very much." She was making a mess of his coat. Jane wiped her eyes with her fichu. "I was wondering if anyone has done a comparative study of the language of glamour. That was one of our chief difficulties today."

"I can think of papers that describe the effects, but nothing, off the top of my head, that gets into how the African system of glamour is described and the structure of its use." He stared into the distance, considering. "It would be interesting to talk to her."

"We might invite her to the house." Jane knew that she had changed the subject from her fears, which they both seemed to be doing too much of late. Still, she was grateful to Vincent for letting her. "I also thought. . . . She has a daughter who is very near her term. What if we brought Amey to the great house for her lying-in?"

"As a kindness, you mean. That it might be something to bind Nkiruka to us?"

"That, and it would allow us to bring in a doctor to examine me as well."

"That strikes me as making excellent sense, and I will own that it would provide a great deal of relief. I have been worried that we have not had anyone to consult with."

"Then we are agreed? I shall make the offer tomorrow?"

"Yes. By all means." He raised her hand and kissed the back of it. "That will be one trouble resolved, which is a blessing."

"And how are we doing with our other difficulties?"

Groaning, Vincent fell backwards on the bed and covered his face with both hands. "I have been staring at record books and examining buildings until my eyes cross and have yet to find anything to make my father weaken his hold on Frank's family."

Jane settled beside him. She rested her free hand on his chest and rubbed circles upon it. "I begin to think that this is a fool's errand. Nothing will make that man release his hold on anyone."

Vincent's silence agreed with that estimation.

Jane found that she was counting their days in Antigua as a way to remind herself that this was not a permanent situation. On Tuesday, their fourth day on the island, with only ten days remaining in their sentence, Jane went to Frank about her desire to bring Amey to the house to have her baby there.

He was in the counting house with three young men of

colour discussing maintenance to the carriage house. When Jane and Louisa came up the tall stairs, he raised his head, brows rising in surprise.

"Excuse me, gentlemen." He rose, coming around the table. "Mrs. Hamilton. Your husband has ridden down to the distillery to oversee an inventory."

"Thank you, but I am here to see you." She glanced past him to the young men. "I do not want to keep you from your business."

"No, please. What may I do for you?" He waited, with his hands by his sides, in an attitude of civil attention.

"Do you know Nkiruka?"

"Ah—yes. What has she done?" A slight frown bent his mouth down.

"What? Oh—no. No, she was actually lovely." Jane wondered if her recollection of the name was mistaken. "Amey's mother?"

"Yes."

"You had spoken of having an older woman assist me. I should like it to be Nkiruka."

He glanced beside Jane to Louisa, raising his brows slightly. In reply, the maid spread her hands a little with a small shrug. Frank frowned, returning his attention to Jane. "She will most likely not be willing."

"Forgive me, but I feel as if we are discussing two different people." And yet, Jane remembered Zeus's response to the older woman, and his obvious deference to her. "She is an older glamourist, and we had an interesting talk about the art. I mentioned the possibility of her coming to the great house for both further discussions and to help with the records. She seemed quite willing."

"Well. Well, if she is willing, then we can make the arrangements." He turned over his shoulder and said, "John, will you make a note that I should discuss an alteration of staff with Mr. Pridmore?"

Jane frowned, trying to understand why the overseer needed to be involved in her project. "Mr. Pridmore?"

"Nkiruka is a field slave—retired, due to her age, but still. She is under Mr. Pridmore's direction. I have charge of only those slaves involved in maintenance of the great house."

Jane nodded slowly, absorbing this information and altering her picture of how the plantation was run. "So . . . the safe house. Is that your charge as well?"

"Ah. No. Mr. Pridmore saw to that himself." He gave a cold, bitter smile that put her in mind of Vincent. "In any event, I am certain he will have no objection to giving Nkiruka over to my charge."

"Perhaps . . . this is more complicated than I thought. Her daughter, Amey, is very near to her lying-in, and I thought that moving her to the great house would make everything easier. Nkiruka would not need to go between her quarters and here so often, and it would be more comfortable for Amey."

Frank's expression became carefully reserved. "You want to bring Amey to the great house. And for Nkiruka to live here?"

"There are empty rooms enough."

He tucked his chin into his cravat and studied the floor. "And after the birth, you would return them to their own home?"

She had not thought of after the birth. "I . . . surely it is safer for Amey to give birth at the house, where there is less dirt and ready access to water."

The young men waiting for Frank had become quiet. Their bodies leaned ever so slightly towards the conversation, though their faces all gave the impression of being intent upon their papers. Frank worked his jaw for a moment, then nodded. "I will speak to Mr. Pridmore. Louisa? Please arrange for the yellow bedroom to be made up for two."

The maid curtsied. "Yes, sir."

He looked back at the young men, whose attention to their paper increased. Compressing his lips, he turned back to Jane. "Will there be anything else, madam?"

He possessed an unnatural ability to make an entirely civil query into a dismissal. "No, thank you." Jane took her leave and retreated with as much grace as she could.

Zeus met the women at the bottom of the counting house stairs. He carried a giant Chinese parasol that cast enough shade for Jane and Louisa both. He fell into step behind them as they began their walk down the hill to the slave quarters. They had entered the orange grove halfway along the route when Louisa cleared her throat.

"Madam. May I speak to you about a matter of some delicacy?"

Jane's heart clenched. A matter of delicacy could only be

Jane's condition. She glanced around to see if anyone besides Zeus were in hearing. "Please, continue."

"Mr. Frank's concerns about Nkiruka. I think that he did not explain fully what those were, out of consideration for your sensibilities."

"And you have no such consideration?" Jane almost laughed at the reprieve. Nkiruka? That was a topic she would willingly discuss, so long as it had nothing to do with increasing.

"It's part of my job to help you get settled and to keep your name out of people's mouths . . . that is, madam, I have been instructed to help you acclimate and to avoid lapses that may expose you to public disapprobation." Her brows were drawn together. "Please believe that I speak only out of concern for your reputation."

"My reputation?" That was the last thing that Jane had expected. "Oh, my dear, you will have to explain yourself bluntly, because I have not the least idea of what you are speaking."

"Lord Verbury cannot be pleased that you wish to bring a black woman into the house. It is not the done thing in Antigua. It will reflect poorly on you and, by extension, on Mr. Frank."

Jane gaped. She reached for something to say, but could only stare at Louisa with her brown skin, and Zeus who was lighter, but no less brown. Jane tried again, aware that her mouth was opening and closing around half-formed responses. Finding her voice, she finally chose, "It does not seem that we have any scarcity of blacks in the house."

Louisa's eyes snapped up, meeting Jane's gaze. She so rarely made eye contact with Jane that the moment astonished her, in part because Louisa's anger was very clear. Then she looked at the ground again, masking the anger with submission. "Madam is under a misapprehension. We have only mulattos in the house. Blacks are not suitable for anything other than field work. I am certain that you will find that Mr. Frank agrees with this determination. He does not wish you to bring Nkiruka to the big house either, but is too gentle to explain the circumstances to you."

This was beyond Jane's understanding. At no point in their dealings with the Worshipful Company of Coldmongers did she notice any difference in the way the variations in their skin tone affected their ability to be employed in using glamour to create cold. . . . Her thoughts tripped over themselves. No. That was not quite true, was it? The leaders of the group did tend to have lighter skin than not. How had she not noticed that at the time? Or here. She had been all too aware of the number of Hamilton offspring and what that must mean about Lord Verbury's relations with the slaves, but she had not recognised that all of the house servants were mulattos or quadroons. The nicer houses, the better clothes, the better positions . . . no wonder Vincent thought that Verbury could command loyalty among the house slaves when being his child here had clear advantages.

And that difference made securing Nkiruka's aid all the more important, because she would have no cause to be loyal to Lord Verbury. Jane took a breath, wetting her lips. "Thank you for your counsel, Louisa. As Frank did not make an objection on that point and did on others, I am satisfied that if it had been a concern, he would have mentioned it. We are not likely to entertain, and even if we did, she will not be serving at table."

"But you must understand that—"

"I assure you that I do." Jane resettled her basket on her arm. "My decision is made."

Louisa turned her face forward again so the deep brim of her bonnet hid her face, but her hands were tight on the handle of her basket. "Yes, madam."

They said nothing else for the rest of the walk. When they arrived at the collection of wattle and daub houses, their reception was quite different from the previous excursion. Upon spying the giant parasol, the children came running up the road to meet them. Apparently, the memory of candied ginger was enough to make them lose some of their shyness—at least, of Louisa and Zeus. Around Jane, there remained a sphere empty of activity, filled only with the darting glances of the children. Louisa's left hand had been claimed by the little girl with the braids. Zeus had two of the older boys vying for the privilege of carrying the big parasol. Jane had only stares.

She tried to smile assurance at the children, but even her most polite "Good afternoon" met with only giggles. When they reached the dirt yard, Nkiruka and the other old woman were sitting on a bench in the shade of one of the sheds. The old man seemed to have moved not at all, and his gentle snores were still occasionally audible over the children's babble.

Jane turned to Zeus. "I am going to talk with Nkiruka in the shade, so I shall not need you. Please feel free to carry on any instruction you like in the finer points of parasol carrying."

"Thank you, madam." When he stepped away, his language changed, taking on the broad vowels and soft consonants of the children. "Here, now. Who wan hol' it, eh?"

Louisa stayed by Jane's side. The likelihood of her spying for Lord Verbury would complicate any of the conversations that Jane planned on having. Putting on a smile with the practised ease she had acquired as a spinster while watching others dance at balls, Jane said, "I do not require any assistance, and I believe your new friends may like the treats you brought. Please be at your ease."

Louisa lifted her head, opening her mouth as though to speak, then thought better of it. "Thank you, madam." She dipped in a curtsy, then turned to the children. "Good afternoon, children." Curiously, Louisa's voice shifted the opposite direction from Zeus's when she spoke to the children. Her consonants became crisper and her vowels were an exaggeration of the fashionable set. It did not seem to impress them, but when she turned back the cover on her basket to disclose the Shrewsbury cakes inside, she received a rapturous "ooo," such as an audience at the Prince Regent's might make in response to a particularly inspired *tableau vivant*.

Jane watched this tableau for a moment longer before making her way across the yard to Nkiruka. The old woman waved, but did not rise.

"Good afternoon." Jane inclined her head to Nkiruka,

who answered in kind. Jane turned next to the other old woman. "I do not believe we have had the pleasure. I hope you will forgive my presumption in introducing myself. I am Jane Hamilton." The name sounded foreign still, even after using it for the month of their ocean passage.

"Dolly." She was broad where Nkiruka was thin, and she looked to have been tall in her youth, but a stoop bent her forward at the shoulders. She had a wide nose and an old scar running along her right brow. "Please sit."

"Thank you," Jane said as she settled on the bench next to Dolly. "I admired your work yesterday, with the spider."

Dolly broke out into a laugh. "Work? Ah, play, dat. You should see festival days."

"I should very much like to." This was true, except for the greater desire to be gone from the island long before then. She glanced at Nkiruka. "I have spoken with Frank. He says if you are willing, that having you at the great house to help would be agreeable. Would you still be willing?"

Nkiruka shrugged and nodded, then tugged at her ragged dress. "Need new clothes. Look bad fu massa have me dressed like dis at big house."

"Of course." Jane set her basket on the ground and pulled out her drawing book. "I also arranged for a room for you and Amey. I thought that it would be easier for you to not go back and forth, and that she might like to stay at the great house for her lying-in."

Dolly nudged Nkiruka with her elbow, with a sly smile. "Look you. Stone under water no know when sun hot."

"Mebbe." Nkiruka shrugged. "But always try de water befo' you jump in it."

Jane had not the least understanding of what they were saying. "Pardon?"

Nkiruka said, "Let me try work before I stay at de big house."

"Oh . . . yes, of course. It might not appeal at all. But the offer of the room still stands for Amey's lying-in."

"Amey go wan' stay ya. Bet."

"Might we ask her?"

With a grunt, Nkiruka pushed herself to her feet and walked to the door of the shed. "Amey! Lady from de big house here again." She paused, then spoke in her own language.

Jane glanced to Dolly and asked, in a low voice, "What is she saying?"

Dolly shrugged. "Don't know. She Igbo. I Asante."

Different languages? It had somehow not occurred to Jane that Africa must have different languages. It made sense when she thought of it, given the continent's vast size.

From within the shed came a sigh and a groan. A few moments later, Amey shuffled into view, eyes hazy with sleep. She braced herself against the door and gave Jane a curtsy.

"Oh! Oh, I am so sorry. I did not mean to wake you." During Melody's last month it had been so difficult for her to find a comfortable position to sleep in. Jane would not for the world have awakened Amey if she had known. She could only repeat her apology. "I am so, so sorry. I only wanted to let you know that I have arranged for a room for you at the great house. I thought you might prefer that for your lying-in."

Amey's head came up sharply and the lingering shade of sleep vanished. "No. Thank you, ma'am."

"Really, it is no trouble. The rooms are plentiful, and your mother has agreed to help me with some work. I thought it would make it easier on you both."

"I appreciate your kindness, ma'am, but thank you, no." She stood in the doorway of the low shed. Her bare feet were dusty with the red dirt of the floor.

To bring a child into the world in such a place . . . Jane could hardly comprehend it. "But what will you do when your time comes?"

"Have my baby at home. Like I do with the other two." A vein in her neck beat rapidly.

"But would it not be nicer to have a real bed?"

"My father built this house. What I goin' to the manor for?" She slapped the rounded flesh of her stomach. "This happen to me there. No. I stay here."

She was nearly to term. Nine months. That would have been shortly before Lord Verbury had his stroke.

"Of—of course. My apologies." Jane looked at the ground, and at the building, and at the doorway in which Amey stood, but she could not meet the woman's eyes. "I am so sorry."

Nkiruka spoke to her daughter in that unknown language. Her tone was soothing and penitent. Amey answered her mother with two short sentences, then turned and disappeared into the dark interior of the shed.

Biting her lip, Jane turned to Nkiruka. "I deeply apologise for bringing any contention into your day. And for . . . other things. If there is anything I can do . . . if she should want for anything. A doctor . . . ?"

"Yes." Nkiruka gave a decisive nod. "A doctor. And better food."

"Of course." And clothes for the baby, and any other comfort Jane could provide besides. Lord Verbury had much to atone for, and if he would not, then Jane would undertake that herself.

Eleven

Tea and Conversation

Jane had intended to get Amey a doctor on Wednesday, but Frank informed her that the doctor would not be able to attend until Thursday. Jane thanked him. Before she had time to wonder if she should start her day with work on her book or on inquiries into better clothing for the slaves, her decision was made for her by the arrival of a note from Mrs. Pridmore inviting her to take tea. It was more than a bit presumptuous of Mrs. Pridmore to invite her husband's employer's wife to tea. More properly, such an invitation should come from Jane, if it were to come at all. Still, this was not England, and she had seen enough of Mrs. Pridmore to know that she was both lonely and more than a little silly. Besides which, more than one policy in Parliament had been settled by tea between the wives of peers. If Vincent could not find accord with Mr. Pridmore, perhaps she could do so with his wife.

With a sigh heavier than such an invitation perhaps merited, Jane altered her plans and sent a note back to accept "with delight."

Fortunately, she had put on her long stays that morning with Vincent's help. The stays were not, strictly speaking, comfortable, but the long bones to her hips and the stiff busk down the front smoothed her form. She was grateful that the Pridmores' cottage stood not more than a quarter mile away.

It was, as promised, a charming cottage with a good prospect overlooking the fields. It had broad stone stairs leading up to a deep porch by the front entrance. Jasmine vines had been trained to run up the support pillars and lend their verdant growth to the little house's sense of invitingness.

As Jane arrived, under Louisa's perpetual parasol, Mrs. Pridmore came out to meet her with a little squeal. "Oh! I am so glad you were able to come. Cook has made cake for us, is that not lovely? I sent the invitation because we had just received a delivery of tea that Mr. Pridmore ordered all the way from China, because he knows how much I miss dear London. Is he not considerate? I hope that you are as fortunate with Mr. Hamilton, and I am certain that you must be." She took Jane's arm as they went up the stairs. "Truly, I have not seen a man who cut such a dashing figure since I was last in London. You must tell me how you attached him. I adore love matches, and all the details of them. Have you read Mrs. Radcliffe's books? Oh, she is a wonder at recording the details of true love."

Jane was certain that Mrs. Pridmore must draw a breath at some point, but she had not yet seemed to require air. She cast one glance backwards at Louisa, who could not quite manage to cover a smile as she followed them inside. The front door opened directly into a broad hall, which also served as the parlour.

"Ladies! Mrs. Hamilton has joined us. Is that not wonderful?" She paused, which seemed to take everyone by surprise.

In the room were four women. One of them was white. For a moment, that was all Jane could notice about her. In the five days since their arrival, she had become so used to all the shades of brown that the putty-coloured skin startled her. Jane bent in a curtsy, out of preservation as much as habit.

Two of the women rose and returned the courtesy. The other two remained against the walls, gazes cast down in the obvious attitude of servants.

"Mrs. Hamilton, may I present Mrs. Ransford from Sarah's Hope—" This was the white woman, an older lady whose translucence seemed a relapse to some elfin ancestor. "And Mrs. Whitten from Weatherill." The latter was a mulatto woman of not more than middle height, well made and with an air of healthy vigour. Her skin was very brown but clear, smooth, and glowing with beauty, which, with a lively eye, a sweet smile, and an open countenance, gave beauty to attract, and expression to make that beauty improve on acquaintance. "Her father is Lord Calcott, and she is married to Mr. Whitten, from a very respectable old Antigua family that has owned an estate here longer even than the Hamiltons. Their property borders yours to the west."

Jane could not help but note that Mrs. Pridmore felt the need to give Mrs. Whitten's particulars but not Mrs. Ransford's.

Mrs. Whitten inclined her head gracefully to Jane. "Indeed, we would not be above two miles away, but for a ravine between our properties. As it is, I am afraid that it requires going down to the base of Green Hill and then back up again, so it feels as though there are two properties between us. Still, with a carriage the trip is a trifle. You must come to visit."

"I should be delighted."

In short order, the assembled ladies worked through the ordinary pleasantries, establishing that it was uncommonly hot for this time of year, that they were thankful that they had coldmongers on staff who could use glamour to make the air cooler, and then moving on to admiration of the newly arrived chest of tea. Nothing was so cooling, was the general consensus, as a cup of strong tea on a hot day. Jane found herself seated on a sofa with Mrs. Ransford, who seemed to have never ventured into the sun.

"And how are you finding Antigua then, Mrs. Hamilton?" The pale woman had the remnants of a Scottish brogue. She set her cup of tea down in its saucer and turned her pale blue eyes upon Jane with the interest one might give to a stuffed bird.

"We have only been here since Friday evening, so not quite five days. I have seen little beyond the estate, but the landscape quite astonishes me. The southernmost clime that I have visited was Venice, and it is not a city known for its trees."

"No, I suppose not."

"Venice?" Mrs. Pridmore bounced up a little in her seat. "Oh! I should adore going to Venice. I have read all of Lord Byron's poems and have dreamt of going ever since then." She set her cup down on the table and, pressing her hands to her bosom, began to declaim.

"In Venice Tasso's echoes are no more,
And silent rows the songless Gondolier;
Her palaces are crumbling to the shore,
And Music meets not always now the ear:
Those days are gone—but Beauty still is here."

With a little sigh, she wrinkled her nose and relaxed her posture. "I sometimes feel that I must remind myself that even though 'those days are gone,' so far from England, 'Beauty is still here,' and I suppose that is why those lines particularly called to me. The songless Gondolier is so moving, do you not think?"

Mrs. Whitten studied the tea in her cup. "I remember when you recited that at our amateur theatricals. I was most struck by the lines, 'Existence may be borne, and the deep root, Of life and sufferance make its firm abode, In bare and desolated bosoms . . .'

"There! See how delightful he is? Such wonderful metre. Oh, I do so adore Lord Byron's work. If I should ever have half the ability I should count myself well satisfied. Are you familiar with his work, Mrs. Hamilton?"

It would be for the best not to mention that Jane was acquainted with the poet himself, or she should likely never hear the end of questions. "Indeed. And are you a poetess yourself?"

"Oh. Oh, no." Mrs. Pridmore looked down with a flush to her cheeks. It was the shortest speech Jane had yet heard from her.

"Do not let her be timid, dear . . ." Mrs. Ransford shook her finger in admonition. "She published a little album of verses last year that was well received."

"Oh—oh, but that was only for our charity. Truly, I hope I am not so foolish as to claim more ability than I possess." She picked up the teapot. "More tea? Do say yes, it is so nice to have ladies with whom I can share such a treat."

Mrs. Pridmore seemed genuinely embarrassed by the attention, and her modesty made Jane like her more than she had before. It did not seem a scheme for attention, but a genuine doubt of her own talents. Jane said, "I should like to read one of your poems."

"Oh, bless me, no. Thank you, that is very generous, but it was only for charity that I allowed them to be published at all. Are you sure you will not take more tea? It really is lovely, and has come all the way from China."

Mrs. Ransford turned on the sofa by Jane's side to face her more fully. "Which reminds me . . . you and your husband must come to our charity ball in July."

Jane planned to be long departed from Antigua by then, but with Louisa in the room, to say nothing of Mrs. Pridmore, she simply smiled. "I should be delighted and will do my best to persuade Mr. Hamilton as well. What is the charity for?"

"The Moravian school. Dr. Hartnell has started a school for the poor youth in Antigua, and has spoken with such eloquence of their plight that the ladies of Antigua threw a ball the last two years to raise funds to help purchase books. It was such a grand success that we plan to do it again this summer." Her pale face warmed with enthusiasm as she spoke. "Mrs. Whitten's home has the loveliest of ballrooms, and she has been so gracious as to let us use it."

"It is fortunate that my husband's grandmother loved to dance." Mrs. Whitten leaned forward in her chair. "Now . . . I know this is terribly forward, but I hope you will appreciate that I am asking because it is a worthy cause."

No doubt they wanted Jane and Vincent to buy a ticket to the ball and perhaps fund the printing of another poetry book by Mrs. Pridmore. "You have piqued my curiosity."

"For the ball, would you and your husband craft a glamural?"

Jane's mouth hung stupidly open. She had not expected *that*, of all questions, though they had made their living through just such commissions for as long as they had been married. She had rather thought that Vincent's father would not have mentioned his son's career, given their history. "I will have to speak with him, of course."

"Oh!" Mrs. Pridmore turned in her seat to face Jane. "Have you studied glamour? I think it is such an interesting art. It is not where my talents lie, though Mrs. Ransford is quite good. You should see her breakfast room, which has the most charming roses glamoured in it. They even smell like roses."

"You are too kind." Mrs. Ransford's cheeks burnt a little, the spots of red standing out almost like rose petals on her pallid skin. "I have been accustomed to creating the glamural for the ball, but should be glad of assistance."

Mrs. Whitten looked between the ladies with some astonishment. "Do you not know who she is? Forgive me, but it was all that filled the *Times* for several weeks last year."

Jane did not know where to look. She picked up her spoon so that she had some form of employment, even if it were nothing more than stirring her tea. Of course news of the trial would have made it here, and any thinking person would have remembered the connection, as Vincent's name had been reported along with his relation to the Earl of Verbury. To have it come up now was something of an agony. The evident confusion on the other ladies' faces made it clear that they did not, in fact, read the paper.

With a little laugh, Mrs. Whitten settled back in her chair. "Mrs. Hamilton should more properly be styled Lady Vincent, wife of Sir David Vincent. They are the Prince Regent's glamourists."

Mrs. Ransford nearly choked on her tea. "Not *the* Sir David!"

"Yes." Jane cleared her throat. "However, the new Earl of Verbury asked my husband to come here as a brother, so I should prefer it if you would continue to call us Mr. and Mrs. Hamilton."

Mrs. Ransford shook her head, resting her hand against her bosom. "I am appalled that I invited you to assist me. But of course, you and your husband should have charge of the entire glamural—if you are willing, of course. I hope that such an assignment is not beneath you after the work you did at Carlton House. I did not see it, but a dear friend in London sent me a souvenir brochure of your last New Year's fête and the illustrations alone made it seem a wonder."

"I am cross that Mr. Pridmore did not tell me. Really, it is quite thoughtless of him." Mrs. Pridmore brightened. "Oh! Might we prevail on you to favour us with a little glamour today?"

To announce in this room that she was unable to perform glamour would be the same as painting a banner and marching through the streets of London with the news that she was with child. Jane ducked her head and turned the spoon over in her fingers. Nkiruka had said that a little glamour was safe. Could she chance it?

She could not. One voice saying that it was safe could not undo the accrued wisdom of the best British doctors. She turned the spoon again, the silver flashing bright against the dull black of her dress. Her black mourning dress. "Ah—" Jane lifted her head, relieved to have an answer that would serve. "I wish I could oblige you, but alas, we are still in mourning. Until the term has passed, we are not performing glamour."

As the women accepted her reason with good grace and many apologies, Jane felt much safer than she had since the topic first arose. She had never thought she would have reason to be grateful to be in mourning, but in this instance, she very much was.

Twelve

A Matter of Timing

On Thursday, Jane and Louisa walked down to the slave huts carrying new clothes for Nkiruka and some treats for the children. Dolly sat on one of the benches with a young girl whom Jane had not previously seen. In fact, when she thought upon it, she had seen no one in these quarters who was not of advanced years or extremely young. The girl appeared to be perhaps sixteen and had her leg propped up on a log. A tidy bandage, shockingly white amidst all the dust, wrapped around her calf.

She had a pile of reeds in her lap and was handing them to Dolly, who had the beginning of a basket constructed in her lap. As Jane and Louisa entered the central yard, Dolly looked up and gave a little nod.

Jane gestured to the bandage on the girl's leg. "May I take it the doctor is here?"

"Inside." Dolly nodded towards the girl's bandage. "Good thing, too."

Jane was aghast to understand that medical emergencies would have gone unattended were it not for her own selfish needs. "Is there anyone else that needs attention?"

"Ole Pappy, he ask why he tired all the time." She snorted. "He old! Sent him to bed. He can sleep just fine out here. Better. Too hot inside. No breeze."

"And Nkiruka?"

"She inside. With Amey."

Jane turned to Louisa, who had acquired a trail of children. "I think I may just step in to see how this doctor is doing. Would you distribute the peppermint sticks?"

"I scarcely think I have any choice, madam." Louisa smiled down at the youngest girl and tugged one of her braids.

"Well, we would not want to keep them waiting. I shall just take the clothes in to Nkiruka and have a word with the doctor." Jane took the package from Louisa and left her with the children.

Through the door, the interior of the hut looked completely black. Jane stared at it stupidly for a moment before understanding. A glamour had been laid across the doorway to obscure the interior. It was only a crude stretch of black, designed to convince the eye that the interior was not lighted, but it cut so sharply across the door that not even the dirt floor inside was visible. If the interior were actually dark, then there would be a few feet lit by the glow of the exterior. This was nothing but black.

Jane paused by the door. "Nkiruka? May I come in?"

After a moment, Nkiruka's head abruptly appeared in the middle of the darkness. Jane embarrassed herself by letting out a small yelp of surprise. The older woman chuckled. Jane could hardly blame her for being amused. It was absurd. She beckoned Jane. "Come in. Expecting you."

Stepping through the glamour, Jane needed a moment to orient to the interior of the hut. Her eyes had been confused by the glamour into expecting a completely dark room, and while it was darker than the yard, the rough-cut windows on each wall let in plenty of light. Jane assumed that they were also obscured by glamour from the outside, which made good sense for a temporary examination room. Rough wooden beams lifted the roof into a high peak. Thatch made from palm fronds was visible in the broad gaps between the boards. There were no walls breaking the space into separate chambers, so it was easy to find Amey lying on a low litter, with a well-dressed woman seated beside her on one of the crude benches. They spoke in low voices about the frequency of Amey's courses and diet.

The woman wore an India-print day dress in a rich salmon patterned with twisting vines, which was a sharp contrast to Amey's threadbare shift. In an effort to distract herself from overhearing the conversation, Jane handed Nkiruka the sturdy calico gowns she had brought. "There are two dresses for you and one for Amey."

Nkiruka fingered the cloth and nodded. "Good, good."

That part of her errand accomplished, Jane peered around the room for the doctor. "Where is he?"

"Who?"

"The doctor."

Nkiruka laughed, a deep belly laugh that twisted her wrinkles so that they completely hid her eyes. "Hey, doctor!"

The well-dressed woman peered over her shoulder. "Yes?"

Jane gaped. "But you are a woman."

"Also coloured. You may as well express surprise about that whilst you are about it." She appeared to be between thirty and forty and was very attractive; her figure was rather small and slender, and her whole appearance expressive of health and animation. In complexion she was a clear brunette with a rich colour; she had full round cheeks, with mouth and nose small, and well-formed dark eyes. Black hair formed natural curls close round her face.

"I beg your pardon. I had not realised that a woman could be a doctor. I have been intolerably rude."

"As I could not be admitted to any current institution, your surprise is understandable. 'Doctor' is a courtesy title. Most white people call me Jones." She turned back to Amey and dipped her hands into a basin of water. She then lifted Amey's dress. Jane found it necessary to study the window. "There is a white doctor for the white people, but I find enough employment among the blacks and coloureds. Most of my work is childbirth and sugarcane injuries."

"Like the young woman outside?"

"Correct. Amey, roll onto your left side for me . . . good. Thank you." After a moment, she continued. "I understand that your husband is interested in making some reforms, Mrs. Hamilton."

"Oh. Yes, we both are." Jane was not certain how the doctor would have heard about that, but she supposed that it was a small island.

"Mm . . . may I suggest then that you consider having an hospital built for the Greycroft estate? Monk Lewis, here in Antigua, had one installed, and found that it increased his productiveness due to the reduction in the amount of time it took slaves to recover. I would be happy to send the documentation around for Mr. Hamilton's consideration." She sighed, followed by the sound of water splashing. "Well, Amey, you show no signs of dilation, and the baby has not turned, so I think you have a while yet. You will send for me when the bearing pains are half an hour apart. Do you have a means of telling time?"

Nkiruka said, "Frances built a sundial on the wall of his house. Amey's youngest boy can keep watch when the time comes."

"Good." Cloth rustled and the wooden bench creaked. "Mrs. Hamilton, you may look again. We are all decent now."

Jane blushed, but turned.

The doctor smiled as she helped Amey lever her swollen figure off the litter. "My apologies, Mrs. Hamilton, for my brusque manner. I am sometimes too attentive to my work to be suited for polite society. I am grateful to you for arranging this visit."

"Oh, well, Frank did all the arranging."

"But you made the request. It has been months since I have been called here. Not since the last time the boiler blew." She nodded towards Amey. "May I assume that you are willing to have me sent for when it is her time?"

"Absolutely. And with any of the other women who are approaching their lying-in. We will also see about an hospital."

"Forgive me if I feel that would be too good to be true, but it does lead to an indisputable improvement in production. I honestly do not understand why plantation owners are so reluctant. Less sick time. More live births. Fewer permanent injuries. . . . It makes economic sense, even if they are indifferent in humane reasons."

"All of which are irresistible arguments." Jane took in a breath and held it for a moment. "Now . . . I must ask your assistance with a matter requiring some discretion."

The doctor raised her eyebrows, waiting.

"May I ask you to examine me?"

Without a moment of hesitation, the doctor's gaze dropped to Jane's midriff and her eyes narrowed slightly. Looking back up, her expression was carefully blank. "The late earl kept a white surgeon on call, Sir Ronald. He might be more appropriate."

The difficulty was in explaining why she did not wish to go to Sir Ronald, without mentioning that the late Lord Verbury was very much alive. Jane wet her lips and made an attempt. "For a variety of reasons, neither my husband nor I wish to consult with Sir Ronald. We also do not wish anyone to know that . . ." It had to be said, and the doctor had clearly guessed. "We wish to keep the fact that I am with child a secret for as long as possible."

"Hence the long stays."

"Correct."

"I should advise against wearing them. The busk compresses the womb."

Involuntarily, Jane put her hand to her stomach. Her heart gave a kick as though it were an infant lodged in her chest. "I have not hurt the baby, have I?"

"Likely not . . ." Dr. Jones looked at Jane's middle again and appeared to make a decision. With a quick shake of her head, she gestured to the litter. "Well. Shall we see?"

With practised ease, she helped Jane out of her dress, petticoat, and the long stays until Jane stood in only her chemise. Without the confines of the boning, her stomach, though small compared to Amey's, was still quite pronounced. With a glance at each other, Amey and her mother took up a station by the door, watching Louisa. Beads of sweat trickled down Jane's back.

She swallowed. "I am grateful to you for your attention. We have been wanting medical advice, given my history, but with our travels it has been difficult."

"Of course. Lie down, please, and let us see how things lie." The doctor indicated the pallet.

Jane's skin itched at the thought of touching the rumpled, dirty fabric. She reprimanded herself and sat on the edge of the pallet. This was where Amey slept, and Jane had not found that exceptional. The rough patchwork sheet itched against her bare arms as she lay back. Bits of dried grass found their way through the fabric to sting her skin. At least, she would prefer to believe that it was grass.

The doctor slid Jane's chemise up, exposing her stomach to the open air. Gripping the sheet with both hands, Jane counted the wooden beams in the ceiling.

"Now, you said 'your history' . . . may I take it that you have had some difficulty?" The doctor's hands were warm as she pressed against Jane's sides.

"I—I miscarried some years ago."

"How far along were you then?"

"Nearly five months. It was . . . we were in the Netherlands when Napoleon escaped from Elba. I had been running, and working glamour." Jane bit her lip before continuing. "My husband and I have been devoted to our marital duties, but it has been nearly three years."

"Hm . . ."

Her hands moved lower, and Jane discovered that in addition to the sixteen main supports, there were fifty-four smaller crossbeams holding up the thatch. "One of the questions we have is how far along I am. I was sick constantly with my first, and became ill again while we were at sea on the way here. I am not ordinarily prone to that, so we thought perhaps two to three months. But on Monday, the baby started kicking."

"When was your last cycle?"

"It was while we were on the way to Vienna. . . . We were in Udine, so . . . December the first? I truly do not keep careful count, as I am quite irregular."

"Hm." The doctor sat back and dipped her hands in the basin. "You may get dressed again."

Jane fairly scrambled to her feet, without waiting for the offer of a hand. She was not so ponderous as to need assistance. Yet. She picked up her long stays and faced the wall for the illusion of privacy as she dressed. "Is it all right to put this back on?"

"Today, yes. But I do not want you wearing it after this." She stood behind Jane and began working the lace through its eyelets. "It sounds to me as if you were simply seasick on the voyage. It is not unusual for pregnancy to make the body reject things it otherwise tolerated."

"Can you tell how far along I am?"

"Given when your last course was, it seems likely that you are twenty-two weeks along. It is customary to reckon forty-two weeks from the last act of menstruation, by which method, if we are rightly instructed, I would put your parturition as the seventh of September."

Twenty-two weeks! That put her firmly in the middle of her fifth month. Thinking, Jane drew her petticoat over her head. "So am I likely to be sick again if we were to take ship anywhere? I was rather hoping it was morning sickness."

The doctor tightened the lace at the back of the petticoat. "With your history, I would not recommend travel by sea. Or any travel, truly, but the vomiting is what I am most concerned about."

Not travel? But she had to get Vincent away from this place. "What about glamour? I have been abstaining so as not to risk a miscarriage. Have you an opinion on the connection between the two?

Sighing, the doctor handed Jane her gown. "The prevailing school of thought is that it is not safe for the mother, but . . . if it were a certain way of aborting a pregnancy, I would have significantly fewer births to attend to."

"My understanding was that the number of births was low."

"Louisa looking for you." Nkiruka had been sitting so quietly that Jane had quite forgotten she was in the room.

Jane brushed her hands down her dress, hoping everything was in order. "Thank you so much. All of you. May I continue to rely on your discretion?"

"Of course." The doctor inclined her head. "Though you will not be able to hide for much longer."

Jane was aware of that. Having been briefly out of the stays, she felt their confinement all the more. She paused by Amey. "When it is your time, make certain I know as well, please."

The young woman nodded, but looked strangely angry. Jane could not imagine why, after she went to the trouble of getting a doctor for her. Perhaps she was merely uncomfortable on the wooden bench. Her mother patted the pile of clothes between them. "These good. . . . Maybe a new blanket for the baby?"

Jane looked back at the rough pallet. "That shall be my next order."

Jane had to wait until after dinner that evening before Vincent was free to speak with her. The day had taken him to St. John's for further study of Antigua's legal code, and he had not returned to the great house until the sun sank below the horizon. While they dined together, the presence of Zeus, who was serving dinner, kept their talk confined to simple, public things.

Jane suspected that their haste to leave the table made it appear as though they were intent upon amorous congress. In truth, though, when they retired to their rooms at last, Vincent shut the door and immediately said, "Did you see the doctor?"

"I did. To be brief: five and a half months, which means a September lying-in. And . . . she recommends that I should not travel."

His face tightened with circumspection. "Is something the matter?"

"No—or, rather, she thinks that I was seasick and that another ocean voyage would be ill-advised." Jane sighed and reached up to smooth the worry lines from Vincent's face. "I have been thinking on this, and have a suggestion."

"We cannot go to England."

"Are you going to listen to my idea, or would you prefer to panic on your own?"

He rewarded her with half a smile. "I will listen to my Muse, always."

"Jamaica is not so far away that my health would be at risk. It is large enough to have a good doctor, and it gets us away from here."

He nodded slowly. "And we would not have to wait for the next packet ship." He kissed her on the forehead. "You are exceedingly clever."

"May we leave tomorrow?"

He rubbed his hair into a mess. "Shall I help you out of your dress?"

Oh, but it was never good when he changed the subject that openly. Jane sighed, to let him know that she was fully aware of his contrivance and that she would tolerate it for a few minutes. He cleared his throat in understanding. Jane turned and let her husband pick the ties of her dress loose. His fingers were not shaking, at least. He helped her pull the muslin over her head and dropped it on a chair next to them. Her petticoat followed after that, and then he worked the corset lace free.

With a sigh, Jane slipped her long stays off and hung them over a chair back, glad to be able to breathe at last. Sliding his arms around her, Vincent rested his head against hers. "Would you be willing to go to Jamaica without me?"

"Are you mad?"

"I want a few more days. There are issues of safety that Frank cannot address with Mr. Pridmore, but I can. Once the boiler is repaired and—"

"No." Jane turned in his arms. "I will stay confined to this room if I have to, but I will not leave you. Do not—hush. Do not even think of explaining why it seems like a reasonable course to you."

"But—"

"Vincent, husband. No. You asked if I were willing, and I am not. You are not yourself here."

He nodded, still holding her, but studying the carpet. A new line had pinched into being between his brows. "I . . . I think I shall take a walk to clear my head. Will you be all right if I go for a bit?"

"Yes, only . . ."

"Only what?"

"Why are you not working glamour?"

He held his breath, and the small whine of protest sounded. Vincent tightened his hands on her waist for a moment, then let out the held breath with a little laugh, stepping away. "I had hoped you would not notice."

"Is it . . . is it because your father would not approve?"

"God, no. That never stopped me before." Rubbing the back of his neck, Vincent tilted his head to the side. "I stopped when we realised you were with child."

"Vincent! Being exposed to glamour is not dangerous."

"I know. I—I was trying to be. . . . You cannot work glamour, and it distressed you so much before that I thought to abstain, too."

Jane's eyes stung. "That is, without a doubt, the sweetest and most foolish thing you have ever done for me."

"I was trying to be respectful."

"My love . . . if we were not here, you would be giving up our livelihood." That was not strictly true, given the state of mourning in England, but close enough. "More to the point, I would like for you to work glamour. The house feels exposed without it."

"The house is, publicly, still in mourning."

"So do not work glamour in public. But in the privacy of our room, it would be no different than the great houses that shut up their ballrooms rather than tearing out an expensive glamural during mourning." Jane sighed. "Also, you are clearly driving yourself mad without that outlet."

He looked at his hands. "You are not wrong."

"Then I am going to lie down while you work." Jane matched action to words and pulled the counterpane back.

"I am an exceedingly fortunate man."

"Pray remember that."

"Always. Except when your feet are cold in the winter." He took a breath, rolling his shoulders as he always did before he started working. Jane held the retort he deserved, along with her breath, as Vincent dipped his hand into the ether. He pulled out strands of pure yellow, wrapping the light around his hand. His face softened. The remaining tension turned into concentration as he passed the fold from hand to hand. He reached in again, drawing out warmer golds to go with the yellow. He gave a half laugh. "I am out of condition. My heart is already speeding."

"This does not surprise me."

He wrapped the gold around the yellow, tying neither off, but simply spinning them. "I promise not to lose consciousness."

"If you do, I will let you sleep on the floor." Jane settled back in the bed and watched him work. It was not a good sign that she thought that Vincent working himself to exhaustion was better than the alternative. "I might pull a blanket over you if the night is too chilly."

He almost smiled. "Then I will work next to the bed and try to faint on it."

Vincent began with small folds, passing the colours between his hands, wrapping the fabric of light up to his elbows, then sliding it off in a ripple of sunrise. The nuances between a Vincent who was concentrating on work and a Vincent who was angry would be imperceptible to another. Both versions of her husband scowled. Both were abrupt when spoken to. But when Vincent was at work with glamour, he had a fluidity and ease of motion that transported him from being merely an attractive man to one who was dazzling. Each movement extended naturally from the one before it and into the next. Colours sprang from his fingers and followed in the wake of his movement.

He seemed to hold a cloud made of fire, then set it spinning around himself. Vincent's breath was audible now. He reached up with one hand, still swathed in glamour that rippled in response to his movement, and tugged his cravat free. His coat would soon follow, if he stayed true to form.

On one of the turns, he stopped and cocked his head to the side, looking at something in the ether. Vincent kept the glamour moving, but he looked at Jane and compressed his lips in silent warning. Jane raised her eyebrows to ask what was troubling him. He replied with a minuscule shake of his head. His face, which had begun to relax, took on the careful mask of control again. He dipped his head and took the strands he held, pushing them outward until the glamour became quite large.

The room filled with a fog formed of sunset and abandon. While Jane could not see the folds making up the glamour, she could tell when it changed from something that Vincent was directing to something that he had tied off. It still spun and seemed to be made of disorder, but she knew his work. The glamour did not continue to develop and alter as it had. Vincent was no longer holding the threads.

Bearing the concern he had displayed in mind, Jane did not ask what he was doing. She clenched her hands under the counterpane but kept her outward demeanour as passive as she could. The glamour was so large now that it overspread the room, obscuring Vincent from view. Jane waited in that tempest composed of fear.

After a few minutes, the glamour shifted minutely, as though Vincent had taken control of the threads once again. It spun twice more, then dissolved, leaving her husband standing in the middle of the room. His coat was on the floor and his shirt clung to his chest. Sweat shone on his brow. Vincent bent at the waist and rested his hands upon his knees, panting. "I am, indeed out of condition."

"Then you clearly need to be working glamour more often."

"Indeed." He straightened slowly, steadying himself with a hand against the chair. For a moment his eyes were bleary with dizziness, but the spell appeared to pass quickly. "I shall join you, I think."

Vincent removed his shirt and hung it over the back of

the chair. As he walked to the washbasin, his back was to Jane, so the scars from his flogging by Napoleon's men were clearly visible. They had faded with the passing years from an angry red to a dull grey-brown. Some had left permanent scores; others were twisted and raised in knots. Vincent poured water from the pitcher into the basin and removed the worst of the sweat from his back and face. He extinguished all but the candle by the bed before he finished dressing. The whole while his motions remained controlled. Jane was nearly ready to scream with anxiety by the time he settled into the bed next to her.

"Good night, Muse." Vincent put his arm around her and nestled against Jane's back. Then he wove a sphere of silence around them. The quality of sound changed so that the humming of insects outside and the rustle of the household staff about their work all vanished. Even so, when Vincent spoke next, his voice was low. "There is a coldmonger in an alcove, masked by glamour."

Thirteen

Parasols and Packet Ships

Jane had to stop herself from rolling over to look at Vincent. If either of them had been working glamour during their time here, they would have seen the threads of both the masking glamural and the ones which cooled the room. In retrospect, the temperature difference between the great house and the exterior made it clear that there must have been a coldmonger present, but in England, coldmongers were only employed by the wealthy, so their presence was a mark of station and they were kept on display. It had not occurred to Jane that things would be different here, but engaging a coldmonger was expensive in England, since the occupation was so dangerous. Spending a man's health was common practise here, so it could be hidden away with a glamoured façade.

Jane lay on her side and forced herself to breathe calmly. Even with the sphere of silence that Vincent had woven, she felt the need to be as discreet as possible.

"I suspect that he, or one of the estate's other coldmongers, has been present the entire time that we have been in residence. They have heard everything."

Jane shivered in spite of the warmth of Vincent against her back. "May I ask you to reconsider leaving tomorrow?"

"You may. The only question is one of how."

The night passed with Jane and Vincent discussing the "how" of their departure in low tones while pretending to be asleep. Sleep was far from either of them. They considered and discarded several plans as too complicated. If they had learned nothing else in Murano, it was in the importance of robust plans.

What they finally settled upon was the plan that Jane had proposed upon their arrival. They would use the *Verres Obscurcis* and walk to St. John's. From there they would take the first ship to Jamaica.

Using the cover of darkness and a goodly helping of glamour, Vincent crept out of bed and collected the *Verres* from their case. Jane was relieved to see that they were still there—after Vincent's revelation, she had half convinced herself that they would have been removed by someone.

The chief difficulty lay in delaying notice of their departure until they were safely off the island. Vincent's routine was varied enough that they thought he could slip away simply by going for one of his walks. While Jane could walk out on the veranda with the *Verre*, her absence would be noted and an alarm raised.

They must, therefore, behave as though they had not noted the coldmonger. Vincent rose at first light, as he was often wont to do, and sat on the edge of the bed. They had acted before, in Murano, and applied the same diligence to this scene and all its details.

Jane stirred and feigned languor. "Can you not sleep?"

"I did not mean to wake you." With a groan, he stood and stretched. "I am going out for a walk to clear my head."

"Will you be back for breakfast?"

"Likely not. I shall probably continue on to the distillery or the fields." He pulled on a clean shirt and the breeches he had worn the day prior. They would have to abandon most of their clothing, but they had faced worse. As he pulled his boots on, Vincent asked, "What will you do with yourself today?"

"The slave quarters again. I promised Nkiruka a blanket for Amey's baby, and I have some questions about glamour that I did not ask yesterday. After that . . . I may make a call to Mrs. Pridmore."

"You should go back to sleep."

"I shall, as soon as you stop making a racket."

He stopped with his waistcoat half buttoned. "Being chased out by my own wife . . . this is a sorry state." But he hung his coat over his arm and picked up his hat. If the hat was heavier than it should have been, or the coat's pockets bulged, neither was apparent. He walked to the bed and leaned down to kiss her on the cheek. "I shall see you at dinner."

"Hush. I have sleeping to do." But though Jane closed her eyes, she lay awake, listening to the sound of Vincent's footsteps carry him out of the great house.

As expected, Louisa wanted to accompany Jane to Nkiruka's. Jane charged her with gathering a basket of provisions from Cook. Some sweets, yes, but Jane also requested cheese, some good bread, and a bit of cured meat to go with the sweets. The bottle of lime juice she added as a neighbourly gesture to enjoy with Nkiruka. Louisa did not seem to think that any of these were out of the ordinary, but the young woman was so good at governing her countenance that Jane could not be certain.

As for herself, Jane carried a blue and white quilt. Held in front of her, it nicely hid her stomach, as well as the spare dress and petticoat tucked inside its folds. Her bonnet had her necessaries hidden up in its high crown.

As they stepped from the porch, Louisa unfurled the parasol. "Are you certain you would not like Zeus to come? With the heat today, it might be good to have the larger parasol."

"It is not so hot as that." In truth, the parts of her black dress that peeked out from under the parasol seemed to turn to hot metal in an instant.

As they walked to the slave quarters, the baby kicked

against Jane's sides in a mirror of her own agitation. It made her aware of how much he or she must have been confined while she was wearing the long stays. Under the cover of the blanket, Jane pressed a hand against her stomach, wishing she could soothe her child.

They passed through the hedge and carried on down the hill. A grove of orange trees marked the halfway point. The shade, even with the parasol, was a welcome relief, and yet Jane's nerves made her seem hotter still.

Vincent appeared directly in front of them. Louisa shrieked at his sudden appearance, dropping the parasol. He sprang forward and took hold of her arms. "There is a sphere of silence around this spot. No one can hear you."

That appeared to frighten her more. She twisted in his grasp, turning desperately towards Jane. "Please ma'am. Please. Don't let him."

"I will not hurt you." Vincent was a large man, and strong. He held Louisa easily as she squirmed.

"No! No. Please—ma'am, please. I been good. Please don't let him. Please, please—"

Jane took too long to understand that Louisa's fear was not of being tied or whipped. The alternative threat was so far out of character for Vincent that she could not imagine anyone thinking it of him. But he *was* Lord Verbury's son. "Vincent—wait."

He looked at her, confused, but did not slacken his grip.

"Louisa—he is not going to . . . do anything to you. We need to leave, and we need for you to not tell anyone."

Understanding blanched the colour from her husband's

face. "Oh. God." He kept his hold on Louisa's wrists, but stepped away so she was extended at arm's length. "No. No. I swear to you that I am only going to tie you up—which may not seem like the comforting statement that I intended it to be."

Louisa caught her breath in hiccoughing sobs. Her person and countenance so clearly marked her as Lord Verbury's daughter, yet her mind had leaped so quickly to the expectation that Vincent would—

Jane covered her mouth with one hand to keep from retching.

As gently as if he were speaking to baby Tom, Vincent said, "I will not touch you in any other way. Will you let us tie you up, without fighting? Neither of us wishes to see you hurt."

"I will not tell anyone." Her voice still shook.

Jane said, "Am I correct that Lord Verbury wishes you to report upon my movements?"

Louisa bent her head so her bonnet hid her face. After a moment, she nodded.

"Then if you do not tell him, he will punish you, will he not?"

Again, Louisa nodded.

Vincent took a slow breath and let it out. "If you have clearly been overwhelmed by us, it will go better if you can tell him something of our plans. If you escape . . . he will reward your ingenuity." He nodded to the side of the road. "Look. I am going to tie you to that tree, with glamour around you to keep you from being seen or heard. I have anchored both with poorfire threads, so you will be discovered before too long."

The poorfire threads unravelled with notorious speed, within four or five hours. They were of some use for certain parlour tricks, but they were unsuitable for longer works, which was why they had been considered useless for so long.

Used as a sort of fuse, though, they would keep Louisa from being able to report for several hours, but not endanger her by hiding her permanently. Jane explained further. "You will be in the shade, and we have the lime juice for you so you do not suffer from the heat. Will you—will you let Vincent tie you to the tree?"

Head still bent, Louisa gave another nod. Vincent sighed with relief and led her to the tree. She sat when asked, and submitted to having her wrists and ankles tied. As Vincent bound her, Louisa lifted her head a little. "What should I tell the master when he asks where you have gone?"

The question was precise. Not "Where are you going," but "What should I tell the master?" Jane wondered if she had mistaken the young woman's loyalties. "Tell him that we discussed Falmouth and packet ships." That could mean either the Falmouth here on the island, or the one in England.

"Will you . . . will you take me with you? That would be the surest way to be certain I did not say anything."

Vincent paused as he secured the last knot. He met Jane's gaze and shook his head. Even if she trusted the young woman without reservation, buying passage for two on short notice would be delicate enough. Passage for two and a slave for whom they had no papers was out of the question. "I am sorry, but we cannot."

"Then, Godspeed, madam. It has been a pleasure serving you."

Jane had not expected to regret leaving Louisa behind, but as they collected their effects and left the grove, she very much did.

Vincent had brought the *Verres* in his hat. With the perfect Antiguan sun, the glass caught the light and wove the *Sphère Obscurcie* around them. They had left Jane's parasol with Louisa, and Jane missed it almost from the first, but the shade would have interfered with the *Verres*. Beneath her black muslin, every pore emitted sweat. It trickled down the back of her neck and stuck her chemise to her skin.

They had transferred their possessions into the basket, along with the blanket. Jane peered at the slave quarters as they passed but could not see a way to deliver it to Nkiruka without exposing themselves. Far, far more than she regretted leaving Louisa, she regretted going without keeping her promises to Nkiruka and Amey. She could only hope that the doctor would be allowed to continue to tend to Amey.

When they were safely established in Jamaica and had sent word to Richard about the true state of things, perhaps they would be able to make changes. She wiped the sweat from her brow and sighed.

"Are you all right?"

"Yes, of course."

"You have been sighing rather a lot."

"Have I?" Jane adjusted her fichu to try to let in more air.

"Indeed."

"I will own that I am hot. Truly, I do not understand how gentlemen can wear coats in weather such as this."

Vincent chuckled. "I made the same argument several times as a child, but have been convinced that propriety requires it. One does become accustomed. Somewhat."

"I remain dubious."

"As well you should." He took her free hand and tucked it over his arm. "There is a grove of palms not far ahead. We can rest there."

"I am perfectly well."

He patted her hand. "I remain dubious."

For all of her protests, Jane found that she leaned upon Vincent's arm more than she had intended. By the time they reached the palm trees, she was deeply grateful for the shade and did not protest that she was well. They stood at the edge of the grove, looking around them for anyone who might notice them appear. The road was thankfully empty. Nevertheless, Vincent wove a *Sphère Obscurcie* around them after they had settled under one of the trees.

Jane abandoned all dignity and lay down with a groan. "I am terribly sorry, but I suspect I shall have to stop more often than I would like."

Brushing a sweat-damp strand of hair from her cheek, Vincent frowned. "Are you certain you are equal to this?"

"Equal, yes. Pleased, no." She caught his hand and kissed it. "Only give me a quarter hour to cool myself and we can begin again."

As promised, a quarter hour's time restored much of Jane's spirits. When they set off, the sun did not seem as oppressively hot as it had previously. A gentle breeze stirred the air and gave surprising relief. Jane reminded Vincent that she had also been walking with Louisa before they reached the orange grove, so she had really gone farther than he thought before wanting a rest. This seemed to prove true as they continued on. Aside from stepping off the road once when a carriage passed, and a second time to make way for a gang of enslaved Africans on their way from one field to another, they made good time down the hill.

At the base of the hill, however, they lost the breeze. With each step, Jane felt heavier. The air burnt her lungs. She took Vincent's arm when offered and leaned upon him. Her back ached, and her stomach felt uneasy. One part of her consciousness was turned inward, feeling for any signs of distress. Each flutter of movement from the baby assured her, but still her pace lagged as they went, and they had not even reached the Greycroft property line yet.

At last, Vincent stopped and wove a sphere of silence around them. Until the world quieted, Jane did not recognise that she had been hearing voices. Rubbing the sweat from her brow, she lifted her head. Cane fields surrounded them.

On the left side of the road, a group of field slaves worked. Sweat gleamed on the bare shoulders of the men and stuck the dresses of the women to their bodies.

Vincent indicated a tamarind tree by the side of the road. "It is not ideal, but I see no other opportunity for some distance. Shall we stop?"

"Please, yes."

He pressed her hand where it held his arm, and undid the silence surrounding them.

Vincent directed her to the tree and wove a *Sphère Obscurcie* to mask them in the shade, followed by a silence. Jane dropped heavily to sit in the tree's shadow. Scant though it was, she welcomed the break from the direct sun. Across the road, men and women worked in the full sun. Surely, she could tolerate sitting in the shade.

Vincent stood over her, frowning. "Should we turn back?"

"And climb that hill? Absolutely not." Jane rubbed her stomach, which seemed to have grown just on their walk. The skin was tight and itched as sweat rolled down it.

"Is anything hurti—"

"I am perfectly well, Vincent." Her voice was more cutting than she had intended. In truth, he looked to be in little better shape than she. Sweat dotted his brow, and his cravat had wilted into a sad knot. Jane drew her knees up, though she had to spread them wider than was modest to accommodate her stomach. She rested her arms upon her knees and let her head drop forward to rest with a sigh. If she had reckoned on how much hotter it would be without the parasol, Jane would have asked Louisa to bring two bottles of the lime juice. Her stomach was a little uneasy, and some lime juice would have settled it. "I am only hot. Give me a quarter hour and I shall be refreshed."

"Of course." The brittle grass crackled as he settled beside her. "Take all the time you need."

With her eyes closed, Jane could pretend it was cooler. If she could only sit here for a few minutes, then she would be equal to another half hour of walking. Jane concentrated on her heart and her breathing, trying to slow both, as she would if she were working glamour. Slow, deep breaths would cool her quickest.

Beside her, Vincent sucked in a sharp breath. In the glamoured silence, the fabric of his clothing hissed as he rose quickly.

"Vincent?" She lifted her head.

He had stopped on one knee and was staring across the road with his jaw tight. "Just rest, Muse." Then he flinched, and his breath hissed out in a high, thin keen of protest.

Jane followed his gaze and uttered her own exclamation of horror as one of the gang drivers brought his whip down. It struck a slender young man, leaving a crimson line across his dark shoulders. Blood already flowed from two previous lines. If the youth cried out, Jane could not hear it. The other field workers continued on with their tasks, stooping, twisting, and driving cane shoots into the ground. Their heads stayed bent as they worked.

The driver's hand rose again.

"Stop him!"

"Then they will know we are here." Vincent's voice was as tightly controlled as she had ever heard it. "Look away, Jane."

"I have seen a man flogged before." The scene brought back too-sharp memories of watching through the trees as Napoleon's men flogged her husband. She had been unable to stop them. In the silence, the arc the whip made was almost like a piece of glamour unfurling. Jane could not look away as it painted another bloody line. They could stop this. "We will find another way to leave."

Vincent needed no further urging. He was on his feet and out of the *Sphère Obscurcie*'s influence as if a spring had been released. His chest expanded, and she could see the force of his bellow as all of the people in the field turned to look at him.

One of the drivers, a thickset man with shoe-leather skin beneath a tall straw hat, shouted at the field slaves and they ducked back to their labour. Vincent strode across the dusty road, coattails flaring. Even damp and disordered with heat as he was, his colour and clothing made him an incongruous part of the scene.

He stopped by the driver with the whip and held out his hand.

The driver glanced over his shoulder to a wagon that stood at the edge of the dusty field. A man uncoiled from the shadows. Slender and blonde, with a light linen coat, Mr. Pridmore took a sip from a canteen and set it upon the bench of the wagon before advancing to speak to Vincent.

Jane could not hear them, and she ground her teeth in

frustration. That they were arguing was clear enough, and that the substance of their argument was the whipping was obvious as well, from the way Vincent gestured at the driver.

Meanwhile, the young man who had been whipped had dropped forward to rest upon his knees and bent elbows, head touching the ground. This was intolerable. She knew well how many months it had taken Vincent to recover from his ordeal, and that was with the attention of Lord Wellington's personal physician. She could not imagine that Dr. Jones, no matter how much care she took, would be able to be so thorough, given the circumstances in which she had to work. Likely the man would be put back into the fields tomorrow, judging by the healing stripes on the backs and shoulders of the other men. Would she have seen the same on the women if they were not covered?

Jane's stomach turned at the thought. Well, she knew how to nurse a man who had been flogged, and if she could do nothing else, she could at least provide some immediate relief. She reached into the blanket they had brought and pulled out her shift. It would mean doing with only one on board the ship, but their passage to Jamaica would not be long enough for that to be an inconvenience.

She forced aside the question of whether they would be allowed to continue on their way. With the *Verre Obscurcie*, she and Vincent could easily elude pursuit—they need only continue walking to town. It would make taking ship more complicated, but not unreasonably so. She hoped. Be that as it may, she could not sit idly by while she had power to affect things. It may not make any difference to anyone but this man, and then only as long as they remained, but if that were Vincent there . . .

. . . and it had been, once.

Jane stood, and familiar grey spots swam across her field of vision. Slapping her free hand against the trunk of the tamarind tree, Jane waited for the dizziness to pass. In only a moment, she felt steadier, so she walked out of the *Sphère Obscurcie*. When she stepped into the sunlight, the heat became a tangible force, pressing against her dark dress and folding the hot air around her face. She swallowed and continued on. She had reached the verge of the field before anyone was mindful of her presence.

A scrubby woman with two fat braids hanging out from under her kerchief saw Jane first. A dark scar at the corner of her mouth disfigured her deep brown complexion and twisted as she frowned at Jane. The braided woman glanced away to where Mr. Pridmore and Vincent argued.

Vincent fairly growled. "I made it very clear that I did not want to see any more whippings occur on the estate."

"If you had stayed at the manor house, you wouldn't have."

"You are not a child. My intent was clear."

"No. But I am in charge of managing the estate. Your *father* approved of my methods."

The woman with braids stared openly at Jane as she slipped past the taller driver. The driver made a grunt of surprise and stepped back a pace, as if uncertain what to do with the white woman who had suddenly appeared in their midst. She knelt by the young man who had been whipped. The damage to his back was worse when viewed at close range, and worse too than her memory of Vincent's wounds. Not for the number of strokes, but for being fresher.

At least, *these* marks were fresher. They were laid over older scars that made it very clear that this was not his first time being whipped, nor even his second. Jane had to swallow hard at her rising gorge. Blood ran freely from the rent skin of his back. The flesh beneath was raw and bright red. The wounds shifted and stretched wider with each pant.

Jane looked up to the woman with braids. "Will you bring me some water?"

Again, the woman looked to Mr. Pridmore, but made no effort to move.

"What the devil—Hamilton, what is your wife doing?"

As calmly as she could, Jane tore a strip from the bottom of her chemise. "I am seeing to these wounds, since no one else was."

"Those wounds are of his own making, and—"

Vincent cut in. "That, they are not."

"Of course they are. He broke the rules, knowing full well the consequences."

"Gentlemen! I need water." Jane lifted her head and glared at Mr. Pridmore. "If you will tell me where to find it, I will fetch it myself."

"There ain't none." The woman's voice startled them all. The woman with the braids had stepped a little forward from the other workers.

"Sukey!" The tall driver snapped his whip so that the tip

just touched her bare forearm, leaving a stripe. "Don't talk to the master without leave."

"I wasn't talking to the master, I was answering the la—" She cut off with a cry as the whip caught her again.

"Stop!" Jane staggered to her feet and stepped in front of the man. The fields pitched around her, greying at the edges. Jane fixed her gaze on the horizon and pulled on the resources that she used to keep from fainting when working glamour. Her stomach heaved as if she were on the ship still, but she would *not* faint. "I asked a question, and Sukey answered me. You do *not* have leave to . . . do not have leave to use the whip. You do not . . ."

She did not faint, but she did vomit, with a force that bent her double. The driver stepped back as her sick spattered his shoes. Strong arms braced her shoulders as she was ill a second time.

"Jane!" Vincent ran to her. His hands replaced the ones currently holding her. As Jane straightened, Sukey stepped back and gave something like a curtsy. Vincent's features were tight with fear. "Are you—"

"Only hot and angry," Jane interjected before he could ask if the baby was all right. Marshalling a smile, Jane squeezed his hand and tried to appear calm. "May I have your handkerchief?"

He fumbled in his pocket for it. "Mr. Pridmore, please send a messenger to the house to ask for the carriage, and another to fetch the doctor."

"At once, Mr. Hamilton." His tone had lost its mocking edge and presented only an earnest concern. "Julian, house.

Smart Martin, doctor. Thomas and Sukey, make up a litter under the wagon for Mrs. Hamilton so we can get her out of the sun."

In moments, the field workers jumped to their assigned activities. Two of the younger boys dashed off in opposite directions on the road. Vincent had Jane in his arms and was halfway to the wagon before she could protest. She twisted around to look behind them. "What about the man who was whipped?"

Vincent's hands tightened, and he made his small whine of distress. "Muse, you are not well."

"I was not *whipped*." Raising her voice, she said, "Mr. Pridmore. Please, let him into the shade at least."

Mr. Pridmore stared at her, and then he sighed. "Against my better judgement, because it distresses you so. Thomas and Sukey, when you're finished with the litter, drag Octavio into the shade, but not too close to Mrs. Hamilton. There are limits, madam, on what is acceptable on Antigua. It would be easiest for everyone if you and your husband learned that this is not England."

Jane hardly needed to be told that. Still, she held her tongue. She had at least won the point of having Octavio tended to. That it had taken being ill gave her a better appreciation for her mother's methods, though she still did not like them.

When Vincent had set her down in the shade of the wagon, she caught his hand. "Vincent . . . would the tamarind tree not be better?"

"I think this has more shade."

"Yes, but . . . for later."

He sat back on his heels and studied her with that perfect and almost indifferent calm. "We are going back to the house as soon as the carriage arrives."

"Truly, Vincent. I have walked farther than this so many times."

"But not in this heat."

And not while with child. "But—"

"No. I know what you are going to suggest, and no." His cool composure cracked for a moment as a line of concern appeared between his brows. "Please, Muse. As you yourself said, we will find another way to leave. But we cannot do it this way."

Fourteen

A Faint Hope

Jane had not intended to fall asleep. As she awoke, it took her a moment to identify that what she was hearing was horses and a carriage. A cool breeze fluttered around her forehead and against the bare skin of her throat. Her head rested on something soft, but she still lay on dusty ground. Jane opened her eyes, feeling a little more like herself. She lay under the wagon.

Octavio lay face down in the dirt in the shadow at the front end of the wagon. Flies buzzed over the bloody cloth stuck to his back, but, thanks to her shift, they could not reach the wounds themselves. On her other side, Vincent sat in the dirt. He had removed his coat and his cravat. His coat . . . that was the pillow beneath her head. Vacantly, he stared into the ether as he worked glamour that was no doubt the source of the cool air. He was breathing rapidly but held his mouth open to reduce the sound.

Lord Verbury's carriage slowed to a stop by the field. Someone got out of the carriage and strode towards them. "How is she?"

Frank had come with the carriage? Jane lowered her hands and tried to raise herself to her elbows, but Vincent caught her shoulders. "Overheated."

She tried a joke to lighten his mood. "I am not a china cup."

"Today you are."

"Do you need any assistance?" Frank asked.

"No, thank you." Vincent slid his arms under her neck and knees and pulled her out from under the carriage. Holding her close to his chest, Vincent stood, and the full brunt of the sun hit them.

Jane's head throbbed and she turned her face into Vincent's chest. His waistcoat was soaked through with sweat. He carried her to the carriage with Frank at his side. "Thank you for coming so quickly."

"Of course." His frown was nearly as deep as Vincent's. "I understand Mr. Pridmore has sent for the physician."

"She should see Octavio, too."

Frank grimaced. "I will get word to Dr. Jones, but Lord Verbury's physician will attend to you."

"I would rather have Dr. Jones, too. Please." Even as Jane protested, she knew that it was too late to keep her condition a secret, but she did not want to be examined by anyone connected to Lord Verbury. "It was only the heat."

Vincent said, "Please follow his advice. I would like to ensure that you experience nothing worse."

Jane's protestations were effectually stopped at the carriage door. Frank climbed in first and helped Vincent get her settled on one of the benches in a prone position. She sat up, though it was clear from Vincent's frown that he would prefer for her to lie upon the bench. As the carriage began to move, the breeze stirred through the open windows. Jane sighed a little at the air. Even filled with dust as it was, the effect was invigorating.

Frank removed the stopper from a bottle and poured her a copper mug of lime juice.

"Please drink this, slowly." He handed it to Jane, who sipped it. No liquor could taste so perfect. Frank poured another and handed it to Vincent. "You as well."

"I am not—"

"I have seen enough Europeans come to Antigua for the first time. Please trust that I am familiar with the effects of heat and how to counter them." Frank settled back in his seat. "What I should like to know is what prompted your walk today. You were en route to St. John's, I presume?"

Vincent studied his lime juice, rubbing his thumb against the metal. He tilted his head to Jane and raised a brow in question. They would have to bargain with Frank. It was not possible that he could still be ignorant as to her condition. Jane sighed. Vincent compressed his lips and nodded in agreement.

He faced Frank. "I found the coldmonger last night."

"Found the . . . ? I thought you knew." He turned to look at Jane. "So then . . . you *are* with child?"

Jane was too tired to dissemble. Her expression must have been answer enough, because Frank sat back in his seat with a huff of surprise. "Well . . . this changes things. I thought that, as a glamourist, you must be aware, and were engaging in some subterfuge."

Vincent frowned with confusion, then his face cleared and he nodded. "Ah. You believed we were feigning Jane's 'delicate condition' because my father thinks she is barren."

"Indeed. The incident in the counting room seemed to be a performance for my benefit." Frank's nod was a mirror of Vincent's as he ordered information into new piles. "May I inquire what you have done with my daughter?"

"Your—Louisa is *your* daughter?" Jane had been certain that she was Lord Verbury's. Perhaps she had not needed to be so suspicious of the maid. "We tied her up. In the orange grove." The shade would surely keep her from feeling the same effects of the heat that Jane had.

"Thank you." He leaned out the window of the carriage. "Jove! Stop the carriage in the orange grove, please."

When Frank settled back in his seat, Vincent leaned forward. "What does my father know?"

"I said nothing about Mrs. Hamilton's expectant condition or your plans for departure. So he still believes she is barren."

Jane swallowed. "But you sent for a doctor."

"Ah . . . so that is why you wished for Dr. Jones." Frank

tilted his head to the side. "She has examined you, correct? Or have I missed my guess in why you requested a doctor for Amey?"

"I—no." Jane's head was spinning from more than the effects of overheating. "I mean, yes. She has examined me."

"Given that Jane is with child . . . what of the coldmonger? Or, coldmongers, rather. Is there danger that they will tell?"

Frank shook his head. "I am very particular about who I have serve in the house, for good reason. Dover is my cousin's son. And February has no reason to love Verbury or Pridmore. He lost the use of his legs in an explosion at the distillery and was then trained as a coldmonger."

With a sigh, Vincent let his head drop. Jane felt the same relief. If Verbury did not know, then there was still hope that they might be able to leave. "Would you have the carriage take us to St. John's?"

"I deeply regret that I cannot. The circumstances that we faced at the beginning are unchanged. While my family is at risk, I am bound to obey Lord Verbury, or at least appear to. Taking you to St. John's would be remarked upon and reported to him. I trust that in the present circumstances, you understand my feelings on this matter."

"So gather your family and go with us. Once we are in England, Richard will manumit them."

"Forgive me, but I have heard similar promises of manumission from other Hamiltons."

Vincent lifted his head. "I am not my father."

"No. You are the man who offered to help my family and

then ran away. Were you going to send for them when you reached the dock?"

A flush of anger lit Vincent's cheeks. Without his cravat, the tension in his jaw was all too obvious. Jane put a hand on his arm. "But even if Richard did not manumit them, once you were in England, your family would not be slaves any longer."

Vincent looked as though he had tasted something bitter and shook his head. "The Somerset ruling. . . . It is widely misunderstood, and would not necessarily be upheld. The presiding judge confined himself only to the narrow question of whether a slave could be removed from England against his will. My professor made it very clear to us that abolitionists stretch the ruling when they claim the judge ruled that slavery was illegal in Britain. He did not. Slaves have been returned to their owners since then."

Frank snorted. "I had forgotten that you studied law."

"You may thank my father for that." Vincent tilted his head, brows contracting. "You knew—you must have known that I was the wrong son when we arrived."

"Yes." The careful stillness that Frank had cultivated reminded Jane of Vincent in so many ways, but beyond a sensation that Frank was taking their measure, she could not guess what he was thinking.

"And yet you took me straight to him, without warning him. Why?"

Frank flashed a sudden and rare smile. "I have found that moments of surprise are greatly instructive."

"And what did you learn?"

"That you were not involved in Lord Garland and Lord Verbury's plans."

Jane rubbed her forehead, which still ached abominably. "I may simply be stupid because of the heat, but I cannot understand why we do not all take ship and go."

Frank's smile vanished. "My mother is here, my sister, my wife, and I have five children besides Louisa. And then what of my children's families? Do I leave my eldest daughter's husband behind? Or his parents? And of course there are grandchildren. Jove would also suffer if he drove us to the docks. Where would you acquire papers to transport so many Negroes to England without question? And if only I left, in the months it would take us to sail to England and back, Lord Verbury could have Mr. Pridmore sell my entire family." He sat forward in his seat, elbows resting on his knees. "Here, I am in a position to do some good. With a different overseer, it would be possible to have the plantation be profitable and humane."

"What can Lord Verbury do, confined to his rooms as he is?"

Frank and Vincent shared a look as though they had carried on this very discussion already. Frank said, "He has Mr. Pridmore and Sir Ronald to help him. One controls the slaves on the estate, the other has the support of the navy. Between the two of them, they would have no difficulties stopping any of us."

Jane shook her head. "He cannot have all the officers. You said that there were forty British forts surrounding Antigua."

"But imagine what happens if you march up to an officer, say that Lord Verbury is still alive, demand his arrest, and then it turns out to be an officer he owns."

Frowning, Vincent rubbed his hair into a mess. "Even if he went to prison, my father would still have the ability to make decisions for the estate while the treason charges were impending. It would tie up the estate, because Richard would no longer be the earl, which would effectually remove what authority I have."

"Yes. It is one of the many complications—" The carriage slowed to a stop in the middle of the orange grove. "Ah. Here we are."

Vincent peered out the window and frowned. "The glamour has been untied."

Jane pushed herself up a little so she could see past him to where they had left Louisa. She could not tell if the glamour was present or not, but she could see the untied ropes on the ground. Louisa was gone.

Frank sighed heavily. "Well . . . I think we can safely assume that Lord Verbury knows you are attempting to leave the island, and likely that you are with child."

Jane said, "We told her she would be safest if she gave him some information about our plans."

"True." He straightened the cuffs of his shirt. "Though she would have told him regardless. Louisa, I am afraid, is not entirely faithworthy."

"But she is your daughter."

"And Mr. Hamilton is Lord Verbury's son." Frank gave a thin smile. "I love my daughter, but she and I do not have an easy relationship. I am required to be a figure of authority both at home and at work, while Lord Verbury has always been kind to her."

"I do not call it kind to threaten to give her to Mr. Pridmore."

"She does not know that Lord Verbury has so threatened. Telling her would frighten her without helping her in any way. I cannot do that." Frank spread his hands and looked inexpressibly sad. "You should know . . . you should know that when she was sixteen, Pridmore was . . . paying her attentions. I could not do anything. Lord Verbury made him stop. Louisa . . . did not understand the difference between 'could not' and 'would not,' and has resented me since then. And his lordship . . . well, she has been a useful instrument for him ever since."

Fifteen

A Choice of Doctors

It took such a short time to drive back to the great house that Jane realised exactly how little ground they had covered in their walk. Far from being a four-hour walk, it likely would have taken them six to reach St. John's at the pace she could manage. Assuming she had not overheated, of course. As the carriage rolled to a stop, Louisa came out the front door and stood at the top of the stairs. She wore a different dress than she had earlier, but seemed none the worse for wear from her brief imprisonment. That gave Jane a measure of relief. She had worried about the young woman.

Jane tucked her fichu back into place around her neck. "If I may take your arm, Vincent, I should be able to walk into the house. I would prefer not to be carried."

"If you should feel faint—"

"I will tell you."

After he handed her down from the carriage, Vincent kept her hand upon his arm, and walked very slowly. Though Jane dearly wished to insist that she was well, he had correctly judged the pace.

Ahead of them, Frank climbed the stairs two at a time. "Louisa, tell Cook to send an ice to Mrs. Hamilton's room, and—"

"Lord Verbury has sent me to invite Mr. and Mrs. Hamilton to take tea with him."

Frank stopped, halfway up the stairs. It was difficult to tell if he were more surprised that she had interrupted him, or by the message. "Please tell his lordship that Mrs. Hamilton is not well." He glanced back at Vincent.

Vincent's arm tightened under Jane's hand. "I will attend him after I see Mrs. Hamilton settled in our room."

"He was most particular." Louisa waited, her chin tilted up.

Another day, Jane would have been willing to face him, but it was all she could do to climb the stairs with Vincent supporting her. It was not a question of keeping her secret any longer, but simply of remaining upright. "I must send my apologies. I truly am unwell."

"Yes. I imagine the heat must have affected you severely without a parasol. We must not let that happen again." The confidence in Louisa's voice and stance did little to reassure Jane. The fear that the maid had shown earlier had been replaced by a familiar bitterness.

She could think of nothing to say to counter the young woman, and that, in itself, was reason enough to avoid Lord Verbury. Jane's mind turned too slowly to be of any real use.

"Louisa." Frank glowered at his daughter. "Has the doctor arrived?"

"I settled Sir Ronald in the white parlour to await Mrs. Hamilton."

The chill that Jane felt had little to do with entering the cool air of the long gallery. The idea of being attended by Lord Verbury's surgeon gave her no comfort. "Thank you, but I have a doctor who is already familiar with my history. I would prefer to be attended by her."

Footsteps sounded, then, on the polished wood of the gallery. Jane turned to look towards the parlour, from which a white man with thinning grey hair strode towards them. He wore a naval uniform, all polished buttons and sharp corners. "Doctor? I presume you are speaking of the negro Jones. She is no more a doctor than my hound."

"Sir. You overstep yourself." Vincent turned Jane away from him. "Frank, please send for my wife's preferred physician."

"Are you really going to trust your wife's health to someone without training?"

Vincent's stride faltered. Jane gripped his arm and murmured, "Not him."

He gave the slightest of nods and continued down the gallery.

"Well, I tried. Let it be on your head if her health suffers."

The floor creaked, accompanied by a slight squeak of a metal rubbing against metal. "Vincent? Jane. Please wait."

At the sound of Lord Verbury's voice, the tension in Vincent's figure changed. His posture remained absolutely the same, but it hardened, as though he were keeping himself from running by sheer force of will.

"Please—please do not let your anger at me stop you from making use of Sir Ronald. I owe my life to his care, and can vouch for his skills. Please . . . at least speak with him." The tremor in Lord Verbury's voice seemed remarkable, even to Jane.

Vincent came to a halt, head erect and staring straight ahead. The blue parlour lay not ten feet in front of them. Nothing on his face showed that he was aware of what he was seeing.

From behind them again, that voice. "I am sorry. I do not expect either of you to accept my apology, but I beg you not to let the lines between us put Jane's health at risk."

A tremor ran through Vincent's features, and he squeezed his eyes closed. The disturbance smoothed, leaving his face composed again. "Apology? Beg? These are novel words." If he had spoken so coolly on the road, Jane would not have needed a coldmonger.

A ragged chuckle sounded behind them. "I know. I am

sorry for that as well. The loss of Garland was an unexpected blow, and I have been behaving badly."

"I think your behaviour precedes my brother's death."

"It does, which is why I do not expect you to accept my apology. I do not think I can atone for what I put you through with the coldmongers or as a child. I have no right to expect you to trust me, but my physician . . ." His voice trailed away. "Roll me closer, please. It is difficult to speak so loudly."

Jane looked back, then. Lord Verbury sat in a wheeled chair, wrapped in a blanket in spite of the heat outside. A tall, stately woman stood behind him, pushing his chair. One could not call her elderly, though her hair was white through, but her clear brown skin had little in the way of lines around the eyes, and her carriage gave an elegant grace to her bearing. She wore a simple white gown, topped with a dress of black net, which was ornamented with embroidery at hem and neck. A cloud of lace formed her fichu and perfectly framed the column of her neck. As she pushed Lord Verbury forward, her gaze darted briefly to Frank, who met it with a slight contraction of his brows. Seeing the three of them together, the resemblance was unmistakable. Her features accounted for those parts of his face that were not from the Hamilton line.

Vincent was still facing the blue parlour, eyes shut. His breath was fast and shallow, but nothing in his posture indicated that he felt any emotion at all.

"That is close enough, Sarah. I do not want to alarm them." Lord Verbury's chair came to a stop just past the front door. Sir Ronald, Louisa, and Frank remained behind, strange stage dressing to this tableau. "Vincent, I am beyond grateful to you for coming here to run the estate. Even though you thought I was dead, it was still generous. That you have remained was unexpected."

"You threatened to have us killed if we left." Vincent opened his eyes and dropped his chin into his cravat—black, to mourn a man who was not dead. He turned to face his father, shifting Jane's hand to his other arm. His free hand, he tucked behind his back, the fist tightly clenched. "I trust you will understand why I have difficulty accepting your apology as sincere."

Lord Verbury looked out the window. "I do. Lord help me, but I do." He reached up with his good hand, and Sarah placed her hand in his. He squeezed it with surprising tenderness. "After the stroke . . . there was a long period in which I could not speak. It was . . . difficult, but gave me much time for reflection. Sarah stayed by my bed and prayed, which I will admit enraged me at first, but . . . but her thoughts and prayers have been deeply persuasive."

"You threatened my wife."

He winced, and it seemed unfeigned. Jane did not trust him, but when he turned back from the window she was stunned to see that his eyes were wet. "I was—am—grieving, and I reverted to old habits from the shock. I think . . . I think you know what that is like."

"These are very pretty words, but the fact remains that we are prisoners in your house."

Lord Verbury dipped his head. "Frank? See to it that

Mr. and Mrs. Hamilton are given safe passage to St. John's whenever they wish to go." He looked back to Vincent. "Now, I presume?"

"Yes."

"All I ask—and I want to make very clear that this is a request, and not a disguised threat—all I ask is that you take advantage of Sir Ronald's expertise, or at least speak with him, if you do not trust him with an examination. Or allow me to call back the Negro, if that is truly your preference. But please, please do not go without a doctor's advice." He wet his lips. "I will admit to having an interest, given Jane's condition."

Vincent's breath stopped altogether. Jane clutched his arm to keep from wrapping her arms around her stomach. She stared from Frank to Louisa, wondering which had told him. Likely Louisa, given everything that had occurred.

Lord Verbury indicated Louisa and Frank with a little turn of his head. "They both knew? Well . . . the fact that neither of them told me is something to consider." He reached into the pocket of his dressing gown and pulled out a piece of paper. "I learned of the child from Vincent, via the laundress."

He held the note that Jane had given to Vincent when the baby kicked.

The paper trembled in his grasp. "I have known for two days and done nothing. Will you not take that as a sign of my good intentions? When I heard that Jane—"

"Do *not* use her name."

Red flooded Lord Verbury's cheeks, but Sarah put a hand

on his shoulder. He clenched his jaw and nodded. "Of course. It is too familiar, given our relations. When I heard that your wife was with child, I consulted Sir Ronald. That is all I have done, and you know well that I could have done more."

Jane had no doubt of that, though she very much doubted his reasons. "This all comes as a shock. Will you give us leave to discuss it?"

"Of course. We shall be in my rooms."

Vincent led Jane back through the blue parlour to their bedchamber. He shut the door with his foot and took Jane straight to the bed.

"Vincent, are you—?"

"Not yet. Please." He threw the counterpane back with one hand and helped her sit. Once she was settled, he stepped back from the bed and rolled his shoulders. Reaching into the ether, he wove the shape she recognised as a *Sphère Obscurcie*. She could tell by his concentration and the spread of his arms that he had widened the fold to cover the bed and half the room. Its edges must pass the outer wall, but the gossamer thinness of the strands would wrap around any corporeal objects, leaving only those in its centre invisible. He followed this with the weaves for silence, executed with precision.

"Vincent, are you all right?"

He turned from the bed and walked to the washbasin. "Would you like to wash your face?"

"I am more concerned about you than my cleanliness."

With his back to her the way it had been to his father, he

seemed at his ease, but he stopped with his hand on the pitcher. For a moment, she thought he was not going to answer her. When he spoke, his voice was low and flat. "I am very close to breaking."

"What may I do?"

"Please pretend that I am not and allow me some time." He poured water into the basin and dipped one of the linen cloths into it. "Now, you once told me I would feel better if I washed my face, so I shall apply the same theory to you."

"It was my governess's theory, but I have adopted it." When he turned back to her, she tried not to search his face or let her concern show, but she did not need to worry about being immoderately expressive, because Vincent kept his attention fixed on the cloth.

He handed it to her and sat on the edge of the bed. "I am only sorry that I do not have any lavender soap."

If Jane had not raised the cloth to her face, her spasm of grief for her husband would have been all too clear. She pressed the cool fabric against her face and breathed through the damp fibres. That horrible man turned kindness into cruelty. She wiped the cloth across her face, removing much of the grime from their walk. While Jane did not feel anywhere near restored, the cool cloth soothed her.

Vincent took the dirty linen from her and folded it into a square. Not even a hint of a frown spoilt his façade of composure. He smoothed the cloth with his thumb, the way he might straighten a fold of glamour. Abruptly, he stood and walked back to the washbasin. "What would you like to do?"

"Leave. Immediately."

"I mean about the doctor."

"Oh . . ." Jane rested a hand on her stomach, feeling for movement within, but found only a faint whisper that might simply be digestion. It was not enough to be truly assuring. Given her sickness earlier, the generally inelegant state she was in presently, and the miscarriage . . . she should take no more risks. "I should like to talk to the doctor, just to be certain."

Vincent let out a breath. "Good. Thank you. I will feel better after he examines you."

"He? I meant Dr. Jones."

He dropped the cloth in the basin and turned. "The Negro? Sir Ronald seems the more experienced of the two."

"You have not met her."

"No, but as a Negro and a woman, she cannot possibly have had the opportunity to receive the same level of training."

"As a navy surgeon, I cannot imagine that he would have had much experience with expectant mothers. I should rather trust myself to someone who has delivered babies in practice."

"But what of the low birthrate among the slaves? Might that be related to who attends them?"

Jane had no ready answer for that. If he had met the doctor, then he would have seen how competent she was and would be less uncertain. "I do not trust him."

"I would not either, except—" He was still for two moments, then crossed the room to the windows to stand with his back to her. He cleared his throat. "I think my father is sincere insofar as his concern for the health of a possible heir goes, and hence will do nothing to place you at risk. It is consistent with his character."

"It would also be consistent with his character as I understand it to instruct Sir Ronald to say that I was unfit for travel, regardless of my general health."

"He said he would let us go."

Jane stared at Vincent, utterly confounded. "I do not understand you. Why would you trust that statement, given your history with him?"

"Because he has never—" He stopped and cleared his throat. Jane very much wished he would turn around so that she could see his face, but right now she had only the set of his shoulders to guide her, and those said that he was in control of his sensibilities. "As a contrivance, there are times when it would have made considerable sense to . . . and yet, he has not. I cannot understand why, so I am . . . struggling. Some of my disquiet is lingering fear from this afternoon, but most of my confusion stems from . . . I do not understand why he would . . ."

"Why he would what?"

"Apologise. To me. He has never—" Vincent's voice cracked and he stopped, putting a hand over his mouth. The thin keen leaked around his fingers, and then even that cut off.

"Vincent . . ." Jane slid her legs to the side of the bed.

"No." His voice sounded torn from cloth. "Please. Do

not. Please—I do not want to grant him this. Let me . . . just give me a—"

His hand flashed to the side, and Vincent disappeared. Jane stared at the spot where he had been, where he still was, wrapped in a preservative sphere. The cry that had not escaped from him swelled in Jane's own chest. She clenched her jaw around it, knowing that Vincent could still see her. Even with something that looked like humility, Lord Verbury had the power to hurt his son.

Only once previously had Vincent hidden from her in this manner. That time, she had pushed into the sphere. Today, she thought it would do more harm than good. Let them escape this place, and then he could unravel safely.

If Vincent needed a moment to govern himself, then she would give him that. Jane pushed herself back up onto the bed and leaned against the pillows with her fingers laced over her stomach. Looking out the window at the unbroken blue sky and the orange trees, she waited.

Perhaps no more than ten minutes passed before Vincent reappeared. His eyes were shot with red and his hair disordered. He walked straight to the washbasin and filled it with water from the pitcher. Eschewing the linen cloths, Vincent splashed water on his face and let it dribble back into the basin. Only after he had dried his face did he turn to face Jane. Even then, he addressed the pillow by her head.

"I am—I would rather be too cautious with your health

than not enough. You were . . . unwell today. My concern seems reasonable to me, but I am . . . I am aware that my thoughts are disordered." Vincent glanced at her and away, swallowing. "Tell me what to do."

"I would not trust anything Sir Ronald said to us. As you said, it is likely that this is a contrivance of your father's to convince us to stay. Dr. Jones is a disinterested party, so I would set more stock by her recommendation."

He stared at the carving on one of the bed's posts, breath a little too quick and too shallow for comfort. "That seems sensible." Vincent rubbed his forehead and closed his eyes. "I am sorry that I am . . . that I am having such difficulty."

Jane had to swallow to answer him. "You have no need to apologise."

He made a low rattling moan and turned from her again. His hands clenched into fists at his side. For a moment, Vincent held his breath, and when he next spoke, his voice was creditably steady. "If you do not mind, may I ask that you avoid being expressly kind to me?"

Now Jane had reason to be thankful that his back was to her. She pressed both hands over her mouth to hold in a cry of anguish for her husband. When she could, she said, "Of course."

"Thank you. I will fetch Dr. Jones." As Vincent turned to go, he caught sight of himself in the mirror. He hesitated, then pulled the stained and dirty shirt over his head. He quickly donned one of the clean ones they had left behind. The shirt was followed quickly by a clean waistcoat, cravat, and coat, creating a fashionable young man out of the deranged glamourist. The last touch was to run his hands through his curls and sweep them into something resembling order. It was an unexpected effort from a man who would rather wear a coat out of fashion than suffer a tailor.

"Do I look less . . . disordered?" He gestured towards his face, and not his clothing.

The red had faded from his eyes, which she suspected was his real concern. Jane nodded. "It will do."

He stepped out of the door, shutting it carefully behind him. Jane listened to his footsteps fade and judged that she had perhaps twenty minutes in which to indulge in hysterics before he returned. She rolled onto her side and pressed her face into the pillow.

As quietly as she could, Jane wept, but before even a minute had passed, two sets of footsteps headed back towards her room down the long gallery. Their echoes gave her plenty of time to return to a seated position and turn the damp side of the pillow down. There was a gentle knock at the door.

Jane sat up further in bed. "Enter."

Sir Ronald opened the door, carrying a leather satchel. He was accompanied by Zeus, who gave Jane a brief smile before shutting the door and taking up a place by one of the walls.

"Good afternoon, Mrs. Hamilton. Your husband asked me to look in on you."

Fury sent a wave of heat through Jane. She knew that Vincent was upset, but that did not give him leave to completely disregard her wishes. "I appreciate your time, but I am afraid there has been a misunderstanding."

"I do apologise for the irregularity of our introduction earlier." He drew a chair up to the side of the bed. He had with him a black leather satchel, which he set on the side table. He glanced over his shoulder. "Face the wall, boy. I have asked Zeus to act as my assistant, thinking that you should prefer someone familiar to a stranger."

"Thank you, that is very kind. But I do not require an examination."

"Oh dear . . . forgive me, but this is an awkward situation. Because your husband made the request, I am obliged to carry through at least a passing examination. I believe we can confine it to questions only. Would that be acceptable?"

The difficulty that Jane faced was that Sir Ronald seemed genuinely concerned that she be comfortable—it would be far easier to resist him if he acted the villain. Given that Vincent had asked him to attend her—and Jane would have serious words with her husband about that—she did not feel entirely able to rudely dismiss Sir Ronald. Her distrust of him came largely from a violent dislike of Lord Verbury. That dislike, however, made her wonder how her answers could be twisted and used against them. "What sort of questions?"

"Your courses, diet, general history. . . . I understand your concern, since we shall be discussing matters of some delicacy. Allow me to assure you of complete privacy and discretion." He paused and glanced over his shoulder at Zeus. "Sometimes they peek. Let me know if he so much as glances this way. Now, we shall start with some simple questions."

Jane relented. For all that she had complained about a navy surgeon having little experience in childbirth, Sir Ronald was thorough and seemed to know his business. He was gentle with his questions and apologised for those which bordered on indecorous.

Nevertheless, it reminded her so thoroughly of the last time a military surgeon had examined her that Jane found that the tears she had not shed when she miscarried were now on her cheeks. "I am so sorry. It has been a difficult day."

"Of course." He settled back in his chair. "Well, I am happy to report that you appear to be in good health, in spite of today's mischance. I would need to do an examination to be certain, but given your history, I should judge that you are well into your fifth month."

"Thank you." The fact that his verdict matched what Dr. Jones had told her made her feel a little more confident about Sir Ronald's judgement.

He stood and walked to the end of the bed. "Boy. Bring me that washbasin." Sir Ronald opened his leather satchel, digging through the contents as Zeus complied with his order. "My concern, Mrs. Hamilton, is that you appear to be suffering from an inflammation of the brain. I would like to bleed you to restore some tranquillity to your system."

"Thank you, but I would prefer not to be bled."

He held up a lancet. "Have you been bled before?"

"I have not."

"Then allow me to reassure you. After your time in the sun, bleeding is necessary to reduce the inflammation. Lessening the quantity of blood will diminish its stimulant quality, which will calm your nerves. It will also diminish the force with which your heart propels blood, and thus meet the same end by lessening the rapidity of the current. Lastly, it will have a direct sedative influence on the nervous centres, which is important in this circumstance, as that is the most reliable method to lessen the inflammation of the brain."

"I am only tired because of our walk today." Jane followed the blade as it caught the afternoon light. Her stomach tightened at the thought of being bled. She had never experienced the antique practice, but her mother's physician had been very fond of it. "The heat overcame me."

"I am certain you are correct that much of your fatigue traces to the heat. However, the decision to walk in it displays all the symptoms of a fevered mind." He took the basin from Zeus and set it beside the bed. "Take her shoulders, please."

"No." Jane slid further back on the bed.

In a practised movement, Sir Ronald knelt on Jane's thighs and grasped her right arm. "Now, boy."

Zeus met Jane's eyes and hesitated, his hands lifted. A crease formed between his brows.

"Please, Zeus. Get my husband." Whatever Vincent had thought he was asking for, it was not this. Jane twisted under the heavy pressure of Sir Ronald's knee. "Please!"

"Do as I say, boy."

Still, Zeus hesitated, glancing to the door.

"Now, or I will have you whipped!" Sir Ronald barked, every inch of his military bearing becoming clear. "Remember who your master is."

Bending his head, Zeus took Jane by the shoulders and held her down.

She screamed, as loud and hard as she could. Jane did not bother with Vincent's name, knowing that he would hear. Whatever his intent, it was not this. She screamed again.

Disregarding her cries, Sir Ronald held Jane's arm firm and put the blade to her arm. It stung only a little. For a moment, she thought it but a scratch, until the blood began to pour forth into the basin.

Outside, she could hear Vincent running down the hall. The latch on the door rattled, but it had been locked. With a thump, it bounced in the frame. Then again. "Jane!" And again. But the house was old and of stout construction. The lock gave not at all.

Jane still struggled against the hands that held her down, but without as much strength.

She could follow Vincent by his footsteps as he ran down the hall, through the blue parlour, out onto the veranda, and down the echoing wood to the balcony door of their apartment. He flung the door open with such force that a pane of glass shattered. She lifted her head to call him, but the room spun about her as if she had been working glamour.

The rage on Vincent's countenance had turned it into a snarling red mask. He dashed across the room, knocking over a chair in his haste.

Sir Ronald did not look around. "If you touch me, your wife will bleed to death."

Vincent checked his flight against the bedpost. His teeth were bared like a mad dog. "Step away from her."

"If you insist. Although, again, if I leave, she will bleed to death." Sir Ronald watched the bowl and kept a firm grip on Jane's arm.

Jane did not hear Vincent's reply. It was lost in a multitude of grey spots and the buzzing in her ears.

Sixteen

Prescription and Proscription

Jane woke to the light of a single candle. She lay on the bed with her feet upon a pile of pillows. Blankets and quilts covered her, but in spite of them she felt cold. She slid her hand under the blankets to press against her stomach. It still belled outward, but she held her breath, waiting for the baby to move. Vincent's stocking feet were propped on the edge of the bed. She followed the length of his legs up to where he sat in a chair, reading a book. A book. After sending that man to bleed her, Vincent was reading a book. Her heart raced with anger, and the room spun about her.

Her body weighed on her, and even breathing seemed to take too much effort. She tried to moisten her lips but her tongue felt stuck to the roof of her mouth. The question she most wanted to know—if the baby was all right—was too frightening to begin with, so she swallowed her fear and held on to her anger for a moment longer. "Why?"

Vincent dropped the book, sitting up with a speed that threatened to upset his chair. "Jane!" He turned his head and spoke to the wall. "She is awake!"

Outside their room, someone ran down the hall towards the back of the house. Vincent sat on the edge of the bed, taking possession of her hand with such care that he seemed afraid he might break her.

"I am furious with you." She tried to pull her hand away.

Vincent let her, but leaned closer. "I am so sorry. I should never have left you alone."

"You should not have sent him at all."

"I did not. He lied to you." Vincent shook his head, eyes glimmering in the candlelight. Above the open collar of his shirt, his neck was flushed an angry red. "I asked Frank to send for Dr. Jones, then my father engaged me in a discussion, which seemed sincere. I can only apologise again, and again, for leaving you alone. But I did not send Sir Ronald to you."

"You did not?"

"Unequivocally."

"Oh." Jane reached for his hand.

He raised her hand to his lips, kissed it, and held it there with his eyes closed. His fatigue and strain had pressed dark circles under his eyes. The mask he had worn cracked into deep furrows across his brow. Underneath that lay anguish and rage.

Light, rapid footsteps sounded in the hall, followed by a knock at the door.

"Enter." Vincent stood, retaining Jane's hand.

The door opened and Dr. Jones entered, wrapped in a white dressing gown. Her heavy dark hair hung down over her shoulders in a pair of braids. A young man in shirt-sleeves followed her.

"How is she?"

"She is alert, this time."

"Good. Will you light more candles, Zeus?"

"Yes, ma'am." Without his livery on, she had not immediately recognised him.

The memory of being held down returned. The weight on her legs. His firm grip on her shoulders. Her heart beat wildly, and Jane could barely draw breath. Spots of grey swam over her vision as though she were working glamour. Jane pressed back in the bed with a low moan.

Zeus lit the candle near her, but paused after lighting the one on the far side of the bed. "Should I go out, sir?"

"Yes . . . I think you had better." Vincent squeezed Jane's hand before releasing it to walk around the bed. He took the taper from Zeus. "I will finish the candles."

At the door, the young man paused. "I am so very sorry, madam. I did not think it would be that bad. Sir Ronald, he bleeds Lord Verbury nearly every visit."

The doctor snorted. "There is a good deal of difference

between bleeding a man who is sitting up and a reclining woman who is with child."

The door shut behind Zeus and Jane slowly relaxed. Sir Ronald had threatened to beat Zeus. Jane was aware of that fact and knew that the young man had little choice, but she could not forget the strength of his grip so readily.

As Vincent lit candles around the room, Dr. Jones leaned over Jane and felt the pulse at her wrist. She frowned, shaking her head. "Mm. How is your hand, by the way?"

Vincent flexed his right hand, the knuckles of which were swollen and bruised. "Better, thank you."

Jane frowned. "What happened?"

"I . . . I hit the wall." He nodded to a place by the door where the plaster was cracked.

The doctor said, "I wish you had followed your original impulse."

"My original impulse was murder."

With a chill, Jane understood that "murder" was not a figure of speech.

"As I said . . ." The doctor reached for a little pot sitting on a small copper brazier and poured some of the steaming liquid into a mug. "Mrs. Hamilton, I have some beef tea. I want you to drink as much of this as you can."

"Delightful."

"It is indeed." She slipped a strong arm around Jane's shoulders and helped her sit up a little.

Even that slight motion made Jane's head swim and the room turn circles around her. She stared at the bedpost and breathed slowly, waiting for the dizziness to pass. It did not.

Neither did it grow worse, so Jane did her best to pay it no mind. She raised her hand to the mug but was still grateful for the doctor's help. She had not had a beef tea since she was living with her parents. The warm, salty drink restored some of the moisture in her mouth.

She finished the mug, and the doctor eased her back to the bed. "Good. We shall try you with some liver and greens next." She set the mug on the side table and turned the counterpane back. "I just want a quick look at the baby. This will not take a moment."

Vincent hovered at the foot of the bed, arms crossed over his chest. He bit his lip, shifting from one foot to the other. Jane stretched out her right arm to the far side of the bed, beckoning him, for his comfort as much as hers. He moved to sit on the edge and laced his fingers through hers. His gaze darted between her face and the doctor's activities.

He cleared his throat. "Have you attended many births?"

"Mm . . . close to forty this past year. Roll on your left side for me, Mrs. Hamilton."

Jane complied, trying to recollect how many she had read about in the estate records. It had not seemed like half so many. "Were those all live births?"

The doctor's hands paused on her stomach. "Some are at other estates or among the free coloured population, of course." She drew the quilts back over Jane with a smile. "Everything seems in order. Now, I want you to keep your feet up and drink plenty of the beef tea. I shall be just down the hall tonight if you need anything."

"You are staying here?"

"At your husband's request."

"What about Amey? And your other patients, and—"

"It keeps me closer at hand, should Amey begin her labour. My assistant knows where to send for me should I be needed. He is used to me moving from time to time." She brushed the hair back from Jane's forehead and laid her warm palm against it again. "I shall see you in the morning. Mr. Hamilton? A word, please."

Jane clutched his hand. "Not in private."

"Muse—"

"I have nothing very alarming to report, but wanted you to rest." Still, the doctor addressed her comments to Vincent rather than Jane. "She is not to be moved until she regains some strength. Even then . . . Mr. Frank told me that you had intended to take ship, and I must advise against that. A week in bed. Then she might move about the house, but no agitation. I cannot stress this enough. No agitation or exertion. Another two weeks should see her fit enough to venture out for gentle exercise, but I should still be cautious about travelling far for a month or more. I will stay here tonight and tomorrow, after which she should be out of immediate danger. Have you any questions?"

"Is there anything I should be doing to help?"

The doctor looked from him to Jane and gave a little smile. "In the ordinary course of things, I often advise the husband to sleep elsewhere so that my patient's rest is not disturbed. You, I think, should stay with your wife as much as you can. Am I correct, Mrs. Hamilton?"

"Yes. Thank you."

"Very good." She gave a brisk nod and blew out the closest candle. "I shall see you in the morning." As quick as that, she was across the room and out the door.

Vincent let out an unsteady breath. "Well, Muse. Shall I blow out the rest of the candles so you can sleep?"

"I think I shall sleep regardless of the light in the room." Jane had never been so tired. "What were you reading before?"

"I have no idea. It was something about plantation management, but I think I read the same paragraph all evening." The slight compression of his lips as he bent his head spoke volumes. Vincent ran his thumb over the ends of her fingers. "It is very dull. Shall I read you to sleep?"

"Would you . . . would you work some glamour?"

His brows rose in surprise.

"Not much. I am certain you are tired as well. I only want . . ." She wanted a change in the room so that it looked different from where she had been held down and bled. But a full glamural was too much work for a night. "I like to watch you work."

"Of course." Yet, he paused, gazing at her. The candlelight played around the planes of his face and smoothed them into an expression of earnest concern. Her breath stopped at the unexpected openness. Without the sharp line of a collar guarding his jaw, he always seemed younger somehow. "Jane . . . I do not say this often enough: I love you. Very much."

Even without stays, Jane could barely draw breath. She offered him a smile that threatened to dissolve into tears. "I love you as well. Rogue."

"Muse." Vincent leaned down and kissed her cheek, dark circles under his eyes.

Jane stopped him as he pulled back. "How long was I unconscious?"

"Nearly fourteen hours. You opened your eyes twice tonight, but did not seem aware—" He stopped and cleared his throat. "You did not seem to be aware of your surroundings. Thank God you insisted that Dr. Jones come, or—well, she has been good enough to stay. I have been . . . worried."

Without the cravat, and with his shirt open, the frantic beat of Vincent's pulse was obvious. The layers of gentlemen's clothing usually served to hide all but the deepest of emotion, but without that disguise of fashion, his struggle lay clear with each uneven breath. Worried. He worried when the baby kicked. She could not imagine the blow to his sensibilities that the past days must have dealt him, and she knew that he would try to shoulder the burden alone.

"This was not your fault."

He closed his eyes, stopped breathing, not even the protest of air escaping. Only that vein in his throat beat on. Vincent turned from her, squeezing her hand as he stood. He wiped a hand down his face and rolled his shoulders. "You asked for glamour. Have you any requests?"

"Vincent . . ."

"I should probably mention that Dover in the coldbox

can hear us. His son is waiting as an errand boy in case either of us needs to call for anything." He walked to the foot of the bed. When he turned to face her, his composure was once again restored. "We are not in view, though."

"Thank you for explaining. I hope that, later, such a measure will prove unnecessary."

"As do I." He reached into the ether and pulled out a fold of glamour that he fanned into a rainbow. "Until then, what shall I perform for you?"

"Artist's choice. I am too tired to make a decision."

He nodded, rolling the folds between his hands. The furrow reappeared between his brows as he stared deep into the ether. She had expected him to work the rainbow into the foundation of one of his abstracted clouds, but he let it dissolve and turned to the nearest bedpost. Dipping his fingers into the ether, he pulled out strands of brown and wrapped them around the wood so it began to appear to sprout branches. He worked steadily, with a delicate precision that was at odds with his person. One expected a man with his height and build to be rough or coarse in movement. The grace of his hands as they twisted and shaped skeins of glamour into the first blush of a glamural made Jane's breath catch in her throat with a sudden yearning.

He twisted the vine up the bedpost till his head was tilted up, revealing the strong column of his neck. In spite of the coldmonger chilling the room, the effort of governing the folds soon raised sweat upon Vincent's brow. The familiar wonder of watching her husband work warmed Jane into a sense of security.

As she drifted, her vision fogged till the lines and threads that made up his work stood out in a web that glowed in her second sight. Some part of Jane noted that she was watching the ether, but she was too tired to remember why she should not, and then she was asleep.

When Jane woke next, Vincent lay curled beside her with one hand resting on her shoulder. The warm weight comforted her. His face had slackened, making it more apparent how strained his waking hours had been. Midmorning light filtered through the mosquito curtains and softened his face further. He snored, though to describe the small wheeze as a snore was perhaps unfair. In spite of his broad chest, Vincent's snore bore more resemblance to that of a kitten. He wore the same shirt he had last night, and Jane rather suspected that he had worked until he was dizzy.

Her guess was further supported by the glamural that shrouded their bed. Passionflower vines wrapped the bedposts, bobbing in an imaginary breeze. He had added a faint trace of their honeyed scent, but not so much as to be cloying. Knowing his work, this was far from finished. The vines on the headboard had only been roughed in, with simple brown threads to indicate where they would be. At the foot of the bed, he had gone farther with the detail so that delicate purple blossoms fluttered on their stems.

Shortly after they had first met, Vincent had given her his drawing book, which was filled with his thoughts on the nature of art and glamour in particular. In it, he had described the idea of putting one's passions into art. Tension might become the tight cling of a vine to a post. The tremble of a hand might make its way into the movement of flowers on their stems. The desire to hide could translate into a bower woven of sweet, aromatic vines whose flowers faced the sun.

Vincent had put himself into the glamural, and that familiar act comforted Jane more than the art itself.

Over the next several days, Jane became acquainted with the variety of ways in which liver could be prepared, learned the joys of boiled greens, and drank more beef tea than she wished to consider. She had not been so exhausted since her miscarriage, and the similarity made her uncomfortably aware of the risk she was in. It took three days before she could sit up without dizziness.

During the first days of her recovery, Jane had alternated between staring out the window, drinking endless gallons of beef tea, and sleeping. She was now beginning to have enough energy to be restless, though not so much that she could leave the bed, so her thoughts had turned to exterior matters such as her book and conditions in the slave quarters.

Vincent, however, could think of nothing else but The Incident, seeming to alternate between worry and anger. If he had not had the glamural to work on, she was not sure he would have survived. He added hummingbirds to the bower, a sky that changed throughout the day, and he resolutely refused to acknowledge any of his distress.

When she pressed him, he replied, "The doctor says you are not to be agitated."

"I will become agitated if you continue to be so remote. I am imprisoned in bed, and lost, and more than a little afraid because I do not know what is happening."

He became even more still. Then he stood from the small table he had taken to using as a desk and came to sit on the bed. He only sat for a moment, then wove a deep silence, cutting off all sound. Jane settled down to wait for Vincent to collect his thoughts, but he only bowed his head and continued to sit. One hand dipped in and out of the ether, drawing a small trail of red along with it, a seemingly unconscious motion. The swelling on his hand had gone down, but the bruises remained in dull greens and yellows. Vincent clenched his fist, wiping out the trail of glamour.

"Jane . . . I am sorry for leaving you in the dark. Truly, I am protecting myself as much as you." His voice was low and faltering, as though he were finding his way through a darkened room. "I have no practise at. . . . I know how to survive when I have only myself to worry about. But with you? Here? I do not know how—" He sighed and ran a hand through his hair. "I feel like a glamourist trying to walk and hold two different glamours. One of them is always about to slip. I cannot breathe, and I am about to lose my grip on all the strands."

She took his hand and ran her thumb gently over the bruises. "You worry me."

"I worry myself." He gave a little smile that might even have been genuine. "But worrying you is the opposite of my intentions. So I am going to ask for your indulgence. Will you let me change the subject? Your breath is distressingly quick and you are pale."

Jane regarded him. The visible bruises were confined to the knuckles of one hand, but, much like the scars on his back, the damage ran deeper. It frustrated Jane that she understood him well enough to know that speaking of such things took effort, and that his reserves were greatly diminished already. When he requested a change of subject—and she was grateful that he at least acknowledged the retreat from the topic today—he often did so to preserve his resources for battles outside their sphere. Still, it vexed Jane that he was correct. She was having difficulty catching her breath and felt as though she were in the midst of working a large fold of glamour.

She sighed to cover her agitation. "You are insufferable."

"I prefer 'inscrutable.' " He smiled, softening a little at her teasing tone, and because she had allowed the change of topic.

"Inexplicable would be more accurate."

"Inconceivable!"

She rested her hand on her ever-increasing stomach. "Not any longer."

He laughed and kissed her on the forehead. "I do not think that word means what you think it means."

"Humph!" But Jane was delighted that she had managed to make him laugh. She would mangle all the words in the dictionary if it would help. "I return to my previous assertion of 'insufferable.' "

"I accept. Tell me about your book."

"Insufferable man. I have been thinking of how to structure it." Truly, she had little to do *but* think. Still, she was always somewhat nervous about discussing theory with Vincent because he had the benefit of formal training, while Jane had only books and a tutor in her history. "My plan is to approach the comparison between European and African methods of glamour as a sort of school. That is, I will treat it as a primer, documenting basic techniques and how our European method approaches teaching them. When I can once again visit Nkiruka, I shall ask her how the African schools approach early training. By comparing the training methods, I hope to illuminate any material differences between them."

"Do you expect significant differences?"

She gave a little shrug. "I am not certain. We were hindered by vocabulary and my inability to see or show folds. I am hoping that this approach will also allow us to build a shared vocabulary of technique. Then I shall be better able to document more advanced theories."

"Perhaps . . ." Vincent rubbed his chin, thinking. "Shall I be there at the next meeting? I can watch what she is doing and exhibit the European folds in your stead."

"Thank you, but you already have more than enough responsibilities." In truth, she would very much have liked to have him there, but she was not certain if Louisa would be entirely comfortable with him present. In spite of Jane's own discomfort, she wanted to make amends with the maid. Her actions when Jane and Vincent were attempting escape made Jane feel that she had mistaken the young woman's loyalties. "I thought to ask Louisa if she worked glamour. Even a little would be sufficient for the initial work."

"Louisa? Truly?" Vincent raised his brows.

"Yes, of course." A sudden concern struck Jane, and she was ashamed that she had not thought of it sooner. She had been exhausted, but that was little excuse. "She has not been sent back to the fields, has she?"

"No. No. The doctor said that you were not to be agitated, so I thought it best to avoid any possible upset."

"I want it to be clear between us that my health is not a permanent condition." Jane had no intention of becoming her mother, prone to palpitations at the slightest provocation. "Are you certain that Louisa is well? You saw the look that your father gave her when he realised she had known about my condition and said nothing."

"I will ask Frank and will report back on her health."

Jane narrowed her eyes at him. "Or . . . you might simply tell him that I am in need of a lady's maid again, and then I can see her for myself."

"I will now remind you of what Frank said about her. And she did report to my father that we left."

"Well, we told her to do as much." Jane rubbed her forehead and sighed. "I thought about it a great deal. Given that I suspected her of reporting to Lord Verbury the entire time she was serving me, the fact that I now know she is doing so changes nothing. What has changed is that I no longer have anything to hide."

Vincent rubbed the back of his neck, frowning at the ground. "I do not like it."

"Vincent, you cannot stay with me all the time. I shall need someone to run errands, and she is accustomed to my ways."

"Is she? Perhaps I might ask her for some advice . . ."

"Rogue." If Jane could have thrown a pillow at him, she would have. "Insufferable rogue."

"Inscrutable." He leaned forward and kissed her. "And you are my Muse."

Seventeen

To Write a Book

Louisa entered Jane's room with her customary knock and curtsy. Jane sat up in bed as much as she could. "How are you, Louisa?"

"I am well, madam." Her gaze was cast down in its usual pose, as though nothing untoward had occurred between them.

"I am very sorry about the way we treated you last week. If you can, please accept my apology."

"Of course, madam."

Perversely, Jane would have felt better if Louisa had shown some trace of anger or resentment. She would have trusted those as being true responses to the mistreatment the young woman had suffered at their hands. This tranquil countenance seemed too smooth to be honest. "Thank you for not telling Lord Verbury that I was with child." She smoothed the counterpane, which belled over her middle in ways that left her condition in no doubt. "Was he angry that you did not?"

"No, madam. I told him that I thought you were only stout."

"And is that what you thought?"

"I would never say so, madam."

Jane sighed and rubbed her forehead. Perhaps Vincent was correct about avoiding fuss. It was clear that Louisa had inherited the Hamilton tendency to keep her true feelings well hidden, and now that Jane knew about it, she could not help being bothered by it.

Given a choice, Jane would be planning their removal to Jamaica, or even St. John's, but right now she was doing well to simply walk from her bedroom to the blue parlour. She sat at the round table in the middle of the parlour with her papers spread in front of her. Voices at the main entry caught her attention, and she lifted her head from the pages.

She had sent Zeus to see if Nkiruka was willing to come to the great house today. He had been so eager and thankful for being asked that Jane had nearly wept. She did not want him to feel guilt for whom he served or what he had been made to do and was glad for evidence that he did not. Still, such an embarrassing display would have confused him, so she was grateful that she had been able to contain the outburst.

She listened to the voices. They were too indistinct for Jane to be certain who had arrived, but she had hopes. She turned to Louisa. "Would you see who that is?"

Louisa curtsied. "Yes, madam."

Jane straightened her papers, trying to put them into some order in case it was Nkiruka. After a few moments, Louisa returned to stand at the door, letting her annoyance show clearly as she said, "Mrs. Nkiruka Chinwe of Greycroft and her daughter, Mrs. Avril."

With great ceremony, Nkiruka stepped into the doorway, wearing the new calico dress Jane had given her. Her gaze wandered over the room, taking in the furniture, the rugs, the gilt frames, and the crystal decanter of lime juice that sat, sweating, on the side table. She finished with a little smile at Jane, and gave an excessively formal curtsy. She could not quite mask her laughter as she declared, "I am delighted to call upon you, Mrs. Hamilton." Then the laughter broke forth in earnest. "Eh! Who'da thought I would be here? Come, girl."

To Jane's very great surprise, Amey walked into the parlour. The new calico dress had been made large enough to accommodate her stomach, but she was still clearly heavy with child.

"Amey! What a delightful surprise."

"Mammy thought I might help with translation. Mr. Pridmore said I could do this instead of my other work."

"Your other . . ." Jane faltered, staring at Amey's stomach. In England, Amey would already be in confinement, awaiting her lying-in. "Well, then I have more than one reason to be pleased." Jane started to push herself to her feet, keeping one hand firmly on the table in the event that her dizziness returned.

Nkiruka waved her hand and bustled across the room. "No, no. We heard 'bout what happen with you. Sit, sit. Don't stand for us." She winked. "Besides. People laugh, you stand for slaves."

"Oh—I . . ." Jane kept thinking of Nkiruka and Amey as she would her father's tenants. People who, while not her equal in social station, were free and deserved her respect with all the correct social forms. That the field labourers with whom she now spoke were enslaved . . . Jane had difficulty not only reconciling herself to their status but even knowing the correct manner in which to interact with them. It was one thing to speak of abolition in England, where the talk was abstract. In some regards, the etiquette of speaking to the house slaves was easier for Jane to understand because it differed so little from the way one spoke to servants in England. At least, it differed little on the surface. She sighed. "Well, I have invited you here as a fellow glamourist. Please, have a seat. May I offer you some lime juice?"

Nkiruka drew out a chair, dropping into it without hesitation. "Thank you."

Amey looked past Jane's head. Her gaze narrowed before she lifted her chin and lowered her gravid form onto the cane seat.

Jane glanced back at Louisa, who was glaring at the other woman. Jane cleared her throat. Louisa's gaze dropped as though she had been burnt and she poured glasses of cool juice for each of the women.

Small talk seemed quite out of the question, so Jane pulled the papers forward. In all likelihood, the surest way to set Amey at ease would be the same trick which she used with Vincent: a discussion of glamour. "I thought that we might talk today about how one begins training in glamour in England, and you could tell me about how the training occurs in Africa."

Nkiruka shrugged further into her seat. "Only Igbo way. Dolly, she do glamour different from me. You interested? Give you list of people to talk with. Bring them here. They show all different ways."

Jane nearly shivered with delight at the thought of so many different variations to explore. If only she could see what they were doing directly. For now, she would write the rudiments down. Then, after her confinement, when she could actually practise glamour again, she could discuss more advanced techniques. "That would be lovely, thank you. Meanwhile, with your help, we might settle upon a common vocabulary. Amey, may I ask you to tell me about how you learned glamour?"

"Mammy teach me, early enough I don' remember no knowing. Then I was sent to the coldmonger's factory for a time."

"Coldmongering? Truly?" Jane was all astonishment. "In England, only young men or boys learn to coldmonger. It is widely accounted too dangerous for young women. Or will you assert that it is as harmless as working glamour while with child?"

Amey cocked her head with a grimace. "No. It hard on

the body. Mostly it was boys with a twisted body, or man that get damage in the field. Some girls got send too, so they could do coldmongering as lady's maids."

Jane lifted her head in surprise and turned to Louisa. "Is that where you learned glamour?"

"No, madam! I learned from Miss Sarah. Greycroft is a large estate, so there are coldmongers enough that Mr. Frank can even hire them out." Louisa gave no hint that Frank was her father or Miss Sarah her grandmother. "The coldmongers are part of the great house staff, and his management of them has made the coldmongers a significant income for the estate."

"Yeah, until Mr. Pridmore—" Amey cut off abruptly with a brief glance at Louisa. "It was an interesting education. My nephew, Winter, just come back and might have some more information for you."

Jane's interest in coldmonger training faded. Vincent had been concerned that Mr. Pridmore was misusing estate funds, though at this point only a sense of responsibility to Frank impelled him to take any action for the estate. This sounded like something he would be very much interested in. She frowned and wiped the excess ink from her pen. "Louisa, might I ask you to go to the counting house and ask Mr. Hamilton to come here?"

Though clearly knowing exactly what Jane was about, Louisa curtsied promptly. "Of course, madam."

As Louisa left the room, Nkiruka's hands dipped into the ether. Jane watched them fixedly. She could just look. Surely it would take no energy to look. Yet she could not walk from the bedroom to the blue room without being a little out of breath. Jane ground her teeth in frustration as the weave took shape around her. Sounds outside their immediate sphere became indistinct. It must be different from Vincent's technique, as it did not cut out all sound but merely made it garbled.

Jane cleared her throat and turned her attention to Amey. "Now. We have a few moments, so allow me to say that if you are holding your tongue because of fear that I will report your words to Mr. Pridmore . . . I am no admirer of his."

Gnawing on her lower lip, Amey turned to her mother. Nkiruka spoke in that unfathomable language, and Amey answered, although her speech was awkward. She made a face and asked a question. Nkiruka patted her on the hand. Amey repeated whatever the question had been.

Nkiruka gave a sharp nod, then finished in English. "Talk."

She sighed. "Mr. Pridmore used to turn out the slaves that get damage. Field accidents. People born ben' up. That sorta thing. Mr. Frank take them, and somehow talk his lordship into sending them for training instead. Sort of. He get permission to send them, but had to use his own money."

"And now, if I am to understand you correctly, Mr. Pridmore wants to take the income from trained coldmongers without having put forth the expense of training them?"

Amey nodded, and Jane drummed her fingers on the table in thought. Given the signs of neglect on the estate that Vincent reported, she had to wonder where the money was going. And then she recalled Mrs. Pridmore's tea—"imported from China at great expense"—her harp, and the printing of her book of poetry. This would be something to discuss with Vincent at the first opportunity.

"Thank you for your candour. I shall speak to my husband about this, but not where I learned of it. If there is anything similar, please let me know at once."

"Just . . ." Amey turned her glass in the circle of condensation it had left on the table. "Just, Mr. Frank, he let the coldmonger an' dem keep some of the money they get for being hired out. An inducement, he call it. For working extra. Mr. Pridmore, he said that's wan waste ah estate resources." She did not actually ask if that practise could remain in place, but the question was clear enough.

Jane had heard that masters sometimes let their slaves earn some money by hiring themselves out or making handicrafts, but she had not realised that Verbury's estate did so as well. "That seems like a sound practise to me. I have always favoured the carrot rather than the stick." Jane sighed again, more fatigued than she should have been from such a short visit.

"You tired?"

Not from exertion, but tired nonetheless. Still, she straightened her shoulders and returned the smile to her face. "I have not asked half the questions I had about glamour." The conversation then turned to one of craft, which saw some of the tension ease out of Amey's figure. They were encumbered somewhat by vocabulary, since even though Amey spoke Igbo, she did not have sufficient foundation to be able to translate some of her mother's terms into European terms. They wound up returning to Jane's original plan of discussing the rudiments of technique.

At one point, Jane found herself using a cat's cradle made of ribbon to try to show a *tordre le fil* hook. They passed the ribbon back and forth with the learning verse that went with it.

Chasing a rat
Came a little cat
Over the table
Underneath the cradle,
Around, around
Upside and down
There goes the rat
Running from the cat.

Nkiruka picked it up quickly, but Amey kept missing the "over the table" pass as she twisted the string the wrong way.

Laughing from deep in her belly, Amey held up the square of ribbon they had once again created. "Is a box useful for anything? Because that seems to be all I can make."

"Can hold your brain, mebbe." Nkiruka reached through the square and tugged her daughter's kerchief.

"Mammy!" Amey laughed and squirmed away.

Amidst the laughter, Jane's fatigue was quite forgotten. Even unable to actually perform glamour, she was still able to find satisfaction in discussing the craft.

"See. Is why reeds better." Nkiruka tossed the string on the table. "Me go mek wan model."

"Reeds?"

"Like for basket? Make shape. It dry. Then . . ." She broke off and said something to her daughter.

She nodded. "You can trace the form, because it keep the shape even without somebody holding one."

"Can't mek square from circle." Nkiruka winked at her daughter. "Except mebbe you." She broke into laughter again.

"Well, that will make an interesting addition to my book."

"Book?" Nkiruka tilted her head and then looked at the paper on the table. "You ah write wan book?"

"Oh . . . yes. It was at first only a way to amuse myself while . . ." She passed a hand down her front. "While I could not work glamour. But I think it has some merit, so I might see about having it published when we are back in London. It is a comparison of African and European schools of glamour."

Nkiruka slid out one of drawings she had done for Jane of an Igbo training exercise. "You go use this?"

"Indeed. If I were able to see glamour right now, I could take notes myself, but since I cannot, this was very useful."

"If you were able—" Nkiruka broke off and scowled at the paper.

"I know you say that it is safe, but I would rather you

think me silly for not looking than take the chance. It is not so long, and—"

The older woman made a sudden rude noise and pushed her chair back from the table. "We gone."

Jane turned from her to Amey, who was also rising, to see if she could explain what had just occurred to make Nkiruka angry. Neither of them met her gaze. Jane stood. "Forgive me. I have done something to offend you, but know not what. Will you tell me?"

"You take . . ." Nkiruka growled and turned to Amey, speaking rapidly with phrases accented by gestures at the paper then at Jane.

The young woman shook her head as she replied. Jane could only watch the conversation with an increasing want of comprehension, until finally Amey turned to her. "She upset that you writing a book and taking credit for her drawings and ideas."

"Teach each other. That ah one thing. Book? No. Done tek enough, done profit enough."

"Oh, but . . ." But . . . that was precisely what Jane had been prepared to do. It had not been her intention to steal Nkiruka's ideas or to take credit for them, but nowhere in the structure of her book had she allotted space to acknowledge that half the ideas were not hers. Jane recalled when a pamphleteer had referred to the first glamural she and Vincent had made together as "created entire by Mr. Vincent" and how troubled she had been by it. Vincent himself had always acknowledged her work, but if he had not?

Jane's face heated with embarrassment. "I am so very sorry. You are quite correct to be angry."

Nkiruka stood with her arms crossed over her chest and stared at her as though she had grown snakes for hair.

"Would you . . . that is, if it would not be an imposition, would you like to author the work with me? I think the topic is of interest, and I cannot possibly undertake such a project without your experience." Jane's heart was beating too quickly, as it often had since she had been bled. She put her hand on the back of the chair to steady herself. "If we did publish it, you would be entitled to a share of the proceeds, of course."

"Proceeds?" Nkiruka looked to her daughter for an explanation. After Amey said a few words, Nkiruka's eyes narrowed. "You pay? Fu talk 'bout glamour?"

"Yes."

"Mi na read nor write."

"That has an easy enough solution. I can teach you to do both, or simply transcribe your words, if you prefer."

"Huh. Ah wha ya tarl!" Her eyes were narrow still.

Before Jane could ask Nkiruka what she meant, the clap of swift bootheels sounded upon the gallery floor. Vincent entered, almost at a run. He drew up at the sight of Jane's guests and attempted to disguise the fear that had been briefly visible. "Louisa said you were unwell."

"No . . . I am afraid that was not true." Jane sighed at the petty revenge and pulled out the chair she was holding. "Vincent, will you show your silence weave to Nkiruka? We were just discussing glamour, and I have some things

I should like your thoughts on." They had other topics to discuss. Too many, it seemed.

And once they were wrapped in silence, she would tell him about Pridmore, and then she would ask if it was legal to have a letter of agreement with a slave.

Eighteen

The Sound of Footsteps

One of the interesting side effects of having spent a week in bed and another venturing no farther than the blue parlour was that Jane had become adept at recognising the footsteps and knocks of the people who passed in the hall. Given Frank's similarity in build to Vincent, she would have expected the two men to sound much alike. Vincent's stride had been designed to exemplify all that was masculine. He moved with firm vigour, and his bootheels hit the floor with force. Frank, however, had been taught to be invisible. She rarely heard him before he was close to the door. His knock, when it came, had two raps that were just loud enough to be heard if one were awake and unoccupied.

Such a knock sounded each evening after

the Incident with Sir Ronald, as they had begun to call it. Each evening, he came with a request from Lord Verbury for an audience with Vincent. Since the Incident, Vincent had seen his father only once, and that while Jane was unconscious. The substance of the conversation had not been conveyed to her, but she could guess it well enough.

Tonight, at the sound of the knock, Vincent lifted his head from the book he was studying and glanced at Jane. She had been resting upon the sofa and now sat up, nodding to let him know that she was fit enough to receive Frank.

"Enter."

Frank opened the door smoothly and stepped into the room without a sound. He shut the door carefully behind him. "My apologies. His lordship has sent me to again request your company."

"No."

This was how similar requests had been met on other evenings. Tonight, however, Vincent cleared his throat and then wove a small sphere of silence, using Nkiruka's method to cloud the sound. "It should be safe to speak freely now."

Rather than abating the tension in Frank's frame, this seemed only to increase it. "This implies you have something you wish to discuss privately."

"Jane introduced me to Nkiruka and Amey today. They had interesting things to say about Mr. Pridmore."

"Ah . . . yes." Frank hesitated, and revealed a rare moment of indecision. He dug his thumbnail into the side of one finger and studied the floor. "I am going to ask you again to talk to your father, but this time I am asking for me and for my family."

"Frank, I am willing to help you in those ways I can with the running of the estate, but I will not speak to my father."

"Hear me out, please. I am aware of what I am asking you." Frank drew in a deep breath and pressed his long fingers over his eyes. "People talk when I am in the room. They forget that I am there, or that the coldmongers can hear. Your father . . . I have never seen him so enraged as he was with Sir Ronald over the Incident. His instruction had been that Sir Ronald was to delay your departure until Lord Verbury had an opportunity to make amends with you."

Vincent's fingers tightened on the book he had been reading. "Did you know? That night, did you know that Sir Ronald was sent into the room?"

"No." Frank dropped his hand. "Though I will not be so insincere as to affirm that I absolutely would have let you know. I like to think I would have, but . . . my family. I might equally have chosen to believe that no harm would come from my silence. My point in telling you this, however, is to say that I have seen signs of genuine distress and remorse. I believe that if you speak to him about Mr. Pridmore, he will listen to you."

"He has not in the past."

"But in the past . . . in the past he did not have a reason to try to make amends. If you wait too long, his remorse will turn into resentment and anger."

Vincent rubbed his forehead, squeezing his eyes closed.

He dropped his hand and pushed himself to his feet. "Stay with Jane."

Jane's heart sank at this. Since the Incident, Vincent's tendency to turn inward and brood had asserted itself, though he made an obvious effort to be open with Jane. Still, it seemed that every conference with his father had further oppressed his spirit. "Must you do it this evening?"

"I shall spend the night thinking on it, regardless. And Frank is correct in the timing. It is the andiron again."

Jane knew the story, but Frank shook his head in confusion. "Pardon?"

"When I was twelve, my father hit me harder than he intended. I fell and struck my head on the hearth andiron. Badly concussed. Very badly, and apparently for a time my recovery was in question. His contrition . . . he did not apologise, but there was a period after that in which he did anything I asked." Vincent shrugged. "And then for a time he resented any reminder that he had made a mistake. So, though I do not relish it, I shall speak with him. For you."

"Thank you."

He leaned over the back of the sofa to kiss Jane's forehead. "I do not suspect this will take long." The conversation would be brief, of that Jane had no doubt, but its effect on Vincent would last.

He went to the door without further delay. Jane could not fault his choice, or Frank for acting as he must to protect his family. No matter if the reasons were valid, or how well the conference went, Vincent would be full of agitation when he returned. Jane sighed.

"Is anything amiss?"

Everything was amiss and had been since they received the letter from Richard. What a mistake of duty that had been. Jane sighed again. "No. I was only wishing that I understood the power Lord Verbury had over Vincent."

It startled Jane at times, those moments when she recognised a characteristic of Vincent in Frank. In this case, Frank stopped making eye contact with her. He frowned and studied the floor. "Regardless of anything else, Lord Verbury is his father. It is . . . it is difficult to break a lifetime habit of obedience."

"But he has not always obeyed. Vincent broke away from the family and escaped this madness."

"As you say, madam." The return of his formality was a mark of his disquiet as surely as Vincent's silence. "That is why I hope that he will be well suited to discuss matters with his lordship."

Jane managed to convince Frank to sit while they waited for Vincent and to tell her about his family. He had been reluctant at first, because it was improper in his role as house steward to be seated with his employer. By pointing out that he sat in the counting house when he worked with Vincent and that it was fatiguing for Jane to be looking up constantly, she managed to get past his reservations. He sat perched on the edge of his seat, but when she turned the topic to his children, he relaxed.

Like Vincent, Frank had a naturally mobile and expressive face when not on his guard. His youngest daughter, Rosa, was the subject of discussion.

"She is only eight, and draws as if she were born with a pencil in her hand. I should show you the drawing she did of Louisa—it is quite a good likeness." He laughed, shaking his head. "Her mother and I do not know where she got this talent from, because none of our other children has the slightest inclination. Rosa, though . . . she is a wonder."

"Has she begun to work glamour?"

"She is just showing an interest, and I suspect she will excel there as well. In the normal course of things, my mother would teach her, but . . ." His ease faded somewhat. "My mother's time has not been her own recently."

"Is . . ." Jane hesitated to ask, but the resemblance between Frank and the woman who had pushed Lord Verbury's chair had been notable. "Is Miss Sarah your mother?"

"She is. Zeus's as well."

"What? Zeus is your brother?" Jane was all astonishment. Nothing in their manner to each other had given that away at all, though the Hamilton stamp had been clear enough.

Frank nodded. "Our sister, Milly, is the upper housemaid." He raised a finger. "Actually . . . now that I think of it, Milly used to draw quite well when she was younger."

Footsteps in the hall caused them both to still, listening to Vincent's approach. Frank stood, straightening his jacket, and turned to face the door. Vincent's tread was slow and heavy. He paused outside the door for half a minute before opening it. His expression had shut and dimmed, as though there were a candle in him that someone had extinguished. "Ah. Thank you for waiting, Frank."

Jane could see the answer in his face, but asked anyway, in hopes that giving Vincent leave to express himself might help. "How did it go?"

In his left hand, Vincent carried a folded sheet of heavy white paper, which he set on the round table. "On the subject of Mr. Pridmore, he is not willing to fire him, because my father is concerned that Pridmore will tell people that he is alive. But if I can find proof that Pridmore has been embezzling money or involved in some other criminal activity, then he feels that it would be sufficient to protect against revenge."

Frank rubbed the bridge of his nose. "Well. That is more progress than I have made."

"Do we have proof?" Jane asked.

Frank shook his head. "I will have to go through the accounting carefully."

"I can help with that." Vincent shrugged out of his coat and hung it over the back of a chair. He paused, leaning against the chair back. "Frank, do we have any sherry?"

"Yes, sir." The retreat to formality showed in his posture as well. "Have you a preference?"

"Whatever is closest at hand. Bring a glass for yourself, as well, if you like." He tugged his cravat free, still staring at the paper on the table as Frank bowed and left the room.

Jane stood and moved to Vincent's side. He rarely drank, and she could recall seeing him inebriated only once during their marriage. That he was asking for sherry was unprecedented in her memory. "Was it very bad?"

"He was civil, gentle in his manner, and contrite." Vincent drummed his fingers on the back of the chair. "He sends his apologies, and actually confessed that he had detained me on purpose to give Sir Ronald time to examine you." His grip tightened and Vincent broke off, turning his head a little away from her. After a moment, he cleared his throat. "He maintains that it was supposed to be an examination only, but acknowledges that even that was a breach. Jane . . . his behaviour confounds me."

"But an apology is the most natural thing in the world, under the circumstances."

"For anyone else, yes. I do not exaggerate when I say that I have never seen him apologise before. Let alone admit to a mistake. And—and, he wept." Vincent turned fully and walked away from Jane. "God. It is . . ."

Frank's quiet double knock sounded on the door.

Vincent wiped his hand across his face. "Enter."

Carrying a decanter and three glasses, Frank slipped into the room. He shut the door behind himself and carried the decanter to the table. "Shall I pour?"

"Please. And sit, if you will. I have need of some advice." Vincent pulled out a chair from the table. "Jane?"

She settled into the chair as Frank poured the amber liquid into small cut-crystal glasses. The scent of honeyed almonds and lemon rind filled the air almost like a glamour.

Vincent took his glass and sat to Jane's left, with the paper in front of him.

Frank hesitated only a moment before settling opposite him. He turned the glass and the crystal caught the candlelight. "I selected Manzanilla. The Oloroso had also been decanted, but I find it too cloying."

Taking a sip, Jane nodded in appreciation. It reminded her of roasted nuts, figs, and caramel. "Lovely choice."

Vincent picked up his glass but barely touched it to his lips before setting it down again. He looked at it, and then very deliberately pushed it aside. He sat forward, sliding the paper to the centre of the table. "My father gave me Zeus."

"What!" Jane could not contain her astonishment and repugnance. She knew that Zeus was enslaved, of course she did, but to be given the young man, and by Lord Verbury, made her stomach churn.

"I praised Zeus's steadiness of character and spoke of what a help he has been during our time here." He rubbed his brow with both hands. "Before I understood his purpose, he had Miss Sarah pull out a deed and give it to me. It is dated prior to his supposed death, and I am to claim to have discovered it in his office as part of my inheritance."

Frank had frozen with the glass of sherry in the air, his eyes wide. Swallowing, he set the glass down with care. "His handwriting has changed since the stroke. May I look at the deed?"

"Please." Vincent waved his permission. "The implication was that there are other deeds for me to 'find' if we continue to stay here, though I do not hold much stock in that."

Frank unfolded the paper and studied it. "Ah . . . this is my mother's hand, which is a credible match." He lowered the document. "You said you wanted advice."

"On three points, yes. The first two are related." He listed them on his fingers. "What is the best way to tell Zeus? And is freeing him advisable?"

Jane stared at Vincent in disbelief. "But of course we must free him. How could you consider keeping him a slave?"

"Because I need to make certain that it will not open Zeus to the same prospect of criminal charges that Frank faces if Pridmore exposes my father. As a slave, he is bound to obey, but as a freedman, the fact that he has been helping keep my father hidden could be a hanging offence."

For the first time, it occurred to Jane that the same might be applied to them. "Are we liable as well?"

"Likely not, given my very public break with the family—though being here may complicate that somewhat. Still, my chief concern is what happens when Pridmore is fired. If he chooses to expose my father, then he will attempt to shift the blame to Frank. I think we can manage that, but do not want to unintentionally endanger Zeus. So the question is whether to free him before or after we take action."

Frank placed the document back on the table. "Explain the circumstances and ask him what he prefers, but I will lay money on him choosing to be freed."

"Even with the risk?" Jane asked.

"Better that than the risk that he might never be freed." Frank shrugged. "Ask him. As for how to tell him, I would wait until the morning, so that when he gives you his answer, you can file the papers and pay the fee directly. You will need to go to St. John's for that, so I will arrange the carriage with Jove."

Vincent nodded. "We shall need to discuss a salary, if he chooses to stay on."

"Very good." Frank picked up his glass and raised it to Vincent. "Thank you. Now, you mentioned three things. What is the third?"

Vincent inhaled very slowly, before turning to Jane. "This involves you, Muse. We have been invited to dinner."

The room grew cold, and Jane was fairly certain that she had gone quite pale. She picked up the glass of sherry and took a sip to hide her distress. She did not want to see the man or have anything to do with him, apology or no. It was not enough. Nothing he said could ever be enough to atone for what he had done and continued to do to Vincent. "You are considering accepting."

"It is his condition for looking at our charges against Pridmore." Vincent reached for her hand. "If you are not willing, then I shall decline. There will be other options."

"But?"

"But . . . I think—and I want Frank's opinion on this—that having you present and visibly with child would remind my father that he wants to continue to mend relations. I think that might make him more disposed to a discussion of Mr. Pridmore's mismanagement."

Frank grimaced. "It might. I am sorry, I wish that were not the case."

Beneath the table, Jane tightened her free hand into a fist until her nails dug into the palm. "And declining will almost certainly make him angry, which will hurt your cause."

"Muse, if you are not comfortable, there are other ways. I have weathered my father's displeasure before."

Comfortable? Having seen the results of Vincent's other conferences with him, Jane expected nothing of comfort from an evening with Lord Verbury. "When?"

He grimaced with annoyance. "He wanted us tomorrow, but I put him off for a week, in deference to your health."

Deferring to her health was not much of an exaggeration. Could she do this? She became short of breath simply walking from one room to the next. Even this much agitation made her heart race far too quickly. Jane closed her eyes, thinking over the conversation. It seemed to her that Lord Verbury's remorse was an instrument to force Vincent to do what he wanted him to do. If Lord Verbury was truly concerned that Mr. Pridmore would expose him, which seemed a likely consequence of firing him, then having a safeguard would be a sensible goal—for Lord Verbury.

She opened her eyes. "The evidence he asked you to look for . . . am I correct that he wants you to extort Mr. Pridmore on his behalf?"

Vincent's breath whistled out. "Yes. And for his benefit."

"No." Frank sat forward, face stern. "No, it is not for Lord Verbury. It is for my wife and Louisa and Rosa and getting everyone else on this estate out from under the influence of a reprehensible man. We will not be using any invented evidence, and not requiring Pridmore to do anything but hold his tongue."

Though the goal was worthy, Jane could see Lord Verbury's hand there as well, using their noble impulses against them. He truly did twist everything and everyone around him. And yet, she did not know that there was much choice. Jane clenched her jaw and nodded. "Very well. Let us accept his invitation in the spirit that it was offered."

Nineteen

A Matter of Appearances

Shortly after breakfast, Frank brought Zeus to the blue parlour. It was clear that he had told the young man nothing save that he was wanted. Jane tried to catch Zeus's eye and smile at him, but Zeus, mindful of Frank's presence, kept his eyes cast down.

Vincent stood when they entered and rounded the table to stand in front of the young man. "Zeus—your real name is Zachary, is it not?"

"Yes, sir."

"Lord Verbury has given me the deed for you."

For a brief moment, the young man's eyes flashed up, and then he resolutely studied the floor.

"There are some circumstances that we must

explain to you, but at the end of that, I will free you, if you would like."

At that, Zeus—Zachary—stared at Vincent, mouth ajar a little. Heedless of the etiquette for a servant, he turned to Frank. In the nod that Frank gave in return, Jane could, for the first time, see that the two men were brothers. Frank's gesture carried assurance and comfort. Zachary's face worked with great emotion. He lifted his hands, then tightened them into fists and returned them to his sides. A muscle at the corner of his jaw tightened in a way that reminded Jane painfully of Vincent.

Zachary swallowed with his head bent. His voice was thick with feeling. "Please tell me the circumstances."

"Will you sit?" asked Jane.

Frank put his hand on the younger man's shoulder and gave it a squeeze. Moving almost blindly, Zachary sank into a chair at the table with his hands clasped tightly in his lap. Frank sat on his other side, and together he and Vincent explained the situation.

At the end of their explanation, Zachary stared at the table, arms drawn tight against his sides. He swallowed several times before opening his mouth to speak, and even then had to clear his throat. "I should like to be freed."

"Good." Vincent pushed his chair back from the table, looking across to Frank.

"The carriage is waiting."

Zachary's eyes flashed up, brow raised. "Now? Truly—I mean, right now?"

"I would rather it done immediately." Vincent stood, and on instinct Zachary sprang to his feet.

Frank pushed his chair back, standing only a trifle slower. "I shall stay with Mrs. Hamilton."

"Thank you." Jane was certain that he would prefer to go with his brother, but it was not yet safe for her to leave the house. Though it was not spoken, none of them put it past Lord Verbury to take advantage of Vincent being off the property.

After the visit to the courthouse, where Vincent paid the emancipation fee of three hundred pounds, Zachary was given a day of liberty to decide what he wanted to do: either strike out on his own, or stay on at the estate in his role as footman. He chose to accept the position offered, though made it clear that it was only acceptable under the current conditions—"current" being the Vincents' continued presence on the estate as a guard against Mr. Pridmore.

It should have come as no surprise that Zachary moved with more assurance, though he sometimes still wore an expression of shock in unguarded moments. An unexpected benefit was that there was one more person in the house who they absolutely knew owed Lord Verbury no loyalty.

Another five days passed before Dr. Jones declared Jane safe enough to leave the house, though even that report came with the warning against travel until after Jane's confinement. So though Jane was safe, neither she nor Vincent had anything like peace. The thought of dinner with Lord Verbury haunted them.

It nettled to have to think of clothes and gowns, but none of Jane's evening dresses fit properly. Appearances would matter a great deal, so she arranged to be fitted for a frock of black net and a gown of black silk for under it. She would be able to wear the net with grey or lavender gowns when they moved to half mourning. Later, she could trim it with embroidery and wear it over more vibrant colours. She had seen a black net worn over a red silk gown to great effect in London. It was all very practical and elegant, and she had never abhorred having a gown made more.

Vincent continued to have difficulty sleeping. He and Frank had been studying the bills and the accounts of rum and sugar production, looking for some inconsistency. They knew it must be there, because the larger estate seemed constantly in need of funds, though by their sales of sugar and rum it should have been seeing a profit. As the days passed with nothing that would prove Mr. Pridmore was appropriating funds, Vincent sank deeper. He tried to rally. Jane could see the effort he made to be present and attentive when with her, but more than once she awoke to find him sitting in the dark. Not working glamour, not reading, but simply sitting.

Seeing what a month in Antigua had done to him, it pained her to think of what enduring three more months might do. When she reflected on it, in all likelihood they would be even longer than that. Her delivery might be expected in September, but her confinement would carry them into October even if there were no complications. Travelling with a newborn seemed rash, so Jane was bracing herself to be in Antigua for Christmas.

Anxious for any opportunity to distract Vincent, Jane read with interest the note she had received from Mrs. Whitten. Clearing her throat, she looked across the breakfast table to where Vincent sat pushing a slice of toast around on his plate.

"Vincent . . . would you like to go with me to Mrs. Whitten's to look at her ballroom? She has invited me to consult about the glamural for the charity ball."

He looked up from his frown. "I thought you declined because we were in mourning."

"Well, it had seemed a good excuse while I was attempting to hide the fact that I was increasing, but . . ." She looked down at her stomach. It astonished her, the difference that only a few weeks could make in her girth. Their first week in Antigua, she might have only been stout, but the last three weeks had made her condition quite clear. "The mourning period ends in August, and no one would think ill of us if we went to half mourning now. It would give me something to do, and I am in want of some activity."

"What of your book?"

"I shall still work on it, of course. My hope is that Nkiruka will assist us on the glamural." Jane felt as if she were pressing too hard, but the circles under Vincent's eyes alarmed her. "We shall not go until the afternoon and be gone a little more than an hour, so you would still have plenty of time to go over the books with Frank."

"I worry less about that than your health, to be honest. I do not know if it is wise to be involved in so large a project."

"I will not be working glamour or exerting myself beyond drawing and consultation." Jane sighed and reached across the table to rest her hand on his. "I know you are only concerned, but I was not seeking advice on whether I should go. My question was if you wanted to join me."

He regarded her without expression. It pained her that she could not guess his thoughts. In private or with his few trusted companions, he was generally amiable, with an easy laugh and mobile features. But even in unfamiliar company, when he became more reserved, Jane had become used to the subtleties of his expression. Over the past several days, he had adopted a withdrawn expression that went beyond his usual reserve. Vincent lowered his hand and gave a brief nod. "Thank you. I shall."

Jane was not entirely certain if he was humouring her or if he had any interest in the glamural. Either way, it would get him away from their troubles for a time.

The Whitten estate occupied the land next to theirs, although the broad ravine and treacherous ground between the two estates required a roundabout route to reach the Whittens' great house. It sat atop a ridge with a good prospect of the sugarcane fields. It was an older building than Greycroft, with two long wings stretching back around a central yard. Wide verandas, which seemed to be a prevalent feature in Antiguan architecture, graced the sides of the building, but the front was in a Palladian style that would not have been out of place at a country estate in England.

The ballroom, to Jane's surprise, occupied its own building set between the two wings. Tall windows opened all the way to the floor, letting a breeze flow through the gracious room. A glamural of what might have been a rustic English landscape occupied the space with a succession of box hedges and strangely lit cottages. A pack of hounds stood among the trees along one wall. Jane frowned. The animals had antlers. Perhaps not hounds, then.

She glanced at Vincent, who was scowling at the unfortunate deer. His gaze went vacant as he looked into the ether, shaking his head with familiar offended disdain. Never had Jane been happier to see poorly rendered glamour.

At the far end of the room, Mrs. Whitten sat at a table with the other ladies who were throwing the charity. She rose with a smile and hurried across the room to meet them. "I am so grateful that you were able to join us. I trust your health is improved?"

"Much, thank you." Jane wondered how many details had made their way through the gossip lines. "The heat surprised me."

"I quite understand. When I returned from my Season in London, I was nearly done in, in spite of having been born here."

"Mrs. Whitten, may I introduce . . ." Jane hesitated before she said his name. Mrs. Whitten was thoroughly familiar with his career, so it would come as no surprise, and it might help restore Vincent to himself. "My husband, Sir David Vincent."

Vincent had shown no surprise that Mrs. Whitten was a mulatto, but his brow rose a fraction at the sound of his own name. He covered any further surprise with a bow. "Madam."

"I am happy to hear you introduced thus, since, as you see, we have need of a glamourist." She looked at the antlered hounds and gave a little wince, then she turned to Jane. "Shall I call you Lady Vincent, or would you prefer Mrs. Hamilton?"

Before Jane could answer, Mrs. Pridmore settled the question by rushing across the room with her hands outstretched. "My dear, dear Mrs. Hamilton! Mr. Hamilton! You have my most sincere congratulations. When Mr. Pridmore told me about your impending joy, I was so delighted for you, but of course I was not surprised. I had wondered, you see, though one never likes to ask, as sometimes the subject of one's curiosity is merely stout. But you had such a glow about you that I was fairly certain, was I not, Mrs. Ransford?"

Mrs. Ransford said, "I am such an admirer of your work, Sir David."

This caused Vincent's brow to go up. "That is kind. What have you had the occasion to view?"

"Oh . . . I am afraid I have not yet had the privilege, but I have read about it. Indeed, being a fellow glamourist, I have made it my business to stay current in the fashions in London, and everyone there is full of praise for your work.

I have it on the highest authority that your glamural of a Midsummer Night for the Prince Regent was absolutely thrilling."

Vincent gave a short bow of thanks.

Mrs. Whitten indicated the table that had been set up at the far end of the ballroom. "May I invite you to sit? We have some drawings I should like to show you." As they walked, she said, "The reason we are particularly glad to see you is that we are having some difficulty deciding upon a motif. The opinion of a professional glamourist would be most welcome."

Vincent's gaze slid a little sideways to Jane. This was familiar ground for both of them. All too often, when they took a commission, the gentleman and lady of the house had differing views of what constituted an appropriate glamural for a dining room or parlour. One might want hunters and hounds, the other would perhaps favour roses in a folly. Having three opinions to contend with would be a challenge, but so petty after the trials of the last weeks as to seem almost welcome.

Jane smiled at Mrs. Whitten. "What are the motifs you are considering?"

"We have narrowed it to two." She gestured to the drawings on the table. Some of them showed talent, while others showed merely that someone possessed a set of pastels.

"Hm." Vincent slid a paper to the side and exposed another, which was drawn with some competence. "The Arabian Nights, I believe?"

Mrs. Ransford nodded, straightening in her chair. "I

thought a touch of the exotic would be welcomed by our guests. Then, during the course of the evening, we could have a few *tableaux vivants* of different stories. We could also dress some of the mulatto slaves as Indians to make the scheme more fully realised. Some mulattos can be exceedingly handsome in the right clothes and the right setting."

No one looked at Mrs. Whitten, keeping their attention firmly fixed upon the drawing, but Jane felt her own face flush on the gentlewoman's account. Clearing her throat, she picked up one of the pastels, which held an awkward view of a canal. "And this?"

"Oh, Venice!" Mrs. Pridmore clapped her hands together and gave a little shrug of delight. "Your recent visit inspired me. I thought we could do the ballroom in the Italianate style and have glamour in the windows so that it appeared we were at a palazzo looking out over the Grand Canal. It would be so cunning to see a gondola go past, do you not think? I am so enchanted with Venice."

The Venice idea had some merit, but the gondolas would be rather more difficult than Mrs. Pridmore thought, simply because it would involve either multiple illusions to create the effect of a ship passing from one window to the next, or a single enormous fold that stretched the length of the exterior of the building. And of course it would then need to be masked so it was not visible on the approach to the building. It was not impossible, but it was more complicated than it sounded. Then, too, Jane was not entirely certain she wanted to relive Venice quite so soon.

She glanced at Vincent, who was tapping his finger upon

the drawing of the canals with his eyes a little narrowed, as though he were playing out possibilities. He then turned to the Arabian Nights. It would be much simpler to achieve, and it had some merit, but Jane felt ill at ease on Mrs. Whitten's account. Though perhaps she was being too quick to guess at the other woman's feelings on the matter. Jane tilted her head, considering, then looked up. "Mrs. Whitten, did you have an idea as well?"

"Oh, no. I am happy to provide the ballroom. I feel no need to do more when we are already so well supplied with ideas." Her manner was tranquil and she gave an easy smile.

Vincent rubbed his chin, still considering. He turned from the table to regard the ballroom as a whole. Jane rose to stand beside him, considering the prospect.

Behind them, Mrs. Pridmore said, "Oh, I do so love to see a gentleman at work. Do not keep us in suspense, Mr. Hamilton. Which one do you think we should do?"

"If you will give us a moment of privacy." He and Jane walked a little away from the group, then Vincent brought his hand up, swiftly weaving a small sphere of silence around them. With their backs to the women, it would be obvious that they were conversing, but their subject would at least be obscured. "This is truly awful."

"It is not so bad as that. The cherry tree is quite nicely done."

"And wildly out of proportion to the hill upon which it is supposed to rest." Vincent shook his head, grimacing. "Muse, do you recall when we met and I said that I expected your glamour to be like that of any accomplished young lady? This . . . this is what I had come to expect from the accomplished ladies of the fashionable set."

"But you had seen the glamural in our parlour by then."

"I . . . I thought a professional had done it." Vincent blushed charmingly and shrugged. "Allow me to apologise again for undervaluing your skills."

"You were forgiven long ago." She very much wanted to take his hand, but with their assembled audience, it seemed best not to. "As for the task at hand . . ."

"Ah. Yes . . . which awkward choice interests you?"

"It seems to me that if we pick either of them, there will be difficulties and more than a little enmity. The points they have in common are a desire for the exotic, though achieved in different ways."

"So perhaps we can guide them to a different kind of place. Russia? That is cold, which surely must be a rarity here."

"Oh!" Jane recalled something she had read in the paper about Britain mounting an expedition to seek a path to China through the Arctic Circle. "The Northwest Passage Expedition."

"Ah . . . glaciers. Icebergs. An ice palace?" He nodded. "That might do. There is a Scottish fellow in charge of the expedition, if I remember correctly, so that should please Mrs. Ransford. We can suggest that it represents the superiority of the empire in an exotic locale."

"Shall we?"

"You lead, please. I am still . . . irritable."

"Oh, love. You are always irritable with clients."

He gave her the smallest of smiles. "More so than usual, then." He undid the threads keeping their conversation private.

Dropping those threads returned them to a room in which a heated conversation was taking place. Mrs. Pridmore was in the midst of saying, ". . . no use at the estate, so I am certain he will not be missed."

"Even so, if she cannot work . . . and in her condition, I hardly see how she . . ." Mrs. Ransford's voice trailed away and she coloured, with some degree of consciousness. "Oh. Have you decided? We are most particularly keen to know what your opinions are."

Jane had doubt on that score. There could be little question as to what the women had been discussing, or of Mrs. Pridmore's opinions of Vincent's efforts at managing the estate. He had grown still and grave again at her side. Jane chanced a smile. "We were discussing your disparate schemes. My husband and I found that there were motifs among them that suggested they had more in common than at first blush."

"Yes, but which does he prefer?"

She had long since become accustomed to clients using "he" and "him" when they were working together, yet she still sighed. Before she could form a response, Vincent said, "My wife is my equal partner in our work. On this matter, we agree."

"If you wish to help your guests escape from the fatigues of running their estates, then you must provide novelty. In truth, we think that Venice and the Arabian Nights both express a desire for novelty and the exotic, but they share a common flaw. You are too much in the English habit of thinking of warmer climes as exotic." She nodded to the window. "But that is hardly the case for the patrons you most seek to impress. They spend the day in the hot sun and want nothing more than to forget it."

Mrs. Whitten said, "What do you recommend?"

Jane answered her, "In honour of Captain John Ross's expedition to find a Northwest Passage, we thought to suggest an ice palace."

"Ooooo!" Mrs. Pridmore clapped her hands again and bounced in her chair, apparently delighted by any novel idea. "And our estate has ever so many coldmongers. It is my husband's especial project, and I am certain he will be willing to loan them to the ball for the occasion."

"Your estate?" Vincent only smiled, and yet the room grew colder by degrees. "I was unaware that you and Mr. Pridmore had purchased any land. I must congratulate him."

"I—oh. That is to say—"

He turned from her to address Mrs. Whitten. "Since it is your ballroom, may I assume that questions about our working hours should be directed to you?"

Mrs. Ransford replied instead, "No, those should be directed to me, since the coordination of the glamural has been my charge in previous years."

"Ah . . . did I misunderstand?" Vincent offered a little bow. "I had thought you wished us to create the glamural."

"Well, yes, but Mrs. Hamilton can hardly work glamour in her state."

Jane stepped in before Vincent could reply. While he was often irritable with their clients, there was a difference between an eccentric curmudgeonly artist and an arrogant nobleman. His manner in that moment tended towards the latter and made Jane uneasy. "Mrs. Ransford, I am so glad to hear you offer your help. We shall certainly need it, although in truth I had been looking forward to continuing my involvement. I am half mad from want of activity."

Mrs. Ransford looked frankly at Jane's stomach. "But you cannot work glamour."

"I can still do drawings and paint. My husband can work some of the glamour, and when he is occupied, I have found a glamourist of some talent who can assist."

"Oh?" The pale woman raised her eyebrows. "I thought I knew all of the glamourists of any skill on the island."

"Her name is Nkiruka. She is a retired field hand."

Laughing, Mrs. Ransford shook her head. "I quite misunderstood you. When you said you had found a glamourist, I thought you meant someone with training."

"She does have training, although I will grant that it is not in the European tradition."

"To be certain." Though her manner said she was anything but certain. "Still, you must understand my confusion when I thought you were comparing the work of a folk glamourist—and a slave, at that—to what a lady of refinement might produce."

Vincent looked around the ballroom. "Is this your work?"

"Indeed it is."

"Good. I am glad to have a measure of your abilities. It is everything I would expect from an accomplished and fashionable lady."

Jane had to cover her mouth as Mrs. Ransford gloried at the supposed compliment. It was enough to conciliate her and allow them to settle a plan that would allow Jane to oversee the glamural through the use of drawing, which would make coordination easier. Vincent would do the finer, detailed work, and they would have the aid of a number of assistants. Privately, Jane expected that he would also wind up laying some of the larger folds, which required more stamina than she expected Mrs. Ransford was capable. All in all, this endeavour was as much like their lives in London had been as they could expect from Antigua.

Twenty

Drawings and Measurements

The next morning Jane settled in her accustomed spot at the round table in the blue parlour to do some drawings of their proposed ice palace. They had taken measurements of the ballroom, which would allow her to make a scale plan that several glamourists could execute in concert. For clients, they ordinarily did a rendering of what the finished glamural would look like. As much as Jane wished that they could create that representation in glamour, the fact that glamour could not be transported made working on paper rather more practical.

What differed in this instance was a consciousness that having drawings alone of the finished effect would not suffice, since she would not be doing the work. Jane would need to also show the foundations, since those were the most easily assigned to the less accomplished glamourists. Over the course of the next several hours, Jane worked on her rendering of the full effect as it would be seen from the entrance to the ballroom. The curtain of snow across the musicians' gallery would need to be woven from several extraordinarily long threads. She thought that they were well within Vincent's abilities but would feel better if she could show it to him before Nkiruka and Amey arrived.

She rang for Louisa. The young maid appeared in the door quickly and curtsied. "Yes, madam?"

Jane straightened, her back cracking audibly from her time hunched over her paper. "Do you know where Mr. Hamilton is?"

"He is in the counting house."

"Thank you." Jane made her papers tidy and stood. For a moment, grey spots swam in the edges of her vision, and she had to press her palm against the table to steady herself until it passed. The doctor said that some dizziness was not unusual for expectant mothers, but it still vexed Jane. "Could you ask Cook if we might have some of her delicious Shrewsbury cakes with tea? Nkiruka and Amey are coming to consult on our plans, and Nkiruka especially likes them."

"I have already done so, madam." She gave a curtsy. "Shall I help you with your drawings?"

Jane looked at the album of drawings and sighed. Given how easily she became dizzy, it would be best to have both hands free while climbing the stairs to the counting house, so she could manage her gown and hold the rail. Though she felt more like her mother with each passing day, Jane nodded. "Thank you, I think you had better."

She was finding that the difference between being nearly six months along and actually in her six month was significant. She had begun to feel somewhat ungainly.

She led Louisa down the hall past their bedroom, out the back door of their wing, and to the counting house. A horse was tied up at the rail, eating the flowers planted at the foot of the stairs as if that were its normal fare. Jane frowned, unable to imagine Vincent being so careless, which made it likely that it was someone else's horse. Lifting the hem of her gown, she started up the stairs, but had achieved only the third when Mr. Pridmore emerged from the counting house.

He was still facing half inward, addressing the occupants, "Thank you for your time and consideration, sir." Putting on his hat, he turned and saw Jane. He lifted the hat again and greeted her before settling it upon his head. "Mrs. Hamilton, so lovely to see you up and about again. Feeling better, I trust?"

"Much, thank you." She managed to keep her dislike hidden.

"I am glad. My wife was delighted that you were well enough to help her with the charity ball. It is a favourite project of hers." He lowered his voice to a confidential aside and took a step closer. "I do know how important it is for ladies to have their favourite projects. In fact, I was just discussing yours with your husband."

Jane stepped back until the rail pressed against her. "My book, you mean?"

He looked confused. "Pardon? Have you the poetry ailment as well?" Shaking his head, he laughed. "I refer to your engaging that negro 'doctor' and promising to build a hospital. I know you mean well, but there are budgets to consider. I should advise, most strongly, to choose another amusement for yourself."

"I hardly think that the health of the people working for us is a subject of amusement."

"Then we are agreed." He smiled and leaned even closer. "Pray, do not amuse yourself in like manner any further."

"Jane?" Vincent appeared in the door, frowning.

Mr. Pridmore straightened, still all smiles and easy manners. "I was just complimenting your wife on her improved health. Good day, madam." He stepped around her and continued down the stairs.

Behind her, Louisa gave a sudden startled exclamation. When Jane turned, the girl's face was flushed and she was smoothing her dress with one hand, clutching Jane's papers tight to her bosom with the other. Her discomfort was all the more apparent in contrast to her usual composure. Mr. Pridmore was past already, walking to his horse as though nothing had occurred. Jane went back down to stand by Louisa. "Are you all right? What did he do?"

"Nothing, madam." She looked at the ground and wet her lips. "An insect flew into me. Nothing more."

"If he touched you in any way, you must tell me." No matter where the girl's loyalties lay, certain things were not acceptable under any circumstances. Jane glared at the man as he rode away, but he took no notice beyond touching his hat in farewell.

Vincent came down the stairs two at a time. "What is the matter?"

"I think he . . . was impertinent with Louisa."

This attention seemed to distress the girl more. "Please, madam. Please do not say anything further about it. I was only startled. It was only an insect."

"Your father is inside." Vincent gestured to the counting house. "Shall we go to him?"

"No! He will—you mustn't say anything. Please? Please do not. Is better if Papa don't—truly, it was nothing." She looked between them with anxious entreaty, a more open display than Jane was used to seeing from her. She was shaking. "Please?"

Vincent's scowl darkened as he turned to look after the man. "If . . . if anything untoward occurs, I should be honoured if you would trust me with your confidence. In certain matters, I have more liberty than your father."

Louisa managed to give a curtsy, even standing on the stairs as she was. She had composed her features, but her colour remained high. "We should not keep Mrs. Hamilton in the sun, I think."

Inhaling, Vincent gave a tight nod. "Of course."

If Louisa came in, red-faced and trembling as she was, Frank would know in an instant that something had occurred, and given the timing of Mr. Pridmore's departure, no doubt he could make an accurate guess as to what had happened. Jane bent a little to try to peer into Louisa's face. "Should you like to go back to the great house to . . . fetch something for me?"

"Yes, madam." Louisa turned, then turned again in a full circle and held out the album of papers. "Your drawings, madam."

Vincent relieved her of them. "Thank you, Louisa. Take all the time you need."

"Thank you, sir. Madam." She dipped in another curtsy and hurried off.

Jane let out a heavy sigh. "That odious man."

"Yes." Vincent rubbed his hand through his hair and grimaced. "Come inside?" He transferred the drawings to his right hand and offered her his left.

As they entered the relative cool of the counting house, Jane said, "I wanted to ask your opinion about the drawings I have been working on, before Nkiruka and Amey arrive."

Vincent's stride checked for a moment. He looked across the room to Frank, who met his expression with some gravity. Pulling out a chair, Vincent guided her towards it. "Sit down, please."

"You are alarming me a little." But Jane sank into the chair. She put a hand to her side as the baby kicked in agitation. "What is the matter?"

Vincent set her drawings on the table. Drawing out another chair, he sat in front of Jane, then took both her hands. "I am . . . I am very sorry to report that Amey has died."

She could only stare at him. His concern, and the tenderness with which he delivered the news, carried with them a tremor of fear. For a brief moment, his gaze dropped to Jane's stomach, then out the window where the slave huts were just visible in the softening distance.

Amey had died? It hurt to inhale. "In labour?"

"Yes."

"And her baby?"

"A stillborn daughter." Vincent's hands were warm and strong around hers. "I am so sorry, Muse. I know that you had taken a keen interest in her welfare."

"I do not understand. Was Dr. Jones there?" Jane looked up sharply. "Mr. Pridmore did not keep her away, did he? He has not called her for months, and was just now wanting me to stop my 'project' of worrying about their health."

"She was there—at least, according to Mr. Pridmore."

"He must be lying." Jane withdrew her hands and clenched them together in her lap. It was too awful. Yes, Jane knew women died all too often, but Amey had borne children before. She had been strong and in good health. How could she so simply be dead? And poor Nkiruka, to lose a daughter in such a way.

Frank cleared his throat. "I am afraid not. He came expressly to complain about the expense when, to him, it served no purpose."

"If there had been a hospital—if she had not given birth in a dark, stuffy, and dirty room." Jane covered her face with her hands, pressing her fingers against her forehead. He was a terrible man. All his concern had been about the expense, and none for the lives that had been lost. Dropping her hands, Jane lifted her chin. "I told the doctor that I would inquire about having a hospital built, and I have done nothing beyond inquire."

"Jane . . ." Vincent shifted in his seat. "There was nothing to be done."

She stood, clasping her hands in front of her again to hide their shaking. "The doctor made some very sound economic arguments about improved recovery rates and reduced sick days."

"I know." Frank nodded. "She has presented the same ones to me, but Mr. Pridmore convinced his lordship that we were spending enough on medical care and that converting land from agriculture to a hospital would be a poor return."

"So, let us look at land that is not suitable for agriculture."

"Muse, I do not want you to upset yourself over this."

"I am already upset!" She swallowed her rising shrillness and took a shuddering breath before she attempted speech again. The doctor had not been enough to keep Amey alive. Would a hospital really have made the difference? Jane turned again to Frank. "Are there maps we might look at?"

He looked past her to Vincent before he answered. Her husband must have nodded, because Frank turned to a set of long flat drawers. On another day, she might have been annoyed that he felt the need to get permission from her husband, but it was a petty concern today.

Pulling open a drawer, Frank said, "I have the plan of the estate, but since there are not enough house slaves to justify more than a sick room inside the house, a hospital will principally relate to the field hands. Its construction is likely to belong to Mr. Pridmore's budget."

"If we must, then we make the argument that a hospital is necessary for my health and the health of Lord Verbury's heir."

Frank laid the paper out on one of the broad desks. "He will still want to see numbers."

"Why must we continually indulge that man!" Jane slammed her palms down on the table. "He cares for nothing but profit and power. People are but tokens for him to spend upon whatever he desires and—and . . . I am sorry, Frank. I know that your family is one of those tokens for him, and at risk. I know why we must indulge him."

Letting his head drop forward, Frank leaned on the table. "I should acknowledge that my experience with his lordship has been very different from yours. Before the stroke, he was a demanding master, but liberal so long as you met his expectations, and not arbitrary. He could even be generous." His fingers flexed on the table. "For instance, my wife was a lady's maid on another plantation. We met in the course of events held around the island and began a doomed courtship. Lord Verbury took note and bought her. She has never been required to work on the estate. So . . . so it is important for you to understand that I follow his wishes not only because my family is hostage."

Behind Jane, Vincent said, "And when you did not meet his expectations?"

Frank lifted his head. "As a slave, you expect to be beaten.

He is methodical and careful not to cripple or leave scars. It was never without cause."

Jane could only stare at him in horror. "How can you possibly—"

"Because I cannot say the same for Mr. Pridmore." Clearing his throat, Frank pushed the map towards Jane. "After the stroke, Lord Verbury has been exceedingly arbitrary, and Mr. Pridmore was given full leave to run the estate as he sees fit. Since your arrival . . . Lord Verbury has been almost constantly angry. He is in conflict. On the one hand, he wants to punish you both for not acceding to his wishes. On the other, you represent his only hope to preserve his legacy."

Vincent gave a cold chuckle and walked a little away from them. "So he will want to deny the hospital simply because we ask for it, but also wants to ingratiate himself in order to be close to the child. How lovely."

"Just so. Presented with numbers, it might remind him to reply with rationality rather than emotion."

"I can attend to that, since I am having no success in finding anything to help us against Pridmore." Vincent crossed to the ledgers. "If you will provide me with the doctor's notes about the economic benefits of a hospital, then I can compare that to the current cost to the estate."

Jane studied the map. It would not restore Amey to life, but it might save some other woman. "Frank and I will attempt to find a location for it."

The map had been clearly drawn, with the neat rectangles of the great house and counting house surrounded by acres and acres of cane fields. They had been broken into smaller plots, each delineated with a careful line. The distillery was closer than she had expected, on the road to St. John's, but in the opposite direction. Only a few spots were not developed for agriculture. Jane pointed at one of those. "What about here? The land between us and the Whitten estate."

He answered quickly, "There is a ravine between us."

"It is barely more than a gulley on this map."

"Alas, that is one of the places where the surveyors failed in their duty. The ground is quite treacherous there, and erosion has widened and deepened it over the years. Even if we were to build well back from it, I worry that the building would fall."

Vincent made a humphing sound from where he sat. "There is currently no sickroom?"

"Correct—or, rather, there is one in name, but it is only a room in the basement of the great house with a cot in it. I keep it supplied with some bandages and a few medicines for the use of the house staff." Frank turned his attention back to the map. "Perhaps something near the distillery? That is where the worst injuries happen."

"Is there room to put another building on the site?" Jane tilted her head to consider the plans. "On this small rise, for instance? That would not be in the way of the wagons or other work, I think."

"It would take some effort to level the top of it for building, but you are correct that it is of no utility to the factory."

"Jane . . . did you say that the doctor had not been here

for months?" Vincent called, his finger on a line in the ledger.

She turned away from Frank. "Yes. Her visit to Amey was the first in months. I am not certain how many months, though."

"But she certainly has not been here once a week." Quite astonishingly, Vincent began to smile and then to chuckle. "Oh, the devil. The devil. She could not testify against him because she is coloured. Nor could Frank."

Jane pushed away from the table at almost the same moment that Frank abandoned the map. He strode briskly to Vincent and leaned over his chair. "What have you found?"

"I found where the money is going." He tapped the page. "I know how Mr. Pridmore is embezzling from my father."

Twenty-one

Invitations

According to the books, Mr. Pridmore had been paying Dr. Jones a regular and healthy sum to call upon the estate weekly, in addition to any other emergencies—of which he had several listed. More money appeared as a transfer to Frank for supplying the sickroom in the great house. Based on those amounts, it should be handsomely equipped. That it was merely a room with some bandages could easily be reflected to make it appear that Frank was the one stealing funds. The laws of Antigua stipulated that no person of colour could testify against a white person. Therefore, neither of them could appear in court to say that the listed amounts had never been paid nor engaged.

Now that they knew the pattern to look for,

Frank went through the books looking for other tradespeople that he knew to be people of colour. In one instance, Pridmore had recorded a repair to the number two boiler, which Vincent was certain had not been done by a professional. In another, he had paid top prices for bolts of fabric to make clothing for the slaves and had "ordered" the cloth from a mulatto haberdasher in St. John's. They found dozens of cases hidden among the accounts, and Jane had little doubt that there were more.

While Vincent and Frank organised their arguments, Jane sent Zachary to Nkiruka with a basket of provisions. Consultation with Frank had suggested that that would be rather more appreciated than the letter of condolence she would have sent in England. Zachary returned with Nkiruka's thanks and said that she seemed very low. Jane counted the days until the propriety of mourning would allow her to call.

At the end of the week, Jane's new gown was delivered. It was black, avowedly because they were still in public mourning for Lord Verbury and Garland, but privately Jane wore it in honour of Amey, and for Nkiruka's loss.

As they dressed for dinner, Vincent slowly stiffened. His movements became more precise and controlled. At times, he would halt with a cravat half lifted, or in the act of buttoning his waistcoat, and close his eyes tightly. A line would appear between his brows for a moment, then his eyes would open and he would carry on as though the pause had not occurred.

While Louisa did Jane's hair, she used the mirror to watch Vincent. He scowled as he attempted to tie a second cravat. The first had not pleased him. He stopped in the middle of arranging the silk into a waterfall knot, closed his eyes, and that line reappeared, then deepened.

"Not again." Eyes flying open, he covered his mouth and strode to the balcony door.

"Vincent?"

He shook his head when she rose to follow him, holding up a finger to indicate he needed a moment. On the balcony, that same hand dipped into the ether and he vanished. Even the sound of his footsteps cut off.

"Louisa, I think that will do." He would almost certainly not want her to witness this and report it to his father. "Thank you."

In the mirror, Louisa glanced at the balcony and then curtsied. "Yes, madam."

When she had left, Jane picked up the black ostrich plumes, watching the balcony in the mirror. She had all three plumes pinned and trembling above her head before Vincent reappeared. His face was grey, with red splotches on his cheeks. Beads of sweat dotted his brow. He walked back in, carefully not looking at her, and went straight to the washbasin.

"Were you—?"

"Yes." He splashed water on his face. "Better now than during dinner, I suppose."

She stood and poured a glass of water for him, dropping in a slice of lime from the little crystal bowl on the side table. She offered it to him. "I have some ginger as well, if that would help."

"No, thank you." He took the glass of water, though, and carried it out to the balcony. He did not disappear, but rinsed his mouth and spat into the flowers. He turned the tumbler, staring at the water. Grimacing, he scrubbed his hand through his hair as though wiping a thought away. "Will you help me with my cravat? I cannot seem to tie it tonight."

"Of course." Jane went to the drawer where his cravats were kept and pulled out another silk one. "Come in when you are ready and I shall see if I can make you respectable."

"That may require more than a cravat." He took another sip of water.

"Shall I have Louisa follow you with a glamural of youthful vigour?"

He rewarded her with something that might have been a chuckle. "Perhaps she could paint a halo over me?"

"Nothing so explicit. Simply a ray of light emanating from heaven, as if you are favoured by God."

"Ah, for that, I only need you seated at my right hand." Vincent came back inside. His colour was a little better, if a trifle pale. Later, she might ask him how often he had been ill since their arrival, but now her goal was to help him steady himself.

"You flatterer." She held up the cravat. "Will you accept this as a token of my favour?"

"My lady honours me." He gave a deep, full court bow, with a very pretty leg. It was clear that he was pretending to be in good humour, and that the pretence helped him come closer to a state of calm.

She beckoned him. He stood in front of her and bent his

head to let her wrap the silk around his neck. Beneath her hands, his pulse was wild, but he did not flinch as she had been afraid that he would. His composure was tolerably tranquil. She murmured, "I honour you, because you are a very handsome man with well-turned calves."

"Not for my skill? My wit? My inscrutability?"

"Those are admirable, I grant—lift your chin, please—but you must not depreciate the power of well-fitted breeches upon a lady's admiration." She tucked the end through and adjusted the knot into a waterfall of silk. "Though I would argue again that you are insufferable, not inscrutable."

"We return to this." He gave a mock sigh. "I shall have to ask you to prove your case."

"First." She stepped back to admire the knot. "Lower your chin carefully to crease the silk."

He did, and then examined the result in the mirror. Even without his coat on, Vincent cut a dashing figure. "Thank you, Muse."

"Who knew that years of tying glamour would help me with the art of a valet?"

That coaxed a smile that was almost real. He picked up his coat and shrugged into it. "You have managed to avoid the issue of my inscrutability. Therefore, I must assume that you tacitly acknowledge that I am."

Jane came up behind him and slipped her arms around his waist. She had to lean forward a little to reach past her own increasing waist. "To be inscrutable implies that you are a mystery beyond understanding, am I correct?"

"Yes."

"And yet, I understand how to make you laugh." With that, Jane tickled him.

The tension that Vincent had been carrying exploded out of him in a laugh from the belly as he bent forward and twisted away from Jane. "I yield! I yield!" He held up his hand, retreating from her. "Careful, or you shall make me wrinkle my cravat."

"We would not want that." Jane smiled. "Not until later."

Vincent's expression changed, softening, and he crossed the room in two quick strides. Pulling her into his arms, he bent his head to kiss her. His skin, fresh shaven for the evening, was soft against her and tasted of lavender. The kiss was chaste at first, and then deepened.

It would not be accurate to say that they left the room immediately. Jane's ostrich plumes needed to be reseated and Vincent required a fourth cravat. Nor would it be correct to say that all their good humour survived the walk to the dining hall.

Zachary waited in his livery, ready to serve, but was the room's only other occupant. The table was set with places for four. Jane's brow contracted. Lord Verbury had invited them to dine with him but had not mentioned a guest, and yet one was clearly expected.

As they waited, the squeak of Lord Verbury's chair caused Vincent's shoulders to set. He pressed Jane's hand where it rested against his arm. Vincent dipped his head to murmur, "If Sir Ronald is our fourth, we shall take our leave."

She lay her free hand on top of his and murmured. "I love you very much. If you should have . . . difficulty, look at me and remember that."

He gave a sad smile. "Ah . . . I am not inscrutable after all. You know me too well for that." He inhaled, and his posture transformed into that young man of fashion who was so foreign to her. The elegant, erect carriage, the easy grace of his stride, the expression of good breeding—all of them belonged to some other man.

That man inclined his head as Lord Verbury appeared in the door, pushed by Miss Sarah. Vincent's voice was modulated and civil, without being coldly formal. "Good evening. Thank you for inviting us."

"Thank you for accepting." With an awkward twist, Lord Verbury waved his bad hand. "We have few options for dining in company these days."

With a smile, Jane released Vincent's arm. "Then let us hope that this is the first of many agreeable evenings." She clasped her hands under her stomach in a pose that she had learned made her increasing figure even more apparent.

As she had hoped, Lord Verbury's gaze was drawn there for a moment, though not so long as to be improper. He allowed a small smile to answer hers. "Let me perform the introductions, then. You have not had the opportunity to meet Sarah, who has been my preserver during this ordeal."

"It is lovely to meet you." Jane covered her surprise at the introduction and stepped forward to meet his mistress as a peer. It seemed that she was to be their fourth, though Jane could not imagine Lord Verbury inviting a mulatto to the table in London, slave or no. Even here, Lord Verbury had not granted her a surname or title, as though to make her position clear. Still, Jane resolved to use at least the style that she had heard from Louisa and call her "Miss Sarah."

Jane had taken the opportunity offered by the ledgers to gather some information about Miss Sarah. She had borne Lord Verbury four children in addition to Frank and Zachary. Only three had survived childhood. The remaining child was a daughter, Milly, who served as an upper maid in the house. Lord Verbury had sired other children by other women, but not so many as Jane had at first thought.

Regardless of Miss Sarah's official station as a slave, it was clear that Lord Verbury regarded her as something more by the very fact that he ate dinner with her. She lowered her head and curtsied to welcome them. Her elegance would grace any ball in London, even at her advanced years. "My lady is very gracious. His lordship has spoken of you often." It was the first opportunity Jane had to hear her speak. Her voice had the broad vowels and soft consonants of an Antiguan, without any traces of an affected British accent. It was beautifully modulated and even that short speech flowed like a stream.

"Shall we sit and become better acquainted?" Vincent gestured to the table, which sparkled under a profusion of silver and crystal.

Zachary stepped forward to take Lord Verbury's chair from Miss Sarah. As he wheeled it to the empty space at the head of the table, Vincent pulled out the chair at the foot of the table for Miss Sarah. Jane went to stand next to the chair at Lord Verbury's right and waited for Zachary to assist her. Vincent sat opposite, and, in very short order, they were assembled.

The soup course proceeded with cautious conversation. As a group, they all seemed to be committed to the most unobjectionable of topics and confined the discussion to the flavour of the soup and the preparation of turtles. Jane offered compliments to Lord Verbury for his selection of a chef, and he returned those to Miss Sarah, who had handled the interviews while he was in England. The conversation nearly faltered there, because they were obliged to discuss the difficulties of finding a good chef here and the comparisons to those who could be engaged in London. That seemed certain to bring to them to a discussion of why Lord Verbury was confined here, but Miss Sarah managed to divert them by making a comparison to the different climes, and then artfully shifted the topic entirely to one of the local weather in Antigua.

There are few topics safer than a discussion of the weather. All can agree that it is too hot or too cold, or that it should certainly be more agreeable if only it would rain or cease raining, depending on the circumstances.

As the first course was laid, Jane found herself saying, "I was surprised in Venice, to discover how grey and cold it was in the autumn. There were days in which I thought I should never be warm again, so to find myself here is quite lovely."

"You must be careful of the heat, though." Lord Verbury lifted his glass of claret. "I should not wish to see you overcome again."

The atmosphere in the room changed almost imperceptibly. Jane paused as she sliced her lamb. "That was unfortunate. You may be certain that I have learned not to go out without a parasol."

"Yes, the shade helps." Miss Sarah took a delicate bite of turbot. "Hm . . . Cook has outdone herself with the turbot. Have you tried it yet? Zeus, please do take the plate down to his lordship."

Vincent slid a piece of that same turbot across his plate. He had been artfully arranging his meal and lifting his fork at correct intervals, but Jane was not certain he had taken more than three mouthfuls all evening. "Everything really is quite wonderful. In general, I must say that I have been very impressed with how the great house has been run."

"But not the rest of the estate?" Lord Verbury raised his brow.

"I can hardly compliment Miss Sarah on the rest of the estate, and I thought that some of the credit for the house belonged to her." Vincent reached for his glass of claret. "Speaking of compliments . . . your cellar, sir, is everything I recalled it to be. Some excellent vintages. Truly."

The side of Lord Verbury's mouth twisted into a half smile, as if he was acknowledging the successful change in subject rather than the compliment. He lifted his own glass and offered a toast in return. "I have always believed in proper management of barrels. However, the credit for this vintage belongs in part to your grandfather, who had the foresight to lay down wine for me." He swirled the glass, watching the deep, sanguine liquid legs drip back down the crystal. "I have endeavoured to do the same for the next generation. You should . . . you should feel free to add to it."

"Thank you." Vincent regarded his father before lifting the glass to him. "I shall."

Jane let out a slow, careful breath. Though the conversation had, on the surface, appeared to be about wine, in a very real sense what they had been discussing was dynasty. It was a very small part of the negotiation that this dinner represented, but Jane nevertheless felt a great deal of relief to have any agreement between the two men.

The conversation continued on the topic of food and wine for some time, with Lord Verbury even sharing an amusing story of a dinner with an ambassador from the Ottoman Empire and a blunder his lordship had made when young, involving an embarrassing mistake in translation. That he was willing to share a story and invite them to laugh at him, Jane marked as a great victory. She still did not trust him, but she acknowledged that he could be a charming conversationist when it suited.

Vincent's countenance began to open, and he shared a story about his first experience with an Italian pasta dish called *vermicelli*, which was a flour paste drawn out in long threads. "You would think that, as a glamourist, I would be able to handle multiple strands, but no matter how I twisted my fork, it would all slip off and then splash in the sauce, which was a shocking red. My cravat looked as if I had been shot."

Lord Verbury wiped his eyes, laughing. "Oh . . . my first encounter with it when I took my Grand Tour went much the same way. Except that it was a sauce made from squid ink. Delicious, but very black. You could have mistaken me for an apprentice clerk who was soon to be let go for wasting ink." He turned to Jane. "Did you have the opportunity to try *vermicelli* in Venice?"

"No, the local cuisine largely favours a dish called *polenta*, which is a sort of porridge made from corn meal and cream. It is buttery, delightful, and eaten with a spoon."

Miss Sarah sat back in her chair as Zachary cleared the first course and prepared to turn the table. "Oh, yes—tell us more about Venice. Mrs. Whitten lent me a copy of Lord Byron's *Childe Harold*, and I was enchanted by his descriptions of the canals."

"To be honest, we did not spend much time playing the tourist." Partly because they had been there to work, and Jane did not wish to open a discussion with Lord Verbury of either glamour or of their business with the glassmakers in Murano.

As Zachary laid the clean cloth on the table, Vincent shifted in his seat and directed the conversation back to his father. "Did you make it to Venice on your tour? It must have been astonishing before the fall of the Republic."

"Alas, no. I chose to go to Cyprus instead." Lord Verbury cleared his throat. "Speaking of Venice, Pridmore tells me that you dissuaded his wife from a glamural of Venice for the charity ball."

"I—yes." Vincent's shoulders tightened ever so slightly.

Jane sat forward to draw Lord Verbury's attention away from Vincent. "We are doing an homage to the Northwest Passage expedition. Have you read anything about it?"

Miss Sarah smiled. "Oh yes. I saw that in the newspaper. Ah—here is Zeus with the second course."

As Zachary carried in the dishes for that course and set them on the table, the conversation turned again to the quantity and quality of the food and gave them safe ground for some time.

Miss Sarah sent the dish of sliced pineapple around to Jane. "Please have more. It is accounted to be excellent for an expectant mother."

Discussing her expectant condition openly in mixed company caused Jane's cheeks to warm. At home a woman's state was only ever alluded to as being "in a family way."

Jane lowered her gaze as if more embarrassed than she was but silently thanked Miss Sarah for reminding his lordship of Jane's state. The blush could only make the topic seem more artless. This was the first time that Jane had ever had the occasion to thank her transparent complexion.

It was interesting to see that she and Miss Sarah had a mutual goal. "We have not wished you joy, yet." Lord Verbury lifted his glass. "To your health."

The glasses flashed in the candlelight as each member of their small dinner party joined in the toast. Jane blushed again, in more earnest, and murmured, "Thank you."

Setting his glass down, Lord Verbury turned to his son. "Have you thought of names?"

"Some. . . . Nothing we have settled upon."

"I should like to make the request again that you consider Frederick." He held up his hand to forestall any protest. "It was my father's name as well, so he need not be named for me."

"I will take that under consideration."

"You do not need to decline so quickly."

"I merely said that we would consider it."

"Recall who taught you how to say 'no' without using the word."

Jane laughed, trying to lighten the moment. "I do not think we shall be able to name the child until we meet him. My own father was originally to be a Gilbert, but upon his birth my grandparents decided that the name did not suit and chose Charles instead."

Lord Verbury snorted. "If all children were named in that manner, they would all have the names of drunken old men, for I have never seen a baby yet who did not appear thus."

Vincent inclined his head. "You may have something there."

"Children grow into their names. Your first mark of shaping them is by your choice of names." He nodded to Vincent. "Vincent Daniel St. Lawrence Erasmus Hamilton. It has a balance and masculine rhythm to it, but you see how I had to offset the weakness of the first name with the latter ones?"

"I have always liked the name Vincent." Jane applied herself to the asparagus in front of her. She had expected to spend the evening helping Vincent govern his temper, but her own was in danger of expressing itself. "I thought it was lovely that you chose to honour his maternal grandparents by using their surname in that manner."

"His mother expressed such a wish for it that I could not do otherwise." Lord Verbury smiled and for once looked the very picture of a proud father. "And he has certainly grown into it."

One might almost miss the cut and mistake it for a mark of affection, but Jane could not overlook the fact that he had so recently expressed an opinion that the name "Vincent" was weak.

Her husband replied, "I shall have to write to my Latin professor to let him know that he was incorrect about the definition *vincere*. I had been taught my name had the root 'to conquer,' but now I find it means 'weakness.' Of course, I should not be surprised, since 'Erasmus' means beloved."

Verbury cocked his head in acknowledgement. "Looking at the root of a word is much like looking at the roots of a tree. The foundation is important, but even a tree with a strong root can still bear sickly fruit if it is subject to mismanagement."

Jane looked across the table hoping to catch Vincent's eye. "The naming of children is such an *inscrutable* thing."

Vincent had been giving his plate an intense scrutiny, but now lifted his gaze to meet hers. The corners of his mouth tightened in the slightest hint of a smile. "It does seem so.

Besides . . . it may be a girl, and then all this consideration of boys' names will be for nothing."

Lord Verbury waved for Zachary to clear his plate. "For now, perhaps, but this will hardly be your only child since you have given up glamour."

Vincent stopped, fork half raised and set it down again. "I beg your pardon?"

"It cannot have escaped your notice." Lord Verbury sat back in his chair in frank astonishment. "Good lord. It has."

"Your meaning is obscure."

"Surely, you can consult a calendar as well as the next man. You were travelling and not working when your wife conceived. There is a reason glamour is considered a 'womanly' art, after all."

The muscle in the corner of Vincent's jaw bunched. He swallowed and turned his attention to Miss Sarah. "Speaking of glamour, I must thank you for training Louisa. She has been a great help to my wife."

"There it is . . ." Lord Verbury shook his head and sighed.

"What?"

"Nothing. Nothing . . ." He leaned towards Jane and lowered his voice as if he were confiding in her. "I forget that he is a tender soul, and I have made the mistake of pushing too hard in the past. It is unnatural for a father to not want his son to excel, but I must remember that he does not like difficult conversations and respect that."

Vincent tilted his head and gave a short smile. "I have not avoided them while here."

"No . . . I suppose not." Lord Verbury rested one finger along his cheek and regarded his son. "Shall we excuse the ladies, so that we can drink our port and discuss your concerns?"

"Perhaps that is best, as we are starting to move that way already." Vincent laid his serviette carefully on the table and slid his chair back. He rose to help Miss Sarah, while Zachary came around to assist Jane with her chair. She rather wished it had been Vincent, but given the nature of the dinner she could not expect it.

If she felt half the strain that Vincent did, she did not know how he managed. Her heart stammered against her ribs and she had to keep one hand on the table to steady herself while the grey spots clouded the edges of her vision. She would not faint. Not here. Not in front of his father. Jane smiled. "I shall be glad of an opportunity to better acquaint myself with Miss Sarah."

"Yes, the evening has been so pleasant. Do not keep yourselves from us too long, gentlemen." Miss Sarah put a hand gently on Vincent's arm and said, "I hope you will oblige us with a *tableau vivant* this evening. Your father speaks so highly of your work."

"You will have me take you for a flatterer." Vincent bowed over her hand with the fluidity of a courtier.

"Ah . . . but I do praise you." Lord Verbury lifted his chin. "I may not have wanted you to pursue glamour, but you have always been good at it."

Vincent's face stilled with a casual smile etched upon it. He stood with his chin tucked into his collar and his hands clasped behind his back. "I appreciate your consideration in saying so. *Now.*"

That conversation was not going to end well. Jane walked to the end of the table in order to break Vincent's gaze on his father. Affecting a light tone, she said, "You gentlemen are speaking too much of the ineffable art of glamour! You must leave some of the conversation for us."

"Yes, Frederick." Miss Sarah shook her finger at him with a little smile. "Promise me that you will not discuss glamour without us."

Both men made the same sort of little inhale, as if they had been called back into themselves. The similarity of movement made the hair on the nape of Jane's neck stand on end.

Vincent ducked his head—not a tucking of the chin, but a gesture of submission—as he reached into his coat and pulled a set of papers from the interior pocket. "Rest assured, we shall only discuss men's business."

Across the room, Lord Verbury inclined his head towards Miss Sarah in a similar gesture. "I promise, Sarah. No discussion of glamour without you."

Jane followed Miss Sarah into the parlour, very much wishing that she were staying in the room with Vincent. Never had the proprieties of being a lady been more vexing than now, with the necessity of retiring to the parlour. Nothing of note ever happened there.

Twenty-two

Constant Vigilance

No sooner had Zachary shut the door behind them than Miss Sarah turned to Jane. The easy smile she had worn throughout dinner dropped and she reached for Jane's hand. "Thank you. Thank you so much for freeing my son." The exquisite modulation that had marked her conversation vanished in a tremor. "I could not mention the subject during dinner, but you must imagine my profound gratitude."

"Of course. We could do no less."

Miss Sarah gave a bitter laugh. "I know for a fact that is not true." She glanced at the clock upon the sideboard. "Shall we sit and pretend to be at our leisure? We have perhaps twenty minutes before one of them suffers a defect of temper, and there is much that we should discuss."

"Twenty? You may be more hopeful than I."

Laughing, Miss Sarah wiped her eyes. "Only because I know that Frederick is trying." She gestured to the small sofa set near the window. "Vincent is astonishingly like his father."

"They seem very different to me."

"Given the conditions in which you have met Frederick, I am not surprised." With a sigh, Miss Sarah sat and arranged her dress around her. "I will grant that their interests are very different, but their headstrong nature and temper bear the same stamp."

Slowly, Jane sat on the sofa beside her. "Vincent has never hit anyone, and would not."

Miss Sarah raised a single brow. "You did not see him with Sir Ronald?"

Jane barely had memories of Vincent entering the room that night, but she had seen his hand and the deep bruises upon it. She had seen the lingering rage in his eyes. "But . . . under the circumstances—"

"Frederick always feels justified as well." Miss Sarah glanced at the clock again. "And there is real anger between them, which dinner will not be enough to cool. But—we have other things to discuss."

Jane could not help but compare Miss Sarah with Vincent's mother, the Countess of Verbury. The only other time Jane had dined with Vincent's father, she had progressed to the parlour with the countess and the other ladies. Both the countess and Miss Sarah were elegant and had retained their beauty in their later years. But the countess had been placidly elegant and directed the public conversation away from any topic that might have even a touch of contention. Miss Sarah, in spite of the controlled composure she had exhibited during dinner, showed real emotion. Jane would have expected that, as a slave, she would have been more assiduous about avoiding any topics which might endanger her, but Miss Sarah had been direct.

"What would you like to discuss?"

Miss Sarah bit her lips and lowered her voice. "I can mimic Frederick's hand. When you go—and I know you will the moment the baby is born—will you take Louisa with you? I know it involves asking you to deliberately lie, but will you please?"

"Only Louisa? Why not your other grandchildren?"

"I do not worry about them in the same way. Louisa is too pretty. She done catch Mr. Pridmore eye. He has been kept from her only by constant vigilance."

Jane had seen that interest firsthand and it turned her stomach. "Of course. But I want to also reassure you that Mr. Pridmore is on his way out."

Miss Sarah shook her head. "No. . . . Vincent and Frank found evidence of embezzling?"

"Yes. So you see, Mr. Pridmore no longer has a hold over Lord Verbury."

"He never has." She leaned towards Jane and lowered her voice. "Frederick told him to do it."

Jane stared at her and was aware that her mouth had dropped open. "But . . . but to what purpose? If he wished to pay Pridmore more, why not simply increase his salary?"

"Because Frederick is supposed to be dead. It was presented, of course, as a way of thanking him, with the understanding that Garland would raise his salary when he arrived. But, of course, it was also to create a lever to use against Mr. Pridmore." She clasped her hands together and addressed one of the walls, as though she had gone mad. "I am sorry, Frank. Frederick did not tell me until he and I were dressing for dinner."

Frank was clearly standing in one of the coldmonger's boxes and had likely been there all evening. Jane's instinct was to rise, throw open the door, and pull Vincent bodily from the room. Her mind churned, trying to put together the information that Miss Sarah had presented to her. "But why would he invite us to dinner if he had no intention of agreeing to fire Mr. Pridmore?"

"Because he wanted to see you."

One of the candles on the sideboard fluttered out, caught in a sudden breeze. A thin trail of smoke bent away from the wall.

Miss Sarah glanced from the smoking candle to the door as if it were a signal. "They are coming out." She leaned back on the sofa and composed her features into an easy smile. "The fashion plates from London show such a widening of silhouette that I have half expected hoops to make a return."

The fact that Jane was sitting on the sofa with her back to the door now seemed like a calculation by Miss Sarah. It was appreciated, as Jane could not quite match her ease of manner, though she did manage to appear tolerably tranquil when the doors opened. "I had no complaints when my dressmaker in Vienna suggested corded petticoats, because the extra warmth was appreciated. Here, though, the fashion seems at odds with the climate. I find myself longing for the simple white muslin of my youth."

The faint squeak of Lord Verbury's chair rolled into the room. Miss Sarah smiled and made a show of mock displeasure. "Now we shall have to leave off. The gentlemen will have no interest in a discussion of the most feminine of arts."

"Flirtation?" Lord Verbury chuckled.

Jane turned on the sofa to face the gentlemen. Zachary pushed Lord Verbury's chair into the room. Vincent entered slightly behind them. His chin was buried in his cravat and his hands clasped so tightly behind him that she could see the strain in his shoulders. He met her gaze and held it as a drowning man holds a rope.

"Flirtation is an art that belongs to both sexes." Jane's pulse thundered in the joints of her hands.

"Then perhaps we should turn to an art that is yours exclusively?" Lord Verbury raised a brow. "We were promised a *tableau vivant*."

Jane could not hear Vincent's thin keen of protest. Nor, with the armour of his coat, could she see him hold his breath, but both must have happened in the face of such a request, delivered in such a manner. Verbury's ability to turn any comment into a blade was staggering. With the knowledge that continuing the conversation would do nothing to promote their cause, Jane could find no reason to remain.

"I do hate to break up the evening early, but I am afraid fatigue has been getting the better of me these last few weeks."

Lord Verbury frowned. "Do not let us keep you, then. Although I will ask you to indulge me and let me retain my son for a while. You do not mind, do you, Vincent?"

"I am your servant, as always."

"Of course." Absolutely not. Jane would not leave her husband with that man any longer. But she could do nothing obvious without betraying Miss Sarah's confidence. "Do not keep him too late, though—we have a glamural to work on tomorrow."

The feminine arts contained many permutations, and Jane found this moment an ideal time to exercise one of her mother's favourites. She stood, took a step away from the couch and the small table and into a clear area on the dense carpet, and let herself tumble to the ground in a faint.

The response was immediate.

Vincent shouted her name and sprang across the room. As he knelt beside her, Jane forced herself to stay limp, while wishing she could signal to him that it was entirely feigned. Miss Sarah called for Frank, but Jane suspected that she recognised the ruse.

In moments, Vincent had lifted her. "Send for Dr. Jones, please."

Jane fluttered her eyes open. "No . . . it was only a faint." She kept her voice weak but pressed her hand against his chest as firmly as she could. He looked down sharply and she thought, but was not certain, that he understood. "You know how easily I have fainted since . . . since I was bled. I only stood too quickly, as I did in Murano."

"It is common with expectant mothers." Miss Sarah stood behind them. "It happened frequently when I was with Zeus."

Lord Verbury grunted in response, no doubt studying Vincent and Jane closely.

Vincent's frown deepened as he studied her. "I will insist on staying with you."

"I want nothing else." She leaned her head against his chest and took comfort in his warmth and solidity.

Without another word, Vincent carried her towards their rooms. Frank met them in the passage, appearing from a hidden panel in one wall. He held the door for Vincent, face tight with concern, though Jane thought it was about what he had overheard more than her state.

Only when they were safely in the room with the door shut behind them did Jane lift her head. "You may set me down. It was entirely feigned."

"When you mentioned Murano, I hoped as much." In spite of that, Vincent set her down on the bed, not on her feet. "Since you never fainted there."

In fact, she had fainted in Murano, but this was perhaps not the best time to enlighten him on that front. "I am sorry I could not alert you ahead of time."

"Understandable." He brushed a strand of hair off her brow. "Now . . . why?"

Jane sat up and met Frank's eyes. "You heard?"

He nodded and pulled out a chair at the table. He rested

his hands on the back of it and regarded Vincent. "Will you sit?"

Looking very grave, Vincent sat at the table across from him. As Frank explained what his mother had said, Jane rose from the bed slowly and kept her hand on the bedpost as she did. The last thing she needed to do was faint in earnest. She crossed the room and sank into the chair next to Vincent. Frank's account was quick and methodical. As he spoke, Vincent's face grew more grave, and new lines appeared around the edges of his mouth.

When Frank finished, Vincent bent forward and rested his head on his hands. "We should not have freed Zachary."

Jane was at a loss to see how he could have reached that conclusion from Frank's recital. "But it puts him, at least, beyond Pridmore's reach."

"But we have done it with forged papers." He had never sounded so dispirited.

Frank cursed a moment later, as he apparently understood something that remained opaque to Jane. How could the papers be forged, when Lord Verbury had given them to Vincent? She chilled as comprehension took her. Because Lord Verbury's handwriting had changed after the stroke, Miss Sarah had drawn up the papers. It would be easy for him to claim that they were counterfeits. The resemblance to Mr. Pridmore and the embezzled funds became clear. Lord Verbury had caught them by encouraging them to commit a criminal activity. If Vincent had merely held the deed and done nothing with it, that would have been one thing, but his father could have made an accurate guess that Vincent would free the young man. Once the manumission entered into the public record, it became a different matter.

Vincent wrapped his fingers in his hair. "I had thought that my very public break with my family would protect me from being seen in collusion, but that same history will be very good for presenting a case that I kept my father a prisoner."

"But he is still a traitor," Jane protested. "That has not changed—"

"I hope not." Vincent sat up, rubbing his brow. "But I cannot help remembering that the reason he was caught during the coldmonger's affair was because his papers were entered into evidence. If there is a forger . . . with the right solicitor and the right judge, there is no telling what he might accomplish."

"But this is far-fetched, surely." And yet, as she spoke, she could see the webs of intrigue as clearly drawn as the lines of a glamour. "Surely this has not all been to get you here and create a case that you forged the papers used in the trial."

"I do not know. It may be an action of opportunity, or perhaps he is merely manoeuvring out of habit, and wants nothing more than to ensure that I do not take him back to England to face trial." The tension seemed to have drained out of him, leaving only exhaustion behind. Every line in his figure bent down. Vincent pushed himself out of the chair. "Now, if you will excuse us, Frank."

Rising, Frank showed every evidence of confusion, but

settled back into his role as house steward quickly. "Of course. If there is anything you require, please let me know."

"I shall. Thank you." He walked Frank to the door and closed it behind him. Then Vincent leaned his head against the wood. When Jane stood, he did not acknowledge the sound of her chair sliding back, nor the rustle of her gown. Cautiously, Jane rested her hand against his back. Through his coat, the steady rhythm of his heart soothed her. Jane had expected it to be racing, but it beat as though he might actually be calm.

He lifted his head, and turned to her. "Do you trust Frank?"

Jane's first instinct was to answer that she did, but she paused to consider before speaking. "When we first arrived, I did not, but I do now. I take it you do not?"

"I do not know." Running his hand through his hair, he shook his head. "I had a realisation during dinner about why it took me so long to be comfortable with your family, and before that with Herr Scholes."

"Oh?"

"I could not believe that their warmth was genuine. I kept looking for hidden mockery and insult. There were none. I am having the same thoughts about Frank now." Grimacing, he dipped a hand in the ether and began rolling a thread of yellow between his fingers. "I am aware that my judgement is poor right now, but . . . but the thoughts are still there."

To live with so little trust would destroy Jane, and it was breaking Vincent. She had been watching the slow erosion of his sense of self and worth without any ability to halt its progress. The revelations tonight had left Jane staggered, and she suspected that there were still more things undiscovered. Almost worse was the understanding that this want of trust was how Vincent had lived for years before breaking away from his family. It repulsed her. The baby kicked against her side, and she put her hand there to try to soothe it.

Vincent caught the motion. "Are you all right? Truly?"

"Your child is practising pugilism tonight." She slid her hand into his and pulled it against her stomach so he could feel.

He bent his head, closing his eyes as their child beat a protest against Jane's side. The hand that had been working glamour stilled and let the thread dissolve. Against Jane's stomach, the warm pressure of Vincent's hand comforted her, and, just for a moment, nothing beyond them mattered.

Then his composure crumpled. The panic he had hidden earlier twisted his features into a tight grimace. With a ragged growl, Vincent pulled his hand free and shoved away from the door, putting his back to Jane. He strode to the table and leaned against the back of one of the chairs with his head bowed. Even through his coat, she could see the tension in his back. He stood like that for a moment and then slammed his palms against the wood. "God. This is tiresome."

He was not addressing her, she thought, but rather speaking to himself. That Vincent had not woven a *Sphère*

Obscurcie and hidden she took as a sign of trust, which, after this evening seemed infinitely more precious. Jane crossed to stand behind him, careful not to touch him in this state. "What may I do?"

Still leaning against the chair, he shook his head. For a moment, he held his breath, and then let it out in a slow, careful stream. "Muse, I am sorry you have to witness this."

"I hope you know by now that I do not mind it."

"Nevertheless, it is embarrassing."

"Embarrassing? What am I doing to make you feel embarrassed?"

"It is my own inability to govern myself. What do I truly have to weep over? That my father spoke harshly to me? That he forbade me to use glamour as a boy? I go about the estate and I see men and women who are beaten and living in the most execrable of conditions and bear it. Yet I am unmanned by . . . dinner?"

Jane held out her hand so he could take it or not as he chose. "Come sit down with me?"

Slowly, so very slowly, Vincent straightened. He did not meet her gaze, but, even so, she could tell that the rims of his eyes were reddened. Jane bit the inside of her cheek and kept her hand out. After too long a moment, Vincent slipped his hand into hers. His palm was slick with sweat and he trembled a little.

Jane led him to the sofa and pulled him to sit down beside her. She retained his hand and the other rested on his thigh. "You know it is more than that. You have been under a very great strain since we received the letter from

Richard, and you had not, I think, fully recovered from Murano."

He did not reply, but neither did he deny that.

"I am going to suggest that the stress of our situation is not going to dissipate until well after the baby is born. If you continue to try to contain the . . . the struggle within yourself, I do not think you will survive."

"It is not so bad as that."

"How often have you been sick since our arrival?"

He bowed his head and that muscle in his jaw tightened. She could almost see him building a reply word by word. Long practise kept her silent, giving him space to answer. Vincent grimaced and opened his mouth twice before speaking. "I will grant that the appearance can be alarming, because you have not seen me go through this before."

"Even if I had, I should be alarmed. But you did not answer my question."

"Five."

That gave her more than a little pause. They had been in Antigua for a month, and Vincent had been ill more than once per week. "To give me some context, how often—as an adult—did that happen before coming here?"

He tilted his head to the side and his eyes moved as though counting motes of dust. "Four." Looking down, he rubbed his free hand along his breeches. "I take your meaning."

"Vincent . . . love. This is destroying you."

"What do you propose I do?"

She slid her arm around his back and pulled herself closer.

"The difficulty is not you. The difficulty is your father, and some difficulties are insolvable."

The air hissed out of him in that small thin whine and his hand tightened in hers. The other one clenched into a fist. "It is difficult to see things that I know are broken and could be made better, such as the boilers, or the slaves' conditions, or the embezzling, and not attempt to affect a change."

"*Can* you make changes? When you try to run the estate, he impedes your efforts. It does not seem to me to be anything except a means by which to further degrade you." She paused to let him consider that, then said, "Why do you keep handing him weapons to use against you?"

Vincent's breath was shallow and rough. Beneath her hand, he trembled like a snared bird, but somehow he kept his countenance calm save for a contraction of the brow. He stared into the middle distance, gaze darting from nothing to nothing.

After some moments, he wet his lips and swallowed. "You are correct. If I keep engaging, there can only be Pyrrhic victories." He nodded slowly, and his breathing steadied. "He will, of course, see this as one more example of running away."

"I know." It pained her to see him struggle, but to hear Vincent say that he would not engage with his father was an immeasurable relief.

"I cannot win."

"I think you just did." Jane lifted his hand and kissed the tips of his fingers.

Twenty-three

To Be a Glamourist

When Jane awoke the next morning, Vincent was already up and sitting at the table in their room. He wore his nightshirt, which she hoped meant that he had spent at least some time asleep, though she had no memory of him coming to bed. When he saw her sit up, he greeted her with a smile, as though nothing had happened the night before. His only nod to the events was to make arrangements to go with her to the Whitten estate rather than working with Frank as he had originally planned. Indeed, throughout the morning, Vincent seemed resolute in pretending that they had nothing more pressing than working on the glamural.

In moments when he thought he was unobserved, the ease of his manner vanished, and it was clear that his spirits were oppressed. But whenever Jane or anyone else spoke to him, he rallied and made every effort to seem unaffected.

Jane wanted to shake him.

But she also honoured Vincent for attempting to prevent his father from having an effect on him, so for their trip to the Whitten estate, she would let him be only a glamourist again. Having nothing to think of but where a fold was placed seemed a luxury beyond measure.

As the day passed, however, Jane began to reconsider the pleasures of working on a glamural. She bent over the table that Mrs. Whitten had supplied for her drawings. It felt decidedly strange to be surrounded by people working glamour and to confine herself to paper, but there was nothing for it. In truth, the glamourists from Mrs. Ranford's and Mrs. Whitten's estates had a degree of craft that would be enviable in London. There was Jeannette, whose skill with finer weaves was wasted as a field slave. Imogene had an exquisite sense of colour that served her well as a lady's maid. Indeed, the largest challenge was that many of the glamourists could only be spared from their duties for a few hours at a time, so much of Jane's effort was spent in managing the work.

Tilting her head to the side, Jane considered the ice floe she had planned to surround the stairs to the balcony. A *répétition mousseux* would provide the necessary transparency while appearing solid, but it might be too busy to have it as well as columns of ice going up on the bannisters.

Vincent's footsteps approached the table, and a shadow

fell across her page. "Muse . . ." Beads of sweat stood upon his brow from the glamour he had been doing that morning. She suspected he was suffering from the heat more than usual, since he had kept his coat on due to the presence of ladies. He leaned on the table as though consulting with her about the plans and wove a muddied silence around them. "What are we going to do about Mrs. Ransford?"

Jane lifted her head. "Oh dear."

The pale woman stood at the side of the ballroom working on one of the ice columns. Jane had based that part of the design on a memory of visiting an icehouse on one of the grand estates for which she and Vincent had created a glamural. Packed in layers of sawdust lay milky blocks of ice harvested from the estate during the winter. The translucent striations of white and pale blue had put Jane in mind of an ethereal marble. She had intended to suggest that sense of marbling in the columns, but use the translucence to allow parts of the original ballroom to show through.

What Mrs. Ransford had rendered had the correct shape, but was an opaque white with dark blue streaks. "Perhaps she is not finished?"

"And how would you thin the folds to create the translucence at this stage without spoiling the form?"

Jane sighed, knowing he was right. "Oh—wait. Perhaps if one were to use the blue streaks to create fissures. . . . Imagine using an anchor thread here, like so, to bend the blue around."

Jane moved her hands in the motions that she would use if working glamour, but kept herself carefully free of the ether. She held her left hand out at the angle of one of the blue striations. With her other hand, she turned the palm flat to the floor and pushed it under her forearm as though sliding a curtain aside.

"You see? By taking hold of the blue and white together, we might stretch it into a gossamer weight into the column. It should actually provide some depth, and . . . in fact, if we use Nkiruka's muddling, as she does with the muddied silence, we might even get some diffraction." Jane squinted at the air, trying to imagine the effect without actually looking into the ether. "Do you think that would . . . what?"

Vincent had the most interesting consciousness about him. A slight smile played at his lips. Compressing his lips, he shook his head and looked away.

"Why are you smiling?"

When his gaze returned, a flush of warmth swept over Jane at the brightness in his eyes. He leaned in so that his breath brushed her cheek. "When you work, you develop the most becoming furrow between your brows. I was distracted."

It was a very great pity that they were standing in the middle of a ballroom. Jane's knees felt weak enough that she rather thought she would like to lie down. She swallowed. "I am hardly working at all."

"Hm. It is perhaps best for me that you are not. Now, your idea . . ." He pulled a fold of white out of the ether and stretched it as she had suggested. "Huh. That could . . . you would need to add a glaze on the exterior—say, something like a Chatel finish, to give a lustre. I think."

He could be so wicked at times. "You are correct. Otherwise it will have a matte finish, which is all wrong."

Vincent wiped the experiment from the air. "Do you honestly think that is what she is going to do?"

"Well . . ." Jane studied the column, where Mrs. Ransford was adding another stripe of blue.

"You just came up with a technique that does not even have a name, and you did it without being able to handle folds." He leaned in and whispered in spite of the silence. "You forget how good you are at this."

Blush overspreading her cheeks, Jane bent to study her drawings. "I think she is leaving after tea, so we can tear it out then. I say 'we,' but . . . perhaps Louisa can do it? She is proving to be quite adept, and I think enjoys the work." She glanced over to where the young woman was engaged on another ice column. With her head tilted up, her habitually guarded expression was more open. Even with the abstracted gaze of a glamourist deep in the ether, her eyes were bright with interest. "Meanwhile . . . how to redirect Mrs. Ransford so she does not feel slighted." Jane tapped her pencil against her chin as she considered the designs.

"Perhaps we should ask her to do some reindeer without antlers, and then we might have some credible sled dogs?"

"Please be kind."

"That was." Sliding one of the other drawings over, he indicated the front of the ballroom. "What about your snow curtain? It is central, which should make her feel important.

If she spins the threads, we can always alter the placement later if need be."

"That is a good thought. The snowflakes themselves are not that different in effect from cherry blossoms, and she did do a lovely job with that cherry tree. I will use you as an excuse, since she seems still in awe of 'Sir David.' "

He snorted at that. In spite of Mrs. Pridmore's preference, while working on the glamural Jane had taken to calling Vincent 'Sir David' again, professedly to remind Mrs. Ransford that he was the Prince Regent's glamourist, but truly to remind him of himself.

"You do not mind speaking to her?"

"Given that we want to retain her good opinion, I think that is probably best." Jane patted his arm. "You can be curmudgeonly."

He shook his head and pretended to scowl, but the corners of his eyes creased with a suppressed smile. He unstitched the muddied silence and returned to the folds he had been laying in one of the upper corners of the ballroom. Most glamourists would need a scaffold to reach, but he stretched glamour and threw it into place as if it were the most natural thing in the world.

Jane waited for a few moments so that it was not quite so obvious that they had been discussing Mrs. Ransford. Armed with the drawing of the snow curtain, she approached the woman and waited until she tied off the thread she was working with. "Mrs. Ransford, may I trouble you?"

Breathing quickly, with a flush to her usually pallid cheeks, Mrs. Ransford stepped back from her work.

"I am only too happy to take a break, so please trouble away."

"Would it be possible to move you to a different project?" She showed her the drawing of the snow curtain. "I need a touch of delicacy here, and thinking of your cherry blossoms, I wondered if I could ask you to take this on."

"Certainly." Mrs. Ransford straightened a little. "I should not be much longer with this."

"I can have Jeannette or Louisa finish that for you."

A little frown creased Mrs. Ransford's mouth. She glanced at where the stout, matronly woman was working on one of the other columns. Her eyes narrowed a trifle and slid back to her own work. Jane had the uneasy sense that Mrs. Ransford recognised the inferiority of her own work.

Jane held up the drawing again. "I do not know that Jeannette has the necessary refinement." Though of course, she knew that Jeannette did. "As the centrepiece of the room, it is so important to have it done well. I shall want the curtain in place before Sir David weaves the aurora borealis effect, and I am afraid that he is working faster than I anticipated. I do hate to pull you away, but I do not know who else to ask. I would do it myself, but . . ." She let her sentence trail off as she ran a hand over her increasing stomach, though that hardly needed any attention drawn to it.

Still, her flattery seemed to have the desired effect, because Mrs. Ransford took the drawing from her and looked at the front of the ballroom where the curtain was intended to go. "It goes all the way to the ceiling?"

"I know it is a tremendous distance to span, but Sir David

already laid an anchor thread across the ceiling. The warp threads for the snow are quite thin—filaments, really—so you should be able to fling them over the anchor rather carelessly and then alter their placement afterwards."

Mrs. Ransford's gaze went vacant as she looked into the ether to where Vincent had placed an anchor thread across the ceiling of the ballroom earlier. "It seems as though it is the sort of thing that might be done by rote."

"The spinning of the filaments, yes, but it will need a discerning eye to make the snow fall in a pleasing manner. It must be regular, but not unvarying, with the occasional flurry. . . . Of course, if you want an assistant to help with the weft, then I can arrange that, but you still remain my first choice to oversee it."

"Mm. I can see why you would not trust it to one of the slaves." She sniffed. "Folk glamour can be charming enough, but cannot compare to English training."

"Quite." Behind Mrs. Ransford, Jane caught Dolly rolling her eyes and had to suppress a smile. "Should you like an assistant?" With any luck, Mrs. Ransford would delegate the majority of the work to the assistant, and they would not need to make any changes afterwards.

"No, thank you. I did the whole of the previous glamural with only a little help from the other ladies. Negroes want a tasteful eye."

"Ah. Well. If you change your mind I should be happy to—" She broke off as a movement at the main door of the ballroom caught her attention. Nkiruka stood on the threshold. She had not expected Nkiruka to come, given that she was in mourning. The older woman, who had never been tall, seemed to have shrunk in the three days since Jane had seen her last. Her skin had an ashen cast to it, and her shoulders hunched forward. "Forgive me, but she recently lost her daughter. Do you mind if I . . . ?"

Mrs. Ransford wrinkled her nose. "That is very Christian of you. Go ahead."

Absently handing Mrs. Ransford her drawing, Jane hurried across the floor.

As she approached, Nkiruka gave Jane a smile. "Thought mebbe you need help. Look good."

"Oh, my dear. I am so, so sorry for your loss."

Nkiruka looked down, face twisting a little. She shrugged and shifted her weight. "She gone somewhere better. Miss her." She thumped her chest twice. "But it better so."

The thought that death in childbirth was better than life as a slave could not escape Jane. She compressed her lips in frustration at their inability to effect changes on a large scale at the estate. It was too much to hope that small changes like a blanket or a dress could provide any comfort, but Jane had nothing else to offer. "If there is anything I can do . . ."

"You got work? House too empty. All the picknee an' dem . . ." She shrugged again, shaking her head, which was still inclined towards the floor. "Need something to do."

It would be difficult to find two individuals whose person was more distinct than Nkiruka and Vincent, yet Jane was put very much in mind of him in that moment. "Of course. I should be very glad of your assistance."

Almost immediately, Nkiruka threw herself into the project with vehemence and proved to be an invaluable help. Jane and Vincent usually worked alone, with the occasional use of assistants in the early phases of large glamurals, such as their cloudscape for the Duke of Wellington. That piece was very large and had been commissioned with only two weeks to create it, so they had, by necessity, employed assistants for much of the foundation work. The finish of the piece, however, had just been the two of them.

And yet, Nkiruka's suggestion that they bring in several glamourists from other estates had been entirely correct. From the harvest festivals, Nkiruka knew exactly who the best artists among the slaves were. Mrs. Whitten offered to make contact with the slave owners and arrange for the loan of their labour for the charity, and in short order they had slaves coming in from all parts of Antigua. It was one of the unexpected advantages of being on such a small island.

Nkiruka was present daily and helped Jane make arrangements with the slaves, being well aware of their abilities. After consulting with Frank on the usual practises in Antigua, Jane and Vincent had determined that it would not raise any eyebrows if they were to offer the slaves a small fee for their labour.

Some of these were older women that Nkiruka had suggested Jane speak to about her book, but some were young men or women who were quite gifted. The young women, in particular, had been trained in European-style glamour for their roles as lady's maids, but several had begun by learning Igbo- or Asante-style glamour from their mothers. None of them could be engaged for long, perhaps only two hours one day and then not again for another three days, but it was well worth it. It relieved Jane to have glamourists who could take some of the burden off of Vincent.

Still, she and Vincent were often the last ones to leave the ballroom. He had stopped trying to help at the estate altogether. Whether it was that or sheer exhaustion, he had been sleeping deeply at night. The dark circles under his eyes had begun to fade, and his appetite seemed to have returned.

As they were working one evening, Jane amending her notes by candlelight and Vincent putting the last touches on a frozen waterfall, a sudden boom cracked the air. Jane dropped her quill. It sounded like nothing so much as cannon fire. Vincent spun towards the open doors of the ballroom. He staggered for a moment and caught himself on a chair.

"Vincent!"

"Only dizzy. I turned too quickly, nothing—" He broke off as another crack sounded, this time with a flash of red.

Straightening carefully, he stepped towards the doors, Jane close behind him. Three more of the cracks fired in rapid succession, each accompanied by a different colour of light. Jane relaxed as they walked outside. "Fireworks."

From the prospect of the Whitten estate, they could look south towards English Harbor. From the fort that stood on the hill over the bay, a series of fireworks painted the sky.

Vincent smiled at them for a moment, then sobered. He slipped his arm around Jane and pulled her close. "Let us go back in."

"What is—oh." She had forgotten the date. For most of the United Kingdom of Great Britain, Ireland, and Faerie, the sixteenth of June represented a major holiday. It was the day that Wellington had defeated Napoleon in the Battle of Quatre Bras.

It was also the day that Jane and Vincent had lost their first child.

She pulled his hands down so that his arms went around her stomach. They stood thus, leaning against one another so that it was not possible to say who was supporting whom. Jane leaned back and rested her head against him, caressing his hands where they held her. "It seems strange to think that we would have had a three-year-old with us."

"Mm . . ." He kissed her temple. "I doubt we would have come."

"No. Nor to Murano, for that matter." She sighed. "I might have resented that, but for now all I can think is that after we return to England, I never want to leave home again."

He chuckled. "Travel is not always this fraught. Most of our tour of Europe was completely without incident, your mother's nerves excepted."

"Agreed, though I suppose the presence of a child would at least have made your father more reasonable on the subject of heirs."

"Not—" Vincent cut himself off and sighed, apparently

recognising that it was too late to stop the sentence. "Not really."

Jane had never asked about the sex of their child. She had been too frightened of all that being with child had entailed, so when she miscarried, her guilt made her want to pretend that it had never happened. Vincent must have asked, or been told. "A girl?"

She felt him nod more than saw it. Perhaps because of Melody's son, Jane had somehow expected it to have been a boy. Though her own parents had had only daughters. "Did you name her?"

"It did not seem right to do so without you." He left unsaid that she had not wanted to know.

Knowing that it had been a girl, a daughter, made the loss tangible in ways that it had not been even in the immediate aftermath. Somewhere, among the soldiers who died at the Battle of Quatre Bras, Jane and Vincent had a daughter buried. Jane found herself weeping.

They remained thus until the fireworks had faded and only the stars and moon lit the sky.

They had been at work on the glamural for a little over two weeks and their team of glamourists had developed a good working rhythm. Though the charity ball was only eleven days away, the ice palace showed every sign of being finished on time. The bulk of the large effects were in place, and their efforts had moved to finishing touches.

Jane was outwardly discussing the floor of the glamural with Nkiruka and Louisa, but she was in fact watching Vincent. He was placing the enormous folds that would make the icy ceiling of the palace. Overhead, a deep night sky sparkled with stars that peeked through the aurora borealis. Its greens and purples rippled in slow waves across the length of the ballroom. Though the ceiling of Jane's design had been separated into crystalline fragments, each piece was so large, that even Vincent needed to take frequent breaks as he worked. Glamour's tendency to drift towards the earth before it was tied off made creating the sharp edges of the ice at that distance a challenge.

Vincent had created two of the pieces thus far, and after the second, he had been so dizzy that he had been compelled to sit for a time. Not long enough, Jane thought. His cheeks were still quite flushed.

She became aware that Louisa was waiting for a response. "I am so sorry. I was distracted for a moment. Could you repeat that?"

Nkiruka snorted. "That man of yours, eh?"

"Yes. So sorry. He has a history of overworking himself, and I was trying to decide if I should intervene." Jane resolutely pressed her hands together. "Now . . . Louisa, you had a question about the snow?"

"Yes, madam. I was thinking about the frost on the windows and how we used the Hobbson's pleating to make that and the snow. Could we use it on the floor as well?"

"Instead of the Vantrose plait? It will require longer to place."

"But it slower, so it is not so wearying." Thanks to their efforts on the book, Jane and Nkiruka had a much larger common vocabulary of glamour than when they started. Nkiruka stretched a piece of blue-white glamour between them. "Look. Use *a me ka ọ dị ka mmadu jịrị anya na-ebe akwa ahu uzọ* with your Hobbson's pleating. Is so snow look?" She slid the flat of her palm in a peculiar sideways motion that Jane was eager to try herself. Where her hand passed, the blue-white sparkled into something that looked like thousands of ice crystals.

"Oh—that is much easier than what I had planned. Yes. Let us do that." She glanced to Vincent, who had tied off the folds and stood bent over with hands braced upon his knees. "Will you excuse me?"

With a knowing look, Nkiruka waved her away and returned to conversation with Louisa. Jane hurried across the ballroom as quickly as she could. A run was not possible, but a hurried waddle soon had her by his side. He was panting and sweat-soaked. "Are you all right?"

"Stupidly dizzy." In spite of the speed of his breath, he did not sound distressed. "I keep forgetting that I am out of condition. No glamour for months. Then two weeks back at it."

"Shall I get a chair?"

"I only need a moment." His breathing did seem to be calming. "Oddly, I think I have missed this."

"Missed being dizzy? This may explain much in your work habits."

He chuckled, head still bent down. "Did you not spin in circles when you were a child?"

"Yes. When I was a child." Though her own dizziness had become less frequent, Jane still took care when standing. As much as she rebuked him for overwork, she would rather have a fatigued and laughing Vincent. After the months of seeing him slowly break from the strain of dealing with his father, being merely dizzy seemed a delightful change.

"There is something about pushing to the edge of what one can do . . ." He tilted his head to the side and looked at the ceiling out of the corner of his eye. "It turned out well, though, eh?"

With the panels of crystalline ceiling in place, the edges of ice caught the aurora borealis and refracted the light into glimmering beams. The night sky seemed almost like a velvet setting for jewels, so deep and rich was the blue. He had added pale wispy clouds, just enough to diffuse the light as they drifted across the sky. "It takes one's breath away," Jane said.

"I can vouch for that."

She laughed. "You do make me worry sometimes."

"Since I worry all the time about you, that seems only fair."

"You need only watch me waddle as proof that everything is well." She had passed the seven-month mark, and it seemed their child had celebrated by suddenly increasing in size.

"You do not waddle."

"Then you are not paying attention, for which I am glad."

"I assure you that I most decidedly pay attention when you move, or speak, or laugh. You do not waddle."

"And I assure you that this last week, I have most decidedly begun to waddle. Shall I take a turn around the room to prove it?"

"Muse." His smile, even when his head was upside down, had a decidedly rakish cast. "If you want me to prove that you still have my full attention, it will require the carriage and a return to our chambers. A turn around the room will not suffice."

Blushing, Jane glanced around to see if anyone had heard. Doing so, she spied a horse galloping up to the ballroom. A moment later, Zachary flung himself from the saddle, striking the ground at a run.

"Mr. Hamilton!" The young man burst through the door of the ballroom. "Mr. Hamilton!"

Straightening with alarm, Vincent turned. He took one step and his knees buckled.

Jane reached for him, but he slipped from her grasp and dropped heavily to the ground. With an ungenteel curse, Jane sank to kneel beside him. Unconscious, he lay with his legs splayed awkwardly.

Zachary hurried towards her. Jane raised her head and found Louisa. "Do you know how to weave cold?" she called.

"Yes, madam." With no further instruction, she rushed over and wove a sphere of cool air around Vincent to try to bring his temperature down.

Jane returned her attention to Vincent and, with Zachary's help, eased him onto his back. His collar was already open, and he had long since abandoned his waistcoat, so she could do little to cool him beyond Louisa's efforts. She felt for Vincent's pulse, which was wild and fast.

He groaned and blinked back into consciousness. For a moment, he frowned at the ceiling before comprehension came back into his eyes. Vincent raised a hand to pinch the bridge of his nose. "Well . . . that was appallingly stupid."

For the second time that day, Jane asked, "Are you all right?"

"The room is spinning as if I were on a pirate ship, but other than that, yes, I am well." He lowered his hand and held it up for her to see. "No shakes. No nausea. Nothing except the amateur mistake of standing too fast."

Her tension relaxed only a little at his words, but she had to admit that his hand was steady. "Then, may I expect you to remain lying down for a while?"

"Perhaps." He lifted his head, and just as quickly lay back down, squeezing his eyes shut. "Allow me to amend that to a 'yes.' Zachary? You came with a message?"

"Yes sir." The young man's livery was flecked with dust, as if he had ridden hard to get here. "The number two boiler has blown."

Twenty-four

Fire and Water

As if the prospect of the boiler blowing were not bad enough, Zachary's next words chilled Jane. He said, "There's a dozen or more wounded bad. Mr. Pridmore won't send for a doctor."

Vincent's eyes snapped open. "Tell me that is not true."

"He won't even let us move them. Frank tried to insist, but Pridmore said he'd whip anyone who touched the wounded instead of helping save the stock. Frank send me to ask you to come."

Jane put a hand to her bosom in horror. All those people burnt and scalded, with no hospital, and Pridmore would not send for medical help? It was beyond monstrous.

"Why does he think I can get Pridmore to do anything different?"

"You're white."

The blunt reality sat between them. Regardless of Frank's competence or the correctness of his position, he could not argue with Mr. Pridmore and hope to win. Pushing himself up, Vincent pitched over and had to catch himself with a palm slapped to the floor. "Damn. Someone help me up."

"Vincent—"

"Jane, I am not going to lie here." He held out his hand to Zachary. "Steady me, please."

Zachary hesitated, looking to Jane for guidance. In the time it took for her to nod, Vincent growled and rolled onto his hands and knees. He braced himself there, head hanging, and let out a steady stream of profanity.

Jane slid forward on her knees and put a hand under his arm. "Lean on me."

With a hand on her shoulder, Vincent got one foot under himself and pushed upright. Even so, he swayed, and would have fallen again if Zachary had not rushed forward to catch his waist. Not yet fully upright, Vincent stood, balanced between the two of them. "Wait. Give me a moment."

"Would it not be better to wait until the dizziness has passed?"

"It can pass in the carriage." He nodded to Zachary, face set. "All right." With painful care, he let go of Jane's shoulder and straightened slowly. Another string of curses in at least three languages emerged as he stood, Zachary bracing him.

Keeping his arm around Vincent's waist, Zachary moved to his side. "Put your arm over my shoulder, sir."

With a grunt, Vincent did so. The activity in the ballroom had come to a complete stop as all of the glamourists watched Vincent's halting progress across the floor. Without a doubt, all of them recognised the pitching, spinning sensation that came of working too much glamour.

No. No, that was not what the looks of concern were. How stupidly self-centred of her. Some of them had friends or family who worked at the distillery.

Jane gathered her gown and began the process of raising her gravid form off the floor. When Louisa appeared to help her to her feet, Jane was deeply grateful. Standing, she faced the women and young men in the room. "If any of you have nursing skills, I would be most obliged if you could go to the great house at our estate. We will be sending the wounded there. Likewise, if you have family there . . ."

Nkiruka stepped forward from where she had been working. "You go with him. We'll take care of the house."

"Thank you. I will send a message to Frank to let him know you are coming." Jane hurried across the floor to catch up with Vincent.

He had become steadier but was still clearly using Zachary for support. As Jane caught up with them, Louisa turned and darted across the room. Jane spared her a glance, but Vincent occupied most of her attention.

His eyes were squinted nearly shut with concentration. "Jane, I do not want you to come."

"I will make a note of that, but you are mistaken if you think I will remain behind."

"I do not think you understand how bad this will be."

"That is not a reason for me to stay when I might be of some use."

"Jane—"

"Besides, unless I miss my guess, you will be occupied with Mr. Pridmore. I can direct the care of the wounded." Jane tightened her mouth. "When you can stand unassisted, then you may argue with me."

"I will not." They arrived at the carriage. Vincent transferred his grip from Zachary to the carriage door. "Thank you."

"Good." Jane turned from Vincent as Louisa ran up to join them, a bundle of cloth in her hands. "Please go to the great house. Mrs. Whitten will give you the use of her carriage if you explain the situation. Ask your father to arrange for the spare rooms to be used for the wounded—"

Zachary interrupted her. "He is at the distillery, trying to see to the wounded there."

"I will see to it, madam." Louisa held out a bundle for Jane, which she took mechanically before recognising it as Vincent's coat and her bonnet. The young woman turned to Nkiruka. "May I ask for your assistance? You have more experience nursing than I do."

"Sure, sure."

"Thank you. My father has some bandages prepared, but we shall need more."

Jane said, "Sacrifice the sheets if there is no other clean linen."

"Yes, madam. I will arrange the carriage." The young maid did not wait to be thanked or dismissed, just hurried back into the Whittens' great house.

Jane spied Zachary's lathered horse tied outside the ballroom. She turned to the young man, pulling on her bonnet as she did. "Zachary. Please go fetch Dr. Jones at once and ask her to meet us at the great house." Over a dozen wounded, he had said. That would be an enormous undertaking for just one doctor, even with the help of the women here. She swallowed. "Please also fetch Sir Ronald."

Vincent turned with alarm and had to fling out an arm to steady himself against the carriage. "You cannot be serious."

"With the number of wounded? Yes." Serious, if still uneasy at the prospect of being anywhere near the man. "He is a competent doctor, and Dr. Jones will need the help."

"I cannot call a man who nearly killed you competent."

"Nearly, but not quite. Given everything, you cannot still believe your father's claim that what Sir Ronald did was not calculated?" Jane wiped her hands on her gown, trying to brush some of her fury away. "I am sorry. My anger is not directed at you."

"I know. God . . . I know that feeling well enough." Vincent nodded to Zachary. "Do as she says. And during this, if we disagree, trust her over me. My judgement may be clouded."

Jove guided the carriage down the winding road at the quickest pace that was safe. During the first part of the ride, Vincent sat with his eyes closed and his hands clenched into fists upon his thighs. Watching him, Jane wet her lips. "Nausea?"

"Yes." After a few moments, he added, "It is the motion, not the . . . the other."

She had wondered if his nervous condition would be a concern, since she felt sick with anger at Mr. Pridmore and she would not be the one confronting the man. "Try watching the horizon. It helped during my seasickness."

"There are only horses in front of us."

"Ahead and to the right." She glanced over her shoulder at the view across the cane fields. "You can see the horizon."

Vincent cracked his eyes, looking where she indicated. The fields stretched across the plateau at the base of the hill in green waves. The wind stirred eddies of grey and brown through the leaves. The set of Vincent's face relaxed a little, and he nodded, not taking his eyes from the horizon. "Thank you."

When the carriage swung around a bend, he transferred his gaze to the horizon on the left side of the carriage and cursed. Sitting forward in the seat, Vincent's face tightened again as he leaned towards the window. Jane sucked in a gasp of dismay. Ahead of them, a double plume of smoke billowed into the air.

With the twists in the road, it would take them another twenty minutes, at best, to reach the boiler. As the carriage jostled and bounced closer, Jane could only stare in horror.

There must be significantly more than a dozen wounded, with the size of those clouds.

They rounded the next bend, and the smoke was hidden behind them. Vincent sank back against the seat, his face grave. "When we arrive, I am going to help you out of the carriage. If I am still unsteady, I shall offer you my arm. I hope I will not need to, but . . ." His face twisted in a grimace. "It will be hard enough to play the nobleman in my shirtsleeves, without worrying about pitching onto my face."

"Oh, I have your coat." In their haste, Jane had forgotten the bundle. She lifted it from the seat where she had tossed it. Louisa had snatched his waistcoat and cravat as well, thank heavens.

"You are a wonder, Muse."

"It was Louisa. I should not have thought of it myself." Jane leaned to the window and looked up the side of the hill towards the Whitten estate. Close to the top, a cloud of dust indicated that another carriage was on its way down. She sent a silent thank you to Mrs. Whitten and to Louisa. She held up his waistcoat and helped him slip his arms into it. "If you are steady on your feet, I will help Frank with the wounded. Otherwise I shall stay by you."

They discussed their plans as Jane helped him dress in the carriage. Though slightly wrinkled, by the time they arrived, he once again looked the part of Lord Verbury's son. If that look were confined to his clothing, Jane would not have minded, but the cold and bitter expression regained its hold on his face.

Simply rolling into the yard of the distillery was enough to make Jane's stomach churn. The baby kicked wildly in answer to her agitation. Through the windows of the carriage, the sweet scent of rum mixed with smoke and cooked flesh. Audible over the sound of the horses' hooves, ragged screams cut through the air. In the centre of the long stone building, the smaller of the two plumes of smoke rose from a yawning hole in the roof. The larger column of smoke came from a flaming mass that lay twenty feet away.

"It blew through the roof." Vincent ground his teeth together. "I told him that the patch would not hold."

Jove pulled the carriage to a halt in a cloud of dust. His outrider jumped down and ran to catch the horses' bridles as the beasts snorted with fear at the smoke billowing across the yard.

Though it looked as if Vincent wanted to spring from the carriage the moment it stopped, he rose more deliberately and held the door as he stepped out of the carriage. Jane watched his face as he turned to help her out. When she was out, he gave a tight nod. "Help Frank."

She squeezed his hand, reluctant to let him go. "Be careful."

He gave that cold, bitter smile belonging to a man she did not know. "I think we are beyond that." And then he was gone, striding through the dust and smoke to where Mr. Pridmore stood. With him, in a cluster of pristine linen and cotton, stood a small collection of white men. Their faces were pink with the heat, but none of the soot or blood had stained their trousers. Their contrast to the rest of the scene appalled Jane.

Vincent had been right. Jane had not understood how bad it would be. A woman, bleeding from a cut on her forehead, staggered in circles. A severed arm, twisted and blackened, leaked blood into the dust. Bodies lay sprawled on the side of the low hill that Jane had chosen for the site of the future hospital. The screaming sobs continued, coming from that area. The explosion had been more than an hour ago, and these people had been in agony that whole time.

Her first instincts were both to run towards that sound and to run away from it. The indecision held her, frozen, in the shade of the carriage. The carriage. She must find Frank. They could put some of the wounded in the carriage.

Between her and the hill, black men in ragged clothing were rolling enormous barrels out of the rum factory. One of them had removed his shirt, and the sweat on his back had varnished a twisted mass of scars. Another had dried blood crusted on one arm. If not for her conversation with Louisa, Jane was not certain that she would have noticed how very dark these men were compared to the house slaves.

They laboured to roll one of the massive barrels down a long, gradual ramp. At the foot of the ramp, a line of five low, open wagons waited to be loaded. Other men stood by the wagons, soothing the mules or oxen harnessed to them. At the foot of the ramp, a thickset man with freckles upon his deep brown skin directed the loading of barrels.

In the other direction, Frank knelt, consulting a woman of colour in her middle years. The woman's ragged calico dress had bloodstains at the waist, but Jane did not think the stains were hers.

She swallowed and smoothed the folds of her dress. "Jove? Can your outrider manage the horses without you?"

"Yes, madam."

Pointing to the woman who staggered in circles, Jane said, "Help her into the carriage and then follow me." Clenching her jaw, Jane strode towards the hill.

Doing so required her to pass close to Mr. Pridmore's group. He had turned to meet Vincent and seemed to be smiling at him. "Of course, but we have to save the stock first."

"The rum does not have precedence here." Vincent's hands were clenched behind him.

"Your liberality is to be honoured, but there are practical matters to running an estate. If Captain Caesar is to sail with the tide, we need to get the stock to his ship quickly. Let me do my job without interference."

"You forget whose estate this is. My apologies, Captain Caesar, but we have wounded people." The man he addressed was a black African with a long narrow nose that put Jane a little in mind of Ibrahim from the ship.

The part of her mind that was desperate to think of anything except the gruesome details of the scene wondered if the captain was Somalian and if his ship was bound for Africa or somewhere else.

Pridmore cut in before Captain Caesar could answer.

"We'll send them back to their homes as soon as we're done here. Everybody will get the day off tomorrow, but we have to get the rum out before we lose it."

Then Jane was past them, and the screaming drowned out Vincent's reply. Frank looked up as she approached. His cravat was missing, and blood flecked the cuffs of his shirt. For a moment he did not seem to recognise her, then his face cleared and he looked past her to Vincent. "Thank God."

The person he knelt by was identifiable as a woman only by her dress. The skin on the right side of her body was raw and weeping and her ear was completely gone. Jane had to cover her mouth to keep from being sick on the spot. Swallowing heavily, she gestured to the carriage. "I thought you could put the worst of the wounded in the carriage and send them to the great house directly."

"Good." He turned to the woman beside him. "Ellen, help me get Kate into the carriage."

Ellen moved to the woman's feet, which were bare and swollen with blisters. "It goin' hurt her more."

He nodded grimly and slid his hands under Kate's shoulders, provoking fresh cries of anguish.

Jane took an involuntary step back; then she braced herself and stepped forward again. "What should I do?"

"Secure some wagons for us. While Mr. Hamilton has Pridmore occupied, you can cow the wagon driver into obeying." He looked across to Ellen. "On three."

Together they lifted the shrieking woman from the ground. Jane followed, feeling utterly useless, but she had to acknowledge that in her state, she could not carry anyone.

The sound dragged the attention of one of the wagon drivers towards them, and he stared at Frank and Ellen as they carried the woman to the carriage. He did not see Jane until she cleared her throat.

The freckled man stared at her in some surprise and jerked his hat off his head, revealing a frizz of black hair around a bald brown pate. "Ma'am?"

"We need to transfer the wounded to the great house. Bring your wagon around to the hill."

"I—um." He glanced to the cluster of men. "I have orders from Mr. Pridmore."

"And I am the master's wife, on an errand from him. I am afraid that his orders overturn Mr. Pridmore's."

"I goin' need to ask him."

If he asked, Pridmore would say "no" at best. Jane bit the inside of her cheek in vexation. "You must see the desperate need these people are in. Surely your compassion alone tells you what is right."

"Compassion don't nothing to do with it. Ah have orders."

Jane turned her face away so the frame of her bonnet would hide her distress. The view of the thickset man was replaced by the smoke-covered yard, and across it, the carriage. Frank and Ellen had help from Jove now to load the wounded, but the carriage could hold no more than four. Why had Frank thought she could sway this man when he could not?

Because she was white. Jane swallowed and lifted her chin. Then she would be white. She turned back to the man. "What is your name?"

"My—um. Silas."

"Silas." She thrust her stomach at him like the prow of a ship-of-the-line, using every weapon at her disposal. "You will release these wagons or I promise that I will let the master know who left me standing in the heat and argued with me."

"I—"

"Now! Or I shall have you whipped." The scars on the men rolling the giant hogshead of rum and the sudden tension in Silas's frame made it clear that whippings happened with some regularity. Just having to make the threat made Jane's skin crawl. If he still refused, Jane could not have it carried out.

Silas stared at the swell of her figure and swallowed. "Ben! Lady want the wagons."

A tall mulatto with stooped shoulders and a scar along his nose turned and scowled. Ben held a whip, which he tapped against his thigh. "What?"

"De boss wife say dem wan' take the wounded to the manor."

He spat on the ground. "Pridmore not goin' like it."

"And my husband is his employer. I promise you, you do not want to face his displeasure."

"Pridmore say he's soft."

Jane took a step closer to him. "He is Lord Verbury's son. Do you truly doubt that he will hesitate to punish you if you continue to disobey me?"

Ben pursed his lips at that, studying her, then shrugged. "Rum or wounded. Make no difference to me." He turned back to the three ragged black men rolling a barrel towards the ramp. He snapped the whip over their heads and bellowed, "Hold!"

They slowed the great barrel, bringing it to a halt on the broad flat area at the top of the ramp. One of the men behind the barrel bent down and drove two wooden wedges under the curved wood to keep it from rolling. The most heavily scarred of them leaned against the barrel and crossed his arms over his sweating chest. He glared past them towards the hill, jaw clenched tight.

Shaking, Jane clasped her hands under her stomach to hide their tremors, then lifted her chin still higher. "I shall also require those men to help load the wounded."

Ben rolled his eyes. "You lot! Move! You hear she."

He cracked the whip towards them again, but they needed no encouragement for this task. As Silas urged his mules forward, the barrel rollers jumped off the ramp, racing towards the hill. Jane turned to Ben as they went. "The other wagons, too. I shall not brook delay."

He grunted in reply and with shouted orders quickly got the line of wagons in motion after Silas.

Only the second had moved away from the rum house before Pridmore noticed. He turned from Vincent and shouted, "What the devil is happening?" Charging across the yard with Vincent close behind, he snatched the nearest mule's reins and brought it to a halt. "Ben!"

"Lady say the master wan' move the wounded."

"Absolutely not. I cannot spare the labour for that."

Looming over him, Vincent said, "You can, and you will. Your treatment of these people is inhumane."

"God spare me from Londoners who come crying about humanity. You do not understand the least thing about managing slaves or a plantation." He flung an arm out towards the hill of wounded. "If those were oxen, you would not hesitate to put them down. The cost to nurse them back to health would not be worth the while. This is—"

"You are fired." Vincent's calm might have been mistaken for indifference.

Pridmore gaped at him. "You cannot."

"It is absolutely clear that your incompetency and refusal to do adequate repairs caused this accident. Your treatment of the slaves—or, in terms you can understand, your neglect of my property—is indefensible. If you press me, I will see you brought up on charges."

"On what grounds?"

"Even in Antiguan law, the deliberate death of a slave is murder. If any of those people die, it lies on your head alone."

Pridmore turned to the white planters who had followed them over. "Explain to him, gentlemen, the realities of running a plantation."

The oldest of the men, face weathered with sun to a rough red, spread his hands and shrugged. "I am not going to presume to tell Mr. Hamilton his business."

Swallowing, Pridmore turned back to Vincent and opened his mouth to speak. His lips shaped words, but no sound came out. Grimacing, he finally said, "I will remind you that I was a favourite of your father."

Jane clenched her fists. It was as clear a threat for retribution as he could make without saying that Lord Verbury was alive.

Vincent's voice went colder still. "I wonder that you claim to be the favourite of a man who committed treason against the Crown. It does nothing to recommend you. You are fired."

Pridmore's face turned red and white by degrees. He stepped closer to Vincent, shaking his finger at him. "You have no idea what you have done."

"I assure you, I know exactly what I am doing." He leaned down. "You have until tomorrow to get off my land."

"I—I—I'll take my quietus payment, then."

"Your what?"

"Louisa. I was promised Louisa."

Vincent laughed outright. "By whom?"

"Your father—"

"Have you papers? Have you witnesses? No? Unless you can raise him from his grave, then I suggest you stop trying to hide behind his name. It carries no weight here." Vincent turned his shoulder to Pridmore, delivering the cut direct, and spoke with surprising gentleness to Silas, who stood frozen by the mules. "Please carry on to the hill. He has no power to stop you."

While Silas was still gathering the reins on his mules, the heavily scarred black man stepped away from the group and ran to Frank. With a frown, Jane watched him lean down to whisper into Frank's ear. Eyes narrowing, Frank nodded and directed him to Ellen. Straightening his coat, Frank stood, and then strode quickly across the ground.

Pridmore fairly frothed, hands opening and closing in fists. "You will regret this!"

Vincent did not distinguish him with a response. He stepped away and gave a bow to the planters and Captain Caesar, entirely calm in outward appearance save for having his chin tucked into his collar. "My apologies, gentlemen. I thank you for your patience." He beckoned to Jane. "Have you had the opportunity to meet my wife?"

The eldest of the men set the precedent. He joined Vincent and closed ranks so that Pridmore stood outside their circle. "Charmed, madam. I believe you know my wife, Mrs. Ransford?"

"Oh!" Jane had not expected to add this awkwardness to the day. "Yes, she created an absolutely beautiful curtain of snow for us." It took all her powers to pretend to be unaffected. Jane used her bonnet to block out the horror around them.

Mr. Ransford smiled, glancing past her to where Pridmore stood, and shifted his position to draw her slightly further away from Pridmore. "She speaks very highly of your ice palace. I cannot wait to see it."

Jane could not give him her full attention. A series of curses and footsteps indicated that Pridmore was storming away. Jane swallowed and attempted to remain properly

British. "That is very kind. Please give her my regards." The conversation was intolerable.

Beside Jane, Vincent had turned to meet Frank. She could not quite make out what Frank murmured to him, but whatever it was caused Vincent to spin and shout, "Pridmore!"

"What!"

Snapping his gaze to the captain, Vincent said, "Did you pay him for the cargo already?"

"Yes, sir." The captain's face hardened with sudden understanding. "Yes, I did."

This caused angry muttering among the planters. Jane wanted to scream at them. They would let Pridmore do what he wanted to human lives, but God forbid he should steal a purse.

Vincent strode across the yard to where Pridmore stood by his horse. "I require my funds."

Pridmore laughed nervously and took a step back. "The money is in the distillery, in my office. It's unfortunate that the entrance fell in when the boiler blew."

Frank cleared his throat. "The purse is in his pocket."

"You're lying."

Vincent stopped in front of him with a palm outstretched. "Sir."

"I have a purse, but it is mine. Are you going to take that from me as well as my livelihood?"

"There is a witness who saw you pocket it."

Pridmore glared past Vincent at Frank. "I cannot believe you are going to take the word of that nasty, lying, nig—"

Vincent punched him hard across the mouth.

Staggering back, Pridmore collided with his horse. A hand went to the blood trickling from his lip. With a snarl, he flung himself at Vincent, fists swinging. Vincent leaned to the side, dodging the first blow. The second glanced off his cheek.

With a speed that astonished Jane, Vincent cracked two blows against Pridmore's chin, then planted a third firmly in Pridmore's stomach. The man folded forward with a grunt until a fourth blow snapped him upright.

Pridmore hung for a moment, balanced on his toes, then fell to the ground, unconscious.

Vincent put a hand on the saddle of Pridmore's horse and swayed for a moment. Hand tightening, Vincent's spine straightened by careful degrees. Jane hurried forward and put a hand on his elbow, though she did not think she could stop him if he were to fall again. "Are you all right?"

He looked down and compressed his lips in his small public smile. "Better than I have been in a long time, I think." He looked up, past her. "Frank! May I borrow you for a moment?"

"Sir?" Frank left his place behind the white men and came forward with alacrity.

The planters stood in a little group, clearly talking about the fisticuffs with great enthusiasm. As far as Jane could tell, the substance of the fight did not matter to them, but Vincent's performance had somehow left them impressed. The vagaries of men would remain unaccountable to her.

When he reached them, Frank looked down at Mr. Pridmore. His face remained guarded, but his right hand tightened a little. Looking up, Frank inclined his head. "What may I do for you, Mr. Hamilton?"

"Two things. First—" Vincent looked suddenly and unaccountably bashful. "First . . . would you—I should take it as an honour if you would call me Vincent."

Frank's mouth hung open a little at the invitation to such familial intimacy. He shut it and turned to look back at the white planters and then at the wagon drivers, his brows drawn a little together. Putting his fist to his mouth, he stood for a moment before saying, "Thank you."

In spite of his resemblance to Vincent, Frank's position as the estate's steward, the colour of his skin, and his very demeanour had made it too easy for Jane to think of him as only a servant. It was easy to forget that he was Vincent's half brother. The fact was, of all of Vincent's blood relations, Frank was the only one who had never played them false. He had been loyal to his own family first but honest about it, and that was as it should be. Jane held out her hand to him. "I am Jane."

He stared at her hand for a moment, then again at the planters. He murmured, "You know they are watching."

"Am I mistaken that being claimed as a Hamilton relation will help your role?"

Frank took Jane's hand and bowed over it with the precision of any gentleman. "Thank you."

Breaking into a smile that looked genuine, Vincent clapped Frank on the shoulder and held out his hand, turning them both so that the handshake was obvious. "Good. I am sorry. I should have offered much sooner than this."

Clasping it, Frank shook his head. "You did not know me."

"And that is a cause for regret," Jane replied.

Frank looked down at Mr. Pridmore. "Yes. . . . Now, you had two things. What was the second?"

Sobering, Vincent scrubbed his hand through his hair, staring with distaste at the man who still lay sprawled in the dirt. He bent down and felt in Pridmore's coat, coming out with a heavy purse. Scowling, he straightened. "Get him off our land." Vincent looked to the hill. "After we have seen to our wounded."

Twenty-five

Old Scars and New

The badly burnt woman lost consciousness on the ride to the great house, which was the greatest possible blessing for her. Vincent stayed behind at the rum factory to deal with matters there, while Jane and Frank returned with the wounded.

When they arrived at the great house, Nkiruka and Dr. Jones met them at the door, faces tight as the first of the wounded was carried from the carriage. There was little for Jane to do. With quiet competence, Nkiruka and Louisa had organised the glamourists as nurses. Together they had prepared the spare rooms to the best of their abilities, assigning the rooms according to the severity of the injuries.

As the wounded were carried through the

door, Dr. Jones took a quick look and told the bearers where to take each patient. Louisa met the pallet bearers at the end of the hall and helped them settle the wounded. They had to be placed two or three to a bed, and on pallets on the floor, but she found space for them all. Jane's experience in tending to her mother turned out to be of practical use, for though her mother's ailments were frequently imaginary, the methods which their family doctor had prescribed for treating them were real.

She soaked torn linens in rainwater and placed them on Sukey's fevered brow and Julian's angry, blistered skin. She helped arrange pillows so that Fidelia could rest more comfortably while waiting for Dr. Jones to come to her. She sat by Letitia's bed and held her hand while she wept. Her husband had been stoking the furnace when the boiler blew, and no one had seen him since. She stayed there until Zachary brought Letitia's mother, and then moved on to the next bed, and the next, and the next. Through their injuries, Jane met Jos, Bodelia, Thomas, Smart Martin, Jeannette . . . Jeannette had been one of their glamourists and now had blisters over her forearms.

As Jane walked across the hall to the next room armed with her linens and rainwater, she saw Frank coming down the passage. Jane waited until he drew near. "Has Sir Ronald arrived?"

Frank sighed. "I am sorry. I could have saved you the trouble of sending for him. He does not work on Negroes."

For a childish moment, Jane wanted to stamp her foot and throw a tantrum. That hateful, odious man. She swallowed her anger, trying to keep her voice low so that that she did not disturb those patients who had managed to find a troubled slumber. "What about Dr. Hartnell? The gentleman who runs the school that we are holding the charity ball for."

"The wrong sort of doctor, I am afraid. He is an historian of sorts. Jane—" Frank stumbled over the new familiarity "May I speak with you for a moment?"

"Of course . . ."

Without a word, Frank relieved her of her bowl and basin. She would have protested, but her back ached from bending over the beds. He led her to the blue parlour, pausing only long enough to set down her supplies, then he held the door to the veranda open for her. Still, he did not speak until the door was shut and Jane seated in one of the cane rocking chairs. The sun had begun to set while she was indoors, and the clouds burnt red over the hazy green hills, which were spotted with flamboyants and century plants.

Frank leaned against the rail. Lit from behind by the sunset, he looked remarkably like Vincent. "I think we must make plans to hide Lord Verbury. Pridmore will tell in retaliation."

She sighed heavily, knowing he was right. What was more, Pridmore would do everything in his power to get his hands on Louisa. Likely, he would make a direct appeal to Lord Verbury and promise silence in exchange for her and who knew what other considerations. Jane chewed her lower lip, thinking. Slowly, she said, "Your mother . . . she offered to make a deed of transfer for Louisa to Vincent. Do you think she would still be willing?"

"Yes, but that opens the forgery difficulties again."

"I have been thinking on that, but tell me if I am wrong. If she forges papers for Louisa, then we can send her and Zachary to England with messages to friends of ours there. The forgery need only be good enough to get her on the ship and can be abandoned once they are in London. Once there, they will be able to secure help for us."

"It will still take two months, at best, before any aid returns."

"True. But if we are going to hide Verbury, then he will not be able to cause your family to be sold—that is something he can only do if he appears to be alive. If we keep him hidden, that leaves us only Pridmore to manage."

Frank nodded slowly, considering it. While Jane could imagine the course of sending Louisa and Zachary to England, she did not have Frank and Vincent's experience in imagining all the ways in which Lord Verbury could twist and turn their actions against them. It was both fortunate and not that Frank had long practise in it.

"Verbury will still have Sir Ronald and others in his pocket."

"Am I wrong that that is only a difficulty if he knows that Zachary and Louisa have left? So long as he thinks he is being hidden for his own safety, then he will have no cause to deploy Sir Ronald against us. Indeed, he might even have Sir Ronald act on our behalf if we can convince him that it is for his own good."

"If I can speak with my mother privately, I will ask her to try to influence him. The challenge is bringing his lordship around to accepting the need to be hidden . . . or, rather, more hidden."

"And where to put him."

Slowly, Frank said, "When my wife and I married, he presented us with a small house. We added rooms on for the children, and it is quite comfortable. My youngest daughters are still at home, and he was fond of them before the stroke."

"And Louisa is supposedly sleeping in the room next to ours in order to be at my constant beck and call, so she will not be missed at your house."

"Zachary's absence will be harder to hide. But possible."

They stared over the plantation. Even through the glass doors, the moans of the injured filtered out into the night. Jane had not heard Kate, who had screamed so horribly at the factory, in some time. She hoped that it was because Dr. Jones had relieved her pain and not due to darker reasons.

Frank crossed his arms over his chest and sighed. "I wish I could be confident that Louisa would not tell him of our plans."

"But . . . if she understands what is at stake?" Jane sighed, understanding that Frank still had not told her about Pridmore. "You have to tell her."

"She will not believe it." Frank straightened his cuffs, though they were flecked with blood. "She thinks Lord Verbury is her saviour."

Jane had no skill or practise at the conniving and scheming that seemed the Hamilton way. The worst that her family had prepared her for was dealing with an invalid.

A sudden thought occurred to Jane as three disparate pieces came together and she sat straight up in her rocking chair. She was good at soothing invalids. Frank had once said that people talked in front of him, forgetting that a servant could even hear them. And, thirdly, Miss Sarah had said that their dinner had been, in part, so his lordship could see Jane—or, more likely, the baby. "What if she heard it from him?"

Frank grimaced at the thought. "How?"

"I can take Louisa with me when I tell Lord Verbury about Pridmore being fired and our plans to hide him."

"When *you* tell him?"

"Yes. It does not seem as if he would hear it from you. I am an unexpected quarter. Also, I am carrying his heir." Jane pushed herself up from the chair, feeling her fatigue in the swelling at her ankles. "If Vincent returns before I am finished, please attempt to guide him away from the room. I imagine he will be out of humour and . . . meeting his father in that state never ends well."

"I will ask Zachary to catch him." Frank inclined his head with a small smile. "But I think that Vincent will not forgive me if I allow you to go alone. I will be in the coldmonger's box in the wall, in case you need . . . assistance."

"Thank you." Knowing that he would be there relieved her of a fear that she had not recognised until it lifted.

Jane found Louisa cutting bandages in the sickroom. "May I pull you away?"

"Of course, madam." On Louisa, the fatigue they all felt had made her youth more apparent. She was so steady that it was often easy to forget she was only nineteen.

"Thank you. I need to inform his lordship of our arrangements and would like you present to remind me if I forget anything."

"Certainly." Louisa turned and picked up a writing book from the table. "I have the list here."

"You are a wonder of efficacy." Jane did not have to strain to think of compliments. She truly did not know how they would have made it through the day without the young woman's efforts.

Louisa followed her through the house to Lord Verbury's room. Jane had made only the smallest effort to tidy her appearance. The unexpectedly useful thing about wearing mourning clothes was that none of the stains from the day showed. Miss Sarah opened the door, her eyes widening in surprise to find Jane there. Jane was able to keep her own countenance calm.

"Could his lordship spare time for conversation?"

"One moment, please." Miss Sarah made as if to step away and shut the door, but something caused her to look suddenly to her right and open the door further. "Come in, please."

Aside from the first day in Antigua, two months prior,

Jane had not been in Lord Verbury's room. It had made little impression on her beyond his presence. She had thought that he was perhaps confined to one room, but the gracious sitting room she found herself in had three doors off of it. Through one of them, she could see a library. The sitting room itself was done in a soothing green, with elegant furniture in the Egyptian revival style. The most notable thing about the rooms was the space between the items of furniture and the distinct want of rugs. Lord Verbury sat in his wheeled chair, making those features of the room instantly understandable.

Louisa followed Jane into the room and took a place by the door, her eyes cast down. In her role as the perfect lady's maid, she stood so still that she became part of the furniture.

Lord Verbury did not acknowledge Louisa and barely recognized Jane's presence. His face was serene, without the suspicion she had expected to encounter. On the other hand, Jane knew better than to take anything of his appearance at face value. Lord Verbury sat back in his chair. "I will admit this is a surprise."

"To me as well." Jane offered a curtsy, though he had neglected his own courtesies. "I hope I find you well."

"I very much doubt that you do."

Jane disregarded the cut the way she disregarded her mother's petulance and smiled instead. "May I ask for a few moments of your time?"

He considered her, then raised one finger on his good

hand and waved it. Miss Sarah instantly left the sitting room with speed and grace. Jane watched her go, using the movement as an excuse to look at the walls of the room, wondering where Frank was standing.

When the door shut behind them, Lord Verbury beckoned to Jane. "Please, have a seat."

"Thank you." Her heart was beating wildly, but Jane hoped that little of her agitation showed. She settled on the sofa opposite him, judging that that would be the easiest vantage for him to see her without rearranging his chair.

"Delighted though I am to have your company, I must wonder why are you here, and not my son."

Jane folded her hands in front of her, knowing that it emphasised her stomach. "My husband has many wonderful features, but his temper is not one of them. I am hoping that you and I will be able to discuss a few things without unnecessary rancour."

"And do you plan to tell me what those things are, or keep me guessing?"

"If I have satisfied your questions about why I am here and not Vincent, then yes." She was vexed at herself for rising even that much to his provocation. "Shall I continue?"

"By all means." Verbury smiled with just his mouth, while his dark eyes remained fixed on hers.

She swallowed, reminding herself that she could end this conversation at any time simply by standing and leaving the room. "I presume that you have been told about the accident at the distillery. I have a list of the wounded and where they have been placed, if you would like to make any alterations to our plans." If he was anything like her mother, then offering him the chance to consult would remove much of his crossness.

He made a sour face and waved for her to continue.

"Have you been told that Vincent found it necessary to fire Mr. Pridmore?"

Lord Verbury rolled his eyes. "I expressly told him not to do so. He will have to take Pridmore back."

"Mr. Pridmore made the error of challenging Vincent's authority in front of other planters. If they had been alone, I think there might have been another resolution. As it was, Vincent had to do so, or risk losing face for himself and the estate." She would say nothing of the philanthropic reasons for firing the man, suspecting that those would mean little to Verbury. "Regardless of your wishes, it is done, and there is no taking it back. Our concern is that Mr. Pridmore will attempt to expose that you are still alive. Have you any suggestions on how to ensure his silence? He made a request that he said was based on a promise you made to him, but I could not bear to accede to it." Jane sent up a silent prayer that he would stay true to type. She resolutely did not look at Louisa.

"You do not have the right to decline."

"He has made his designs quite clear, and I cannot send an innocent anywhere near such a man."

Lord Verbury barked with laughter. "An innocent? My dear, I promised her to him, because he had already had her."

The room became suddenly, intolerably warm, and Jane

had to clench her fists in her lap to keep from slapping Verbury. She did not care that he saw the movement. She swallowed, and, with as much calm as she could summon, met his gaze. "Be that as it may, I cannot do without Louisa, regardless of promises made. It would distress me."

"Give him the girl. Your distress is worth less than my life."

Jane smoothed her gown over her stomach. "I hope you understand that the distress would affect more than my sensibilities. I cannot do without Louisa."

He stared at her stomach and then grunted, but gave no other sign of acknowledging her point.

"So the matter before us is how to hide the fact that you are alive. I have a proposal, if you will hear it."

What she found most disturbing about Lord Verbury was his resemblance to Vincent. Though he was old and infirm, in his high forehead and strong brow, and even in the line of his jaw, she could see how Vincent would age. If all the wrinkles on Lord Verbury's face had come from sneers and frowns, it would in some ways be easier to hate him. Yet at the corners of his eyes, he had clear laugh lines, as if there had been a point in his life when that had been a frequent behaviour.

He shifted in his chair, picking at his lap blanket with his good hand. "I am curious about your plan."

"With Louisa in residence here, Frank has an empty room at the house you built for him. It has two entrances. We propose to move you there—not permanently, but just until the immediate danger has passed. If Mr. Pridmore brings anyone to the estate to look for you, they will certainly start at the great house, which will give us ample time to get a warning to you and hide your presence using glamour. If you can ask Sir Ronald for assistance in discrediting Pridmore, then we should be able to maintain the deception as long as needed."

"You seem very sure of yourself. And if I refuse?"

"I hope that you would not refuse without reason. You know the principals better than any of us, and certainly better than I. If you see a deficiency in the plan to remove you, I should very much like to know about it."

He snorted. "You are not what I expected."

"I am glad to hear it." He so clearly wanted her to ask him what he had expected, in the same way that her mother would make profligate remarks—though of a wildly different sort—simply to provoke a response. Suddenly, Jane recalled her father saying that all her mother wanted was to know that she was not alone. She tilted her head to one side and gave as much of a smile as she could. "Frank's youngest daughters are still at home. I suspect that they would be glad to have you and Miss Sarah to themselves for a while."

He rubbed his chin. "Have you met them?"

"I have not had the occasion." Jane suddenly felt that that was a great negligence on her part. "Frank says that Rosa is showing a great deal of talent in the arts."

Lord Verbury nodded slowly, as though he were thinking through the various points. He drummed his forefinger on the arm of his chair. "And what are you offering in exchange for my agreement?"

"Keeping you safe is not enough?"

"I *was* safe, until my son defied my directives and you refused to part with your maid. You must know that there will be consequences to that." He narrowed his eyes. "I am being generous in allowing you to set the conditions for his apology."

He was an awful, awful man. Jane had to bless her long training as a young lady, which had given her the ability to govern her expression, although she was fairly certain that her complexion had given away her rise in temper. It was always so much more difficult to maintain her composure when he made an attack on Vincent. Jane sighed, understanding the balance that Vincent had spoken of having difficulty with. Well, then . . . if she was angry, she would use it.

Jane shook her head. "You have a misapprehension about this conversation. My family does not, as a rule, indulge in the same games of intrigue that yours does, so I will speak to you plainly. You speak of wanting an apology, but any 'conditions' you set would clearly be punishing Vincent for defying you."

He clapped slowly. "Brava, for your insight."

"I am not finished." Jane rested her hand on her stomach. "You want contact with this child, because you think it likely that Richard will not sire an heir. My entire knowledge of you gives me no reason to ever allow it."

"I see why Vincent hides behind you. At least one of you has a spine."

"Do you offer insults as a reflex? Because nothing I am

seeing here convinces me that my estimation of you as a dangerous influence is incorrect." Jane leaned forward. "If you want to have any contact with this child, you will need to show that you are capable of kindness and generosity of spirit. I will measure that by how you treat Vincent."

"You want me to coddle him."

"I do not care how you choose to frame it. You are perfectly aware of what behaviour I expcct."

He snorted. "So you expect me to submit meekly to your plan of being confined to a slave cottage, and to dote over Vincent to reward him for defying my direct orders."

"Yes."

He leaned back in his chair. "And when I do not?"

"Then I hope that you have a plan for avoiding Mr. Pridmore." Jane smoothed her gown. "I very sincerely hope that you will not refuse to go to Frank's house simply to spite me or Vincent."

Verbury stared at her until Jane began to grow uncomfortable, but she held his gaze and waited. If there was one thing that a young lady learned, it was how to wait with a tranquil expression. Jane had spent many dances in her youth perfecting an easy and disinterested countenance while waiting for someone to ask her to stand up with them. She counted it as a small triumph when Lord Verbury reached for the silver bell on the table next to him and rang it.

"You may go. Send Frank to me."

"Of course." Jane stood as the door to the library opened and Miss Sarah reentered the room.

As far as she understood Vincent's father, he had been on very good behaviour. He could not agree to her terms immediately without feeling that he lost face. Jane's mother would also lament things, but given time to calm down and reflect in private, she always found a way to justify a decision as being her own choice. Jane had to hope that Lord Verbury would show at least as much sense as her mother.

Her fear was that his bile would outweigh his reason.

Jane curtsied to Verbury and turned to take her leave. Louisa still stood by the door, perfectly composed if you ignored the tears on her cheeks. She turned with exquisite grace and held the door for Jane.

Only when they were out of the room and the door had shut carefully behind them did Jane acknowledge what had occurred. "My dear . . . I am so, so sorry."

"He promised me? To Mr. Pridmore? But he stopped him—he made him stop—" Louisa's voice cracked into silence and she pressed the heels of her hands to her eyes. "Please don't let Papa know about—I never told him. Please, please don't let him know. He would be so angry."

"I promise that your father will not be angry at you." Jane kept her voice low and gentle as a section of the wall opened and Frank stepped silently into the white parlour. The grief on his face nearly broke Jane.

"Not at me." Louisa lifted her face, eyes red with tears. "If he knew, he would hurt Mr. Pridmore, and then they would hang him, and it would be my fault, and—"

"Shh . . ." Frank put his hands very gently on his daughter's shoulders.

She turned and flung herself on her father, sobbing. He folded her in his arms and rocked her back and forth.

Jane stole away as quietly as she could. There were some parts of the story that did not belong to her.

Twenty-six

Good Counsel

Hours later, Vincent returned to the house, bringing Frank with him. The men were discussing something as they came down the hall, and Jane caught only the end of it as they entered. ". . . other daughters will be excited to see him."

Vincent shrugged out of his coat. "Well, he was always kinder to my sisters." His cravat was missing and his waistcoat stained with dried blood. Soot marked his brow. "The sherry is on the sideboard."

"After today . . ." Frank went to the sideboard and retrieved the carafe and glasses. "Thank you, yes."

Jane rose from where she had been resting on the sofa. "How is Louisa?"

"Shaken, but well. Better, when I explained that we wanted to send her to London." Frank's mouth twisted in a grimace. "She is at home with her mother and Zachary. Both are packing, and with luck we will have them on a ship tomorrow."

Vincent added, "And I have written a letter to Richard explaining the whole of the situation here."

"Miss Sarah was able to do the forgery?" she asked.

"Yes, thank God." Frank cleared his throat, and poured a measure of Manzanilla for them each. "Your conversation with Lord Verbury, by the way, was a triumph of negotiation."

"Did he agree to remove to your house, then?"

"Yes. I do not know how you did it, but he did."

"Honestly? I pretended that he was my mother."

"Good lord! Do not let him hear that." Laughing, Vincent leaned down to kiss her on the cheek. "I am glad to see you sitting. I was worried you would work yourself too hard."

Relieved that he had any laughter in him, Jane caught her husband's hand as he straightened. "Me? You were the one too dizzy to stand earlier today." She pulled him down again so she could look at his face, but no bruises seemed imminent. "Well . . . you seem to have been telling the truth when you said Pridmore did not hit you hard."

"I am constantly amazed at how useful my father's insistence that I study pugilism has been." He grimaced and rubbed the side of his face. "It stung a little. No more."

"Should we ask Dr. Jones in to take a look? And perhaps have a glass of sherry with us?"

Frank said, "We asked if she would take a glass, but she had a patient she wanted to sit with until . . ." He sighed. "I think she will not be joining us."

A sobbing moan sounded from one of the rooms. Jane straightened in her chair, relieved only a little when she heard someone moving to help. Face grave, Vincent nodded to the interior. "How bad is it?"

Jane settled back in her chair. "We have eighteen wounded. I am not certain how many dead." She thought of Letitia, whose husband had been working the furnace.

"We have at least six. Four bodies." Vincent rubbed the back of his neck. "Two not accounted for, but both of them were in positions to be caught in the blast."

Setting the glasses on the table, Frank's mouth tightened. "I will ask Ben for the names and let their families know."

"Anthony, Bonthorn, Cuped, Fortune, Jackey, and Handel. I stopped on the way back, but their families had guessed." The anger, which had dimmed earlier, lit Vincent's eyes again. What had changed, for Jane, was that it no longer appeared to be coupled with despair or fear. Vincent picked up the sherry and stared into it. He took a sip, grimacing. "I should have fired Pridmore the moment I saw the boiler. I knew that patch would not hold. And of course there were the inconsistencies in the accounts."

Vincent had always been a man of action, and the months of being unable to effect changes had taken a toll on him. Jane rested her hand on his. "The reasons you stayed your hand made sense at the time, remember that. Aftersight will do none of us any good."

Nodding, Frank sat across from Jane. "I also did things that made sense at the time, but I regret now. I cannot change my actions in the past, but I can work to make sure that I repair their damage in the present." He sipped his sherry and cleared his throat. "May I tell you about one?"

"There is no need, unless it will ease your mind," Jane said.

"Thank you. I would rather you hear it from me. The first day, I lied to you about the ship. Lord Verbury ordered me to tell you that the packet ship, the *Marchioness of Salisbury*, had left. She had not. She was in harbour for two more days. Second . . . there is almost always a private ship bound for England."

"We could have left at any time?" Jane scarcely recognised the sound of her own voice.

"Please believe that I would not make the same choice again."

"You did not know us . . ." Still, the idea that they might have left this place, even be in England by now, made tears of upset spring to her eyes. Jane wiped them away hastily before she could cry. With the hold that Verbury had over Frank, was it any wonder that he acted as he did? "You did not know us."

Vincent leaned back in his chair, face mild, but he drank half the contents of his glass without seeming to notice. "Were there any other deceptions?"

"Nothing after the first week." Frank held up his hands

as Vincent stiffened in his chair. "Those you know about already: the coldmongers, Louisa's spying, my spying . . . but after your attempt to escape your father, I became convinced that you were as you presented yourself to be and not an instrument of his. It is . . . it is not what I had come to expect from the Hamiltons."

Vincent snorted. "Well, I can hardly fault you for that determination. And I am tired as the blazes of not trusting you. So—thank you for telling us." He sat forward and lifted the sherry decanter, refilling Frank's glass and his own. He raised his glass. "May I offer a toast to trust? Better to have it come late than to have none at all."

Raising his glass, Frank tapped it against Vincent's and then Jane's. "To trust."

Jane barely subdued a sob of relief, but could do nothing to stop the tears that flooded her eyes this time. She wiped them away, deeply annoyed to be crying once again.

"Muse?"

She half laughed, waving at her face and then her stomach. "It is just the . . . I seem to cry very easily these days."

"My wife is the same whenever she is in a family way," Frank said. She was grateful to him for making her feel less a ninny.

Jane was aware that they were all pretending, rather desperately, that their clothes were not stained with blood and smoke. Their laughter was louder than the humour warranted and the pauses too long, as they listened for cries from the sick rooms. But she encouraged the gentlemen to relax a little by making sure that their sherry glasses stayed filled.

As the night wore on, Frank's speech shifted at times from the British pronunciations she was used to from him. The softening of consonants and lengthening of vowels happened mostly when he spoke of his children, with a look of relaxed fondness. Once he said, "The boy fu me—" And then caught himself, language stiffening into British starch again: "My son is doing quite well in mathematics. His mother and I are pleased."

Strangely saddened to hear the veil of language in place again, Jane could not think of how to draw it back. "I should like to meet your wife. Might we have you for dinner?"

Frank's brows drew together. "I honestly do not know. I will have to think about the ramifications of your entertaining us . . ." He looked at his glass. "But perhaps I will do so on an evening when I have consumed a little less of your sherry."

"Allow me to join Jane in issuing the invitation, and to add that I care not a grain for the 'ramifications.' "

"Be that as it may . . ." Frank pushed his chair back from the table. "I should bid you both a good night. We will all have a long day tomorrow."

"Indeed." Vincent began to rise and then dropped awkwardly back into his chair, grabbing the table with one hand. He closed his eyes and exhaled slowly. "Well . . . this is embarrassing."

Jane was at his side with no real memory of having moved. "Vincent?"

"I forgot how much glamour I worked this morning." He reddened, eyes still closed. "And that I had not eaten since breakfast. I am afraid that I misjudged and will require some assistance."

"Of course." Frank moved to his side smoothly. "Forgive me for asking, but is the nature such that I should fetch a basin?"

With a breathless laugh, Vincent half shook his head. "No, nothing like that, thank God. Just deucedly dizzy. Glamour and strong drink . . . I am terribly sorry. 'No Drinking' was one of Herr Scholes's three rules, for this very reason."

Jane patted him on the shoulder and exchanged a look with Frank. "Well, I shall not fret, then. I have seen you too dizzy to stand before. At least you have not passed out."

"No. Not yet." Vincent sighed.

Frank crouched by him. "We will stand very slowly, then. Jane and I will assist you to the bed, and then I shall finally have the opportunity to show my skills as a valet."

"Very kind." Vincent transferred his grip from the table to Frank's shoulder. "And again, you have my profound apologies."

With Frank on one side and Jane on the other, Vincent rose slowly and did not lose consciousness. They were able to guide him to the bed, accompanied by a steady refrain of apologies and begging of pardons. Jane had seen Vincent inebriated exactly once before, though in that instance he had not combined it with an excess of glamour. In both cases, though, his speech became more precise and defined, as though he was trying to compensate for a muzziness of thoughts.

As he sat on the bed, Vincent gave a sigh of relief. "If you would not mind helping with my boots, Frank, that would be much appreciated. I can manage my shirt on my own, and Jane is familiar with my bree— God. I really am in a shocking state. So terribly sorry."

Jane had to cover her mouth, torn between laughing and being completely embarrassed at the implications of her intimate knowledge of her husband's breeches.

With a chuckle, Frank knelt to pull one of the boots free. "Please believe that I am glad of an opportunity to help."

Still blushing, Vincent bent his head and fumbled with the buttons on his cuff. Jane stepped in and undid them both for him before he had the opportunity to protest that he retained some dexterity. In very little time, Frank had his boots off, and Jane had helped Vincent draw his shirt off over his head.

"I will take your boots with me to have them cleaned this evening." Frank rounded the end of the bed, turning to look back at them. "Will there be— God." He had stopped, staring openly at Vincent's back.

Jane had become inured to the scars and accepted them as part of the landscape of her husband's body. She had forgotten what it was like to see the knotted mass of wheals for the first time. They had faded over the years to a ruddy grey, though in some places, the skin was white and shiny and bloodless. It looked like a topographic map of some landscape with twisting fjords and unexpected ravines.

Vincent looked over his shoulder, countenance sobering in an instant as he realised what Frank was looking at. "Ah."

"What happened?"

"I was flogged."

"Forgive me, but I can see that. I've seen it often enough, but you're . . ." Frank's expression was confused, and it seemed clear that at least part of it was because Vincent was white. "Did your father—?"

"No. He was always careful not to leave marks." Vincent shrugged, making the mass writhe with his motion. "Napoleon. I was a captive for a fortnight."

Frank drew his hand down his face and shook his head. "Well . . . well. I suppose it makes a little more sense now why you are so opposed to having anyone whipped."

With a bitter smile, Vincent said, "Quite apart from benevolent reasons, I can say with absolute certainty that a whipping will do nothing to make a man more cooperative."

Frank drew breath and hesitated. "May I suggest . . . may I suggest that you find reason to take your shirt off the next time you are in the fields?"

"What happened to me was not the same. It was only a fortnight."

Only a fortnight. He was correct that it was minor when compared with a lifetime of whippings, which made the slaves' reality no less horrible.

"It will lend you credibility." Frank studied the boots he held. "We are very used to Englishmen coming and wanting to make reforms, and then nothing changes. If you are serious that there will be no more whipping here . . . let them see the marks."

"If I had any doubts that you were a Hamilton, that would answer them." Vincent sighed and looked forward again. His face, in profile, was grave. "Let me think on it when I am sober."

Two days after the accident, Jane was helping Dr. Jones with Julian, a young man who had been scalded along much of his right side. Those burns were atop fresher wheals from a whipping, and the wounds showed signs of becoming infected. Dr. Jones had given him a grain of opium, so he was not entirely conscious as they changed his bandage, for which Jane was grateful. She took the soiled bandage from the doctor and dropped it into a metal basin.

Opening a jar, Dr. Jones studied the young man's back with a frown. "I have been asked about your husband's scars."

Startled, Jane paused before picking up a roll of fresh linen. She had not been certain that Vincent would follow Frank's counsel. "What do people want to know?"

"If they are real. How it happened. If he is really white."

"If he is really . . . I do not understand that last."

Dr. Jones peered at her over the young man's shoulder. "You know Mrs. Whitten."

Thrown by the apparent change in subject, Jane could only nod.

"She is in a family way. Her husband is almost as fair as Mrs. Ransford, so their child will likely be lighter than the mother and, to someone who does not know the heritage, appear white."

"Yes, but—"

"But if Mrs. Whitten were a slave, that child would also be a slave." She took the cloth from Jane and dipped it into salt water. "So the fact that your husband has scars from being flogged raises the question for some people of how he could have them if he is truly white."

As she applied the cloth to the wounds, Julian stiffened, even with the opium cutting the pain. Jane was hard pressed to steady him as Dr. Jones worked, and it was some moments before she could answer. Vincent had not been burnt on top of the whipping, but she remembered the saltwater treatment all too well. He would not let her be in the room with him while his wounds were being cleaned, but his exhaustion afterwards had been clear enough.

When Dr. Jones finished with the cloth, Jane said, "My husband was caught by Napoleon's soldiers. He had certain information that they wanted, and he would not give it to them. They had him for two weeks."

"That explains why the scars sound so impressive." She turned to her satchel and searched through it. "Out of appalling curiosity, I would like to see them. I have only seen raised scars on dark flesh. The pigmentation differences intrigue me."

"I will . . . I will see what I can do." Privately, Jane could not imagine Vincent willingly removing his shirt in front of a lady.

Dr. Jones laughed, clearly perceiving Jane's doubt on the subject. She pulled out a jar and, removing the top, turned back to their patient. "When are you going back to work on the glamural for the charity ball?"

"I had not thought to, under the circumstances."

"May I counsel against that?" She smeared a liniment with a sweet, almost honeyed character across the seeping wounds. "Having some activity will help those who lost family."

The number of dead had risen to nine, when they lost Bodelia, Smart Martin, and Jos. Sukey still hung in the balance, but her mother tended her diligently. Having something to do had seemed to help Nkiruka, and Jane knew the value of activity in staving off melancholy. "I suppose . . . I suppose I am simply too Anglican to feel entirely comfortable with the idea. At home, we strip the glamour from houses during the mourning period. But . . . but this is not England." She sighed, a bit annoyed with herself for being even a little surprised that there were differences in customs. "Do you really think it would help?"

Dr. Jones wiped her hands off on a cloth, still looking at the young man's wounds. "All I can tell you is that several of the women have asked when they could go back. So . . . yes. I think it will help." She took the roll of linen from Jane. "And how is your own situation? Seven months now, yes?"

"Well, he or she kicks with astonishing vehemence at times. Is there . . . is there a way to tell the sex?"

"Ha! I can tell you a hundred different ways, and none of them reliable. Lift his arm for me? Like that . . . good."

For a few moments, they were occupied with wrapping the bandage around his chest and shoulder. Doing so, it was difficult to avoid noticing how many times Julian had been whipped. Jane ground her teeth together as they worked. This was not England, but England was still responsible. "I will speak to Nkiruka about setting a new plan for the glamural."

Three days later, with only nine days remaining to finish the glamural, Jane and Nkiruka needed to alter their plans significantly. Vincent could no longer devote his time to working on it, and the last of the ceiling panels remained to be woven. After staring at it for a while, Jane decided to call the opening in the ceiling "intentional" and move on.

Without Louisa to run errands for her, Jane felt every month of her expectant state. She sat at the table going over lists and pressed the fingers of her left hand to her temple. She rubbed a small circle, trying to ease the dull ache. Sometimes it seemed that when she was seated, all of the discomforts of her condition made themselves known with renewed clamour.

Beside her, Nkiruka sighed with sympathy. "Where that Louisa girl?"

"Working on other things, I am afraid." Frank had seen Louisa and Zachary safely on board the ship, so they should be five days at sea by now. "Frank needed her, and after the accident at the distillery, his needs took precedence." That was true, if one omitted what those needs were.

"Mm. Need someone fu care of you." Nkiruka tapped the sheet of paper with a wrinkled finger. "After dis done, you want—you ask me once. Stay in de great house. You still want that?"

Jane lifted her head from the paper and regarded Nkiruka. If she were to interview lady's maids in England, the elderly woman would hardly have merited a single meeting. Here, what Jane wanted—no, what Jane needed—was not someone who could do her hair to match the latest fashion plate from *Ackermann's Repository* but someone that she could trust. In a just world, Nkiruka would spend her declining years spoiling grandchildren and being coddled with possets, not chasing after slippers for Jane. "You could simply stay in the house, you know. You would be welcome. We could just work on the book." Jane had set it aside to work on the glamural, but a return to the project would not be unwelcome.

"Not all day. It get dull." She shook her finger towards Jane's middle. "Besides. You go start get big soon."

"That is alarming, that this is not yet considered large."

Nkiruka laughed. "No! You shoulda min see . . ." Her voice trailed away and she frowned down at the paper. "Let me know. All right?"

On an impulse, Jane reached over and took her hand. "Yes. I would like you at the great house, very much."

Twenty-seven

Shades of Charity

The evening of the charity ball had arrived, and all of the sparkling members of Antiguan society were present. Jane was surprised by how disproportionately white men were represented. While there were white women, there were not so many as Jane had expected, and many of the gentlemen had brought elegant young women of colour with them instead. If she had met them in London, Jane might have mistaken some of them for Italian.

As the lines of dancers formed down the centre of the ballroom, surrounded by pillars of ice, Jane and Vincent stood to the side and watched. She had offered to loan Nkiruka a dress for the occasion, but the older woman had declined, preferring to stay at the great house.

Vincent looked very much as if he wished he could have stayed with her. The early part of the evening had been spent with different benefactors praising the glamural. Vincent, never easy in a crowd, had retreated into his usual taciturn self and let Jane speak to most of the patrons. The presentation of a new glamural was always difficult for him. He so hated being at the centre of attention under any circumstances, and he preferred that people be transported by the work and not think of the effort that went into it.

An elderly Scottish couple had been complimenting them for some minutes now. Even Jane had been reduced to merely nodding and smiling in response to the barrage of flattery. She came back to attention when the gentleman said, ". . . of course, now that I see the glamural, I cannot resent your having Imogene for the past month."

"She is very accomplished." Saying that Imogene had been with them the entire month was a bit much, as she had only been able to attend for two hours a week. "I only wish we could have had more of her time."

He laughed, slapping his belly. "More of her time! That is rich. I tell you, I wish we could have a second just like her, too. We missed her for the weeks she was with you. Missed her indeed. More of her time! Ha!"

As he chuckled, Jane shifted to glance at Vincent. He had a small line between his brows. This was the most conspicuous, but not the only, conversation of this nature. She wanted to question the man further but did not want to get Imogene in trouble if she had been using the glamural as an excuse to have a day of leisure. "Well, it was very kind of you."

The orchestra played the opening refrain for "Lord Nelson's Hornpipe" and offered a welcome reprieve from the string of awkward conversations. It was an easy thing to encourage the gentleman and his lady to join the couples standing up to dance.

When they had stepped away, Jane turned to Vincent. "Does it seem to you as if several of our glamourists may have misrepresented how often they were with us?"

"Given the conditions I have seen, I cannot hold a grudge against them."

"Nor I." She gave a little laugh. "I suppose that explains why I did not know who Tamar was. Likely she never worked for us."

"I find myself not terribly disturbed by this." With his hands tucked behind his back and with his dark coat and elegantly fitted breeches, Vincent cut a fine figure.

Jane sighed. He did have such well-formed calves. If only she could convince him to wear formal attire more often.

"You disagree?" he asked.

"No, I was only thinking how well you looked this evening."

He snorted. "By 'well,' I presume you mean sunburnt?"

"It does not harm your appearance. But, I was rather thinking of—"

"Mr. Hamilton, sir!" Mr. Ransford approached with Mrs. Ransford close by his side. He wore a kilt beneath his formal coat and rolled a bit as he walked. "I must congratulate you, sir, on a triumph. My wife tells me that you are the Prince Regent's glamourist! I had no idea when we met. None. I would expect a namby-pamby man, not a pugilist such as yourself. Eh? Eh?" He held up his hands and mimed boxing. "And you did all this, to boot?"

"Very little, in truth, and none at all this last week. Your wife was in charge of the snow curtain, for instance." Vincent put his hand behind Jane's back. "My wife, who is also the Prince Regent's glamourist, had charge of the project, but given her condition, the bulk of the work was actually done by a group of accomplished local glamourists."

"The column by the entrance has their names written upon it." Though Jane had requested that those slaves who had worked on the glamural be allowed to attend the ball, none of the owners who had been willing to loan them for the project seemed to be able to spare them for this particular evening.

"Well, that's as it should be, eh? Eh? The unpleasant work is always done by the slaves. That's what they are there for. That's what they are there for, I always say. And thank God for that."

God had little to do with it, but this sense of divine right had been a common refrain through the evening. Jane was beginning to suspect that it was the real reason that Nkiruka did not want to attend. Still, though, this was a charity ball, and Jane did not want to create a scene with one of the patrons. It really was too bad that boors were universal. "I must compliment Mrs. Ransford on her work."

"Very kind, I am sure." Mrs. Ransford beamed with

delight. "Though I did miss Mrs. Pridmore's help this past week. I wish you could have waited until after the ball to fire him, Sir David. I do wish that."

Vincent made an indifferent noise that simply acknowledged that she had spoken.

Mr. Ransford gave a belly laugh. "He hardly had a choice, my dear. The state of the things . . . I hear your production is already double Pridmore's, and with a reduction in your slaves at that. How are you managing that? I've got to know. Seems we wear out more leather than you trying to get our production where it should be."

"I am paying them."

With a roar of laughter, Mr. Ransford mimed punching Vincent on the shoulder. "That's rich. Well, I'm surprised you kept Pridmore as long as you did. It was a credit to the memory of your father, dear man. Although Pridmore is now saying the most shocking things in town. Only proves that you were right—quite right, if you ask me. Quite right."

"What sort of things has he said?"

"Trying to convince people your father is alive. Deuced foolishness. But then, drink will do that to a man." He shook his head and looked at his own punch cup. "Deuced foolishness."

"How astonishing," Jane managed. "The subject of drink reminds me to ask you for the recipe for your punch, Mrs. Ransford. I have not tasted its like in England, and should be glad to have it when we next host in London."

As she hoped, Mrs. Ransford caught the phrase 'in London' and leaped upon the topic, moving them safely away from Mr. Pridmore. "You are not going back to England soon, I hope?"

"Not until after my confinement, but not too long after. My parents would never forgive me if they could not see their grandchild." They were safe for some minutes, then, because the subject of children could take over any conversation.

Vincent stood beside her, silent except when compelled by etiquette to speak. He bore the Ransfords' conversation for some minutes, then abruptly put his hand on Jane's back. He said nothing, but Jane recognised this as a silent plea to find an avenue of escape.

Jane gave a sorrowful smile. "As pleasant as this is, Mrs. Ransford, you and I should probably circulate amongst the guests and continue our work for the charity."

"Oh, bless me. You are right. Come along, Mr. Ransford! Come along!" She turned from them, hauling Mr. Ransford in her wake. "Sir Thomas! So pleased to . . ." Her effusions faded into the general bustle of music and dance.

At Jane's side, Vincent let out an audible sigh. "It is not a good sign that I am thinking of the opening nights at Carlton House with sentimental regret."

"Yes, well, having the Prince Regent to distract attention is an unexpected benefit." Jane tucked her hand under his arm. "If I may suggest . . . the columns to either side of the musicians are for show only. You could safely stand within the glamour and no one would be the wiser."

"Is there room for two?"

"Two, yes." She looked down at her stomach. "Three, though, may be another matter."

"Hm . . ." He rested his hand upon hers. "We may need another solution, then."

"My dear Sir David, whatever did you have in mind?"

His lips compressed ever so slightly, and the skin at the corners of his eyes just hinted at a smile. "A discussion of the rigours of glamour, of course."

"I see."

"With a possible exploration of breathing patterns and ways to avoid overheating."

"That would be—oh! Mrs. Whitten." Jane's face must be as red as a poppy.

Elegant as always, Mrs. Whitten wore a round dress of translucent India silk, trimmed at the hem with a fortune of beads reminiscent of frosted leaves. Over the dress was an elegant quadrille robe, fastened on the left side and edged with still more silver beads. With her white gloves and shoes, the whole was exactly calculated to work in harmony with the ice palace motif.

She had with her an elderly gentleman in a black coat of an older style, with a mane of silver hair brushed smoothly back from his face. "Lady Vincent, Sir David. Would you allow me to present my dear friend Dr. Hartnell? It is his school for the poor that we are hoping to fund for another year."

"A pleasure, sir." Jane gave him the deep curtsy his age and gravity merited.

Vincent bowed in a similar fashion.

The old man smiled, his hooked nose bending along with his wrinkles. "The pleasure is entirely mine. I must thank you for your efforts on our behalf. This . . ." He waved at the ceiling. "I have travelled a good deal in my day and have not seen its like before. Remarkable."

It was so much easier to accept a compliment when one had actually done the work. "You are too kind. In truth, though, the credit belongs to the glamourists who worked with us."

"But you designed it, did you not, Lady Vincent?" He tilted his head to the side. "Have you had occasion to visit any of the Arctic countries?"

"Not yet, I am afraid."

"Oh, you must. Iceland, in particular, is one of—"

"You!" In an elegant frock of Venetian gauze, Mrs. Pridmore pushed her way through the crowd. A full plume of white ostrich feathers tipped with amber quivered over her head as she advanced on Vincent. "Mortal! That blush of shame proclaims thee Briton, once a noble name; First of the mighty, foremost of the free, Now honour'd less by all, and least by me. Seek'st thou the cause of loathing? Look around!"

It took Jane a moment to understand that Mrs. Pridmore was reciting verses by Lord Byron. Vincent seemed just as taken aback. Mrs. Pridmore's voice rose as she recited. To do her credit, her elocution was first form and filled with all the loathing of Minerva. The dancers slowed their movements and the crowd turned to watch her chant.

"First on the head of him who did this deed
"My curse shall light—on him and all his seed:
"Without one spark of intellectual fire,
"Be all the sons as senseless as the sire:
"If one with wit the parent brood disgrace,
"Believe him bastard of a brighter race:
"Still with his hireling—"

Mrs. Whitten stepped between Vincent and Mrs. Pridmore. "My dear . . . perhaps this is not the best time."

"He had no right! Grenville worked so hard. All the time." Her voice shook with emotion. "What are we to do?"

"Let us go somewhere more private, hm?" Mrs. Whitten looked past Mrs. Pridmore and caught the eye of one of her servants. He nodded, and, in moments, two men in livery were sliding through the crowd. "I have been wishing you would come to me."

"How could I? After he fired Grenville. With no cause! The humiliation is not to be borne. He is so—we had such hopes, and now . . ." She began to weep.

Vincent spread his hands in distress. "Mrs. Pridmore, please accept my honest regrets that you—"

She screamed and flung herself at him. Without thinking, Jane stepped in front of her husband. At almost the same moment, Vincent took Jane by the shoulders. He turned her, sliding around her, so his back was to Mrs. Pridmore. The breath puffed out of him, but he stood, arms wrapped around Jane, as Mrs. Pridmore rained blows against his back.

For several long moments, the shock held everyone in place. Then, Dr. Hartnell said firmly, "Mrs. Pridmore!"

"Let go! Let me go!" she shrieked, sobbing. "I will see you hanged! We have friends. Do not forget that! We have friends here!" Still sobbing, she was half led, half carried through the crowd, all of whom stepped back with murmurs at the spectacle.

Hands shaking, Vincent released Jane. She turned, her shock giving way rapidly to useless fear now that the danger was past. He had closed his expression off so it seemed severe, but nothing more. Holding her at arm's length, Vincent ran his gaze over her person. "Muse? Are you all right?"

"Shocked, only. You should not have done that, she—"

"The baby." He let go of one arm and wiped his face. "As soon as you moved—her aim changed. Down."

That was the only moment of comparative solitude they were granted. The crowd that had stood back during Mrs. Pridmore's actual assault now rushed around them, wanting to hear all the details.

In the midst of this, Mrs. Whitten appeared. "Shall I call your carriage?"

"Yes." Jane had no need to consult Vincent when his body spoke with such eloquence of wanting to escape. "Forgive me, but yes."

With a sigh of relief, Mrs. Whitten nodded. "Good. Because I suspected as much and already did."

She extricated them from the crowd, making their apologies for them, and in short order, had Jane and Vincent out of the ballroom and in the carriage. Vincent leaned back against the seat with a heavy sigh. He winced and straightened again.

"Did she hurt you?"

"No . . . although, remarkably, she lands a more solid punch than her husband."

On the Sunday following the charity ball, Jane and Vincent prepared for a different event. With the assistance of Frank and Nkiruka, they had arranged a thank-you dinner for the glamourists who had helped create the glamural and their families.

Nkiruka held the violet satin petticoat out for Jane and helped her pull it on.

As the older woman reached for the black net frock she would wear atop it, Jane sighed and pressed her hands against the base of her spine to massage the dull ache there. It seemed as though her back almost always hurt these days.

"De picknee hurting you?"

"Oh no." It was only when Jane stood, or sat, or laid down. She slipped her arms through the full sleeves. She should not complain about the aches attendant on her condition to Nkiruka, of all people. "You should go on and get ready. Vincent can help me with the rest."

"Pfff . . . he ah glamourist. Not hairdresser."

From his place by the window, Vincent raised a brow at that. He had put on his breeches before Nkiruka's arrival, but he had been turning his shirt over and straightening his waistcoat for the past quarter-hour. Covering a smile, Jane leaned towards the older woman and lowered her voice. "I know, but he is too modest to dress with you here."

Patting her hand, Nkiruka winked and left without further protest, although her chuckle was audible after the door closed.

"I could have used the dressing screen."

"I am certain you could have." Still, that was not Jane's chief reason for sending the older woman out. She pulled open a drawer and withdrew a small package. "But . . . it occurred to me that today is the nineteenth of July, and in the nearly four years of our marriage, we have always been in the midst of some crisis on your birthday."

He stared at her and at the brown paper parcel in her hands. The severity of Vincent's countenance made most people assume that he was older than his one-and-thirty years. In this moment, he seemed younger and almost lost. His mouth worked for a moment, until he cleared his throat. "I . . . I am not in the habit of marking the day."

"Well, I will not make a fuss as if you were reaching your majority." She handed him the package and kissed him on the cheek. "But I liked having an excuse to do a little something for you."

"Thank you." His voice was low and rough.

"You have not opened it."

She watched him keenly as he undid the string tying the paper shut. It was not often that she was nervous about what he would think, but this particular gift had enough of her in it to prompt tremors of anticipation. Inside the paper was a case, smaller than the palm of her hand, made of the local sandbox tree. The thorns of the tree had been sanded away, leaving a pattern of small burs in the smooth wood. It had been polished with beeswax until it shone as though glamoured. Vincent undid the catch and opened the case. Through an ingenious system, it unfolded into a small trifold frame. Frank had arranged the case for her, but Jane had painted the small watercolours within it. On the left was one of herself, and the right held one of Vincent.

The centre was empty yet.

"Muse . . ." was all he managed to say before pulling her into an embrace. His other approbations did not require language to understand, which was fortunate, since neither of the Vincents had the ability to speak for some time.

When they emerged from the room to welcome their guests, Vincent had the miniature frame tucked into the inside pocket of his dinner coat. It was so slender the outline did not show, but his hand drifted to his breast pocket from time to time. Jane caught Frank's questioning gaze as they stood in the foyer to welcome the guests. She gave a little smile and a nod to let him know that the gift had been well received.

If Lord Verbury had still been in residence at the great house, Jane doubted that it would have occurred to her or to Vincent to open the dining room for anyone. He would hear of it, of course, but simply having him under a different roof made it easier. By Frank's account, Lord Verbury even seemed to be enjoying his stay, which she attributed to the influence of his youngest granddaughters. At the tender ages of six and eight, they possessed such winning ways that even his lordship was not immune.

They had sent the carriage and the wagons from the distillery for the slaves from the farther plantations. Jane had no idea how Frank had convinced the other estate owners to agree, but she suspected that it involved invoking their station as the Prince Regent's glamourists. As the first wagon pulled up and its occupants alighted, Jane stepped onto the veranda with Vincent to meet them. "Jeannette, so lovely to see you. Is this your husband?"

The stout, matronly woman had recovered from the fire at the distillery quite well. Most of her burns had been mild, as she had been some distance from the boiler, for which Jane was grateful. Jeannette did her best curtsy and poked her husband in the side. "Yes, ma'am. This is William Smith." She wore a simple calico dress, a little faded, but painfully clean. William Smith wore dark trousers, mended at one knee, a white shirt, and a neckcloth of rough cotton.

Jane welcomed them, regretting that she had chosen to wear her formal gown. As they went in, she turned to meet the next couple. The woman bore a strong resemblance to Amey, with round cheeks and the same warm tones to her skin.

"Please be welcome. My husband, Sir Da—" Jane cut off as the pain that had been in her lower back reached around her entire middle and squeezed. On instinct, she reached for Vincent. Jane had felt this particular pain before. That time she had tried to convince herself that it was only a cramp.

"Jane! What is— Oh, God."

"No—wait. This happens to some women." She had to believe that. This had to be a false labour. "Give me a moment."

Vincent turned to the interior. "Frank!"

Jane put her hand on her lower back and forced herself to straighten. "There. See? It has passed." She took a breath, trying desperately not to cry. The front sweep was full of wagons, and she put on a smile for them. The woman still stood in front of them, watching her carefully. Jane could not remember her name in that moment. "Please come inside and be welcome."

Vincent took her arm. "Jane . . . come away."

"There is nothing to be done." She swallowed. "Either I am in labour in earnest, in which case we have some time, or, this was a false labour, which seems likely. Let us see what happens before resorting to panic. You recall how long Melody's delivery was." She was speaking to herself as much as to him, because the third possibility sat between them.

She did not let him argue, simply turned and greeted the next guest. Jane had no idea what she said—she relied on her education to carry her through the social forms of introductions and welcome. What little part of her was not turned inward directed itself towards Vincent, who hovered by her side, going through the same forms as Jane.

He turned away from her only once, when Frank arrived. She half heard the hurried conversation and knew that they were sending for Dr. Jones. Beneath her façade of civility,

Jane was too terrified to tell them not to. Deep inside, she repeated to herself, *Not again. Please God. Not again.*

And then she greeted the next guest and the one after that. As five minutes turned to ten, and then ten to fifteen, Jane began to relax. Women in her neighbourhood had been afflicted with these pains. So long as they were irregular—or, please God, there was only one—she had nothing to worry about.

Then another pain started in her back and her entire middle tightened again. Jane stopped with a word half formed on her lips and closed her eyes. It was not that it hurt. Indeed, the pain was no more than when her flower arrived, but it was so clearly a bearing pain.

Vincent swept her up in his arms, turning towards the house before she could draw breath. She clung to him as he carried her to their rooms. The hard square of the picture frame thumped against her cheek with each step. That inner voice crept out as she pressed her face against his jacket. "Not again. Please, please . . . not again."

"Hush. Shh . . . shh . . . Frank has sent for Dr. Jones, and she will take good care of you." But his grip tightened on her. He knew the math as well as she did. Seven and a half months. Thirty weeks.

It was too soon.

Twenty-eight

The Good Doctor

By the time Vincent had set her down on the bed in their room, the bearing pain had ended. Jane wiped her eyes as he stepped back. Vincent shifted his weight. "What do I do?"

Jane had no idea. She had been with Melody during her delivery, but until close to the end, most of the time had been spent waiting. Even then, Jane's role had just been to hold Melody's hand. Vincent would need some activity, at least at first. It was easier to worry about him than to think about what was happening to her. Near panic already compromised her ability to breathe. She had tried to be so careful. Jane caught her thoughts before they could run away with her. Clearly, she needed some activity as well.

"Help me undress." She sat up.

Vincent leaped forward. "You should be lying down."

"I am not doing this in an evening gown." She slid her feet off the bed. "Besides, the midwife had Melody walking until her time began in earnest."

"But—yes, of course." Though Vincent was well practised in assisting her under other circumstances, his movements were so cautious that Jane could have unstitched the gown faster.

"I am not a china cup." As if to belie her words, another of the cramping waves made Jane stop and close her eyes. God. It was too soon.

The door to their room opened, but she could not bring herself to open her eyes to see who had come. The voice identified her soon enough, though. "De picknee coming, eh?"

Vincent answered for her. "It seems so. Can you . . . ?"

"Sure, sure. You go 'head now."

"I cannot leave her."

Jane was able to inhale slowly and open her eyes. "Actually, I would like for you to go."

His face had already been pale with worry, but now his brows turned up, completely stricken. "Muse . . ."

She put a hand on his arm. "We have guests."

"You cannot think I am going to dinner while you are in here—" He waved a hand at her middle, unable to finish the sentence. "You cannot expect that."

"I want you back later, but it will be hours before there is anything except discomfort. Let Nkiruka get me settled while you at least start the dinner." She could see that he was going to protest again. "I promise I will have someone call you when Dr. Jones arrives."

Vincent opened and closed his fists, jaw tight. At last, he exhaled forcibly and leaned down to kiss her on the cheek. "I love you." Straightening, he looked at Nkiruka. "Call me the moment anything changes. The very moment."

Nkiruka helped Jane out of her gown, petticoat, and short stays so that she wore only her chemise. Over that, she pulled a morning gown, which gave her the illusion of modesty, but would be easy to remove when needed. At Nkiruka's suggestion, Jane took a turn around the room when the discomfort became too strong to sit still. She was walking, hands placed against her lower back, with Nkiruka at her side, when rapid footsteps and a brisk knock announced the arrival of Dr. Jones.

Still in her riding coat, the doctor opened the door and eyed Jane. "You need to lie down. Immediately."

Jane raised her head, frowning. "Nkiruka suggested this, and it does seem to help the pain."

"Has your water broken?"

"I do not think so."

Dr. Jones looked past Jane to Nkiruka and raised her eyebrows in question. The older woman shook her head. "Not yet. The pain just start."

"Thirty weeks. We do not want labour to begin." Dr. Jones set her satchel down and pulled off her riding coat to disclose a simple Pomona green round gown of stout linen. "Mrs. Hamilton, I want you to lie down on your left side, please."

Jane was too unsettled to fully understand her and needed a nudge from Nkiruka to move. Dr. Jones had said, "do not want labour to begin" as if there were a *choice*. Jane sat on the edge of the bed, her frown sinking. "Can you stop the labour?"

"My hope . . ." Dr. Jones pulled a tightly stoppered bottle from her satchel and set it on the side table. "My hope is that you have not begun labour in earnest. If you have not, then we might be able to put it off for a while yet."

While they had been waiting for Dr. Jones's arrival, Nkiruka had stripped the bed down to a single sheet plus some pillows. Jane lay down and then rolled onto her left side, which put the doctor behind her.

"Nkiruka, will you take this to the cook and ask her to steep it in milk? I want it warm, but not hot. Also, a basin of hot water and some clean towels."

Patting Jane on the arm, Nkiruka left her side. "Quick quick."

Jane glanced over her shoulder in time to see Nkiruka take an oil-paper envelope from the doctor. She lifted her head a little. "Will you please tell Vincent that Dr. Jones is here?"

"Na worry." And Nkiruka was out the door.

Not worry? Jane had a better chance of sailing a ship to the Arctic Circle. No. No, she was not her mother. She would not fret before knowing what was happening. Another bearing pain took hold and Jane let her head drop back to the pillow. She tightened against it, trying not to make a sound.

"Bearing pain?"

Jane nodded and managed to say, "Yes," though her voice sounded choked, even to her.

Something light and metal rattled behind her. "When was the last?"

"I do not—do not know. Half an hour?"

"Hm." Behind her, Dr. Jones poured some liquid into a glass. "I shall want you to drink this. The taste will be quite strong, but please drink it all."

"What is it?"

"A strong claret infused with ginger, passion fruit, wild yam, and Hoffmann's anodyne. Let me know when the pain eases." She crossed around the bed to Jane with a glass in one hand and a watch on a chain in the other.

To Jane, the band around her stomach felt as though it were tightening rather than softening. She did not know how much time passed before she could nod that it had dwindled. It could not have been that long, as Vincent had not arrived yet. "It is better."

Dr. Jones snapped the watch shut. "The wine will likely make you dull, but its purpose this evening is to try to relax you, with the hope of stopping the bearing pains, or at least slowing them."

In the hall, rapid footsteps that were not quite at a run gave notice of Vincent's approach. He stopped outside the room. Jane could imagine him composing his expression.

Indeed, when the door opened, Vincent gave every appearance of being quite calm, if one dismissed the rapidity of his breath. He bowed. "Doctor."

"Mr. Hamilton." Dr. Jones handed Jane the glass of wine. It had a distinct spicy resinous fragrance that burnt Jane's nose.

They continued for a moment with formal pleasantries while Jane drank the odd mixture. It made her feel as though her teeth were being sanded with honey. Harder than drinking it was not shouting at them to omit the social forms. She was not her mother, however. Jane could be calm. She could wait until the doctor had something to communicate.

Only when Jane had drained the glass and handed it back to the doctor did the conversation progress. Setting the glass on a side table, Dr. Jones said, "I need to examine you. Do you want your husband to step into the hall?"

"No, thank you."

Vincent looked startled. "You have not examined her yet?"

"I have been here no more than five minutes." Dr. Jones pulled Jane's shift up. "Draw your knees up to your stomach, please."

Jane tilted her head up and studied the glamour that Vincent had wrapped around the bed. She thought it likely that he was using the Wohlreich variation to create guide threads for the hummingbirds to fly along. Without being able to see into the ether, it was as much a mystery as how anyone could have cold hands in such a warm climate. Jane shifted a little on the bed and turned her attention to the feather pattern on the hummingbirds. He had not individually woven each feather, but when the little creations were in motion they gave every appearance of having real feathers. She would have to ask Vincent to stop one of them so she could examine it more closely.

"Mrs. Hamilton, had you experienced any discomfort before you sent for me?"

"No. Not really."

Vincent cleared his throat. "Her back has been hurting for the past two days."

"Oh, but that is normal for a woman in my condition."

"It has been worse lately."

Jane stared at him. Though he was correct, she was certain that she had not complained of such. "How could you possibly know that?"

"You have been knotting your hands and pressing at the base of your spine."

Dr. Jones asked Vincent, rather than Jane, "Has the pain come and gone?"

"I believe so."

"Have you noted the frequency?"

Jane said, "Pardon me, but the wine has not left me incapable of answering questions."

With a touch of asperity, Dr. Jones straightened from her examination. "Will you answer with more accuracy than, 'No. Not really'? Because I will tell you that it is difficult to diagnose a patient who will not discuss their symptoms."

"I did not wish to complain about something that seemed minor."

"When a doctor asks you about pain, answering is not a complaint." Dr. Jones put her hands on her hips and glared at Jane. "Now. How long has your back been hurting?"

"The past two days."

"And has the pain come and gone?"

"Yes."

"Have you noted the frequency?"

Jane hesitated, not certain. "No. I was trying not to pay attention to it, to be honest."

Dr. Jones wheeled on Vincent. "Mr. Hamilton?"

"I was not at home for large parts of yesterday, so cannot account for those, but today it seemed as though she were uncomfortable about once an hour." He looked at Jane with some apology. "You sighed."

"That hardly seems worthy of note."

"Well, you never complain, so I have learned to pay attention to your sighs."

"There was nothing to complain about."

Vincent opened his mouth and then snapped it shut again. He nodded, with his lips pressed tightly together around whatever he was not saying.

"What?"

He shook his head and addressed the doctor. "Can you tell us what is—what to expect?"

He was the most provoking man sometimes. She could not even scold him for the bald change in subject, because it was to one in which she had the keenest interest.

"These are irregular symptoms." Dr. Jones turned the watch over in her hands, opening the cover. "The back pain and the regularity of the bearing pains are consistent with early parturition. But she is showing none of the other signs. Without her history, I would call these false bearing pains and not worry. But with it . . . with it, I think it likely that she will come to term early. The longer we can delay parturition, the better your child's chances."

Jane inhaled sharply at that. An angry part of her wondered what Vincent would make of the breath. Given the tension in his own countenance, she imagined that he was managing a similar terror. Her query of, "How long . . . ?" was met with his: "What can we do?"

Dr. Jones held up her hands to hush them both. "I have read of infants born as early as seven months surviving to maturity. I will feel more secure if we can get you to eight months, but every day will help. So we are going to try to slow the bearing pains, and until the baby comes, you are confined to bed."

Through the night, Jane was turned, given possets, and wrapped in hot flannels, all in an effort to relax her womb. The draughts that Dr. Jones had provided did, indeed, make Jane dull, but not enough to allow her to sleep through the bearing pains. As the ache began in her back again, Jane shifted in bed, surprised to see that morning had broken.

Seated by the bed, Vincent lifted his head from his book and reached for his watch. He still wore his formal clothes from the evening prior, but the cravat was wildly rumpled and his hair looked as though it had been nested in by a frightened owl. "Another?"

"Yes." She sighed as the ache spread across her middle. "It is not as bad, I think."

From her chair by the balcony doors, Nkiruka quietly snored with her head resting against the cushions. More alert, Dr. Jones sat up on the chaise lounge. "How long was the interval this time?"

"A little over two hours." Vincent kept his eye on his watch as he had been instructed.

Jane rested her hand on her stomach, waiting for it to ease. Early in the evening, she had been counting, but now she could barely form numbers in her head, much less string them into a rank. "It is lessening."

"Thirty-seven seconds."

Dr. Jones stood up, stretching. "Good. I think that we can safely say that these are false pains."

Jane did not agree that the pains were entirely false, but she understood what the doctor meant. She closed her eyes in relief.

"But I do not want to chance you standing."

The little bit of relief Jane had enjoyed subsided. Though she would very much have liked to protest that she was well, she was exhausted and frightened. "You think bed rest is still necessary?"

"I do."

Nkiruka snorted and woke, jerking her head up from where it had sagged. The lines of her years were more apparent on her face that morning. She should have gone to bed hours ago. Blinking the sleep from her eyes, Nkiruka sat forward. "Wha happen?"

"Mrs. Hamilton's pains seem to have slowed." Dr. Jones came to the bed and lifted the log that Vincent had been keeping of Jane's bearing pains. "More significantly, they are irregular now. You will likely be fatigued today, but as the time passes, you will become afflicted with ennui. Have you a project with which to occupy yourself?"

Her head was so heavy that she could scarcely imagine being interested in doing anything.

"Dat book? Mebbe you can work on dat?" Nkiruka rubbed her eyes and peered at Dr. Jones. "It all right to bring visitors? Talk glamour?"

They had set it aside while working on the glamural, and then, with the injured here at the great house, Jane had given it little thought. She could not even recall where they had left off, though that might have as much to do with the draughts that Dr. Jones had given her.

Dr. Jones raised her eyebrows and gave Nkiruka a look that Jane did not quite understand. "Yes, one or two visitors a day will do no harm. One or two." She turned back to Jane. "So long as you stay in bed and do not become overexcited."

"It shall be the driest prose imaginable."

"You do not need to go to such heroic lengths. Simply pay attention to your body. If the pains become regular or less than twenty minutes apart, send for me at once." She fixed Vincent with a glare. "And do not agitate her."

"I will do my best."

Dr. Jones turned to Nkiruka with something that almost looked like anger. "May I ask for your assistance with the patients?"

"She need me here."

Vincent cleared his throat. "I will stay with Jane."

She hated being such a bother. If she were going to do nothing but lie in bed all day, all she needed was a bell to ring for someone. It took too long to assemble that thought into a sentence. By the time it was prepared, the farewells had already occurred.

Vincent closed the door behind them and leaned against the handle for a moment. Clearing his throat again, he rounded the end of the bed so that she did not have to strain to see him. "Shall I read to you? Or do you want to try to sleep?"

"Will you lie down with me?"

He looked at the bed with something like fear. "I do not want to disturb you."

"Please believe that you cannot disturb me any more than I already am." Jane rubbed her face, which was sticky with dried sweat from the hot flannels she had been wrapped in. "I cannot believe that you slept at all last night."

He tilted his head in a half shrug. "You may be right."

"So come." She patted the bed behind her. "Lie down and try to get some rest. I worry about you."

He shook his head and snorted.

"What is amusing?" She so wanted to go to him, or at the least to sit up.

"You fret about me all the time, but never complain on your own behalf."

"To be fair, my health has been generally good."

He held up his hands. "I am not supposed to agitate you, so I shall not argue."

"I am not certain whether to be delighted by this new power or dismayed." Jane tucked the pillow more firmly beneath her head. "I shall choose delighted, and further declare that if you do not lie down and rest, I shall be quite agitated."

"Now you are not playing fairly."

"Indeed." Jane beckoned him closer and took his hand. She gave a gentle pull, lifting her head. Vincent bent down to kiss her. When he was close, she gave her most inviting smile. "Just lie down for a little? I will feel better if you do. Besides, you will be able to feel the bearing pains when they occur."

He kissed her again, on the forehead. "As you wish."

Shedding his coat, he walked around to the other side of the bed. When he slid under the counterpane, Jane reached for his arm and pulled it around her. Vincent lay pressed against her back, but though he was quiet, she could tell by his breathing that he did not fall asleep.

Twenty-nine

Contraction and Agitation

Jane had a writing board propped upon her stomach, which was proving a remarkably useful surface. She wiped her pen off, studying the page, and then glanced across the room to where Dolly sat with Nkiruka. "Let me read this back to make certain I understood correctly."

"You go 'head."

"The Asante, in contrast to the Igbo, see glamour as divided into five parts. Two of these are easily explicable as a division of light into the visible spectrum, or *krasodae hann*, and *krasodae esuma hann*, which is all light outside the visible spectrum. *Krasodae dede* is what the British call 'sound' and *krasodae huam* is 'scent.' They have, in addition to these, a fifth form of glamour, which is tactile in nature. Though the effects are faint, they are nevertheless tangible."

Jane sighed and scowled at the page, wishing once again that she could see the weaves. She thought, but was not certain, that *krasodae ka* was, in fact, a breeze that was woven with more precision than she was used to granting it. It was similar to other glamours in that it was largely an illusion, but Dolly could make it feel as though someone had tapped Jane lightly upon the shoulder. When Vincent was home next, she would have to put the question to him.

Dolly nodded. "That right."

Jane gnawed on her lower lip. "Can you show the weaves in the visible spectrum, just so I might see? I should like to sketch them."

"Sure." Her nut-brown face wrinkled in concentration. "But a lot of it have to do with what part of the *akoma so dae* you take hold of."

"Pardon? The *akoma so dae*? What is that?"

Dolly frowned, drumming her fingers on her knee. "Is . . . is the ether."

Jane sat up, then reminded herself to lie against the pillows again. She sank back against the bed's headboard. This was new, the idea that there was more than one part to the ether. "How many parts does the ether have?"

"T'ree." Dolly held up her fingers and ticked off three different words. "*Akoma so dae*, *adwene so dae*, and *asaase so dae*."

"Nkiruka. Does Igbo do this as well?"

Nkiruka looked frankly baffled. "No. Only one: *mkpụrụ obi ikuku*—ether. How come you nuh say before?"

"Arwe nuh talk. Arwe jus' do." Dolly shrugged and sucked her teeth in amusement. "How you nuh say ah only one ether?"

She had a fair point. Jane paused before answering, and, in that pause, heard several horses coming up the drive. They were not expecting visitors today. Feeling very much like her mother, Jane asked, "Can you see who that is?"

Nkiruka stood and went out to the veranda, leaning on the rail to look towards the front of the house. She straightened quickly. "Ah de soldier an' dem."

Jane tightened her hands into fists. The unexpected arrival of soldiers never led to anything good. "Will one of you be so kind as to find Sir David at once? And Frank, as well."

Brushing her hands off on her apron, Nkiruka headed for the door. "Mr. Frank done know. Mi sure smadee done tell he. Where Sir David?"

Jane reached for the itinerary Vincent had left for her. He had written one out every day for the past week so that if anything occurred, she could send for him quickly. "Two o'clock. He should be at the distillery."

"I'll tell Jove. He'll go." As Nkiruka opened the door, Jane could hear masculine voices from the front of the house. She could make out nothing of what was being said, save that the tone was demanding.

Heart pounding, Jane wiped her quill off again, though

it was quite dry. She folded the papers into a neat bundle, but the pages betrayed her by rattling with her nerves. Tightening her grip to stop the shaking, Jane reached over to put the paper on the side table. She would have given almost anything to be allowed out of bed. Without being asked, Dolly came and lifted the writing board from what passed for her lap.

Jane wiped her hands on the counterpane and tried to think of something to say to fill the awkward silence. She could not even offer Dolly a drink without pressing her into service to get it. She swallowed and took a breath to calm herself. "So . . . we were speaking of the ether, I believe. What distinguishes the various ethers for you?"

Compressing her lips, Dolly settled into the chair by the bed that Vincent habitually occupied when he was in the room. She clearly knew that Jane wanted distraction. "The *akoma so dae* closest to . . . to mi heart. Is for—" Dolly sighed, frowning with aggravation. With her fingers curled a little inward, she waved her hand in front of her face. "It here. Is seeing. Is feeling."

"Illusions? Emotions?"

"No." She grimaced. "Next time I bring mi daughter. She tell. She—"

The sound of rapid footsteps stopped her voice. Jane clutched the counterpane and faced the door, trying to at least appear calm. Nkiruka shoved the door open with her hip, looking back down the hall. "Is Pridmore. Mad. Searching for the master."

"For . . ." Jane's voice died away. He had found someone to arrest Lord Verbury. "For Sir David, you mean?"

"No, no. He father. The old master. Say he still alive."

"Really? My husband will be interested to hear that." Jane bit her lower lip. Their reasons for keeping Vincent's father hidden were twofold, both based on their fear of his retaliation. Vincent was certain that, were he exposed as being alive, he would immediately sell Frank's family in a show of sheer malice. The other fear—that he would somehow implicate Vincent in his crimes—was of less concern to Jane. She felt confident that, though Verbury would do everything in his power to make their lives miserable, he could not do any lasting harm to them. Frank had no such assurance.

"What you wan' to do?"

"I cannot do anything, beyond what you have already done for me. I am afraid that we must simply wait to hear what happens after he speaks with Sir David."

"I mean, when he come here." Nkiruka jerked her thumb in the direction of the front of the house. "They searching whole house."

"I—I see. Well, it is vexing, but we have nothing to hide." She wiped her hands on the counterpane again. "Shall we pick up where we left off?"

They spoke for only another twenty minutes—though Jane attended very little of it—before the sound of a horse at full gallop sounded on the front sweep. Nkiruka went to look without being asked and came back as quickly. "Your husband. Whew! He look angry."

"I am certain he is." The helplessness of being confined to this room without any notion of what was happening increased Jane's disquiet more than simply having Pridmore in the house. Louisa, at least, was beyond his reach and should, with luck, be landing in England with Zachary soon.

Her stomach tightened painfully, as if to remind her that she was not to be agitated. Jane closed her eyes and tried to calm herself. She rested a hand on her middle, willing the tension away. Slow and steady breaths might help.

Nkiruka shifted from one foot to the other, dress whispering with the movement. "Mebbe you lie down?"

The urge to scream was very strong—not from pain, but because Jane was so constrained in her choices that *lying down* was her most useful course. She clenched her jaw and drew in another slow breath. "Likely you are correct."

She began to understand why her mother was so often vexed. Jane eased down into the bed and rolled onto her left side. For reasons she did not understand, that seemed to be the most comfortable. The baby thumped against the wall of her stomach. She pressed back against the spot, relieved that some of the tension had faded already. Not a long bearing pain, then, and the last had been several hours ago.

Vincent's unmistakable footsteps pounded down the hall. Jane lifted herself on her elbow to look over her shoulder as her husband burst into the room. His gaze went to her immediately. "Are you all right?"

"Yes. But the message was about—"

"I know." He still held the door with one hand, already halfway back into the hall. "I just needed to be certain that Pridmore had not come anywhere near you." He turned to Nkiruka. "Lock the door behind me. I put nothing past him."

And he was gone again, footsteps retreating down the hall in haste. Nkiruka locked the door, then went and locked the door to the veranda for good measure. Jane was left with nothing to do but lie in bed and try to be calm.

The tension in her chest had nothing to do with labour pains.

Another three-quarters of an hour passed, during which the ladies abandoned all pretence of discussing glamour. Their conversation consisted entirely of speculation about what was happening outside their locked room. That conversation stopped with another set of footsteps. Jane raised her head from the pillow, counting. It sounded as if Vincent were accompanied by at least four men, possibly five.

Though somewhat deadened by the wall, she could hear their conversation clearly enough for concern. Stopping outside their door, a gruff British man said, "And this room?"

"That is our bedchamber. My wife is within and not well." Vincent's cold, aristocratic tones were barely recognisable as her husband, save for the timbre of his voice.

"Bet you anything that's where they are keeping him," Mr. Pridmore said.

"We have been over the whole of the estate. I have been

patient, because I believe that Admiral Cunningham is here in good faith. About you, sir, I have no such belief."

"For diligence, Mr. Hamilton. My apologies, but I must insist."

"And I regret the necessity of declining. She is in a fragile condition and must not be agitated."

It was too late for that. Jane was already agitated beyond what she could stand. She waved to Nkiruka. "Open the door. Please."

The older woman narrowed her eyes at Jane, which seemed best to ignore. Jane pushed herself up in bed. She would not be foolish, but neither was she going to be discovered curled on her side like an invalid. It was bad enough to be in bed in a morning dress that imperfectly covered the great hill of her stomach.

Jane pulled the counterpane up more firmly as Nkiruka opened the door.

Vincent stood framed in the door, arms folded across his chest. He spun, clearly startled, and gave Jane a glimpse of a white man in his later years, with a hoary grey moustache. He wore the uniform of a navy officer. Mr. Pridmore stood just behind him, face mottled red with sun or drink.

Pridmore pushed past Admiral Cunningham.

Vincent stopped him with a hand on his chest. "No." That single word, spoken in a low tone, was imbued with more threat than a dozen syllables.

Pridmore shrugged his hand away, fist clenching at his side. "Never touch me."

"Then do not anger me."

"Vincent?" Jane called from the bed. "I do not mind if the admiral comes in."

At the sound of her voice, the tableau broke and she was able to breathe a little better. With a bow, Vincent faced the admiral, taking Jane's lead. "May I ask that only you enter?"

"What are you hiding, Hamilton?"

Vincent neglected Pridmore and kept his gaze on the admiral. "Please. She is in danger of coming to term early."

With a grunt, the admiral turned to address what Jane presumed was the rest of his attendants. "I will be but a moment." He stepped inside. "The door remains open, of course."

"Of course." Vincent's chin was tucked deep into his cravat. He followed the admiral into the room with his hands clenched behind his back. His voice was coldly formal as he made the introductions.

Dolly and Nkiruka took up stations by the wall, heads bent as if they were only servants, but Jane could see their fingers fidgeting and had a strong suspicion they were using glamour to talk to each other. Jane tried to smile at the admiral, but she felt her chin tremble. There were many things that vexed her about being with child, but the ease with which she cried was one of the more irksome. She was agitated and a little angry, not sad, so the threat of tears perplexed her.

"My apologies, madam, for disturbing you." The admiral gave a superficial glance around the room, taking in the bed and the rest of the furniture. He slowed a little at the glamural Vincent had cast about the bed, but his examination of the room took no more than half a minute in total. He offered Jane a bow. "I thank you for your time, and wish you joy."

"Is that it? What about under the bed?" Mr. Pridmore charged into the room.

Vincent spun and took him by the collar. He shoved him back so hard that Mr. Pridmore came off his feet, slamming into the doorframe. He staggered into the hall, and a uniformed arm caught him before he fell. Another white man stepped into view, holding Mr. Pridmore up.

Vincent, who was not a small man, seemed to have grown even taller and broader. His hands were no longer behind his back, but held ready at his sides. "Do not. Come into. This room."

"You saw what he did, Admiral? You saw that? Verbury must be in there." He waved at the glamural. "Probably hidden in all that whigmaleery."

Jane was fairly certain that Vincent was a paper width away from punching Pridmore again. No matter how justified, it would almost certainly complicate matters. "Admiral, if you would like the glamural to be taken down, I can arrange that."

"And why do they even have a glamural? If Lord Verbury is really dead, should they not be in mourning?"

"We have it because I am confined to bed, and my husband has made every effort to amuse me. Mr. Pridmore, truly, I understand that you are angry because you and Sir

David did not agree about how the estate should be managed, but this is unbecoming."

"I was doing my job! I was doing what his lordship explicitly asked me to do. And if you had not hidden him, he would confirm that."

Admiral Cunningham shook his head. "Thank you, Sir David, for your time. I think we have seen more than enough."

"But they are lying!"

The rub of it was that Jane and Vincent *were* lying, but the accusation still would not rest easy on her husband. She cleared her throat. "Your reasoning is *inscrutable.*"

Vincent pulled his gaze from Mr. Pridmore. Even the residue of his fury was daunting. "Yes. And curious, too. I think that you are claiming that my father is alive, when for that to be the case, *you* would have had to shelter him for the year prior to my arrival. Do I need to remind you again that he was accused of being a traitor to the crown?"

Admiral Cunningham spread his hands in apology. "Truly, that was the only reason I came. Rear-Admiral Hume had delayed Lord Verbury's arrest due to his health, and then he passed away. But Mr. Pridmore claimed he was alive and . . . well. It seemed best to be certain."

"I quite understand." Vincent maintained a remarkably even tone.

"My thanks for behaving like a true gentleman about all this bother." The admiral shot a glance at Pridmore to suggest that *he* was not a gentleman. "Good day, sir. Madam."

Mr. Pridmore gaped in the hall. "You can't—he's here. He's got to be here somewhere." He stepped forward again, but this time the officer in the hall stopped him. He tried to shake the man off but, at a gesture from Admiral Cunningham, was dragged backwards out of Jane's view. "I'll find him! I don't know where you've hidden him, but I'll turn over every stone and smoke him out!"

Admiral Cunningham shook his head as Vincent began to follow him into the hall. "Best to stay here, eh? I would have lost my temper long ago." He pulled the door shut after him, leaving Vincent in the room with Jane.

They all stood, in frozen silence, listening to Mr. Pridmore's rants fade into the distance as he was marched down the passage and out of the building. Without turning, Vincent said, "Nkiruka, Dolly. May I ask you to leave us?"

Though his tone was painfully calm, it brooked no discussion. They broke from their positions by the wall. In moments, the two women were out of the room, and Jane was alone with her husband. Still, he remained staring at the door.

Jane waited, giving him time to collect himself. She looked to the basin, to see if there were clean towels. There were. The side table had a fresh decanter of lime juice. She could not rise to offer him either, but they were there if he needed them.

Vincent drew a sudden breath. "I have just lied to an honourable man." His hands tightened into fists. "I just lied to protect a man I detest, because if I did not, I know precisely what he would do to Frank's family. So I lied, knowing that my father was depending upon my nature, knowing that he was using me, knowing that even when he is not present, he can still twist and shape me to his purpose. Knowing that the lie would be another weapon he could use against us. And still I lied for him."

"Not directly."

"As you have reminded me, lies of omission are still lies. I still did exactly what my father wanted. I *protected him.*" Only the edge of his face was visible from Jane's position, but she thought his eyes were closed. "I keep thinking how much easier it would be if he were actually dead."

"I have entertained the same thoughts."

"But you would not act upon it."

"Nor would—"

"I am so angry that I do not trust myself." He spoke rapidly, as if the words escaped against his will. "Will it alarm you more if I hide or am visibly disturbed?"

"I would rather know. Always."

He grunted in reply and, for two moments longer, remained still. When Vincent moved, he shoved his hands into the ether, tearing great masses of red into the room. With an inarticulate growl, he flung them away, reaching for more glamour as the red rippled and frayed out of sight. Stretching forward with his full body, he dragged folds of black and vermillion into the room. Vincent wrapped them around his body and reached for more glamour till the air around him was heavy with rage.

Jane watched him until she realised that the illusion had made her press back into the pillows in fear. She had told him to stay, and she had meant it. She could not comfort him, but she could at least keep him from feeling that he had troubled her.

Jane shut her eyes and curled onto her side as if she were sleeping. But she could still hear him gasping as he worked.

A rustle of cloth suggested that his cravat had been discarded. The hiss and thump was probably his jacket. The ragged panting might be nothing more than an extremely large fold. If she did not look at the glamour, Jane could almost pretend that those were the normal sounds of Vincent working.

Thirty

A Question of Nature

Jane had not intended to fall asleep, but she did so too easily of late. When she awakened, the sun had shifted towards evening but was still well above the horizon. Vincent lay on the bed beside her in shirt and breeches, utterly limp. Sliding closer, Jane carefully curled up against him. With her head resting on Vincent's chest, she could hear his heart and the hushing of his breath. His shirt was dry to the touch and his breathing calm and regular, so he must have been asleep for some time.

What had been most difficult about their time in Antigua was watching the sharp alteration to Vincent's manner. During the course of their marriage, he had slowly let her know about the abuse that he had suffered as a child. Nothing had driven the point home so thoroughly as being here and seeing him struggle not to fall victim to his father's designs again.

She felt the shift in his breathing before he stirred.

His chest rose as he inhaled, then tightened with a held breath. Beneath her ear, his heart sped. She pressed her hand against his chest and rubbed circles against the tension there.

With a soft exhalation, Vincent brought an arm around her and drew her closer. "I am very sorry." He turned his head to press a kiss against her forehead. "That was an indulgent display."

She rose on an elbow to look at him. The evening light had crept under the veranda and now lay across the bed. The pool of ruddy sun gave some colour to Vincent's face, which was otherwise haggard. Whether it was the colour or the angle, the light caught on three silver hairs at Vincent's temple. Jane ran her finger over them, wondering when they had appeared. "You seem calmer, so I cannot call it unnecessary."

"Well, I am not in danger of throttling anyone, so I suppose that is something." He turned into the pressure of her fingers with a little grunt of appreciation. "And how are you?"

"Much the same as I have been." She moved her attention to his forehead, trying to ease the lines that had appeared there. "Enormous."

Chuckling, he lowered his hand and rested it on her stomach. "You have been saying that since we realised that you were with child."

"Yes, well, I now have a thorough understanding of why it is called 'increasing.' "

"Is it because my affection for you increases?" Vincent ran his hand up her side and pulled her down into a gentle and chaste kiss. Jane inhaled the warmth of her husband and very much wished that he were allowed to agitate her.

On the first of August, Jane woke from an involuntary doze in the late afternoon to the sound of murmured conversation outside her room. Vincent was speaking with someone, but she could not make out what was being said. She pushed herself up to sit against her pillows, blinking the sleep from her eyes. Nkiruka was not in the room. Perhaps they had stepped into the hall so as not to disturb her, but there was Frank's voice as well. She thought about ringing the bell to let them know she was awake, then thought better of it. She was not her mother, to require attention simply because she was afflicted with ennui.

The baby pushed against her side, making a brief visible bulge under her shift. She had reached two-and-thirty weeks, and the baby's activity had increased in strength. Jane smiled and pressed back. The pressure was met with another thump. "Patience, my little pugilist. I know you are crowded."

Jane picked up the bundle of notes she had made during Imogene's visit that morning. Imogene had only had an hour to spare, but she had been able to help translate some of the phrases that Dolly had used. *Kyim homa*, for instance, turned out to be comparable to *boucle torsadée*. Other words simply had no equivalent concepts in European glamour.

The door opened and Vincent entered. "Good afternoon, Muse."

"I had not expected to see you until dinner." She set the papers aside on the bed.

"Yes, well . . . I hope I am not disturbing you?" He drew his chair from its usual spot and turned it so he sat near the middle of the bed rather than at the head of it. He sat stiffly in the chair, face in profile.

"Not at all." The baby kicked again, hard enough to startle an exclamation from Jane. She laughed before Vincent could fret about something beyond whatever was troubling him. For something was troubling him, of that Jane was certain. She would see if she could ease his mind a little before she pressed him to find out what was the matter. "Your child and I have been playing a thumping game today."

"I did not know that was possible."

"I will show you. Here." She took his hand to draw it to her side.

As she pulled on his hand, a glamour tore. It frayed into oily rainbows, obscuring Vincent's face for a moment. He jerked free, turning in his chair so his back was to her before the last edge unravelled back into the ether.

He had been holding a masking glamour in front of his face. Small wonder he had looked uncomfortable. It was devilishly difficult to walk with a glamour in place. Doing so required holding all of the threads in correct relation to each other, to oneself, and to the ether, and none of them could be tied off to conserve strength. Which raised the question of why.

"Show me."

He let out his breath in a long sigh. "I am sorry. I thought you would worry unnecessarily if you did not hear the explanation first, so I wanted to assure you that I was well—and I am—before you saw this." Vincent turned in his chair to face her.

His left eye was swollen nearly shut, and deep purple bruises surrounded it. More contusions mottled his cheek. The skin over his brow had torn and been stitched neatly back together. All of this had clearly transpired much earlier in the day, and no one had told her.

Internally, she again railed about being confined to her bed. "Did Mr. Pridmore do that?"

He snorted. "I have not seen him since his visit with the admiral. With luck, he has taken his wife and left the island. I think word has gone round that he is not to be trusted, so he is unlikely to find work. No . . . this was an accident with my father."

If Jane were allowed out of bed, she would have been halfway to Lord Verbury already. That hideous man. "Hideous, cankered, ill-hearted, splenial spit-poison."

Vincent looked up, eye widening, and Jane realised that she had spoken aloud and with some vehemence. "You see why I wanted to tell you first, before you saw the bruises?" He spread his hands. "The fault resides largely with me."

"I fail to see how you can possibly bear any blame for being so misused."

"I had not been to see him since Pridmore's visit. I had been too angry. But he does not like being kept in the dark any more than you do."

"I do not ever have the urge to hit you."

"Be that as it may, I know that he nurtures a grudge, and I had given him several reasons recently. He complained that he had to hear of Pridmore's visit from Frank and not from 'his son.' I pointed out that Frank was also his son, which started an argument about legacy. He again raised the desire that we should name the child after him, and I, foolishly, said 'No.' "

"You have refused before."

"I have used polite evasions. This time, I was blunt."

Jane waited, but Vincent seemed little inclined to continue the story. He did continue to drive his nail into the side of his thumb. "How did a man confined to a wheeled chair do that to you?"

"I would rather not . . . very well. He seemed to let the matter drop, which is an approach that I really should have recognised. Then his lap blanket slipped to the floor." Vincent's jaw clenched, and, when he continued, his voice was flat and unaffected. "I bent to pick it up, and he struck me with his cane."

"He hit you with his *cane*?"

"Not in the face. Across the back. The blow shocked me enough that he had time to land a second before I took it from him. Then he—he seemed to lose his mind to fury. I have never seen him so . . . but then, I have never stopped him before. He tried to get out of the chair. I was afraid he would do injury to himself, so I restrained him, which was when . . . this happened. His head." He waved his hand at the bruises. "But, as I said, it was my own fault."

"That is not your fault."

"If I had not taken his cane, he would not have had cause to become so angry."

"He *hit* you with it."

"Yes, but I—I know what things anger him, and I did not shy from any of them." Vincent stopped and spread his hands helplessly. Slight tremors ran through them. "At any rate, it was a good reminder."

"Did you really need a reminder that your father is a vindictive fiend?"

"No, that I have—" Again, he stopped himself, this time shaking his head. "So. How is your book coming along?"

"Changing the subject would work better if you at least made an effort to tie the two topics together."

Vincent stared at his hands still longer before pressing them together to quiet the shaking. Jane gave him time to organise his thoughts. Her much-tried patience was rewarded when he sighed and sat forward, turning his face so that the bruises were more prominent. He did not meet her gaze, though, and seemed to be studying the base of the wall behind her. With one hand, he touched the heavy purple under his eye. "This. My response to Pridmore, both when he was here, and when I punched him—I needed the reminder that. . . . It has been easy to pretend that I do not have a temper these past few years, but that is only because it has not been tried."

"I would say that it has been sorely tried on several occasions and that you have exhibited admirable restraint."

"Restraint. You mean when I am afraid to move because if I do I will hit something?"

"But you do not."

"The urge is there." He glanced towards her, but not quite at her. "I needed the reminder of my relationship with my father, because you are with child."

Of all the things that Jane knew, she was certain that he would never strike their child, and she was equally certain that this was a fear his father had deliberately implanted. Jane held out her hand, resting it palm up on the bed until he took it. "You are not your father."

"I am glad you think so."

"You are not like him. You do not use people. You do not beat them for a difference of opinion. The fact that you have the urge to hit . . . *I* have that urge sometimes. What is telling is that you do not act upon it."

"Because I am practised at stifling the impulse does not mean— My capacity for violence terrifies me."

"It does not frighten me." She tightened her grip on his hand. "*You* do not frighten me."

"But I have."

Jane shook her head. "I do not count my nearly constant dread that you will overwork and drop from a strained heart as a fear of you."

"Can you honestly tell me that you have not been frightened *of me* at some point in the past three months?"

Jane sighed, knowing the moments he was thinking of,

when she had taken an involuntary step backwards or when she had flinched because he raised his voice. "Are you able to look at me? I want you to have no thoughts that I am dissembling."

Too slowly, Vincent lifted his eyes to hers. Even with one eye swollen nearly shut, his fear was obvious. Jane held out her other hand, waiting until he placed his there.

Holding tight to both hands, Jane fixed Vincent with her gaze. She made no effort to govern her countenance, because he would note that effort and likely take it as a sign of things concealed. "You have startled me. Several times, I have been alarmed by the strength of your temper, but *not* because I was afraid of you. I have been frightened of what being here is doing to you. Our first day here—after we discovered your father, you said 'Forgive me. I am not myself.' I do not think you have been yourself since we arrived. He has stretched and warped and twisted you out of yourself, until you believe that this extremity is your natural state. It is not. You are not yourself. And you are very much forgiven for it."

Vincent shut his eyes, hands trembling in her grasp.

"You will not hit me. You will not hit our child. It is not in your nature."

In a very low voice, as if he were forcing the words out, he said, "I am afraid it is."

"I know you are. That fear is part—only part, mind you—of why I know that it is not your nature." She lifted his hand and kissed it. "You are obstinate, imprudent, and sometimes rude. You are not cruel. The most I will grant is that you are insufferable and occasionally inscrutable."

His smile, weak though it was, seemed like sun breaking through rain. Jane kissed his hand again, closing her eyes to hide her own anger. When she was allowed out of bed, she had a list of words to present to Lord Verbury, all of which would shock her mother.

The baby squirmed in answer to her agitation. She could do nothing about Lord Verbury for the present, but she could try to help Vincent settle back into himself. Jane opened her eyes and lowered Vincent's hand to her stomach. "Here. I was going to show you the game we are playing. Push and the baby will push back."

"Will I not hurt you?"

"No more than this inconceivable child does." Jane put pressure on the back of his hand, pushing it into the part of her stomach where the baby had last nudged her.

A moment later, an answering bump pushed at Vincent's hand. He let out an unsteady laugh and pushed again. "That is remarkable."

"I try to think of it that way." Truly, every time the child moved it was a good sign, even if there were occasions on which it was a trifle uncomfortable. "I think the baby recognises your voice, too."

"Really?" Vincent lifted his head.

Jane tried to reply only to his surprise, not the bruises. "At any rate, he or she moves more when you talk."

"Perhaps I should sit here and recite the classics, then. Or moralize upon—God!"

Jane's stomach had glowed.

It was only a brief flash of ruddy light, which had seemed to originate deep within her. Suddenly breathless, Jane stared at her own middle. "I suppose that should not be a surprise, given whose child this is."

"And at not quite eight months." Vincent leaned forward and kissed her on the cheek. "I will be certain to boast to Herr Scholes that our child is more of a prodigy than his grandchild."

"You are going to be insufferably proud as a father, I suspect."

He sobered a little, regarding her with earnestness. "I hope I am."

Over the next week, Vincent's bruises turned impressive shades of purple and spread down his cheek in greens and yellows. The swelling reduced, making it more obvious how bloodshot his left eye was. It was impossible for Jane to look at him without recalling what had caused it. If the mere impulse to hit someone caused bodily harm, Jane's thoughts would have flayed Lord Verbury.

But giving way to her frustration and anger would do Vincent no good, to say nothing of her own state. There was a notable increase in the frequency of pains when she was agitated. So Jane turned that weakness into a strength. If she could not leave the bed, and if she needed to remain calm, then she would make their bedchamber a refuge for her husband.

She lay on her left side with Vincent curled against her back. One of his arms lay nestled against her chest. He seemed to actually be asleep, which was not the case every night, so she tried not to move in response to the discomfort that had awakened her. Jane looked to the shelf clock to note the time. Twenty past midnight. Trying to ease the tension, she inhaled slowly.

Jane smelled smoke.

Frowning, she lifted her head, peering through the sheer lawn curtains and out the window. The moon was only a thin crescent, but dull orange glowed at the base of the frame. "Vincent."

He made a soft grunt.

Jane turned and shook his arm. "Vincent. Wake up."

He startled into wakefulness, half sitting. "What is it? Are the labour pains—"

"I think something is on fire."

A glance at the window had him out of bed. He crossed the room and flung the veranda doors open. The charred sugar smell increased. Vincent swore, and then ran back into the room, snatching his breeches from the chair he had hung them on.

He continued on to the door and flung it open. Leaning into the hall, he bellowed, "Fire! Alarm the house! Fire in the cane fields!"

Jane sat up, pushing the mosquito netting aside. She could just see over the edge of the window, but as the house sat on a hill, she could not get a clear view of the fire.

Hastily, Vincent drew his breeches on, not troubling to

change out of his nightshirt. "Ring for Nkiruka. I want someone with you in case the wind shifts or Pridmore shows up."

"Do you think he set it?"

"One field might be natural." Vincent shoved his feet into his boots. "This is all of them."

Thirty-one

Fire and Smoke

For the first quarter hour, the great house was filled with frantic activity, as everyone who was able was roused to try to fight the fire. Pinned in bed, Jane listened to people running past. Nkiruka, wrapped in one of Jane's old robes, lit a candle and sat by the door to the balcony to report on what she could see from the house.

All Jane could do was sit in bed, pick at the counterpane, and listen.

After that first quarter hour, the house fell into deep stillness as it emptied. Even the coldmongers went to help. Still, Jane strained her ears, trying to tease some knowledge out of the air. If Pridmore was out there and setting fires, what might he do to Vincent? With such a slender moon, the night would be very dark. That started a whole new string of worries about what might happen to Vincent near a fire. The memories of the people burnt in the distillery accident rose in her head.

Jane slipped a hand between the pillows and her lower back, trying to massage away a dull ache of tension. "Has anything changed?"

"If anything change, me'll tell you."

"I know. I am sorry. I know you will."

As the ache in her lower back spread in a band around her middle. Jane closed her eyes and tried to calm down. "What time is it?"

"Another?" With a grunt, Nkiruka got out of her chair and carried the candle to the shelf clock. "Ten to one."

That was only a half hour since her last. Jane put her hand against her stomach, which was hard and tight. "I am going to lie down, but I shall not be asleep."

"Na worry, sec. Me'll tell you wha me see."

"Thank you." Jane slid down in the bed. She curled onto her left side, face turned towards the window, and waited. The orange glow had grown brighter against the night sky.

The scent of smoke grew as well as the hours carried it on a steady breeze towards the house. Nkiruka held a handkerchief to her mouth and coughed into it.

"Do you want to shut the veranda door?"

Nodding, Nkiruka stood and bustled to the door. She paused to step onto the veranda and lean on the rail to look across the valley floor. When she came back in, her face was tight. "My house on fire."

"Oh no. Oh, Nkiruka. Your grandchildren . . . do you

need to go?" Jane pushed herself up on one elbow, trying to see out the window.

"Me too slow. Nothing cyan do by the time me get dey. Dolly will mind them." She twisted the tie on her robe, still looking across the valley. With another cough, Nkiruka shut the veranda door. "Dem safe with Dolly."

"I am certain you are right. Of course they are safe."

Jane noted the time of her next bearing pain in the logbook with some trepidation. The last five had been at regular half hour intervals. Dr. Jones had said to send for her if they became regular or more frequent than twenty minutes, but there was no one to send. She looked up from the page to where Nkiruka stood by the veranda door.

The older woman frowned, her hands set on her hips. The light from the fire had grown bright enough to dimly light the room.

Jane set down the quill. "What do you see?"

"We need go." She turned from the door. "De fire closer. Wind blowing towards us. Let's go."

"Go?" Jane stared stupidly at the numbers on the page, as if looking at them would change anything.

"Yes." Nkiruka bustled across the room and pulled a stout walking dress out of the wardrobe.

As if in answer, the baby pushed against Jane's ribs. She swallowed, resting her hand against the spot. "Vincent would come if we were in serious danger."

"Fire jus' cross de road. We haffu go. Now." She carried the dress over to Jane.

Heart pounding, Jane sat up and, for the first time in two weeks, swung her legs out of bed. Nkiruka helped her slip into the dress and then knelt to put her slippers on, since Jane could no longer see her own feet. When Jane stood, she had to grasp the bedpost for support. The room spun a little, as if she had been working glamour. All of the weight she had gained seemed to have doubled in her weeks abed.

"You all right?"

"Dizzy." Jane rubbed her eyes, trying to clear her vision.

"You lean on me. We go."

Standing, Jane could finally look out the window at what had alarmed Nkiruka. The flames had swept up the hill, and one of the orange trees on the far side of the great house grounds had caught fire. Jane put her hand on Nkiruka's shoulder and nodded. "I see the need for haste."

Though Jane felt weak and had to lean on Nkiruka more than she wished, her vision cleared and she seemed to be in no danger of fainting. They went down the passage leading to the back of the house. They scarcely needed a candle—through every window, flames lit the sky. Jane sent up a prayer for Vincent's safety.

Nkiruka opened the door into the yard, provoking both of them to cough. The air was hot and thick with smoke. Nkiruka shut the door and patted Jane's arm. "Wait here. I go get us a couple ah damp cloths."

Jane leaned against the wall with a hand held over her nose. "Excellent thought."

Nkiruka hurried back down the hall and disappeared into one of the rooms they had used for the wounded. Jane thanked providence that they were all out of the house, though she was not certain they were any safer where they were.

Another bearing pain squeezed her. Though the discomfort was not great, Jane winced, knowing that half an hour had not yet passed. She hoped it was a sign that they were irregular rather than becoming more frequent.

In short order, Nkiruka reappeared with two lengths of dripping linen. She slowed as she approached Jane. "Another one?"

"Yes." Jane took the wet cloth from her, trying to ignore the cramp. "How can you tell?"

"You frown, so." Nkiruka drew her brows together and set her mouth in a straight line. Then she crossed her eyes.

In spite of herself, Jane laughed. "I do not."

"Next time me'll hold up wan mirror." Nkiruka tied a cloth around her head, covering her mouth and nose.

Jane followed suit, knotting the wet fabric behind her head so they looked like a pair of unlikely bandits. "I feel as though we should rob a bank."

"Later. Fus, arwe do fire walki—"

"Jane!" From the front of the house, Vincent's bellow cut through the walls.

Jane's knees went weak with relief. Only the fact that she was already leaning against the wall kept her on her feet. She pulled the damp cloth down and drew a breath to reply. It turned into coughing, and then a wheeze with each burning inhalation.

He ran into view in the blue parlour at the end of the hall. Knocking over a chair in his haste, he dashed through the room. "Jane!"

"Here! We are here."

"Oh, thank God." He slid to a halt in front of them. His face was dark with soot, and he had a damp linen cloth hanging around his neck. "The road is closed off, but the way to Frank's house is still open and the wind is blowing away from it."

"Dat too far fu she walk. Take she to the safe house. Good thick stone walls."

"No—there is no ventilation. You would suffocate in short order with the way the wind is blowing." He pulled the cloth up over his nose. Bending, he lifted Jane into his arms. "And I have no intention of letting her walk."

"You cannot carry me all that way."

"It is not fashionable, but Frank is bringing a cart round. Nkiruka, will you get the door?" He was sticky with sweat. "And Muse, pull up your cloth. The smoke is very bad."

Jane pulled up the cloth as Nkiruka opened the door. Vincent swung, turning to smoothly guide Jane's legs through. He stepped on to the back veranda, still looking back into the house to make sure her head did not hit the frame.

Mr. Pridmore stood in the yard.

Jane stiffened in Vincent's arms. "Put me down."

"What—? Oh, rot!"

"Told you I'd smoke him out. Clever, keeping him at Frank's. Didn't think his lordship would stoop to staying in slave quarters." Pridmore smiled rakishly. "Mighty glad to see me, too. Be interesting to see what happens when people hear how you kept him prisoner."

"You have my father, which is what you wanted, and there is a fire that threatens all of us, so this is not the time for discussion."

"From what I hear, your brother is more tractable. Pity that I'll have to tell your father you died in the fire." Mr. Pridmore produced a pair of duelling pistols from behind his back. "Real mother-of-pearl inlay. A present from Mrs. Pridmore. She said all real gentlemen should have a set."

Vincent put Jane down and stepped in front of her. "Then let us handle this like gentlemen. I see you brought two pistols."

Nkiruka stood just inside the door, holding it open. She beckoned to Jane, eyes wide over her mask. Jane shook her head, though she was not sure what she could do.

"I wasn't thinking to duel you." Pridmore raised one of the pistols and aimed it at Vincent.

"You know he wants my wife alive."

"He did say that."

Vincent walked down the stairs, curving his steps away from Jane and Nkiruka. "And I will wager that until he is certain it is a boy child, he does not want me dead, only disabled."

"No . . . that's my own addition to his plan." He cocked the pistol. "I'll tell him you threatened me."

In desperation, Jane clutched her stomach and let out a shriek that would do her mother proud. "The baby!"

Pridmore glanced at her. As he did, Vincent darted to the right and vanished.

The pistol's shot cracked the night. Jane grasped the rail for support. Vincent had woven a *Sphère Obscurcie*, but he could not have gone far holding the weave. There was no way to tell if the shot had hit him so long as he was hidden in glamour.

Clearly shaken, Pridmore took a step back, lowering the pistol now that its single shot was spent. He raised the other pistol and held it at ready. "Where are you, Hamilton?"

In the distance, flames crackled and wood popped. Jane's own ragged breathing caught without feigning as another bearing pain wrapped around her. She kept her eyes on the yard, waiting for Vincent to reappear.

He popped into sight ten feet to the left of where he had been, moving at a run towards Pridmore. The move to the right must have been a feint. Pridmore cursed and swung to aim at him, but Vincent vanished again. Pridmore darted away and turned his loaded pistol on Jane. "Stop! Or I shoot your wife."

Behind Jane, a brief flurry of movement caught her attention. She looked back, hoping that Vincent had somehow made his way behind her. Frank stood in the hall with Nkiruka, heads bent together in furious conference.

Vincent's voice pulled her attention back to the yard. "At

forty feet? With that trinket? Expensive, yes, but unless I miss my guess, it is of Spanish manufacture, and notoriously inaccurate." He reappeared only fifteen feet from Pridmore.

Frank stepped on to the veranda with Nkiruka right at his back. He slowly raised a hunting rifle to his shoulder. "Whereas, you have seen me bring down geese with this. I have two shots to your one and—let me be clear—a very, very strong desire to see you dead. You have until the count of three to put down the pistol."

Nkiruka's head was bent. She panted while her hands worked swiftly in front of her.

"One."

Pridmore turned the pistol back to Vincent. "You really think you can hit me first?"

"Two."

The pistol jumped in Pridmore's hand with a flash, a finger of fire pointing straight at Vincent. Almost simultaneously, the shotgun cracked, sound exploding in Jane's ears.

Pridmore threw his pistols down and ran for the safe house.

Jane did not care for that. Vincent had vanished again. She had just started down the stairs when her husband reappeared twenty feet to the right of where he had been standing. He was breathing hard enough to stir the damp cloth wrapped around his head. Otherwise, he appeared untouched.

Springing forward, Vincent took her by the shoulders

and looked her over. "Muse. Tell me that shriek was a pretence."

"It was." Though the pains were coming with concerning regularity. "A distraction seemed necessary. Now, tell me that you were not shot."

He shook his head. "I was standing nowhere near there. Used Herr Scholes's trick of an inverted Cruikshank's weave. It only worked because of the dark and the cloth over my mouth."

Frank and Nkiruka joined them. "We need to move quickly, before he comes out of the safe house and recognises that I have no gun." Frank held up a broomstick.

Vincent's approbation of Nkiruka was visible above his mask. "Nicely done."

She tapped him lightly on the arm. "You haf fu show me that disappearing trick."

He turned, following Frank towards the side. "At the first opportunity."

"I saw you working behind Frank, but it was still quite convinc—" A sudden alarming wetness ran down Jane's thighs. For a moment, she thought she had soiled herself, before the understanding came. "Oh dear."

"Muse?"

"I believe my water just broke."

Vincent had Jane in his arms before she was aware of being lifted. "Where is the cart?"

"This way."

"Wait, wait." Nkiruka put a hand on Frank's shoulder.

Even with the damp cloth obscuring half her face, her frown was clear. "She need Dr. Jones."

Frank hesitated, looking at Jane and then Vincent. "There is a fire across the road."

Nkiruka lifted her chin and stepped closer to Frank, speaking in rapid Igbo. Jane caught the words, "Dr. Jones" and "picknee" but nothing else.

To her surprise, Frank answered in the same tongue, though even to Jane's ear his diction in that language sounded almost childish. It was a short response.

When he turned back to Jane and Vincent, his expression was guarded and fearful. "You must promise that you will not tell a soul about what I am about to say, not ever. Swear on whatever you hold most dear that you will keep this secret."

Without hesitation, Vincent said, "I swear on my love for Jane, I will keep your secret."

"Yes." Jane did not know what secret they were being asked to keep, but by Frank's expression it was dire. "And by mine for Vincent, I also swear."

"We will take you to Dr. Jones, but I must stress that we are about to place hundreds of lives in your hands." He glanced at the fire again, and gestured for them to follow him towards the slave quarters. "We will not be able to take the cart because the ground is too uneven once we leave the path, but it is not far."

"Where . . . ?"

"There is a secret village. Picknee Town." He looked pained as he said it. "Where the map shows the ravine."

Jane's jaw dropped open and Vincent looked no less shocked. "The birthrate."

"With malnutrition, beating, and overwork? It is already low. But . . . but we want our children to have a better life. When the village was first established, the planters noticed that live births had stopped, so we use a lottery now. Sometimes it is the mother and child, sometimes only the child."

"Is that—was Amey . . . ?"

"Amey had a daughter and they are both doing quite well." Though Nkiruka's voice was still heavily flavoured with an Igbo accent, her speech shifted so it did not sound as though English were a foreign tongue, imperfectly understood. She lifted her dress and tucked the hem into the sash of her robe so she could walk more easily. "I am sorry for that deception."

It was fortunate that Vincent was carrying Jane, because she was not certain she would have been able to remain standing. Nkiruka had been deliberately making her comprehension of English seem deficient. Nkiruka saw her realisation and winked. "I can sound like you, if I want. But still speak language of the heart with family and dem."

Jane began to see all the ways in which she had been carefully managed. "And . . . and the glamural at the Whittens'—all of the slaves who said they were coming to work for us and did not." They had been using Jane and Vincent as a reason to be absent, to visit their families. And then the women—the women that Nkiruka had suggested Jane bring in to talk about glamour had no doubt done the same. No wonder she had been so keen to continue work on the book because it gave her the opportunity to give more women reasons to leave their estates. Jane suddenly remembered Nkiruka helping Louisa organise the wounded and the lists that they had prepared. "And you can read and write, can you not?"

Nkiruka laughed, shaking her head. "No. Reading is what Frank is for. Don't need it for me. I came because working on the book made easy excuse for people to travel. See their families. Doc was mad about it, but I set her straight."

"You used us."

"Yes." Nkiruka's shrug very eloquently pointed out that Jane had no room to be angry about that.

Vincent tightened his grip on Jane. "But why not simply rebel? Why not free everyone?"

"There are forty naval bases on this island," Frank said.

"They tried rebellion in 1736, before my time." Nkiruka shook her head. "No white blood was shed, so the British only executed nine-and-eighty of us. Now, we keep as many children safe as we can. They grow up in Picknee Town. Some stay there. Others slip out and join the free population, or leave Antigua."

Though Jane had dozens of questions, another bearing pain gripped her. She clung to Vincent and tried not to make a sound. It was not so bad. No worse than a cramp in the leg, really.

He looked down, face tight with worry. "Are you all right?"

"Please do not ask me that with every bearing pain."

"Is there anything I can do?"

"Set me down and let me walk. It eases the discomfort."

"But you are supposed to be on bed rest."

"That was to stop labour. We are a bit past that now."

Frank glanced over his shoulder. "As the father of five, allow me to offer this piece of advice: do whatever she tells you."

"Of course." Vincent set her down with exaggerated care.

Nkiruka nudged Jane. "Take his arm, though. You don't want to fall."

As they walked along the rough path, Jane was grateful for Vincent's arm. Looking back at the great house, Jane could now see that the fire near there was separate from the ones in the cane fields. Mr. Pridmore had clearly been busy.

Walking did help with the pains, but her back still felt tight and unpleasant. After two weeks in bed, Jane became quickly fatigued walking on the uneven ground. She disliked requiring help, but if she fell, Vincent would wind up blaming himself somehow. Jane sighed and leaned on Vincent more heavily. She kept her vision on the ground directly in front of her.

So when Vincent stopped dead in his path, she almost stumbled.

In the dark and the smoke, it was hard to make out why they had stopped. Frank knelt in the tall grass next to a cart that had been upset. He lifted his head and his face was terrible. "He is still alive."

With that, Jane's vision resolved, and she understood

that she was looking at Lord Verbury's wheeled chair. "What is he doing here?"

"I have no idea. Pridmore must have been bringing him from my house."

Nkiruka stepped forward and peered over Frank's shoulder. She gave a startled gasp. "He alive?" She stabbed Frank in the shoulder with a finger. "You knew!"

His shoulders sagged. "Yes . . . yes, I was aware he was not dead. I am surprised the news had not made its way to you."

"Why didn't you tell me?"

"Because—because the more people who knew, the more likely the secret was to get out." Frank shifted the cloth mask. "Can you tell me that you would not have used the information?"

"Of course I would have."

"And he would have sold my family."

Vincent looked behind them at the fire. It had gained ground and would overtake this spot. "Can you carry him?"

"Leave him." Nkiruka spat on the ground. "He poison."

Vincent and Frank shared a look that was indecipherable, even to Jane. Then Frank sighed heavily and tugged off his cravat. He tied it over Lord Verbury's eyes in a crude blindfold, then stood, hauling the unconscious man over his shoulder. "Yes. He is poison, but as simple as it would be, we cannot leave him."

Jane wished it were otherwise. If they had not seen him lying there, and discovered the next day that he had expired in the fire, she would not have mourned. Finding him and leaving him to die in the fire, though, would be murder as surely as if they had used a gun. She did not like it, but she agreed that they could not leave him.

Nkiruka glared at him. "You know what he did to Amey."

"And to my mother." Frank shifted the burden higher on his shoulder. "If leaving him were in my nature, he would have been poisoned long ago."

With no more words, Frank led them off the path to the slave quarters and headed straight across the plateau towards the ravine that divided Greycroft from the Whitten estate. Leaning on Vincent as she was, Jane could feel the horrible tension in his body.

As Frank had said, it was not far from the slave quarters. They had been walking for no more than twenty minutes when the ground in front of them dropped away into a craggy ravine. The land twisted along a graceful curve, showing raw, crumbling earth that fell a good fifty feet or more to a winding stream. The erosion from that stream had clearly widened unsteady soil so that the ravine was on its way to becoming a canyon. No one could view it and think of trying to climb down those soft walls.

It looked utterly real. Nkiruka stopped and glanced at them with a mixture of pride and amusement.

Vincent's gaze went vacant as he stared into the ether. He shook his head. Then shook it again.

Jane squeezed his arm. "What are you seeing?"

He shook his head a third time and returned to seeing the corporeal world. "Nothing. There is no glamour visible. How is there no glamour visible?"

"I told your wife thinking about it like fabric limits what the English can do." Nkiruka winked. "After the child is born, we can talk about glamour."

Frank came to stand in front of them, Lord Verbury's form still limp over his shoulder. "The entrance will make you feel as if you are falling. It is only three strides deep, so set your course and walk straight ahead."

"You can make people feel motion?" Vincent sounded almost outraged. Jane understood his frustration perfectly, that there might be something with glamour that he could not do.

"Visual and wind." Nkiruka shoved him from behind. "Not actual motion."

Frank led them forward along no path that Jane could see. It looked for all the world as if Vincent were about to step off the edge of a cliff. And then the view changed so that what had been below them now seemed to be rushing at them with great speed. Wind whistled past Jane's ears and stirred her hair. Her every sense told her she was falling. For three strides, and then it all cleared.

They stood on the far side of a narrow bridge across a ditch. A small village composed of wattle and daub houses stood before them in a gently sloping valley. Frank pulled down his cloth mask. "This . . . this is why I cannot leave Antigua. I have to protect this."

Thirty-two

A Laborious Enterprise

Frank went ahead to let Dr. Jones know they were coming and to secure his lordship, while Nkiruka led them through the lanes of the village. In the cock-crow hours, Picknee Town was quiet and had the tucked-away, snug feeling of many an English village. In the dim light, the wattle and daub houses could be mistaken for stucco and thatched roofs, complete with cheerful gardens set in front. They passed a blacksmith and what gave every appearance of being a haberdashery. There, Jane had to stop and bend to put one hand on her knee. Vincent held her other arm and supported her with a hand on her waist.

Jane ground her teeth. It was not the pain so much as the fatigue, or perhaps the two in combination. "I am very sorry, but I think I do need to be carried after all."

Without a word, Vincent shifted his grip and smoothly lifted her into his arms. He smelled of smoke and his shirt was damp against her cheek. Next to her ear, his heart rattled like a runaway carriage. Through the open collar of his nightshirt, her fingers brushed the riot of hair on his chest. Jane pressed a palm to his chest, rubbing a small circle as if that could calm him.

His voice rumbled through her fingers. "I am supposed to be comforting *you*."

"You are."

Their destination was only two streets from where Jane had stopped. They arrived at a two-story shingled building in the heart of the village. A neat sign hung next to the door: *Hospital*.

As Vincent carried Jane up the stairs of the front porch, Frank opened the door. "I am to ask how often the bearing pains are coming."

Jane had stopped counting sometime after they left the house. "They were every half hour before we left."

"She has had three since then, so every fifteen minutes, I think." Vincent carried her inside.

The door opened straight into a sitting room, which was rustic but very pretty. A pair of candles shone merrily on a small table. A young man of colour sat near it. His round cheeks were slick with sweat, and one leg fidgeted nervously as he stared at a door on the far wall. At the sound of their entrance, he looked round, and his eyes widened.

Frank held up a hand. When he spoke, his voice had nothing British about it. "Dem wid me. Nkiruka, she done vouch fu dem. Dey safe."

The young man looked as if he would protest, but a young woman cried out in another part of the hospital. Head whipping in the direction of the noise, he tightened his grip on his chair.

Frank led them away from the sitting room, through a broad passage, and into a room on the ground floor. A glamural of stars and clouds covered the ceiling and made the plain, whitewashed walls more appealing. Against one wall, a plain cupboard had been painted white to match the walls. A narrow bed stood against the opposite wall with a table and straight-backed chair next to it. At the foot of the bed, a small brazier gave off a pleasant resinous scent.

In the middle of the room stood the birth stool.

It had a rounded barrel back, but the seat was what drew Jane's attention. Carved in an open *U* shape, it was designed to allow an expectant mother to sit without anything to impede an infant's entrance into the world. Vincent passed the stool and lowered Jane on to the bed.

Nkiruka and Frank conferred by the door. Jane suspected that they had a muddied silence wrapped around them, as she could not make out the words of their conversation. After a moment, Nkiruka patted Frank on the shoulder, and then Jane could suddenly hear them again.

"Dr. Jones is with another patient, but should be in shortly," Frank said.

"Where is—"

"You are not to worry about him. Concentrate on your wife." Frank put a hand on Vincent's shoulder and squeezed. "I need to go back to the great house. Will you be all right?"

"Thank you, yes. I know I should come, but . . ."

"There is no need to explain. And truly, unless you have dealt with arson before, you are simply another body to carry water."

The amount of work that must needs be done would be tremendous. Jane squeezed Vincent's hand. "You should go."

"I am not leaving you."

"Sitting in the waiting room will not suit you. You do better when you have some activity."

"I am *not* leaving you." A spasm of fear rattled Vincent's mask of self-control for a moment before he governed himself. He shook his head firmly. "I am not leaving this room without you."

Most husbands would have been shocked to have been asked to even approach a birth chamber. Jane could not comprehend how she had been so lucky as to have one who wanted to be with her. "You understand that it will get worse, and will likely be difficult for you to watch. There will be blood. I will scream. I might hate you. Are you certain?"

"Do not ask me again. Please."

She smiled at him as the tears that she seemed to be plagued with, pressed into her throat. "Well then. Consider yourself warned."

Dr. Jones pushed the door open with her hip, carrying a steaming basin in her hands. Tendrils of her hair had escaped their kerchief and curled against her cheeks. "Mr. Hamilton, you will be more comfortable in the waiting room."

"I am staying."

"We have already had this argument, I am afraid." Jane was taking a turn about the room between pains and had her hands pressed against the ache in her back. Nkiruka followed her on one side, with Vincent on the other.

"Hm." Dr. Jones set the basin on the little table. "Well, lie down and let me see where we are. I left my other patient with one of the midwives but should get back to her quickly. Are the bearing pains still fifteen minutes apart?"

"Yes."

"Good. Let me see if I need to wake another midwife or if we have time."

"Are you not going to attend to her?" Vincent held Jane's arm, unnecessarily now, as she walked back to the bed.

"With two patients in labour at the same time, I have to order my time based on need." Dr. Jones spoke with exaggerated patience, as though this was a speech that she had given many times. "The midwives are trained in this, and I should only be necessary for an emergency. My other patient is farther along, so she is likely to need me before your wife does."

Jane lowered herself to the bed and, without being told, turned on her left side, drawing her knees up. "I quite understand."

Dr. Jones moved Jane's shift out of the way and for the next few moments gave her something to distract her from the ache in her back. Vincent shifted from one foot to the other, staring fixedly out the window.

"Good . . . good." Dr. Jones stood, nodding, as she pulled Jane's shift back down. "You are well dilated, but I would guess that we have another few hours before the bearing pains begin in earnest."

Vincent's voice cracked in disbelief, "In earnest? What has been occurring thus far?"

Though Jane was not at all encouraged by the reminder that her discomfort would grow yet worse, she could not help laughing at her husband. "Are you certain you do not wish to wait outside?"

His jaw firmed. "I am staying."

"Mr. Hamilton. Your wife needs to conserve her energy for labour, not cheering you." Dr. Jones stopped at the door. "If I have any cause to think that your distress, which is only natural, is affecting her delivery, I will ask you to leave. Do I make myself clear?"

He wiped his hand down his face, smearing the soot so it blended with his bruises. "You do. Thank you."

"Hm." She nodded to the basin on the table. "There are towels in the cupboard. Please wash yourselves before I return. This will be a dirty enough business."

Jane paced around the room in random patterns, Nkiruka and Vincent trailing her. At regular intervals, Jane needed to stop and brace against one of the bearing pains. They came more rapidly now. She stood with her hand against the whitewashed wall, arm outstretched and rigid.

Vincent shifted his weight and ran a hand through his hair. "Try breathing rapidly, in little pants."

"I did not know you were educated in childbirth."

"I am not . . . but I have some experience with pain."

At this point, Jane was willing to try anything. So, feeling a little foolish, she panted. Whether it was the shallow breaths or because the bearing pain was ceasing on its own, she felt somewhat better. It would be preferable if Vincent did not have the experience to offer that advice, but the relief was welcome.

Every hour, Dr. Jones returned to review Jane's progress. When Jane's report on the frequency of the bearing pains made her brow furrow, the doctor asked her to lie down on her left side upon the room's narrow bed. Humming a little, Dr. Jones turned to the table and opened a small pot of oil, which she lavished on her hands. "This will be uncomfortable."

She was entirely correct.

After longer than Jane liked, Dr. Jones pulled back and wiped her hand upon one of the linens. "The baby is breach."

Jane felt the blood drain out of her face. Nkiruka said a word in Igbo that Jane suspected was a curse.

Only Vincent looked at a loss, his brows drawn up in worried confusion. "What does that mean?"

"It means that the baby is presenting feet first, so the birth will be more difficult. I am very sorry. It is sometimes a complication of bed rest, that the infant does not turn head down." Dr. Jones folded the towel and blew out her breath in a huff. "I am going to visit my other patient and instruct the midwife that she will need to finish with her. When I return, things will be unpleasant, but we should be able to deliver the baby safely."

"Should?" Vincent took a step closer to Jane.

"Yes. It is fortunate that the baby is early, since it will be small." With that encouraging sentiment, Dr. Jones set the towel down and took her leave.

As Dr. Jones promised, the next several hours were not pleasant.

Jane sat on the birth stool with Dr. Jones on a low seat in front of her. Vincent sat on a taller chair at her back, bracing her with his hands on her sides as she strained with the bearing pain. Her breath hissed through her teeth as she waited for it to pass.

Panting, she ground out, "Are my eyes crossed?"

"What?"

"Do my eyes cross during bearing pains?"

"Um." He leaned forward around the edge of the chair. "No."

"Ha!" Jane glanced at Nkiruka, who stood at her side with a cloth to wipe the sweat from her brow.

The older woman chuckled. "Now you turning purple in the face."

Dr. Jones cleared her throat. "That much is true."

"Lovely— Ah!" Jane had wanted to get through the birth without crying out, but that proved to be impossible.

Well past noon, sweat-soaked and panting as if she had been working glamour for days, Jane leaned her head back against Vincent during one of the respites between her bearing pains. Those had become fewer and shorter. The glamour in the ceiling had shifted with the sun to become a cerulean sky with downy clouds drifting across it. Jane watched one of the clouds simply because it was moving.

Vincent's arms around her had been a constant comfort during this ordeal, for which Jane was grateful. "I think every man should be required to sit with his wife during labour."

"If that were the case, there would be a significant number of only children." He kissed her cheek. "No man who loves his wife could possibly want to make her endure this."

She patted his hand. "Next time will be easier. Or so I have been told."

Nkiruka nodded. "Dat's true. My last baby dropped out

after only two hours. I almost didn't have time to know I was labouring."

"Speaking of . . ." Jane closed her eyes and braced again as the next pain came.

There then passed a period of time in which Jane said many unutterable things.

The afternoon sunlight had flooded the room. Dr. Jones looked up from her stool and gave them a smile. "Ten toes and healthy colour."

"What?" Vincent leaned forward as if he could see past Jane's bulk to her nethers.

"The feet are out." She looked down and moved her hand. "And when I touch them the toes curl, so everything is going well."

Jane began weeping with relief. She was too tired to be annoyed by her tears. With the sweat covering her, she doubted anyone would notice the addition.

"But this means that I need you to push in earnest now." Dr. Jones had sweat upon her forehead as well. "When the next pain comes, you must bear down. I will guide the baby."

Guide was a gentle word. What followed was not. Jane strained to push with her entire body. She clenched her fists, and her face, and everything, trying to push this child out of her. She gasped for air, pushing, and pushing, and pushing.

By her ear, Vincent murmured, "There, there . . ."

"Do *not* 'there, there' me!" She fairly snarled. "And do not even think of kissing me to make it better."

He pulled back a little. Jane could not see his face, but it must have had some alarm on it, because Nkiruka chuckled. "She doing good. Na bite you yet."

"Yet." Jane drew in another breath with which to push. "Give me time."

Dr. Jones said, "You are doing well . . . just keep pushing."

"I *am* pushing."

"Good . . ." She seemed completely inured to the violence of Jane's responses. "Good. And—yes. You are having a boy."

All the frustrated anger of the labour dissipated with those words. Jane found Vincent's hand and clutched it. Turning her head, she leaned back and kissed his bruised cheek. He appeared completely inarticulate, mouth open and eyes wet.

"In the usual course, when I say that, the child has been delivered, but the hard part is next. Shoulders."

The hard part? Nothing about this had been easy. Setting her jaw, Jane returned to work.

"Wait—wait. Do not push for a moment while I draw the arms down."

Jane sagged back in the chair, closing her eyes as she tried not to strain against Dr. Jones's efforts. This was the surest confirmation of original sin that she could think of, but surely after so many generations there was no need to continue revisiting the punishment. Her whole being was fixed upon a core of agony. As things below shifted, Jane clenched Vincent's arms. Sound tore from her throat, completely outside her volition. Vincent held her steady.

"There . . . Nkiruka, will you support his body while I turn the head?"

The rustle of cloth told of Nkiruka taking her position, but Jane could only sit and pant with her head propped against her husband's chest. Why in the name of heaven did any woman consent to have more than one child? This was beyond stupid. At a new sensation below, she tightened her grip on Vincent.

Some part of her was aware that her fingernails were digging into the skin of his forearms, but she could not relax her grip.

"All right. Now, you may resume pushing."

The bearing pains of the last quarter hour of Jane's labour made her fully abandon any attempt to not cry out. She screamed without regret. Even the gaps between the pains hurt as her body felt stretched and burnt and torn all out of proportion.

But at last, on the eighth of August, with one final push, Charles Byron Leopold Vincent fully entered the world.

The sudden relief, the hollowness, almost made Jane faint. She swallowed, still breathing heavily, and used Vincent's strength to stay upright in the chair. Leaning forward as best she could, Jane looked down.

Her son lay in Dr. Jones's arms, with his eyes screwed shut. He was wet, and bloody, and beautiful. Squirming, he drew breath, and let out a cry of glorious outrage. Dr. Jones handed him to Nkiruka, who had a clean linen ready to receive him. With practised movements, Dr. Jones quickly dealt with the cord that still bound him to Jane, while Nkiruka wiped the blood from his small, perfect body.

And then she was laying their son in Jane's arms.

So little. He was an exquisite miniature, red and squalling and angry. The nails on his fingers were wonderfully formed. She touched one delicate finger, and he wrapped his hand around her finger with an implacable grip. A fine tuft of dark hair lay plastered against his skull. His brows were drawn together in a scowl of protest, already recognisable as inherited from Vincent.

She turned to her husband. "Charles, meet your papa."

Vincent's eyes were red and he was weeping without shame, staring in wonder at their son. He opened his mouth, but no sound came. Clearing his throat, Vincent made another attempt, but his voice was still rough. "How do you do." Tentatively, he brought one hand up and, with a blunt finger, traced the curve of their son's cheek. "Charles."

There were a few more indignities for Jane to suffer through, but the pains seemed insignificant in comparison.

When her labour was at last fully completed, Nkiruka carried Charles back over and returned him to Jane's arms. She had tied a red ribbon around his left wrist, and now she tapped it, smiling as she did.

"What is that?" Jane was so tired that even Charles's slight weight seemed almost beyond her abilities.

"Keeps the evil spirits away." She touched the baby's nose, wrinkling her own at him. "But with good parents like aryou, I don't know that he need much help."

"Mm . . ." Jane very much wanted to go to sleep. "May I lie down?"

"Not just yet." Dr. Jones still crouched in front of her, frowning.

The fatigues of the past day seemed to crash over Jane all at once. It was all she could do to keep her head up. "Vincent, will you hold Charles?"

"Of course." As he took her son, she thanked heaven that he had been so involved with their nephew and already knew how to hold a newborn. Even with the bruises on Vincent's cheek, his smile was so open and full of joy that it made her light-headed.

She rubbed her hands together. "May I have a blanket? I am a little chilled."

"Nkiruka, take the baby from Mr. Hamilton." Dr. Jones straightened, her face tight. "Sir, I need you to transfer your wife to the bed."

Answering the urgency in her voice, Nkiruka lifted the baby away, as Vincent said, "What is happening?"

Jane knew before Dr. Jones answered him. Now that she thought of it, the fatigue, her chills, and her own knowledge of friends who had not survived their lying-in all spoke to one answer. It was not acceptable. She had a very clear vision of growing old with Vincent. Of teaching with him.

Of watching her father feed their children strawberries. Of spending time—

"She is bleeding, and I cannot find where."

Jane felt Vincent lift her into his familiar strong arms. She tried very hard to tell him that she loved him. He would need to remember that, but grey swam at the edges of her vision, then crowded together and became a field of black.

Thirty-three

Eyes of the Sleepers

Vincent felt his muse go limp in his arms. Her face was pale and bloodless. The sweat from her labours had not yet dried, but all the tension had gone out of her body. His throat began to close. Vincent held his breath until he was not choking on his own fear. "Jane?"

"Mr. Hamilton." Dr. Jones's voice snapped him back to himself.

He strode across the room and set Jane down as carefully as he could on the bed. Her head lolled to the side as though her neck had no bone in it at all. He stepped back, tucking his hands behind himself to hide the shaking.

Dr. Jones snapped Jane's shift up with frightening competence. Frightening because, as competent as she was, she still looked grave.

The blood that stained Jane's chemise began to pool onto the blankets of the bed. Vincent covered his mouth and turned away. Nkiruka stood next to the brazier, rocking Charles in her arms. All the wrinkles in her face were drawn together in despair.

Vincent turned back to the bed, running his hands through his hair as he tried desperately to restore order to his thoughts. Jane was bleeding. If the doctor could not find and stanch the bleeding—

Vincent snatched the thread of panic, tying it off. He did not have time for that. Jane did not have time for that.

"What can I do?"

"Take your son into the other room." Dr. Jones had put her hand *inside* Jane.

He sucked in a breath and caught the next string of panic, tying it to the first. He shoved both away from him. Dr. Jones must know by this point that Vincent would not get in the way, which meant she did not want him to witness something. She did not want him to watch Jane die.

The folds and threads wrapped around him in a tapestry of fear, nearly driving the breath from his body. He held still until he could push them away enough to draw breath, and while he did, he watched Dr. Jones try to save his Muse.

Dr. Jones had her eyes half closed, brows drawn together in a frown as she concentrated on what she was feeling. Vincent had no understanding of the interior of a woman's body. His education had not included medicine, as that was a trade, and a nobleman's son did not go into a trade. All he was good for were a thousand fashionably useless things, and glamour. Glamour could do nothing except create illusions. What Dr. Jones needed was a way to find out what was bleeding.

And there, Vincent caught a single, slender thread of hope. "If you could see inside her, would that help?"

"Take your son outside."

"Would it help?"

"I do not have the time to explain the curves of the human form that make that impossible."

"I am not—" Vincent broke off with a growl and just wove a *lointaine vision* instead. A *boucle torsadée* could also show something at a remote distance, but it needed to run in a straight line. That would not suit. The *lointaine vision* could be bent and twisted around obstacles. It required constant maintenance, but he could snake it through a keyhole if need be.

Holding the threads, Vincent twisted them past Dr. Jones's hand. This shortness of breath was welcome. This was not one more symptom of his inability to govern his sensibilities. Jaw tight, Vincent made a particular kink in the near end of the thread and stretched it into a thin, flat disc that showed whatever the far end of the thread pointed at. The threads themselves were not visible, save in this one spot. For all the world, it looked as if he held a dish of blood shrouded in shadow. Concentrating, he twisted a skein of the full spectrum around the running thread of the *lointaine vision* and made the image brighter. The tips of Dr. Jones's fingers appeared at the edges of the disc.

Dr. Jones let out her breath in a rush. "Yes. Yes, that

helps." She shook the visible wonder away and her brow furrowed back into concentration as she watched the *lointaine vision*. "Can you move it where I am pointing?"

"Yes."

The space to traverse was small, and it took delicate nudges of the threads to follow Dr. Jones's fingers without touching her arm or Jane's body. The *lointaine vision* did not care what his intentions were—it would show whatever was at its end, and if a solid body crossed its path, then *that* became the end in view.

Vincent could thread a *lointaine vision* through the smallest opening when he was calm, but he was far from calm.

Still, while Dr. Jones was searching, he was able to concentrate on her hand. He could concentrate on managing the threads of glamour and drive out the purpose from his thoughts. The fact that his Muse was bleeding to death billowed at the edge of his mind, but he could not let himself turn to look at it.

"There. Stop."

Dr. Jones pointed to a tear in the deep red wall of Jane's body. The ragged patch was no longer than the knuckle of Dr. Jones's thumb, but bright red blood poured down from it.

"God."

"Hold steady, Mr. Hamilton." Dr. Jones pinched the opening shut between her thumb and forefinger. "I should advise you to look away."

But he could not avert his gaze and still maintain the glamour as it needed to be. He had to stare at the space between his hands and at the blood that still leaked out of Jane.

"Nkiruka, there is a needle and thread on the table. Will you thread it for me? Doubled, no more than six inches."

He tried to take comfort in the confidence in Dr. Jones's voice, but there was so much blood. When Jane had miscarried, he had thought that was a frightening amount of blood. This. . . . The tremors began again.

He inhaled deeply, filling his lungs until his ribs ached, and blew it out. Again. He had to hold the threads steady for Jane. Breathe. Reach for a thread of calm from anywhere. Anything that would steady his hands. He was the Prince Regent's glamourist. He had survived Napoleon, by God. He would *not* be unmanned by blood.

But it was Jane.

And he would break without her.

God help him, Vincent knew the path he had been on before Jane. He could not lose her. The world could not lose her. Their son—

"I need the image steady." Dr. Jones squinted at the *lointaine vision*, which shook between his hands. Pieces of the disc shifted to a view of her arm and then back to Jane's workings.

"I am trying." He ducked his head and concentrated on the glamour. He must think of it as a technical challenge, not as though his Muse's life depended upon it. The glamour was well within his abilities. He need only steady his hands.

He needed to steady his hands.

He must steady his hands.

It was vital that he steady his hands.

Vincent had spent his whole life trying not to be overset by his emotion. His father had always said it was a sign of weakness. When pure will failed, he had learned to hide it and to tie a glamour around himself that looked like control. But the illusion would do no good here. His hands must be steady in earnest.

Nkiruka gave Dr. Jones the threaded needle. He had not even seen her set Charles down on the counterpane by Jane's head. She stared at his hands, her vision soft and vague, as if she were looking into the ether. "Let me."

He wet his lips. This was not a standard technique, and he had altered it even further to brighten the image. "You see what I am doing?"

"Clear enough."

"Then yes. Please, God, yes."

She slipped under his arm to stand in front of him where Jane usually stood when they worked in tandem. With a delicate precision, the older glamourist touched the lines. Her touch was so gentle, he almost could not feel it, but the tremors in the image steadied a little. She nodded, brows drawn together in concentration. "Got it."

Vincent let go, and stepped back.

The image steadied the moment his hands were no longer on the thread. Nkiruka, an elderly woman who must be in her seventh decade, could do what he could not. Out of sheer habit, Vincent swung his arms behind his back and clenched his hands together at the base of his spine.

Without some activity to distract him, even an activity he was failing at, the billowing fabric of fear kept pulling his gaze. It was always worse after the fact. He could brush past when in motion, but standing still and useless, it was too easy to get tangled in the folds. Jane could die. He had been worried that she might miscarry again because it had distressed her so the last time, but bearing his child might kill her.

When she recovered, he was never touching her again without a French envelope between them. He would *not* get her with child again. Watching her suffer the delivery had been bad enough, but to risk losing her again was unthinkable.

His breath was fast and shallow. Vincent held it. Then he exhaled slowly and attempted to hold to a regular pattern, as unnatural as it felt. As he watched Nkiruka and Dr. Jones work to save Jane—and they *had* to save Jane—it was impossible to miss the tension of both women.

God. He could not breathe again.

Vincent took Dr. Jones's advice and looked away. He walked to the far side of the room, trying by some action to trick his body out of its betraying weakness. He reached the wall, turned, and walked the circuit of the room, until his path brought him to the bed.

Jane's head was turned to the side, and her soft mouth hung a little open. Her skin was grey and translucent, making the delicate blue vein at her temple all the clearer. By her head, wrapped tightly in white cloth, Charles lay in ruddy contrast. His son's perfect health, even coming nearly a month too soon, seemed obvious in the roses in his cheeks.

Good. It would kill Jane to lose another child.

Vincent wrapped his hands in his hair. She would be well. Dr. Jones knew her business. His wife, his Muse, his life, would be well. She had the best possible medical care.

Just like the Princess Charlotte.

Vincent's stomach turned. He closed his eyes. Absolutely not. Not now. He would not begin to panic and mourn when there was no need. Dr. Jones would bring Jane through this. His chest ached with every inhalation. Jane would tell him that he needed some activity, and she would be right. He needed to do something before he lost all semblance of control.

Lowering his hands, Vincent opened his eyes and stepped forward to pick up Charles. Jane would not want him to be unattended.

He had been frightened to hold Tom the first time Melody had handed the baby to him. One hand cradled Charles's head, shifting him to the crook of his arm. Then Vincent put a hand under Charles's back to hold him steady. He weighed so little, no more than five pounds. Their nephew, Tom, had seemed impossibly small, but he must have weighed nearly twice that.

Vincent bounced from the knees, twisting a little from side to side in the pattern Tom had seemed to like. It made his rib ache a little, but that was a useful pain. Charles squirmed, frowning at the motion, and then relaxed. His little rosebud mouth opened in an imitation of Jane's. Vincent touched Charles's lips, and the tip of his finger obscured his son's mouth.

His hands had stopped shaking.

Risking a glance at Dr. Jones and Nkiruka, Vincent had to look away immediately to keep the panic from fluttering back. Blood soaked the blankets and covered Dr. Jones's arm.

He bent his head to Charles. His son's eyes were open, winking and staring about without comprehension. The frown came back, bringing with it the little furrow that Jane got when she concentrated. Not yet an hour old and already trying to understand the world.

A heavy sigh from Dr. Jones almost dropped Vincent to his knees. He stared fixedly at the wall and tried to interpret the sound. "Mr. Hamilton, I have stopped the bleeding."

Vincent took firm hold of the fraying threads of control and clung to them. He could no more move than a glamourist could walk with an intricate illusion. Some response was required, though. He formed the thought in his head, made certain that he could speak without his voice breaking, and said, "I am glad to hear it."

"I do not want to cause you further distress, but neither do I want to give you any illusions. Your wife has lost a great deal of blood. More, I judge, than when Sir Ronald attended her."

"Thank you. I recall your cautions from when she was bled. May I assume that our efforts will be the same here?"

"Keep her calm. Keep her warm. Get as much liquid into her as we can. Yes."

"But she will recover." His voice sounded too coldly formal. He was doing that thing his father despised, being unable to make eye contact. Vincent turned to Dr. Jones and tried not to look away.

"She will be in danger for some time yet."

"But you think she will recover."

"That is my hope."

He clenched his jaw and bore down on the threads of his emotions. The effort made tremors of tension run through his frame, but those he knew how to hide. So long as he was holding Charles, they could not see his betraying hands. "I understand. You will tell me if there is anything that I can do to aid in her recovery."

"Naturally."

Nkiruka leaned against the bed, breathing rapidly from her work with the glamour. She wiped her hand across her forehead and nodded to him. "Got some glamour you could do to help."

Dr. Jones rolled her eyes. "It will do no harm, but do not exaggerate it."

"Knew we shouldn'ta sent you to France. You have all these foolish European ideas."

"Those foolish European ideas have saved a number of lives here. And you know that, or you would not have raised the funds to send me to study."

It was insignificant, a safe topic to give him time to regain a little governance. "You studied medicine in France?"

"Paris. With Dr. Laennec." Dr. Jones wiped the blood from her hands on an already bloodstained towel. "My early training was here, as a midwife. I have since realised that a number of practices I learned here were superstitions, but harmless."

"Harmless . . . until you na do them."

"I have not stopped you. We have the brazier at Mrs. Hamilton's feet to draw the bad spirits down, and I see that you have already tied a red ribbon around young Master Charles's arm. Next comes the spirit bower. I am familiar with the routine."

"I show you, Mr. Hamilton."

He was aware that they were managing him. After the distillery accident, he had seen how effectually they managed the family members of the wounded. "Thank you."

Working briskly, they cleared away the blood-soaked blankets and washed Jane. He had to turn his back to stare out the window so he could not see how limp she was. At some point, he realised he had given Charles his little finger to suck on, which reminded Vincent that he would need to arrange for a wet nurse.

"Much better. You may turn around—your wife is decent again."

He almost laughed. They thought he had turned around out of modesty? Of all the aspects of their marriage, he and Jane had never been shy about *that* after their wedding night. He had turned because he could not bear to see Jane suffer, which was why he had learned to be open with her, as well as why he hid his infirmities from her. He was aware how much that annoyed her, but she fretted when she knew. It was the one trait she had inherited from her mother, though his Muse turned it outward rather than inward—her own infirmities she disregarded almost scrupulously. But his she treated like threats to his life.

If, for instance, she had known that Vincent's father had cracked one of his ribs, she would not have let him carry her, even though he was demonstrably capable of it. He was not so careless of his health as she believed, but he drew a distinction between discomfort and disability. If he could learn to dance after being caned, then he could carry Jane with a cracked rib.

And he could turn now. It hurt to see her limp figure, but it would not leave a permanent mark. If she were to die, that would be a very different matter.

They had dressed Jane in a rough chemise and drawn a clean blanket up to cover her. If she were not so drawn and still, with a bundle of pillows holding up her legs to encourage blood to stay near her heart, she might simply be resting after her labour. . . . Vincent swallowed and had to clear his throat before he could speak. "You had mentioned a glamour?"

Nkiruka beckoned to him. "I set it. You can keep it going."

"Is it a running thread?"

"No. Uses what your wife calls 'poorfire threads,' so they fray quick. Gotta to keep refreshing, or it dissolves, but . . ." She gave Dr. Jones a glare. "My people don't get childbed fever. Folks who keep the old ways? Less infection."

"And I am telling you that it is a matter of heritage." Dr. Jones shook her head. "Europeans are more prone to infection than are Black Africans. It is natural that, as populations mix here in Antigua, we should see a rise in infection among the coloured population. It has nothing to do with abandoning the old ways."

"Still, I should like to try it." Vincent would try anything that stood a chance of keeping Jane alive.

"It will do no harm." Dr. Jones picked up the bundle of soiled cloth from the floor. "But I do not want to give you false hope."

She had no worries on that count. Vincent grasped the thread of despair and wrapped it into a tight knot with the others. Later. Later he could let them unravel and find somewhere to hide until he could stitch a plausible countenance back together again.

Thirty-four

A Second Sight

Vincent ran his finger down the length of Jane's strong, proud nose in a way he never did when she was awake. He loved the shape of it and the way it reflected the force of her character, but any attempt to convince her of that had failed. She thought it overlong. If one wanted an insipid lady of the fashionable set, she was correct. But the way the tip of it curved when she smiled, the wrinkles across the high bridge when she was annoyed, the flare of her nostrils when she was working . . . all of these made it so eloquently *her* that he could not fail to adore it.

He straightened and studied the web that Nkiruka had woven over and into Jane. It was largely composed of poorfire threads. Though he did not think they could help Jane, he suspected that Nkiruka had set up the web to give him something to attend to while he waited. He was grateful for that.

Vincent expanded his vision to the second sight. Now the web stood out in glowing lines, which his mind interpreted as a black-purple not-colour. The threads were all tied off, though not with any knot he recognised, so all he needed to do to keep it from decaying was to be certain the thread was spun to the appropriate degree. The high, tight hum of the poorfire threads buzzed beneath his fingers as he made a minute alteration to tighten them.

A brief, familiar knock sounded on the door. He sighed. What news would Frank have for him?

"Enter." Vincent let go of the threads and turned his vision back to Jane, hoping for some reaction to the sound of his voice.

The door opened. "They told me. I am so sorry."

"Mm." He wiped his hand down his face to remind himself to act somewhat human and stood to meet Frank.

Frank had changed clothes since the morning and was in a sensible black suit, cravat neatly tied, with no trace of the fire from the night before. He carried a bundle under one arm. "I brought you a change of clothes."

Vincent looked down, seeing for the first time his own dirty nightshirt and breeches. He had been holding Charles in this? Small wonder that Dr. Jones had insisted on taking him to a wet nurse. Jane would be appalled if she woke to find him in such a state. "Thank you." Something more was required. "How is your family?"

"Shaken, but safe. Mother will be bruised for some time, but Pridmore did her no serious bodily injury when he took Lord Verbury." Frank hesitated as he set the clothes down on the little table. "What is *your* state?"

"I hardly know." He held the tendrils of feeling so tightly that all of them tangled together. He was aware of what that did to his countenance and worked to present a less forbidding expression. It was not welcoming, but given that his other choices were breaking things or breaking himself, placid civility seemed the best option. He looked down at Jane. "I am concerned, but calm enough to hear your news. I assume you have some."

"I do."

The birth stool had been removed from the room and replaced with a soft chair that would be useful when Jane was up and nursing Charles. Vincent gestured to it and pulled his own straight-backed chair from beside Jane's bed. He did not want to be even that far away, but Frank deserved the courtesy of his attention, and more. Sitting, he nodded for Frank to begin.

"I will start with the least important, since it will not require much in the way of remark. I have an early report of the property damage." Frank pulled out a sheet of paper from his coat pocket.

The motion made Vincent think of his own coat, which he had not thought to take from the great house. The miniatures Jane had given him were still tucked inside. He lost his grip on the illusion of calm, and a strand of rage lashed free.

Standing, he walked away to the window until he could tame the urge to hit. Frank was not the object. That was Pridmore, who had threatened Jane and destroyed what might be her last gift to—no. She would wake up. Vincent cleared his throat. "I trust you have that well in hand."

The paper rustled as Frank folded it. "Vincent, all of this can wait."

"I have nothing else to do." He pulled in and in and in until it was safe to move again. He could not act on instinct in this state, but needed to consider every action and measure it against what a rational person would do. Smiling would be too much, but to turn and incline the head would suit. Vincent did so. "Should we go over it?"

"No . . . I wrote it out so you could look at it at your leisure. The irony is that because Pridmore set multiple fires, several of them burnt towards each other, due to the lay of the land or the wind patterns, so the losses were less extensive than they might have been. The great house had damage to the roof and the blue wing, but the stone construction worked in our favour there. There was some smoke inhalation among those who fought the fire and some minor burns, but no loss of life." Here was the hesitation again. "With one exception."

"Who?"

"Pridmore sought refuge in the safe house." He held up his hands. "Not fire, but smoke."

"I see." There should be something there, a sense of vindication or relief, but it seemed to be only a fact that had nothing to do with Vincent. What would Jane make of this? "His wife?"

"I can make inquiries."

"I recall Jane—" His voice cracked on her name, and he had to stop. "I recall being told that Mrs. Pridmore was from London. If she does not have family here, will you arrange for passage for her?"

"Of course."

"Thank you." Vincent nodded. "Is there anything else I should know?"

Even to Vincent, Frank's hesitation made it clear what the next matter would be before he spoke. "Dr. Jones believes your father has had another stroke."

What to do with that information? Vincent would welcome his death. If Jane had not been with him, he thought he might have left his father by the path, but she would not have approved, and she would have been correct. To have him still alive. . . . It did not matter, and Vincent suspected that it had never mattered.

Nothing mattered except Jane.

Vincent held his breath until it was steady, then ventured, "He has recovered from strokes before."

"I—I think that will not be the case here."

"I have already mourned." He had not intended to say that aloud. "The first time. I had forgotten how . . ." He had forgotten how constant the threats and degradations were, but that was not what he meant to say. "I thought that if I had another opportunity, then perhaps—" Perhaps his father would finally be proud of him. "It was foolishness."

With an uncomfortable degree of understanding, Frank gestured to the door. "He is across the hall, if you want to see him."

"I cannot. Jane is—" His voice cracked again, but Vincent could not care. "She is not well. I cannot leave her while she is—" His control slipped again, and he had to stop, staring at the ground with his jaw tight around his fear.

"I understand." Frank's voice was as calm and soothing as if Vincent were a skittish yearling.

He tried to tie off the strands of fear and consider what the appropriate responses were. "Forgive me. How are you taking it? He is your father, too."

"No." Frank shook his head firmly. "No. He sired me, but he was never my father. The man who raised me, when Lord Verbury was not here, was a field slave and a cousin to my mother. He taught me what was good and honourable and decent. Lord Verbury was not a bad master, in the relative scheme of things, but he was never my father."

All Vincent had learned from his lordship was who he did not want to be. "Then perhaps he was not mine either."

The person who had taught Vincent who he wanted to be was lying on the bed behind him, limp and horribly pale.

Vincent's own shout woke him. Tension ebbed out of his body as he understood where he was. He lay curled on a pallet on the floor next to Jane's bed. His heart still beat quickly as he lifted both hands to his face and pressed the heels of his palms against his eyes. The wine barrel dream again. Vincent stretched to his full length, trying to erase the memory of childhood confinement. It had been a long time since he had cried out loudly enough to wake himself. Jane usually woke him, though he had no idea how she knew the nightmares were happening.

He extracted himself from the knot of bed linens and rolled to his knees to check on her. The poorfire web surrounding Jane made her white chemise glow a pale violet. Part of him hoped he had not disturbed her, but every other part prayed her eyes would be open.

They were not.

She was breathing, though. It killed him that he needed to be certain of that. It was fast and shallow, but breath.

Kneeling by the bed, Vincent rested his head against the cool linen of her pillow. Her hair still smelled of smoke. "Jane . . . Muse. Please wake up." In the night, his only answer was the echo of his voice off the plain white walls. "I am lost."

He traced his finger down her nose and let it rest against her lips. They were dry and cracked. Nurses, midwives, and Dr. Jones had been in and out of the room all day, trickling broth into her mouth with care not to choke her. He did not say it again, but he silently pleaded for her to wake. Only to open her eyes, the way she did after Sir Ronald had bled her. It had troubled Vincent then to see her half-lidded eyes open without seeing, but he would take that now. He would take any sign that she was improving.

In the darkness, it was difficult to keep his fear bound up. He would not weep. To do so would be to mourn for her, and he must think that Jane would get well. The web surrounding her twinkled at the edge of his vision. He stood. The tension must have loosened on the poorfire threads if they had shifted to violet. Vincent reached for the ether and, with a few twists, spun the threads tight again and out of visible sight.

It barely quickened his breath, but the feel of doing *something* helped steady him after the nightmare. Bless Nkiruka for giving him a task.

And Frank had brought a distraction as well, with the reports from the great house. Frank needed no help in running the place. The only use that Vincent served was to be the nominal head of the household, who was respected solely because of an accident of appearance. Bringing the reports and the clothing had been an unlooked-for kindness. Vincent pinched the bridge of his nose and bent his head, grateful that there was no one to watch him. He had done nothing to deserve the consideration of these people.

But he would accept it with gratitude. Pulling the chair up to the little table, Vincent prepared to work. He lit the room's single candle and settled into the chair. Frank's tidy handwriting marched across the page, detailing the initial estimate of property lost.

It was dull going, and he was grateful for it.

The next day passed slowly. Vincent had dressed with care in the clothes that Frank had brought him. Jane liked it when he was tidy. He looked at the razor. The way the light danced along the edge as his hands shook told him that he would slice his own throat if he tried to shave now. Vincent closed the blade and set it aside before he was tempted to try.

Around noon, someone brought a bowl of a thick ragout and some aromatic bread for him. He stared at the heavy red broth, and all he could think of was blood. If he were to create a glamural of the ragout, it would bear no true resemblance to blood, being both thicker and more orange, but his stomach turned regardless. He drew the serviette over it and pushed the bowl towards the centre of the table.

He managed a few bites of bread, which stuck to the sides of his mouth. Vincent knew his own tendency to stop eating when distressed and could not allow himself the luxury of weakness. If Jane needed to be carried anywhere, or Charles. . . . He should eat the soup.

Drawing the bowl back to himself, he pulled the cloth off of it. His gorge rose and he stopped, swallowing. The rebellious nature of his own body frustrated him beyond measure. He had learned to hide the shaking and the nausea, to work through dizziness, overheating, and shortness of breath, but no amount of training could make them go away. All he could do was to proceed as if they were of no consequence.

Vincent picked up the spoon.

A commotion in the hall drew his attention, and he was glad for it. Vincent set down the spoon, pushing his chair back. He paused at Jane's bed, hoping the raised voices would cause her to stir. She lay in exactly the same attitude as she had for the past day. Tucking his hands behind his back, Vincent went to the door and opened it.

The door to the room across the hall stood open. Dr. Jones stood over the bed, supporting the shoulders of a figure that convulsed wildly. At the foot of the bed, a coloured man constrained the legs, to keep them from writhing off the bed. The person—a man—had been rolled onto his side, and strangled grunts came in time with his tossing arms.

Vincent knew what a seizure looked like. One of the pupils at the Royal Academy had been coldmongering on the side, to pay bills, and then pushed too hard in a class. "Do you need help?"

Dr. Jones looked up, meeting Vincent's gaze. "Close the door, Mr. Hamilton."

Until that moment, he had not recognised the man on the bed. His back was to Vincent, and the man was too thin to be his father. His father had always been a giant, even when his hair silvered. Even when he was confined to a wheeled chair, the force of his character had overshadowed Vincent. Without the armour of his clothing, the bone-thin man did not seem to be related to the Earl of Verbury.

"Close the door," Dr. Jones repeated, and then she turned her attention back to the figure, who continued to shake in her grasp.

Vincent took a step back into the room where Jane lay and pushed the door to the hall shut. He stood, staring at the white paint, waiting for some feeling. The tangled ball of emotion in his core hung there, heavy and dark, but the idea that his father might be dying provoked . . . nothing. He felt not even relief at the thought.

Turning his head, Vincent looked over his shoulder at Jane. The stillness of her figure pushed the knot of feeling into his throat. He closed his eyes and tightened his jaw around the urge to gag. It took a few careful breaths to steady himself.

When he felt more composed, Vincent crossed the room and pulled the chair from the table to the side of Jane's bed. He sat, took her hand, and waited.

When Frank knocked on the door, Vincent jumped in his chair. His neck had an odd pain in it, as though he had fallen asleep sitting up. "Enter."

He set Jane's hand carefully at her side and stood, scrubbing his hand over his face. His face was damp. God's blood, he was a mess.

Frank slipped into the room, closing the door behind him. His face was too carefully composed to bear any sort of good news.

"He is dead?"

"Yes." Frank stepped farther into the room. "I thought . . . this is vulgar, but, given the previous circumstances, I thought you might want to see him before I made arrangements."

Did he? Vincent could barely think beyond the confines of the room. "I saw . . . I saw the seizure. I keep thinking that I should feel something." He rubbed his hair with both hands and sat back in the chair. "My whole life I fought him, even when he was not present. I have fought and fought against the man he had wanted me to be, and now that he is gone, now that the obstacle is finally removed . . . I do not know what to do."

"Given your history, I am not surprised." Frank crossed the room and sat in the nursing chair. "He and I had a very different relationship, but even for me, very few aspects of my life have not been shaped by his lordship's wishes."

"That is very much it." Vincent drew a breath. "I feel as if I have been pushing against a wall and it is suddenly gone."

"A door, perhaps, that is now open?"

"For both of us, I hope."

Frank sat forward in the chair and rested his elbows on his knees, hands pressed together. His gaze went to Jane and then back to Vincent. "Do you need anything?"

The brief flash of pity in Frank's eyes threatened to unravel him. Vincent looked down, clenching his hands into fists. For a moment—and a moment only, thank heavens—he was tempted to ask Frank to bring him some sherry, but this was not a time to slip into darkness. If Jane woke and he was insensible . . . it would not stand. "Thank you." He forced his hands open, heedless of the shaking and lifted his gaze. "Would you ask them to bring Charles to me?"

One of the nurses had brought Charles in to visit, and Vincent now sat in the nursing chair, which he had pulled over next to Jane's bed.

Each time he saw their son, Vincent was surprised anew by how little he was. In art, even the most detailed miniature was necessarily in want of completeness. Not Charles. His fingers alone were works of the highest order. It did not seem that anything so small could be so exquisite.

Vincent stretched his legs out in front of him and rested Charles on his lap. The midwife who had brought him in had wrapped him in a blanket, so that only his arms were free. The shift Charles wore was an unassuming cotton, without the rows of tucking and embroidery that Tom's dresses had borne. The cap, too, was simple and its unadorned nature made the utility of warmth more apparent. In Vienna, he had thought the ruffled caps an affectation of fashion.

"But you will not be a fashionable young man, I wager." He let Charles grasp his index finger. His son's entire hand wrapped around it with an astonishingly strong grip and still the little thumb did not quite meet the equally small fingers. "You will be handsome in manner though, I trust. Your mother will have to instruct you there. Hm?"

Charles squirmed in reply.

"That is correct. Of the two of us, you should defer to her judgement more than mine."

A little series of grunts was his answer. Charles's hand found his own face and his eyes widened in astonishment.

"I will grant that that is not the common arrangement, but you need not look so surprised. Your mother is kind, with a steady character. She is wiser than I am, and a better glamourist. Yes. You will do well to attend to her example.

I will tell you that I am a better man for doing so." For a moment, Vincent found it difficult to breathe. The little squirms and grunts of their son made Jane's stillness more apparent. His Muse needed to awaken soon. Thank God that Charles was too young to be able to see clearly, or he would be appalled at the state his father was in.

While holding Charles, Vincent was able to sometimes concentrate on just the single strand of joy that their son represented, but doing so meant letting the other strands slip and his glamoured façade of calm fray. It was always the joy that surprised him and made the unravelling begin. Vincent compressed his lips and cleared the emotion out of his throat. "I look forward to introducing you to your cousin. I am glad that you will be of an age together. Tom is an upright young man."

A gentle tap at the door preceded Nkiruka into the room. "How you do, doo-doo?"

"Well, thank you." Vincent shifted Charles to his elbow and stood, relying on old training to steady himself with nothings. "And yourself?"

"Fine. Better yet, if you na lie to me."

"Sorry. I am . . . doing poorly. She is—" And those were words he could not say aloud. "But Charles is well."

Her vision went vague as she looked into the ether. "You do good with the web."

"Thank you for giving me something to do."

"It keeps infection out. I don't know how or why, only that it do."

"I admit that I am used to thinking of glamour as having little practical application."

"That true enough." She laughed and shook her head. "Dat's why bakkra don't care much if we do glamour. T'ink it's only pretty pictures."

"Although one could make the argument that the glamural hiding this village is a deeply practical application." He rocked on his toes a little, dandling Charles. "How are you hiding the weaves?"

"De words an' dem don' have no English."

"Jane said as much when you were working on the book. I am sorry it was lost in the fire." For a moment his fury at Pridmore and his father rushed up. They had caused this. It was their fault that his Muse was—his throat tightened. It did not matter. They were dead, and she would recover. He swallowed and was able to forge ahead. "It is a very great loss."

"Oh, I brought de book with us. T'ink I'm going to let all that work be wasted? Eh eh!"

Vincent had to turn away. God's wounds, was the smallest thing going to make him weep? He stood by the chair and faced the window, though no pretence would hide his difficulty in governing himself. It became harder to keep the snarled mess of his sensibilities in check with each moment that his Muse slept. "I am glad to hear the book was saved." At least his voice was tolerably steady. "I should like to read it."

"Sure. I bring it." Nkiruka came to stand in front of him.

"But let me hold dis picknee dat cause so much trouble first. Ah he mi come for."

"Of course." Vincent was equal parts reluctant to part with Charles and also grateful that he did not have to risk dropping his son. He wanted a moment to restitch the illusion of control. If it were a glamour, he would tear the misshapen patchwork out and start anew, but for Charles, for Jane, he had to keep the façade in place. Once he started to unravel, he was not sure there would be anything left of him.

Thirty-five

Considerations

Jane must have been working a great deal of glamour to be so out of breath. Vincent was talking about folds with someone. She knew the voice that answered him, but she could not place it for the longest time. Dragging her lids open, Jane looked to see who it was. Still, the apparatus of her mind turned so slowly that she stared at the elderly black woman for some time without a name attaching itself. Jane knew that she liked her.

Nkiruka. Yes. That was it.

She stood talking with Vincent, whose back was to Jane.

Jane wanted him to turn, but she was so tired. She would call him in a moment.

A baby was crying.

Jane frowned. Why had Melody brought Tom into her bedchamber in the middle of the night? It seemed rude and unlike her.

Vincent's voice rumbled, "Shall I hold him again?"

"Naaa. I t'ink he wet."

Oh. Jane's eyes were closed. She opened them, blinking against the light. Nkiruka held—oh. Oh, she held Charles. Vincent bent over their son, patting his belly as the infant shrieked his displeasure.

Jane's mouth was dry and she had to swallow several times before she could make a sound. "May I see him?"

Vincent jerked around. His eyes widened. By his expression, he had not expected her to live. Neither had she.

Jane tried to smile at him, and Vincent's composure shattered. He took a step towards her and his legs buckled. Her husband dropped to his knees like a marionette with all its strings cut.

Nkiruka backed away, turning to the window. She wove a sphere of silence around her so that Charles's cries vanished, leaving only the sound of Vincent sobbing.

He knelt by the bed. Vincent found her hand and clutched it with both of his, pressing his face down against it. The sobs were nothing romantic, but ragged and raw. Each breath sounded as though it tore open his throat and choked him. Jane wanted to bring her other hand over to stroke his hair and soothe him, but she had not the strength to do even that.

She settled for moving her thumb along the ridges of his fingers and smoothing his hot tears away.

The storm, when it passed, was not long, nor did Jane think that it had swept away all the clouds from Vincent's mind. He leaned against her, face nestled against the damp fabric of the bed. She stroked his hand and raised a finger to his forehead, which was fevered, as though he had overworked with glamour.

When Vincent's breathing had steadied, he pulled himself up. His face was red, blotched, wet with tears, and, with the addition of his bruises, altogether inelegant. Jane had never seen anything so handsome.

"Forgive me for that." Vincent pulled a handkerchief from his coat pocket and wiped ineffectually at his face. He kept his other hand on hers.

"Nothing to forgive." Speech was laborious but necessary. "Flattered."

His chuckle contained the remnant of a sob. "This is a strange sort of flirtation."

"Inscrutable."

That had been, perhaps, a mistake, as he began weeping again. His breath caught like a child's, and he shook his head. With a sort of mocking smile, Vincent gestured at his face. "Apparently, this is what joy looks like on me." He did not bother with his handkerchief but wiped his sleeve across his eyes. "I always was a backwards youth."

She mustered a smile for him. "You say that as if it were no longer true."

"No, only to prove that I have long practise at being contrary."

"I did not need proof."

Vincent laughed, and cried, and laughed some more. "Do you want to see Charles?"

"Very much."

He rose and walked away from her with clear reluctance. Jane rolled her head to the side to watch him, weariness keeping her pinned to the bed. Her whole core ached, and when sleep came again, she would embrace it gladly. It crept around the edges of her vision, and she had to widen her eyes to keep them from shutting of their own accord.

They must have closed a little, though, because Vincent was at the bed with a wriggling bundle, and Nkiruka was slipping out the door. Jane pushed against the mattress, trying to sit up, but succeeded only in thinking about moving. Vincent knelt next to her, turning so that she could see their son's face.

Charles had finished his fit of pique and stared at her. His eyes were wide and serious with the slightly troubled expression unique to newborns, as if he had come into the world knowing how to right all the troubles but could no longer quite remember how.

He grunted and waved his arm, fingers spreading as if he were going to work glamour. Without thinking about it, Jane shifted her vision to the ether. There was nothing for him to catch, and his motions truly were the random waving of an infant. Still, it felt remarkably good to let her vision relax into her second sight.

Jane pulled it back to the corporeal world with an effort. She was so tired, and she wanted to see as much of her son as possible before falling asleep. He yawned at her, as if in complete agreement.

"Have you been good for your papa?"

"Exemplary conduct." Vincent's eyes were still quite red but had dried somewhat. "And becoming of a gentleman."

"Good." A yawn escaped her to match Charles. "Pardon."

"Shall I let you sleep?"

"I am afraid so." She suspected she had little choice, but there was one matter left unattended. "But . . . kiss me first?"

Still holding their son, he bent down and gave her a tentative kiss. Vincent tasted of salt and strong tea and still smelled of smoke. The brush of the stubble on his chin gave her a rough gauge of how long she had been unconscious.

Jane kissed him again, just managing a touch of the lips. "Poor thing."

As he pulled back, his eyes had again grown wet, but they crinkled at the corners. "You always do worry more about me than you should."

"Because you are a delicate china cup."

Two days after Jane awoke, Vincent finally felt comfortable leaving the room. She was not well by any means and could not yet sit up, but Dr. Jones was willing to go so far as to assert that the danger was past. He was gone for several hours, and when he returned, he had dirt on the cuffs of his shirt.

His face was a little pinched.

"What is the matter?"

"Hm?" He paused in the action of sitting, then lowered himself slowly the rest of the way. "We buried Lord Verbury. Frank and I."

"Oh, Vincent . . ."

"There was no one else we could ask to do it. He is supposed to be more than a year dead." He displayed his hands, which had blisters on the palms. "Oddly, I think it helped. You will find this foolish, but I think I needed to be certain that he was actually dead this time."

She understood and did not have the benefit of having seen the body. "I am not surprised."

He shifted in the chair and reached into his pocket. "I also needed to look for this."

"What is it?"

He put a small, dark rectangle in her hand. It had a cracked, rough surface. Frowning, Jane held it in front of her face. For a moment, she fumbled with it, still clumsy with fatigue, and then it opened into three equal pieces. It was the trifold case she had given him for his birthday.

The two portraits inside had been a little darkened with smoke but had somehow survived the fire.

"When you are well . . ." He paused for a moment, and

when he went on, his voice was rough. "When you are well, I shall require the third portrait."

Tears filled her eyes as she nodded. "Of course."

Vincent reached out. For a moment, she thought he was going to retrieve the case from her, but he slipped his hand into hers instead. They sat in amiable silence as Vincent ran his thumb over the edge of her fingers. He sighed once, before looking up with reddened eyes. Wiping his face with the back of one hand, Vincent shook his head and gave a blushing smile. "I have been thinking . . . or, rather—I spent a great deal of time when you were . . . I talked to you. Or, at you, I suppose would be more accurate."

Jane almost held her breath in imitation of her husband. During the course of their marriage, Vincent had become better about discussing his internal state when she inquired, but it was still a rarity for him to offer anything without prompting. She allowed a squeeze of his hand to encourage him but otherwise tried to wait as he gathered his thoughts.

"As we were burying his lordship, I realised . . . there are things I would regret if I never said to you." He stopped, his gaze lowered and brows drawn together. "I never told you why I fell in love with you. Because it reflects badly on me. Not—not falling in love, but the . . . the circumstances. Or . . . or what it said about me. I mean to say, it was difficult to explain without also explaining my family, and I—" He snarled his free hand in his hair, shaking his head.

Now he needed some assurance, which Jane could provide. She squeezed his hand again. "I trust you know by now that I am not so easily frightened away?" Even so, she was fairly burning with curiosity about something that she had not thought of since the early days of their marriage.

He nodded. "You are a wonder." Clearing his throat, Vincent sat forward in his chair and freed his hand. With both hands clasped in front of him, he appeared to be in a deep study of the floor. "Your skill caught my attention, but—as I am certain you recall—it vexed me. Later, I realised it was jealousy."

"Jealousy!" Jane could not prevent her laugh. She had never met a more accomplished glamourist than her husband, and she privately suspected that time would judge him to be Herr Scholes's superior. "My recollection was that you said my work was stiff and lifeless."

His head came up and he gave a crooked smile. "At the time, your completed glamurals were exquisitely rendered to the point of being somewhat studied, yes. But your *tableaux vivants* . . . Jane. I wish I could make you understand how truly extraordinary you are."

"I will accept your approbation because I am too tired to protest."

Jane regretted teasing Vincent as his brows went up with concern. "Shall I let you sleep?"

"No, no. I want to hear how I dazzled you with my talent."

"Well . . . I wanted to talk with you, and propriety, as well as my own . . . curmudgeonly nature, made that difficult. But there was a day when . . . you were out riding with Mr. Dunkirk and his sister. I was drawing an apple tree when your party came upon me. I had been hearing your laughter for some time before you saw me, I think."

"I recall the day."

"We talked about art and the nature of perfection, and you said that you thought that imperfections helped one appreciate something beautiful more fully. It was . . . it was a transformative thought for me. My entire life, I had been taught that imperfections meant failure, and yet, I could not deny your statement, for I had chosen that tree to draw because its storm damage made it more interesting, and in many ways, more beautiful than its perfect neighbours. And I thought—" His voice cracked and he compressed his lips, shoulders hunching forward. "And I thought that perhaps it meant that I was not flawed past redemption."

Jane would have given much to be able to get out of bed. Her chest ached for her husband. Understanding him now rewove that long-ago afternoon in her mind. She could now see his silence and forbidding nature for what they were, preservative camouflage to survive his relationship with his father. Vincent was correct. If he had told her earlier, she would not have understood, because she would have found it impossible to believe that any father could be so terrible to his child.

"I love you because of your imperfections. I love the way you try to protect me when I do not need it. The way you become cross while working, your stubbornness and independence and that you can be utterly insufferable." She looked down at the trifold case that she somehow still held in one hand and turned its roughened surface over. "I would not wish any of them away, because then you would be someone else."

"And this is why you are my Muse." Vincent came to sit beside her on the bed. He leaned down to kiss her forehead. "Thank you."

"For?"

"Only thank you."

Jane slid over to allow him room to curl beside her. She wanted strength for anything more, but marital duties can take many forms, and in this instance they involved only silence, and understanding, and a release of cares.

Thirty-six

With a Will

It was another week before Jane was allowed to sit up in bed, but she felt no desire to try to leave this time. She was not able to nurse Charles, and she felt a pang of jealousy every time she saw Amey give him suck. With children only two months apart, Amey and Jane had much common ground for conversation. They were thrown together often, as the newborn needed regular feeding.

Jane sat on her bed holding Isabella, a lively little girl with the stamp of a Hamilton, while Amey nursed Charles. Isabella had a decided fondness for the strings of Jane's cap and held one fast in her plump fist. Jane laughed as her cap was knocked amiss yet again. "Very well.

You may have it, though what you shall do with it, I do not know."

The answer was to shove a corner of the cloth into her mouth and chew upon it.

"Don't spoil her, ma'am."

"I think she has other plans." Jane bent her face down to the little girl and blew a rude noise upon her cheek.

Isabella squealed with laughter. Jane did the same upon the other cheek, which was velvet soft, and then laughed herself. "Amey—" Jane stopped, staring at the woman who was nursing her child. The tenderness with which Amey watched him drove whatever insignificant thing Jane had been about to say straight from her mind. What she wanted most in Charles's life were people who cared for him. "Amey . . ."

"Yes, ma'am?"

"Will you call me Jane?" She took one of Isabella's hands in lieu of her mother's. "It seems only appropriate, since I believe your daughter is my son's aunt."

Slowly, Amey smiled and then laughed. "I guess she is." She reached across the space between them and offered Jane her hand. "I would be glad to."

"Would you . . . would you like to come with us to London? With Isabella and your other children, I mean."

Amey hesitated and looked at Isabella, face twisting a little with indecision. "You know that people would think she's your husband's."

Jane looked down at the little girl, clearly a Hamilton, even at so young an age. Amey was correct, of course, that any person who looked at the child would assume that Vincent kept a mistress under their roof. But after months of worrying about what Lord Verbury would think and how he would use things against them, Jane found that her fear of London gossip was very low. To leave Amey here because of that? Noblemen got away with worse, and Vincent was a glamourist, so he had the advantage of already being considered eccentric. It would likely be the subject of gossip for a time but not quite rise to a scandal. It might even help Isabella make a better match when the time came. Jane might be considered a fool or an object of pity, but she could not summon the necessary concern to count that a thing worth fearing. "I think that we can manage. If you want to come."

"And have my children be free in truth? Yes. Thank you. Yes, I will."

Another week passed before Jane was declared well enough to be moved back to the great house. Jane did not know how Frank had managed it, but he had somehow hidden their absence from the neighbours thus far. She was carried there on a pallet and felt almost as though she were a young rajah. Amey and Nkiruka accompanied them, with a promise from Jane and Vincent that they could leave at any time they wished. Dark smoke stains marred the stones of the great house, but their apartments had been cleaned and restored for their use.

One of the things that had been impressed upon them

was that not every slave on the island knew about Picknee Town. The rebellion in 1736 had failed because one of the enslaved had boasted carelessly. So there was a council that carefully selected who was trusted with the knowledge of its exact location. Steady rumours placed it as being in a series of caves accessible from Devil's Bridge, on the opposite end of Antigua, while contradictory rumours said that it was an old wives' tale and did not exist at all. The planters tended to be of the latter opinion since, of course, it was not possible for the slaves to do something so organised and clever.

This careful secrecy meant that only those closest to Amey had known that she was in Picknee Town, though not necessarily where it was. They had put it about that she had been close to death, but had recovered, and in the chaos after the fire, her return went largely without comment. Which was fortunate, as Jane had much need of her assistance.

Jane had an uncomfortable familiarity with being able to go only between their bedchamber and the blue parlour. This time, however, her domain was expanded to include the nursery. The room next to theirs had been converted, and Isabella and Charles settled there. What was most remarkable to Jane was how much more pleasant and inviting the house was, now that she was not dreading what lay on the far end of the building.

She was sitting in the blue parlour making some notes to herself when Vincent arrived with Frank, as she had requested. Jane wiped her pen clean and smiled at the gentlemen. "I have a proposal."

They exchanged matched expressions of circumspection as they sat at the table opposite her.

"We were brought here on the pretext of Lord Verbury's having a will in Antigua. I propose that we deliver one." She slid her sheet of notes across the table to Vincent and Frank.

Vincent looked over the notes and immediately drew a sphere of silence around all of them. "This is a bold plan, Muse."

"One of the chief advantages of being ill is that I have nothing to do but think, and I keep thinking about Picknee Town. It seems to me that it will always be at risk so long as the land is in white hands. The 'ravine' makes it useless land, so I see no reason why the Hamilton family should object if Lord Verbury chose to leave that plot of land to Frank. Amey tells me that there is precedent of other owners leaving land to their children."

"And the deeds of transfer for Frank's mother, wife, and children? That is a significant number of slaves for the estate to part with."

"Yes, but the least expensive route. Freeing them would be the right course of action, but not one that would be believed, I think."

Frank shook his head. "You are thinking my mother would draw this up."

"I am." Jane straightened her shoulders as best she could. Her posture had suffered since the birth.

"But why would he have done this?" Vincent stared at the paper, still shaking his head. "It is not just the list of actions, but making sure that he appeared to be in his right mind. No one who knows him would believe that he would be so generous."

"But he freed Frank before his supposed death, which would be a necessary step to granting Frank slaves of his own. And what is your birth name, Frank?" Jane warmed to her topic. "What did he keep insisting to Vincent? That we name our son after him, as he named you. In a better world, with a better man, I think he would have done this for his firstborn son. So if not for benevolent motives, then to spite Vincent by replacing him in the will."

"And the rest of the estate stays in Richard's control . . . which no one could question." Vincent leaned forward and rested his elbows on the table with his fist over his mouth. His brows were drawn together. Frank drummed his fingers on the table, alternately frowning and looking blank. Sometimes they were so much alike. Vincent scrubbed his hands through his hair and sat back with a little bit of a groan. "It is a legacy of generosity, which is better than he deserves, but one I would rather see in the world. If your mother can create it, I can present it as genuine in London. Since Jane's suggestion would formally disinherit me, I cannot be accused of being partial."

"Are you certain? Not that it would be accepted, but that you wish to give up your inheritance."

"I gave it up years ago. It is better that it stay that way." Vincent reached across the table and took Jane's hand. "We are not Hamiltons."

Sir David and Lady Vincent had many heartfelt discussions about what they would do upon their return to England. The mourning period for Princess Charlotte would be over in November, and new commissions would be plentiful as the nobility restored glamour to their homes for the first time in a year.

Jane still fatigued with alarming ease, and although she had dipped her hand into the ether, she would be in no condition to do serious work for some time yet. It would have caused her more concern prior to the experience of creating the glamural for the charity ball. She could still participate in the design, so long as she had assistants to help with the execution while she regained her strength.

Since both Jane and Vincent had a strong desire to never travel again, they determined to settle in London, where they could be engaged by the most discerning clients and, of course, the Prince Regent himself. They had hopes as well that the position at the school in London, which Herr Scholes had mentioned, might still be open. If not, Jane was of half a mind to begin their own school.

With all of those thoughts in mind, she sat down with Nkiruka to ask her to come to London with them.

The older woman laughed and laughed, wiping tears from her eyes as she shook her head. "Eh. I know you mean well, but no. Thank you. Me'll tap right ya."

"But in London you would be free."

"You saying you only free me if I go?"

"Oh—no." Jane knit her brow, trying again. "I only meant that the society is less restrictive. You would have more opportunities there."

"You t'ink dem will le wan black woman be mayor of London town? Hm? No. I have family here. I have responsibilities here." She spread her hands. "I leave dem for what—sleep on cotton sheets and teach white babies glamour? No. Thank you. I stay here."

Jane and Vincent sat on the veranda with their son, enjoying the afternoon breeze. Vincent was wiping off some milk that Charles had spit up on his lapel. He had a cloth thrown over his shoulder, but at the ripe age of three weeks, their son had developed remarkable aim.

Jane laughed, "Shall I take him?"

"No, no. There are parts of the coat he has not adorned yet." He shifted cloth and infant to his other shoulder as he continued to wipe ineffectually.

Watching them fondly, Jane rocked in her chair. She should perhaps go inside, since she was so close to dozing. It seemed to be her natural state these days, which she chafed at more than a little. She did feel steadier, but that was only by comparison to the days immediately after Charles's birth.

A cloud of dust appeared on the road to the great house, though the direction of the last bend in the road kept its source from being visible. A sound grew to accompany it. A carriage and a number of horses approached the house.

Vincent looked up as they came into view. Jane grew

cold with alarm. These were British soldiers. But Pridmore was dead—how could he possibly have done anything? No. It seemed more likely that this was something Sir Ronald had arranged as a final revenge from Lord Verbury.

"Jane, would you take Charles and go inside?" Vincent stood, not taking his eyes off the soldiers or the unmarked carriage that had arrived in their midst.

She reached out for their son but made no immediate move to go inside. With Charles's comforting weight in her arms, she stood and followed Vincent down the length of the veranda to the front steps of the house. If this were some action against them, there was nowhere she could reasonably go to hide. With her health as poor as it was, Jane was not even certain she could pull a thread out of the ether, much less weave a glamour.

The carriage rolled to a stop at the head of the sweep, and one of the soldiers dismounted to open the door. A military officer got out first, uniform bright with braid, followed by the man Jane had least expected to see.

Her father had come to Antigua.

Thirty-seven

Familial Relations

For a long moment, Jane could only stare at her father, so out of place in the heat and dust of Antigua. His white hair fluttered under his tall dark hat. "Papa?" Without a word, Vincent took Charles from her and freed Jane to all but run down the stairs. "Papa!"

Mr. Ellsworth met her halfway, the tension in his face fading as he pulled her into his arms. His embrace unlocked a fountainhead of emotion, and Jane found herself sobbing on her father's shoulder. He rocked her, smoothing her hair. "There, there . . . shh . . . there, now."

"What are you doing here?" She drew back, still weeping. "I thought you were in Vienna."

His dear face was reddened from the voyage,

and his eyes had a suspicious wetness. He wiped one with a knuckle as though he had something in his eye. "We left for England not long after you. The letter must still be en route, I suppose." He broke off as Vincent's footsteps ground across the gravel behind her. "And is this . . . ?"

It was not how she had pictured introducing her son to her father, but Jane nodded. "May I introduce you to Charles Vincent?"

"Charles . . . ?" Now her father's eyes were wet in earnest. He held out his hands to Vincent. "May I?"

With tender care, Vincent transferred the older man's namesake into his arms, for all the world as if they were not surrounded by British soldiers. It seemed odd to Jane to be suddenly surrounded by so many white faces.

Once relieved of his burden, Vincent eyed them with some concern. "And the soldiers, sir?"

"Those came with me." The voice was so strikingly like Vincent's that Jane felt dizzy. Struggling out of the carriage, assisted by two soldiers, was Vincent's brother Richard. "Received your messengers, old man. Seemed best to bring some support, given our father's past dealings, and the Crown agreed."

His features still had the signs of indolence that are so striking among young men of fashion, but with new lines on top of them, as though he had been quite ill. He leaned heavily on a cane and swung his right leg with a pronounced limp, stopping next to a distinguished white gentleman of middle years.

"General Montgomery, allow me to present my brother, Mr. Vincent Hamilton, and his wife."

Vincent shook the general's hand. "A pleasure. Although I hesitate to correct my brother, and it risks presenting the news in the wrong order, we are more accurately Sir David Vincent and Lady Vincent."

"The Prince Regent's glamourists, yes." General Montgomery held his hat under one arm. "His Royal Highness was most concerned about your situation."

To General Montgomery, Vincent said, "As to that . . . my father died three weeks ago."

"Dead!" Richard's composure divided into a mixture of shock and relief. "Are you certain that he is truly dead?"

"There was a fire. I saw the body, and, believe me, I made a thorough examination. So while I am grateful—beyond grateful—that you came, I am only sorry that you made the trip to no purpose."

General Montgomery shook his head. "Not at all. The fact that your late father was able to remain at will for as long as he did makes it clear that there is rank corruption in the naval forces here. Your message to your brother mentioned Sir Ronald . . . bad business, that. Well. We should be able to clear it up and make good use of our time here. We have three ships-of-the-line in the harbour with steady men who can be trusted."

"May I also recommend Admiral Cunningham? Though I regret to say that circumstances forced me to lie to him." Vincent grimaced. "Still, I believe he is an honourable man."

"Good to know. Given what your brother has shared, I

would be surprised if the admiral did not forgive you the indiscretion."

The successive shocks, welcome though they were, were making Jane's heart race and familiar grey spots swim at the edge of her vision. She put her hand on Vincent's arm. "Forgive me, but I think I am about to faint."

"It is all right, Muse. I do not need to be—"

"No, really."

"Oh!" He lifted her into his arms as grey splotches danced around her vision.

Her faint did not last long. By the time Vincent had carried her into the foyer of the great house, Jane had revived. She lifted her head, turning to look over his shoulder for her father. He followed close behind, holding Charles. Richard limped at his side, but the military officers came no farther than the door, taking up station there while the General supervised arrangements for his men.

Mr. Ellsworth let out an audible sigh of relief when he saw she was awake.

"I am so sorry. The heat sometimes overwhelms me."

Vincent growled, "You mean you almost—gah!" He twisted as she found the spot on his ribs where he was ticklish.

Jane glared at him and gave a little shake of her head. The time to tell her father that she had almost died in childbirth was not now. Preferably not ever, but especially not after he had just spent a month at sea worrying about her.

"I might have dropped you," he murmured.

"There are many things I am afraid of, but that is not among them." Jane looked down the long gallery. "But please do set me down when we are in the blue parlour."

"I was going to take you to our rooms."

"I know. I am asking you not to." Jane's pulse was steadier, and she thought that if she were sitting she would be all right. "I will be more nervous being secluded."

"You really do not play fair sometimes." But he set her down when they crossed the threshold of the blue parlour.

Frank entered from the back of the house. No doubt he had run across from the counting house when one of the other staff told him about the soldiers. Richard glanced idly at him, then again, his brows going up in surprise at the familial resemblance.

Frank bowed to Vincent, slipping back into the role of the house steward as easily as if he had never left it, and took up a station near the wall in case anything was wanted. It was more than a little uncomfortable to have him waiting on them now.

Jane sank onto the nearest sofa, which gave the gentlemen leave to take their seats as well. Her father came to sit by her, held captive by Charles's little fist wrapped around his thumb.

Richard lowered himself into an armchair with a sigh and used his hand to stretch his right leg out awkwardly in front of him. The foot stuck up at an unnatural right angle. "So you said you were Sir David again. May I assume that our dear disgraced father disinherited you?"

"Yes." Vincent gave a quick summary of events to both men, thankfully leaving Jane's hemorrhage in Picknee Town with the parts unsaid.

When he finished, Richard rubbed his temples, mouth slightly open in horror. "I am so terribly sorry for what you have suffered. I thought he was dead, Vincent. I do not know if you can forgive me, but please believe that nothing would have induced me to ask you to come here had I known. I hesitated even then, but at the time, travel was not possible for me."

Vincent cleared his throat, "I was sorry to hear about your leg."

"At least I have an adequate reason for not wishing to dance with young ladies."

Jane said, "We are grateful that you came now."

"I know what my father was. That is why I did not come alone. When I received Sir David's message, I went at once to the prime minister and made arrangements for the arrest of our father." He looked towards the door and frowned. "The Antiguan will . . . if it perchance burnt in this fire, the English will would still stand. You could receive your rightful inheritance."

Vincent ran his hands through his hair. "No. I am sorry that I am going about this backwards, but there is an introduction to make."

"You always were a backwards child," Richard drawled, but Jane had enough practise with Hamilton men to note that though he appeared calm, his gaze rested on Frank a trifle too long.

Vincent tucked his chin into his cravat and his hands behind his back. It became suddenly very easy to remember that he had once studied law. "The Antiguan will—most of the details are items that are best suited for later discussion, and I think you will not find them objectionable, but there is one point I would be remiss to delay. Richa—" He stumbled over his brother's name and cleared his throat. "Lord Verbury, may I present Mr. Frederick Hamilton II, our father's acknowledged natural son. He has been running the estate, and, I truly believe he saved our lives. If the Antiguan will does not stand . . ."

Jane clasped her hands together so tightly that they ached. She had hopes that Richard was a decent man, not because he had made the trip to Antigua, but because he had thought to bring her father.

"I see. Well. That explains why you looked familiar." Richard struggled to his feet, hopping a little on his left foot while he got the right under him. Limping, he held out his hand. "I am pleased to make your acquaintance, but if we are to be brothers, I shall insist that you call me Richard."

Frank stepped away from the wall, his expression carefully guarded, but Jane suspected that his sensibilities were no less affected for it. He and Richard shook hands cordially. To look at them, one would think the meeting occasioned no more comment than any two gentlemen meeting in passing on the streets of London. "My family calls me Frank, and I would take it as an honour if you did as well."

"Am I correct that you are Miss Louisa Hamilton's father?" Upon receiving a nod, Richard continued. "Then

I should have told you directly that your daughter and brother are both in good health. I left them established in my house in London rather than risk bringing them to Antigua while things were unsettled with my father."

Frank closed his eyes for a brief moment, but before he did, the deep relief had been painful to witness. "Thank you, sir."

"Mm . . . as I believe you are the eldest son, I should be saying 'sir' to you. I say . . . any chance we can alter the will to make him the earl? Deuced unpleasant trial, mostly accounts." He chuckled, though Jane thought he was not entirely in jest about wishing not to be the earl. "I can imagine the stir *that* would make in the peerage."

Then introductions needed to be conducted again with Jane's father. There were many repetitions of "How do you do" and "A pleasure" before they were all seated again. At some point in the proceedings, cold lime juice and pineapple appeared, and as the company refreshed themselves, Richard explained all that had occurred in London.

"Not knowing that the Ellsworths were supposed to be out of the country, I sent a special courier straight to Long Parkmead, reasoning that they would like to know of an impending grandchild."

"Which I very much did, though from your letter I thought to find you still expecting." Mr. Ellsworth tickled young Charles under his plump chin. "Not with such a handsome young man already."

"I did not expect you to come."

"Jane . . . even if it had not been my natural inclination,

do you think for a moment that your mother would have allowed any other choice? I did not even trouble sending a reply in return, simply went posthaste that very night to meet Lord Verbury in London."

It was so odd to hear the words *Lord Verbury* and attempt to associate them with anything but dread.

Mr. Ellsworth broke the silence by turning to Richard, as if it were the most natural thing in the world, and saying, "Lord Verbury, would you like to hold your nephew?"

Richard looked at young Charles and chuckled. "Yes, I would. But may I ask you to bring him to me?" He tapped his right shin with his cane and it gave off a hollow wooden thump. "I would not trust myself standing with him."

"Of course." Mr. Ellsworth stood, cradling Charles in his arms, and crossed to Richard.

The new Earl of Verbury took his nephew with the awkwardness of someone who has been little in the company of children. In most households in England, a newborn and his mother would be confined for some time after birth, but Jane had had quite enough confinement prior to her lying-in to want anything more to do with it.

Richard, The Earl of Verbury, studied his nephew, then looked across to Vincent, and then to Frank. He grunted and regarded Charles again. "He has the Hamilton brow, I think."

When Charles Vincent was four months of age, he sailed into England in the arms of his mother. As they docked in the port at Weymouth, the young man commanded a significant entourage, even at such a tender age. In addition to his parents and his grandfather, he was accompanied by his aunt Isabella, two months his senior, her mother Amey Avril, and two of Amey's other children.

The voyage had been uneventful, and Jane was deeply grateful that the motion troubled her not at all. More so, she was grateful that Weymouth harbour was not more than an hour's journey to their own small town in the neighbourhood of Dorchester. Within two hours of arriving in England, she stood in a light fall of snow upon the front sweep of her family's home at Long Parkmead.

The door to the house flew open and Mrs. Ellsworth came out at a run, gown raised and flying. Melody and Alastar followed at not much slower of a pace. With only a bare acknowledgement of Jane, Vincent, and Mr. Ellsworth, she lifted her grandson out of Jane's arms. "What a handsome young man you are. Yes. Such a delight."

Laughing, Jane met Melody in an embrace, while Vincent and her father were all very correct with Alastar. "How is my nephew?" Jane asked.

"Crawling and managing to destroy everything he can reach. I dread the time when he begins to walk." Melody rested her hand ever so briefly on her stomach and blushed when Jane raised her brows. "Shh . . . Mama does not know yet. I can only take so many tonics."

"I will not tell." Jane turned to reach out a hand for Amey, who held Isabella. "May I introduce our friend, Mrs. Avril, and her children Isabella, Solomon, and Eleanor."

Mrs. Ellsworth was too absorbed in her new grandson to pay any mind, but Melody smiled and stepped into the role of hostess without hesitation. "I am so pleased to make your acquaintance. La! But you must be fatigued from your trip, and we are making you stand in the cold."

Amey laughed. "It's all right. I'm still all amazed at the snow."

"Oh! But of course, I should imagine it is a rare occurrence in Antigua."

Mr. Ellsworth broke away from Alastar and Vincent. "Bless me. I was about to forget a promise to Solomon and Eleanor. I have been telling them these past two hours that we should play in the snow when we arrived."

"Shall I go with you?" Vincent asked.

Alastar clapped him on the shoulder. "Go inside with your wife, and I will keep Mr. Ellsworth company."

"And I shall make certain you have hot cocoa when you come inside." Melody clapped her hands. "Oh, but it is so lovely to have you home again."

By mutual agreement the party divided, some going to Long Parkmead's shrubbery, while the rest entered the house and were soon settled in the front parlour with strong tea and good Stilton cheese. Thomas and Isabella crawled across the carpet, managing to find every small thing that they could stick into their mouths. Amey and Melody sat on the floor with them, retrieving objects from little hands and laughing as they compared notes.

Mr. Ellsworth, Alastar, and the children did not stay long out of doors, as neither child had a proper winter coat. Both men were rosy-cheeked and laughing at the children's delight with the new miracle of snow.

With her family thus around her, Jane settled on the sofa next to Vincent and had the satisfaction of watching her husband and mother coo over her son. She had long wished that he could be easy in the company of her family, and the introduction of young Charles seemed to provide exactly the topic of conversation best suited to them both.

Epilogue

In London, Jane and Vincent took possession of a house with an enclosed garden for the children to play in. Their plans to work on new commissions came to nothing as they discovered that Queen Charlotte had passed away in November, putting the nation into mourning again.

This made them deeply grateful to accept the invitation to work at the school for glamourists. They were delighted to discover that they both knew the proprietress, though it had been over four years since they had last seen Miss Dunkirk. It took very little effort to persuade their patron to offer a post to Amey as well. Herr Scholes came from Vienna to consult in setting the curriculum, although he was often distracted by

Charles and Isabella. Still, the school opened in the autumn of 1819 with much fanfare.

In short order, it became quite the thing for young ladies of quality to be trained at Miss Dunkirk's School for Girls. Vincent advocated for opening an adjoining wing of the school for the education of boys in the art of glamour. Though there were fewer applicants by far, those that did attend were deeply enthusiastic.

Their reputation was further increased with the publication of *A Comparative Study of the Glamour Taught in Europe and Africa, with a Particular Concentration on the Traditions of the Igbo and Asante Peoples, by Jane, Lady Vincent, and Mrs. Nkiruka Chinwe.*

At times, Jane felt that she ought to be doing more when she saw the efforts of their niece Louisa and Vincent's half brother Zachary. With introductions from the Earl of Verbury, the two were soon mixing with company of the first order. Jane and Vincent, in turn, introduced them to the coldmongers, who helped them make connections among the coloured population of London. With steady influence, Louisa and Zachary carefully made the right friends, and in 1824, their combined efforts were instrumental in seeing slavery overturned throughout the United Kingdom.

Jane and Vincent maintained a regular correspondence with Frank, who kept them informed on events back in Antigua. His mother lived to see slavery abolished and her children free. Picknee Town was finally unshrouded from its glamour and all the families who had been separated were reunited. The Hamilton estate survived the abolishment of slavery with little ado, as the steward had already been in the practise of treating the slaves as freedmen.

Though the Vincents' later life took some surprising turns, we shall leave them with this final scene from not long after the school opened, to reassure you that they received a well-deserved rest. Jane woke in the middle of the night to find Vincent's finger on the tip of her nose. She wrinkled it, eyes crossing to see what he was doing. "Vincent?"

He jerked his hand away. "Sorry. I thought you were asleep."

"I was, until someone touched my nose." She rolled onto her elbow, just able to see him in the dim light of their bedroom. The new gaslights of London cast an orange glow in the room, so unlike the heavy darkness when they had first moved there. "Are you not able to sleep?"

"No, no. I just heard Charles, so I went to look in on him."

She frowned. They had acquired a nanny after it became clear that Amey's time was better spent teaching than chasing Charles or Isabella. "Mrs. Eccles is supposed to do that."

"But I like to." He leaned down and kissed her gently. "I am sorry that I disturbed you."

"Well . . . so long as I am disturbed." She kissed him more deeply, sliding her hand up his arm to find the collar of his nightshirt and undid a button. "And perhaps a little agitated . . ."

He made a long, shuddering inhalation. "Muse . . ."

"Rogue?"

"Give me a moment—" He rolled to the side and opened the drawer of his bedside table.

She ran a hand down his back to find the bottom edge of his nightshirt. "Inconceivable."

"That is the plan."

They were occupied then and on many nights with duties marital. Jane had found her muse as surely as Vincent had, and both of them, together, discovered that it was possible to receive inspiration from more than one muse. Even if that second muse were smaller and frequently given to interrupting those duties marital.

But that is for a later time. We shall leave them now with the privacy they have earned.

Afterword

First and foremost, I need to thank Joanne C. Hillhouse, an Antiguan and Barbudan author, who helped me with the Antiguan Creole English in the novel. By "helped," I mean "rewrote it." Let me explain why I decided to do this.

I grew up in the American South—specifically, the Piedmont of North Carolina and East Tennessee. The reason I'm being specific about this is that I grew up in a part of the United States that has very clear regional differences. People talk about "the Southern accent" as if it's a homogeneous thing, but it's really, really not. Accent goes far beyond how the words are pronounced, or the cadences used, and very much into the word choices and sentence structures. Language reflects the culture of the people using it, precisely because we use it to express ourselves.

There are also very distinct class differences in the way English is spoken. This is true everywhere, but the American South is one of the places where it's really clear. A Southerner will often try to scrub the "country" out of their voice to arrive at the "genteel" Southern accent so that people won't think they're uneducated. And, if they move out of the South, where that distinction isn't recognized, that requires scrubbing all trace of the South out in order to not be perceived as a "hick."

Yet . . . when I go home, I'll slide back into a Southern accent when I'm in a store so I don't seem like an outsider. It's code-switching at its most basic.

So, when I decided to set a book with a lot of action in Antigua, I knew that I wanted to represent the Antiguan Creole English. I also knew, from having watched people mangle the Southern American English, that understanding the nuances was going to be really, really important and really, really hard.

Harder than making my books sound like Jane Austen?

Yes.

Why? Because Jane Austen has been researched, and studied, and analyzed, so there's no shortage of material available. It's taught in school in the United States. I could grab a representative text and use that as my base. Even when I had characters who were speaking with an East London dialect, I could ask a friend to "translate" it for me.

But the primary text? No shortage of material, and it's material that I have been exposed to since a very young age.

Trying to find a representative text of Antiguan Creole English written by a native speaker in 1818? Welcome to colonialism.

The next best choice was to read a lot of work written by contemporary writers. (I recommend the works of Jamaica Kincaid, Joanne Hillhouse, and Marie-Elena John.) It was very clear to me that I could come up with something that a reader unfamiliar with the Caribbean region would accept. And it was also clear that I would completely screw up the nuances.

So I hired Joanne Hillhouse to translate the dialogue. I also rewrote sections because she made suggestions about places where the communication would be nonverbal. Language is complex and not simply what is said, but also what is unsaid.

Dialect, likewise, isn't just people talking funny. It's a reflection of culture.

While doing so, I knew that it would make parts of the dialogue harder for many of my American readers to understand. While I could have made the dialect less thick, it would have also contributed to erasing the culture of the Antiguan population. In the "A Note on History" section, I'll have some recommended reading, if you'd like to know more about dialect and Antigua.

Justin Roberts's dissertation "Sunup to Sundown: Plantation Management Strategies and Slave Work Routines in Barbados, Jamaica and Virginia, 1776–1810" was invaluable in understanding how a working plantation ran. More on that in the "A Note on History" section.

Megan Eccles mentioned on Twitter that she had named her son after Vincent. I was at a point where I needed Vincent's full name so I asked what her son's middle name is. One of those . . . one of those names is his.

Michael Livingston (for the longtime readers, yes, that's the man I named Captain Livingston after) is a medieval literature professor who I turn to when I need help with archaic language. In this case, it was attempting to come up with a term for ultraviolet light. In real history, UV was recognized in 1801 by German physicist Johann Wilhelm Ritter as "oxidizing rays." So, theoretically, I had a perfectly good period word to use. But . . . but, my theory was that in a world where glamour works, people would have known about ultraviolet much earlier. After tossing around a couple of different ideas, Michael offered "porphyry" as a possibility. This was perfect, because it corrupted so easily into "poorfire," which was a great word for a light that makes things glow.

My husband, Rob, who is my muse, has been wonderfully supportive and lets me talk through plot problems when I am stuck. He doesn't offer answers, but he knows all the right questions to ask.

My agent, Jennifer Jackson, and first reader, Michael Curry, deserve especial thanks this time. During the research process, I realized that the ending I had planned was *not* going to work. Not in a billion, billion years. We sat over dinner and hashed out possible alternates. Jenn pointed out that the thing I keep returning to in these novels are the personal stakes and relationships. Rather than making the conflict larger, I made it smaller and more personal. Otherwise, you would be reading about a rebellion.

Likewise, my editor, Liz Gorinsky, always makes my books better, but with this one, when I was at the mid-point, I realized that my new ending would also *not* work. She helped talk me through the reasons that it was a problem and figure out what I needed to do to fulfill the promises I'd set up at the beginning.

Many thanks to my assistant, Beth Bernier Pratt, who keeps me from double-booking myself and generally makes the world a much better place.

Thanks also to my beta readers: Alycia, Amanda Jensen, Amber Hancock, Andy Rogers, Annalee Flower Horne, Anne, Beth Matthews, Bonnie Fox, Caroline, Carrie Sessarego, Charlotte Cunningham, Chloe, Chris M., Chris Russo, ChristonJP, Darci Cole, David Wohlreich, Denelian, Elizabeth Lefebvre, Faith, Furecha, Gloria Magid, Halley Ruiz, Hilde Austlid, Hope Romero, Jessica James, Jill, Joan, John Casey, John Devenny, Jon Marcus, Julia Rios, Justin Clement, Karen, Kassie Jennings, Katherine Boothby, Kathleen Ladislaus, Katie, Laura Christensen, Lilia Visser, Mark Lindberg, Mary Alice Kropp, Matt, Melissa Tomlin, Mrs. Arkban, Nina Niskanen, Nonny Blackthorne, Norma, Pat, Patrick, Rae Nudson, Ryan LeDuc, Sally, Sara Couture, Sara Glassman, Serge Broom, Siddhartha, Stephanie McDaniel, Tanya Kucak, Terry, Tracy Erickson, Trish E. M., and Tyler Kraha.

I wrote great chunks of this book at Letizia's Natural Bakery in Chicago, where they would let me camp for hours. Always friendly, and they have excellent pastries.

My parents and my husband's parents are wonderful people and both sets recently celebrated their fiftieth wedding anniversaries. So, unlike poor Vincent but like Jane, I have had excellent examples of loving families. I am grateful for them.

Also, my brother, Steve—excuse me, I mean Dr. Stephen K. Harrison—who, by virtue of getting his PhD in history, gave me something to try to one-up. Affectionate sibling rivalry is a great motivator. Five novels, Steve. Ha! Top that. You know . . . by being hired to teach history internationally. And . . . um . . . having grandchildren for our folks.

Darn it.

Thanks to Ebele Mogo, president of the Engage Africa Foundation, who answered my call for help with the Igbo. Much like my work with Joanne, I sent her my clumsy attempts, along with my thoughts and intentions, and she translated the concepts for language and cultural appropriateness. I am deeply grateful to her for sharing her creativity with me.

Thanks to Irene Gallo, Tor's art director, and Larry Rostant, my cover artist, for letting me have a little bit of a hand in the cover. I have been making Regency dresses for "research" since I started the series and asked if I could make this one. They were game and said yes.

So, that dress on the cover?

I made that.

And I also need to thank the unknown embroiderer who did the beadwork on the sari I built the dress from. Everything that is special about the dress is the work of someone who I have no way of identifying. While I know that it's period correct to make a dress from a sari and not know the craftsperson, this is one place where I truly wish I could be anachronistic. It's beautiful and I wish I could thank them by name.

Of course, thanks to Jane Austen. I borrowed a number of lines of text from her to describe the women of color on Antigua. As an example, Louisa shares a description with Emma Watson of *The Watson*: "Her skin was very brown but clear, smooth, and glowing with beauty, which, with a lively eye, a sweet smile, and an open countenance, gave beauty to attract, and expression to make that beauty improve on acquaintance." I'll let you find the others, but just remark that one of them is a description of Jane Austen herself.

And, finally, thank you. Thank you for following Jane and Vincent through the early years of their marriage. May your own Muses treat you with kindness.

A Note on History

I'll be honest: when I sent Lord Verbury to Antigua at the end of *Without a Summer*, I did it before much research about Antigua. I'd picked it because in Jane Austen's *Mansfield Park*, Sir Thomas goes to Antigua to check on his estates. I had the idea of showing part of the offstage action that happens in that novel.

The first place this came back to bite me was that it completely destroyed the plot that I had pitched to Tor. The original synopsis ends with a slave revolt modeled on the 1791 Haitian Revolution. The problem is that when I started researching, there were forty British forts on Antigua. Forty. It was also Britain's major naval base in the Caribbean. There was no way, even if I could make the revolt succeed, that the people of color would be able to hold the island. It had too much military significance for Britain to allow it, which meant that the novel, and the series, would have ended with blood and more blood. I did significant revisions to wind up with the plot you see here.

The other thing that I did not understand prior to researching the novel was the enormous differences between the slave system in the United States and in the Caribbean. Both were horrific, but in different ways. In the United States, there was the prospect of escape to the North. In the Caribbean, the enslaved Africans were on islands. There was no escape. Because of that, they had comparatively more freedom of movement than those in the United States. But "comparatively" is the operative word. The enslaved Africans had to grow their own food, in addition to laboring in the cane fields. The surplus from these "sustenance plots" formed the basis of a second economy on the island, complete with market days. Since these market days formed the basis for much of the food served at the great house, the white slaveholders would turn a blind eye to movement around the island by the women who did most of the marketing.

This was countered by the fact that sugarcane was a year-round crop. In the American South, there was an off-season, but in Antigua, the enslaved people literally worked from sunup to sundown, every day.

In addition, the ratio between blacks and whites in the United States and Antigua were vastly different. In the United States, white people outnumbered the enslaved

Africans. The population was denied access to education as a way to solidify the white slaveholders' claim of superiority. In Antigua, there were approximately ten enslaved Africans to every white person. As a result, there weren't enough white people for the skilled labor required on the island. Slaveholders regarded the ability to read and write as a valuable asset and would make certain that the people they had enslaved were educated. Lord Verbury's decision to educate Frank would not have been the generous gesture that it might have appeared in the United States. He would have seen it as an effective use of resources.

This education also extended to the medical professions. Large estates had a white doctor and a black doctor, who treated the respective populations. The British author and slaveholder Monk Lewis made the economic arguments that I've given to Dr. Jones (whose first name may or may not be Martha . . .) about the importance of hospitals. Many of the black doctors were women in the tradition of midwives.

While Mrs. Whitten is a fictional character, she is based on a number of different free women of color in Antigua such as Anne Hart Gilbert and Elizabeth Hart Thwaites. There were not enough white women for every man who wanted to marry, which meant that women of mixed race were much more likely to be freed and married than in the United States. Even if not actually married, society silently accepted the necessity of mistresses in ways that would be unacceptable in England or the United States. Understand, however, that many of these women faced a choice between two horrible options: work in the fields or have relations with their captor. There were cases of love, but those should not be considered the rule or used to romanticize the realities of being an enslaved woman of color.

One of the other features of Antigua and many of the other islands in the Caribbean was the existence of Maroon populations. These were people who escaped slavery and established colonies on the islands. Periodically, these villages would be raided and the people gathered up and either resold or returned to the estates they had fled.

Picknee Town is based on the Maroons, combined with another historical fact. Antigua had an extremely low birthrate among the enslaved population. Papers from the time discuss the difficulties with "breeding stock" to try to figure out how to increase the number of live births. It does not seem to occur to most of the white slaveholders that malnutrition, overwork, and abuse might be contributing factors. Even so, in *Slave Women in Caribbean Society, 1650–1838*, Barbara Bush points out that the enslaved people on other islands faced similar hardships and did not have such a low birth rate. It's possible that people were using abortifacients to keep from bringing children into these conditions, but it's impossible to know for certain.

It would be nice to think that a Picknee Town existed, but I'm afraid that the reality was likely much, much grimmer.

Jane's experience in childbirth was based on the *A Treatise of Midwifery: Comprehending the Management of Female Complaints* by Alexander Hamilton (1804) and *An Essay on*

Natural Labours by Thomas Denman, M.D. (1786). It is harrowing reading and I do not recommend it. Suffice to say that in the real world, Jane would not have lived.

If you have an interest in learning more about Antigua and its neighboring islands, allow me to recommend the following books:

Anonymous. *The Laws of the Island of Antigua: 1668–1804, Volume 2.*

Beckles, Hilary McD. *Natural Rebels: A Social History of Enslaved Women in Barbados.*

Buckley, Roger Norman. *Slaves in Red Coats: The British West India Regiments, 1795–1815.*

Bush, Barbara. *Slave Women in Caribbean Society, 1650–1838.*

Craton, Michael. *Empire, Enslavement and Freedom in the Caribbean.*

Ferguson, Moira. *Colonialism and Gender Relations from Mary Wollstonecraft to Jamaica Kincaid.*

Handler, Jerome S. *The Unappropriated People: Freedmen in the Slave Society of Barbados.*

Kincaid, Jamaica. *A Small Place.*

Mintz, Sidney W. *Caribbean Transformations.*

Roberts, Justin. "Sunup to Sundown: Plantation Management Strategies and Slave Work Routines in Barbados, Jamaica and Virginia, 1776–1810."

Schaw, Janet. *Journal of a Lady of Quality.*

Walvin, James. *England, Slaves and Freedom, 1776–1838.*

Glossary

GLAMOUR. This basically means magic. According to the Oxford English Dictionary, the original meaning was "Magic, enchantment, spell" or "A magical or fictitious beauty attaching to any person or object; a delusive or alluring charm." It was strongly associated with fairies in early England. In this alternate history of the Regency, glamour is a magic that can be worked by either men or women. It allows them to create illusions of light, scent, and sound. Glamour requires physical energy in much the same way running up a hill does.

GLAMURAL. A mural that is created using magic.

GLAMOURIST. A person who works with glamour.

BOUCLÉ TORSADÉE. This is a twisted loop of glamour that is designed to carry sound or vision depending on the frequency of the spirals. In principle it is loosely related to the Archimedes' screw. In the 1740s it was employed to create speaking tubes in some wealthy homes and those tubes took on the name of the glamour used to create them.

CHASTAIN DAMASK. A technique that allows a glamourist to create two different images in one location. The effect would be similar to our holographic cards which show first one image, then another depending on the angle at which it is viewed. Invented by M. Chastain in 1814, he originally called this technique a jacquard after the new looms invented by M. Jacquard in 1801. The technique was renamed by Mrs. Vincent as a Chastain Damask in honour of its creator.

ETHER. Where the magic comes from. Early physicists believed that the world was broken into elements with ether being the highest element. Although this theory is discredited now, the original definition meant "A substance of great elasticity and subtlety, formerly believed to permeate the whole of planetary and stellar space, not only filling the interplanetary spaces, but also the interstices between the particles of air and other matter on the earth; the medium through which the waves of light are propagated. Formerly also thought to be the medium through which radio waves and electromagnetic radiations generally are propagated" (OED). Today you'll more commonly see it as the root of "ethereal," and its meaning is similar.

FOLDS. The bits of magic pulled out of the ether. Because this is a woman's art, the metaphors to describe it reflect other womanly arts, such as the textiles.

LOINTAINE VISION. French for "distance seeing." It is a tube of glamour that allows one to see things at a distance. The threads must be constantly managed or the image becomes static.

OMBRÉ. A fold of glamour that shades from one colour to another over its length. This technique was later emulated in textile by dip-dying.

NŒUD MARIN. A robust knot used for tying glamour threads. This was originally used by sailors for joining two lines, but adapted by glamourists for similar purposes. In English, this is known as a Carrick Bend.

PETITE RÉPÉTITION. French for "small repetition." This is a way of having a fold of glamour repeat itself in what we would now call a fractal pattern. These occur in nature in the patterns of fern fronds and pinecones.

SPHÈRE OBSCURCIE. French for "invisible bubble." It is literally a bubble of magic to make the person inside it invisible.

Reading Group Guide

1. Did you learn any new historical facts from *Of Noble Family*? If so, what?
2. How did you feel about Vincent's attitude towards his nephew, Tom? Did his regard for the baby surprise you? Why or why not?
3. On several occasions in the book, Jane behaves unfairly towards people over whom she has social power—for instance, when she commandeers Amey's house for her own medical exam and when she plans to use Nkiruka's work in her book without asking. Has anyone ever treated you unfairly? How did it feel? Can you think of a time when you've behaved unfairly towards someone with less power?

4. Vincent and Herr Scholes tell funny stories about Vincent's attempts to sneak out of the house as a young man. Did you ever use subterfuge to try to sneak out? Did you have better luck than Vincent?
5. Jane and Vincent have to engage socially with many people whose views on race and slavery they find abhorrent. Have you ever had to make nice with people whose political views repulsed you, or whose behavior you found unconscionable? How did you handle it?
6. In the book, Jane and Vincent are forced to stay with Vincent's father, who is judgmental and cruel. How do they handle the stress of staying with him? Can you think of anything else they should have done, or of things that work for you that would *not* have worked for them, given their characters and circumstances?
7. Have you ever had to collaborate with someone who wasn't as good at something as you, but who didn't seem to know it, as Jane and Vincent had to do with Mrs. Ransford? How did you handle it?
8. How did you feel when Jane's life was in danger when she was giving birth?
9. In the story, Vincent uses glamour to help Dr. Jones find the hemorrhage. Doctors in the real world did not have the equivalent ability until well into the twentieth century. Do you think medical science would have advanced differently in a world with glamour? How?
10. In *Of Noble Family,* Jane and Vincent interact with people of color from many social stations, including a rich landowner, a free black doctor, and many enslaved

people. Did you find yourself wanting to learn more about what life was like for people of color in the early nineteenth century?

11. How did you feel about Vincent and Jane naming their baby Charles, after Jane's father? Is there anyone else in their lives you think they might name a child after?
12. Medicine in the early nineteenth century was not nearly as advanced as it is now. Many doctors did more harm than good. Given the potential hazards, would you have trusted a doctor with your health?
13. Kowal addresses both family and racial injustice in this book. What do you think the major theme of the story is?